DRAWING HOME

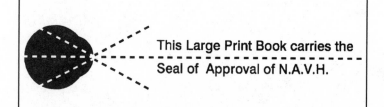

This Large Print Book carries the
Seal of Approval of N.A.V.H.

DRAWING HOME

JAMIE BRENNER

THORNDIKE PRESS
A part of Gale, a Cengage Company

Farmington Hills, Mich • San Francisco • New York • Waterville, Maine
Meriden, Conn • Mason, Ohio • Chicago

Copyright © 2019 by Jamie Brenner.
Thorndike Press, a part of Gale, a Cengage Company.

Thorndike Press® Large Print Core.
The text of this Large Print edition is unabridged.
Other aspects of the book may vary from the original edition.
Set in 16 pt. Plantin.

**LIBRARY OF CONGRESS CIP DATA ON FILE.
CATALOGUING IN PUBLICATION FOR THIS BOOK
IS AVAILABLE FROM THE LIBRARY OF CONGRESS**

ISBN-13: 978-1-4328-7124-6 (hardcover alk. paper)

Published in 2019 by arrangement with Little, Brown and Company, a division of Hachette Book Group, Inc.

Printed in the United States of America
1 2 3 4 5 6 7 23 22 21 20 19

For my Georgia

There's no way to be a perfect mother and a million ways to be a good one.

— Jill Churchill, *Grime and Punishment*

My darling girl, when are you going to realize that being normal is not necessarily a virtue? It rather denotes a lack of courage.

— Aunt Frances, *Practical Magic* (1998)

CHAPTER ONE

On summer weekends The American Hotel in Sag Harbor felt like the center of the universe. If you lived in town, you were stopping by for a drink, and if you were visiting, you wanted a spot in one of the eight guest rooms.

It was the Friday before Memorial Day, not officially summer but close enough. The Hampton Jitney stopped right in front of the hotel and unloaded a fresh batch of Manhattanites every hour.

Emma Mapson, a Sag Harbor native, had watched the summer crowds grow every year. She'd seen fancier restaurants open and higher-end boutiques decorate Main Street. But one thing that never changed was The American Hotel. The red-brick Colonial building looked and felt exactly as it had when Emma was a young girl, with the same antique wood furniture, nautical paintings, and Tiffany chandeliers. The lobby had the same well-worn couch and the same backgammon table where her father had taught her to play and where she, in turn, had taught her own daughter to play. It all seemed to say to her, *Go ahead, live a little.* At least, it used to feel that way.

"I have a problem with my room," a woman said, approaching the front desk.

"I'm sorry to hear that," Emma said, glancing down at the handwritten reservation log and trying to figure out which guest she was talking to. "What's the problem?"

"Everything!" the woman said. "I can't find a single outlet for charging my phone. There's no television, and there's no closet."

Emma arranged her face into a practiced, neutral expression. Too empathetic, and it was like she was admitting there was a problem; too quizzical, and the guest felt even more provoked. Best to look simply blank.

"What's your last name, ma'am?" Emma asked.

"Stoward." She spelled it slowly, as if Emma were barely familiar with the alphabet. Emma flipped through the reservation ledger and found the woman was booked in the Cooper Room. True, there was no television in that room — or in any of the rooms. And although technically there wasn't a closet, the room did feature a large antique armoire. She had no idea why the woman couldn't find the outlets.

"Mrs. Stoward, I'll —" Emma looked up and caught a glimpse of a familiar mop of curly dark hair across the lobby.

The American Hotel's front desk provided the best people-watching in town. Emma never knew who might be sitting on the sofa, which offered views of Main Street on one side and the hotel's always-full bar on the other; she might look up and see the town dockmaster, a tourist from the Midwest, a celebrity chef, or Billy Joel, a local. But she was happiest when the person planted in that coveted spot was the one she saw now, her fourteen-year-old daughter, Penny.

Penny's thin frame was hunched over her drawing pad, as always. Emma couldn't see her face because it was hidden by hair. Oh, that hair. When Penny was a toddler, people had stopped Emma in the street to comment on her daughter's curls. Emma watched her now, willing her to glance up. She could always tell from Penny's eyes — big and dark and so unlike her own — whether or not she was in a decent mood. Emma didn't know if it was Penny's age or just Penny, but the mood roller coaster was something to be reckoned with.

Emma smiled at the hotel guest standing before her. "I'll be up to your room in a minute to see what I can do," she said, buying herself some time to find out why Penny had left school so early. When the woman was out of sight, Emma slipped out from behind the desk.

Penny, busy rummaging through her book bag, didn't notice her.

"Hi, hon," Emma said. "What are you doing out of school?"

Penny looked up, pushing her curls out of her face.

"It's a half day. You know, 'cause of the holiday weekend."

Of course. "Right! I forgot." She leaned down to wrap her arms around her but Penny wriggled away. Emma straightened up, trying not to feel rejected. "Okay. So what's your plan?"

"I'm going to hang out with Mr. Wyatt. But I need to buy a book first." She gave Emma her puppy-dog-eyed *I need money* look.

Emma sighed. "Can't you borrow it from the library?"

"They don't have it yet and I really want to show it to Mr. Wyatt today."

Emma turned to look at the corner of the

bar where the old man, a world-renowned artist and her daughter's unlikely pal, could always be found in the late afternoon. "Don't bother Mr. Wyatt right now. He's talking to someone." She walked Penny to the front desk and handed her a twenty. Her daughter leaned over and gave her a quick kiss.

"I guess now I know the price of a little public affection," Emma said.

Penny rolled her eyes on her way out the door.

Emma answered the ringing house phone, booked a room reservation, and then walked up the stairs to the second floor to see what she could do to placate the complaining guest.

"Finally," Mrs. Stoward said when she opened the door. She was not alone in the room. Emma spotted a man — Mr. Stoward? — seated on the edge of one of the twin brass beds. He was busy tapping away at his phone and didn't bother looking up.

"See what I mean?" Mrs. Stoward waved her arm as if to say *Look at this disaster.*

Emma glanced around, taking in the antique full-length mirror, the red-and-gold-striped couch, and a set of Dominy chairs. The room also featured a beautiful armoire that could hold a full wardrobe.

It made her crazy when summer people didn't fully appreciate the charm of the hotel. The building dated back to 1843 and yet guests expected it to feel like the Four Seasons. And they never had any sense of the village's history. They didn't care that it had been a whaling port, a writers' colony, a historic African-American community, a stop on the Underground Railroad. Did they know that John Steinbeck had called Sag Harbor home? No; all they wanted was restaurant recommendations.

"Let me show you the outlets," Emma said. She bent down and pointed out one hidden by the legs of the wooden desk.

"Well, that solves one problem," the woman said, hands on her hips.

Emma walked to the armoire and opened it. "We have more hangers if you need them. I think you'll find this very spacious."

Mrs. Stoward peered suspiciously at the armoire. "Is this cedar?"

"Just use the damn cabinet, Susan," mumbled the man.

"And what about the television?" she said to Emma.

That got the man's attention. He directed his irritated gaze at Emma. "Yes, we need to get a television in here," he said. "There's

14

a game at seven."

Before Emma could explain that they didn't have televisions at the hotel, she heard a scream from the ground floor.

"Excuse me," she said, and she rushed from the room to the top of the stairs. One of the housekeepers was running up.

"Someone just passed out at the bar!" the housekeeper yelled, almost breathless. Passed out? It was early afternoon. Had someone already overindulged? It had been known to happen.

"Did you call an ambulance?" Emma said, running down the stairs to reach the front desk. She pushed through the wooden door between the stairwell and the lobby, a door she knew was often blocked by a café cart or a table, but she would lose precious seconds if she used the patio door and went around to the front entrance.

Nothing was blocking the door to the lobby today. She grabbed the black landline phone on the front desk and dialed 911.

"It's Emma at The American Hotel. We need an ambulance for an unconscious customer." The dispatcher asked her for some specifics, but from her spot, she couldn't get a good look at the fallen customer, and the phone wasn't cordless. The old-fashioned quirks of the place

15

sometimes posed a challenge. She should have used her cell phone, but service could be spotty.

Waiters and busboys gathered around the person on the floor; the bartender, Chris, was on his knees trying to help. Did Chris have EMT experience? She wouldn't be surprised. Most people working in town were, if not jacks-of-all-trades, skilled at a variety of jobs. The person taking your dinner order one night could very well be operating your water taxi the next.

She scanned the bar, looking for anyone she recognized, trying to get a sense of whether the guest on the floor was a tourist or a local. The bar had a few regulars who came for happy hour every day, year-round. They were the ones at the bar in the middle of a blizzard. The American Hotel was a club to these customers.

Emma realized one bar stool was empty, the one at the corner closest to the lobby.

Oh no. She hoped the person on the ground wasn't who she thought it was.

Penny crossed Main Street, heading for the bookstore. As far as she was concerned, the town had two major things going for it: the bookstore and the self-serve frozen-yogurt shop, BuddhaBerry. Somehow, between

16

these two places, she would find a way to pass the three-day weekend.

Penny didn't do well with lots of free time. It made her anxious.

"Instead of worrying," her mom had said, "think of something you have to be happy about. Just one thing, even if it's small."

One thing she had to be happy about was that eighth grade was nearly finished. It had been a brutal year. She'd almost failed math. Her best friend, Robin, barely had time for her anymore now that she'd become part of the group of "basics" — the girls with the flat-ironed hair and the new iPhones and the right clothes. Then, in December, the town's only movie theater had burned down. Everyone freaked out — it had been a historic building, and that stretch of Main Street smelled charred for weeks afterward. The burned pit was nasty. Still, Penny was amazed how upset people got about it.

"It's symbolic," her mother told her. "It's a sudden loss. And too much about this town is changing as it is. We have to hold on to some things."

Without the theater, there was one less thing to do on the lonely weekends. And now, one less thing to do this summer.

But she still had this place, Harbor Books.

The bookstore smelled like fruit and spices from the Dobrá Tea bar in the back. The owner, a twenty-something woman named Alexis Pine, had told Penny about the tea thing months before it opened. Alexis was obsessed with it — oolong tea, pu'er tea, green tea. Alexis had long hair that had once been blond but was now the pinkish-red hue of hair that had been dyed with Kool-Aid. She had funky, boho clothes and was basically everything Penny wished she could be. Alexis also had two cats in the shop, a vintage-book collection in a glass case in the back, and an impressive working knowledge of graphic novels.

"Hey, Penny," Alexis called from the counter. "Your book came in."

Penny was moving on from her manga and superhero phase and getting into realism with the graphic novel *This One Summer* by Jillian Tamaki and Mariko Tamaki.

Penny slid her mother's twenty across the counter with her fingertips, trying to touch as little of the bill as possible.

"Whatcha doing this weekend?" Alexis asked, handing Penny her change.

Penny quickly shoved the change in her pocket, pulled her forbidden tube of Purell out of her handbag, and squeezed a fat blob of it on the backs of her hands and on her palms. It burned her skin, which was already dry and cracked from overwashing.

"I'm not sure what I'm doing yet," Penny said.

She was embarrassed to admit that she didn't have any plans. Why did she feel like such a loser lately? It wasn't just the usual things, like not having a dad around and living in a house that was small and in the wrong part of town. Her otherness felt deeper, more unshakable, with every passing week.

It was why she felt more comfortable around older people. They didn't seem to notice anything strange about her. Most were just nice. This was why she had gotten into the habit of hanging around the hotel where her mother worked.

That's why she was going back there now to show her new book to Mr. Wyatt.

Mr. Wyatt had white hair and always wore a tweed jacket and carried a nephrite walking stick from Fabergé. His usual seat was in the near corner of the bar, his back to the lobby, and he didn't talk to anyone because he was always bent over a cocktail napkin doodling. It had taken a while before she'd realized some of these napkin drawings were framed in the dining room. The night she'd noticed this, she wanted to ask

19

her mom about it, but the bar had been packed, and if her mother had known she was still there, she would have sent her home. So she asked the old man, "How'd you get them to hang your drawings on the wall?"

"They fished them out of the garbage or retrieved them from a crumpled heap at the end of the evening. I had very little to do with it."

It took her a few seconds to process this, and then she told him, "I draw too." It was one of the few things she enjoyed.

"I'm surprised anyone of your generation lets go of the phone long enough to put pencil to paper," he said.

"I'm not allowed to have a smartphone," she said. Penny had OCD and anxiety, and the doctor said screens were the worst things for her. This didn't help her in the friend department.

"You're not allowed to have a phone but you're allowed to hang around in hotel bars?" he said.

"I'm just visiting my mother at work," she told him.

The old man looked across the room at her mother, then back at her. He smiled for the first time. "Emma's kid. I see the resemblance." He had to be lying. Her mother was beautiful and she was, well, not.

After that night, Mr. Wyatt asked to see her drawings. He met her in the lobby and they sat on the couch; she drank soda and he had martinis and he taught her about contour and proportion. A month or so later, she realized that Henry's drawings were hung in other places besides the hotel. His artwork was all around town. Henry was famous.

Now, as she was leaving the bookstore, her phone, her old, crappy, embarrassing flip phone, chirped with a text.

Don't be mad. You can totally come to the party. I'll send you the address.

Penny ignored it. She didn't need Robin's charity invitation. She had better things to do.

She headed back to the hotel. It took her a minute before she noticed the police cars. Two were parked at an awkward angle right in front of the building. Traffic was being redirected. A small crowd had gathered on the sidewalk.

She ducked her head down and tried to slip across the front porch to the hotel entrance.

"Young lady, step aside. You can't go in there," an officer said.

Ushered to the sidewalk, Penny wondered

21

if she could sneak around back. And then —

"Some old guy dropped dead at the bar," a man announced. "Right over his martini."

"That's how I want to go," someone said.

Penny stood very still. Sirens blared nearby, and she covered her ears, her anxiety officially triggered. In the midst of all this, the four o'clock jitney pulled up to the curb, and dozens of passengers disembarked, lugging bags and talking on their phones. Although Penny was desperate to get away, she was trapped by the swarm of summer people in a hurry to have fun.

CHAPTER TWO

Few things in life gave Bea Winstead more pleasure than a crowded room.

As one of New York's most legendary art patrons, Bea was famous for her intimate gatherings of, oh, a hundred or so people, the kind of people whose deep pockets and eagerness to acquire the next big thing merited an invite. And then there were the guests of honor, the lucky artists who walked into Bea's Park Avenue apartment wondering how they might pay the next month's rent on their studios in Greenpoint and ending the evening with six figures in sales. It was this promise of art meeting commerce that had given Bea's parties the heady air of unpredictability and importance for more than four decades.

But apparently, her power was waning. She scanned the room and noted the no-shows. Had her parties lost their luster? Or was it simply that she could not compete with Memorial Day weekend, when everyone fled to the Hamptons? God, how she loathed the Hamptons.

"Kyle, tell the caterers to keep the drink carts at least five feet from any panels."

Her assistant was a handsome young man with a thick head of hair, vibrant blue eyes, and the chiseled features of a movie star. When she first saw him doing odd jobs around her building, she assumed that was what he aspired to be, an actor, like her favorite waiter at Aureole, who'd ended up on a sitcom.

"No, ma'am. I'm happy to be a handyman," he'd said when she asked.

Bea appreciated that kind of focus. Dedication to work was important, whatever that work might be. It was a sign of good character. And so, when she needed help with a particularly complicated art installation in her apartment, she'd asked him. That same week, her assistant quit. She thought, *Why not hire someone practical, for a change?* Enough with these dreamy art hangers-on with no discernible skills. She offered the young handyman a job with a salary he couldn't turn down.

Bea took a final look at the canvases Kyle had mounted on the wall for the evening's event, paintings of gigantic flowers, amoe-

24

bas, and birds. The artist, Bronx native Frank Cuban, was twenty-six years old. Bea was hosting this show of his work tonight as a favor for an old friend, Joyce Carrier-Jones, an artist she'd known back in the heyday of the Tenth Street galleries. Now Joyce was the dean of admissions at Franklin, the city's top fine-arts high school. Cuban was a former student. In art, as in life, it was all about who you knew.

The artist's show included one panel in acrylic, graphite, wood, and nail polish. Another was an oil pastel on paper with Sharpie and spray paint. Amusing, yes. Groundbreaking, no. Bea missed the days when there were one or two big art movements in any given decade. She missed the sense of discovering a true star.

But the key to longevity was not to look back. Looking back was fatal to the spirit.

Joyce Carrier-Jones walked over and handed Bea a glass of wine. Joyce had a loud manner of dressing, bright caftans and large ceramic jewelry. Her dyed-black hair had a dramatic silver streak in front and she wore oversize square-framed glasses.

"Cheers," Joyce said. "To the rise of another new talent. You know, Bea, I really admire your career. I might want to move into managing artists like you used to do.

Never too late, right?"

Bea barely heard her. She held up her wineglass, incredulous. It was stemless! Did any standards exist these days?

"This is unacceptable," she said.

"Do you see a crack?" Joyce said.

"It's not what I see, it's what I don't see — a stem! You cannot serve white wine in a stemless glass." Her free hand fluttered impatiently up to the large pearls around her neck.

"Oh, Bea, it's fine. You have to get with the times. These are very popular right now."

"A stem is for function, not decoration. It is to keep the chilled wine from being heated by hands."

She charged back into her foyer in a huff, thinking for the thousandth time that the greatest indignity of aging was not watching your body degrade but watching the world around you fall apart.

Bea had been raised in a place where etiquette was second only to religion — Newport, Rhode Island. She was born just a few years after the Great Hurricane of 1938, a night when roads had been washed away along with people's lives. But her parents' story about that infamous evening said everything about the town: When the deadly storm hit, their neighbor Grace Graham Wilson Vanderbilt was preparing for a formal dinner, and she continued her preparations even as a large portion of her porch was swept away by the winds. Roads became rivers, and the invited guests had to decide whether to risk their lives or risk offending Grace Graham Wilson Vanderbilt. Twenty-seven of the thirty invited dinner guests arrived.

She would have her assistant deal with the wineglasses.

"Kyle, I need to talk to you," she said, snapping her fingers and waving him over.

"I need to talk to you too," he said. "There's something you should see."

Kyle handed her his phone, a news alert on the home screen: *Henry Wyatt, pioneer of the minimalist art movement, dead at 83.*

The room blurred around her. The party, the paintings, the wineglasses — all receded, replaced by images of another crowded room decades earlier. A young man with tapered fingers and paint under his nails. She closed her eyes, seeing a railroad apartment filled with canvas after canvas stacked against the walls. The memories rushed at her, vivid and breathtaking. She saw herself as if it were yesterday, sitting with Henry on a bench in Washington Square Park, broke and uncertain but with their entire lives ahead of them.

Bea reached for Kyle's arm to steady herself. "Get everyone out of this apartment. Pack my bag and pull the car around to the front."

"Now?"

"Now!"

"Where are you going?"

"*We* are going to the Hamptons."

In addition to everything else she had to do, Emma suddenly had another major task: maintaining a sense of normalcy.

While she had long heard rumors that The American Hotel was haunted, she had never known anyone to actually drop dead there. That it would happen on her watch was unfortunate. That it would happen to someone she knew and liked, even more so. But there was no time to think about Henry Wyatt when the bar was overflowing and the wait list for a table was in the double digits.

The Henry Wyatt business was being handled by her boss. The owner of the hotel, Jack Blake, had spent a long time huddled in the back office with the police chief and he was now busy keeping out the press. Emma told herself to pretend it was just a typical Friday night and focus on keeping the guests satisfied.

The head bartender, Chris Vincenzi, signaled for her.

Emma had a special affection for the bartenders at the hotel. She knew it was partly because her own father had been one himself. He had died when she was very young, so the hotel bar felt like a link to him. But on a practical level, she appreciated the bartenders because they made her job easier.

The bar was the heart and soul of the establishment. When cocktails were flowing and the conversation reached a fever pitch, when the assembled crowd was that perfect mix of local and transient, moneyed and blue collar, young and old, all was right with the world. Even the most persnickety hotel guest couldn't help but fall under the spell. When she'd applied for a job at the hotel, she'd dreamed of working behind the bar. But Jack Blake had never, in the history of his establishment, hired a female bartender. Sexist? Maybe. The guys at the bar called it tradition. She wondered if her father would have agreed with them.

"Em, can you pull this bottle for me?" Chris said, scribbling the name of a particular bottle of the Châteauneuf-du-Pape on a bar napkin. "I don't think any of the servers will be able to find it and I'm too slammed to go myself."

The owner of the hotel was serious about his wine. Jack had been collecting since the early 1970s, and the wine list was more than eighty-five pages long with somewhere around seventeen hundred selections. Although Emma had been employed at the hotel for almost a dozen years, the intricate maze of the wine cellar still occasionally stumped her. When she was downstairs, wandering through the rows of bottles, a thought popped into her head: *Penny!* It was the first time in hours she'd had a minute to think of her. Penny was going to take the news of Henry Wyatt's death hard. Emma just hoped that she could be the one to tell her what happened, that Penny wouldn't hear about it from someone else or see it online.

The hardest part of her job was that, when she was at the hotel for twelve or fourteen hours straight, she didn't get much contact with Penny. It was a safe town, and everyone knew everyone, but it was still less than ideal to have a fourteen-year-old running around unfettered after school. She was a good kid, but things happened. And when Emma was caught up in a busy wave at work, she felt completely cut off from her other job, her more important job, of being a mother. A single mother.

The wine cellar's numerical system sometimes sent her in circles and made her feel like she was misreading coordinates on a map, but tonight, thankfully, she navigated it correctly and spotted the bottle of Paul Jaboulet Aîné 2010 Domaine de Terre Ferme Red, Châteauneuf-du-Pape. Okay, so something had finally gone smoothly. Maybe the night was turning around.

Upstairs, she delivered the wine to the table and hurried back to the front desk to answer the ringing phone.

"The American Hotel, Emma speaking."

"Emma, Jim DiMartino here."

Jim DiMartino, a ten-year veteran of the Sag Harbor Police Department, had been one of the first responders when Henry Wyatt collapsed.

"Hi, Jim. You looking for the chief? He left a while ago."

"Actually, that's not why I'm calling. I've got Penny here at the station."

Over the din of the bar crowd, she could vaguely make out his words, something about a party and underage drinking and someone backing a car into a house on Fahys Road. Penny hadn't been drinking, but she'd been caught up in the sweep.

Emma looked helplessly around the room at the full tables, the packed lobby, the bar three-deep with customers.

"I'll be right there." Mercifully, the police station was just two doors away. She would go get Penny, and then she would have to call Angus to take her home. Angus, who used to rent the house next door, had moved in with Emma and Penny five years ago, when he lost his wife. Part of the move had been for financial reasons; why pay rent on a whole house when he lived by himself? Angus and Celia had, years before that, sold the house they'd owned together. The increased property taxes were crushing everyone, even people who were living in modest homes in modest parts of town. Now there was no such thing. A lot of people Emma knew had been forced to make tough choices.

But really, the move had been part of a promise he'd made to Celia before she died. Celia, who had babysat for Penny since she was a baby, did not want her husband to live alone after she was gone. "The man has been married for fifty-eight years," she'd said to Emma. "He won't fare well on his own. Good heavens, do you know how he would eat if left to his own devices?" Celia, anxious to make sure her husband would be loved and taken care of, made both Angus and Emma promise they would live in the same house.

Emma hated to call him this late. Angus spent his days volunteering at the Sag Harbor Historical Society or the whaling museum and he was usually asleep before eight. And, really, Emma should be taking Penny home herself. But just as a captain couldn't abandon his ship, she couldn't leave the front desk on a busy Friday night. Emma had long ago accepted that at any given moment, she was dropping the ball either at work or at home.

She turned into the alleyway between the municipal building and Page Restaurant. Page had its windows open, and music and laughter filled the night air.

The small station couldn't house all the teenagers picked up at the party, so they were lined up as if this were a fire drill at the high school. Every young face was glued to a cell-phone screen. She scanned the group for Penny. Her daughter, tall for her age at five foot six, usually stood out in a crowd of teenagers. Her wild hair also made her difficult to miss. And yet Emma didn't see her.

Emma made her way into the station. Sure enough, Jim had kept Penny close. She sat behind the counter at a chair next to Di-Martino's desk.

"Thanks for the call," Emma said, shaking the officer's hand. She turned to her daughter. "You okay?"

"Yeah, Mom. I'm fine." In typical teenage fashion, she seemed irritated, even though Emma was the one who'd been put out. Moments like this would be so much more tolerable if she had a co-parent with whom she could share an eye-roll. But, just as she had countless times before this, she reminded herself that she was in this alone and that she and her daughter were both doing their best.

"You didn't tell me you were going to a party."

"It was a last-minute thing. And my phone died."

Emma didn't have time for this.

"Some night," DiMartino said.

"Never a dull moment," Emma said, though that wasn't exactly true. There were many dull moments. Mostly dull moments, punctuated by minor catastrophes. Was that motherhood — or was it life?

She walked Penny back to Main Street and sat her on a bench in front of a sign for the old jail museum. She told her not to move an inch until Angus arrived.

Only when Emma was back behind the desk at the hotel did she remember the news about Henry Wyatt.

CHAPTER THREE

There were houses that had addresses and houses that had names. Henry Wyatt's home of the past thirty years was the latter. It was nine at night when Bea reached Sag Harbor and Kyle steered the car onto a private street, Actors Colony Road. In the midst of this beautiful stretch of waterfront homes, the house called Windsong sat like the jewel in a crown.

The driveway curved around the side of the house and led to a hidden garage. Of course Henry would not blight the approach to his home with anything as pedestrian as parked cars.

Kyle came around and opened Bea's door, and when the cool night air hit her cheeks, she almost lost her footing. It was real. This was happening. She was at Windsong, but Henry was not. Henry was gone.

Kyle managed the luggage while Bea walked to the door clutching the single key in her hand. The darkness of night lifted when the security lights were activated by their movements. Kyle let out a low whistle as the house, in all of its modern, dramatic glory, suddenly came into view.

It was a masterpiece designed by Henry himself decades ago. Henry was an artist to his core, and he had never been constrained by medium. He painted, he drew, he sculpted, and he created his home. Bea, a nonartist who had always surrounded herself with talented people, did not possess the drive to create, but she was in awe of it.

The one thing all of Henry Wyatt's work shared was minimalism, and Windsong was an absolute extension of that. A combination of wood, stone, and metal, the house had floor-to-ceiling glass walls and an open layout.

Bea put the key in the lock. It had been a few years since she'd used it, but she hadn't taken the key off her key chain since the day Henry had given it to her.

She moved through darkness and found the central light switch from memory.

"This place is insane," Kyle said. Even at night, the spectacular integration of the interior of the house and the outdoors was breathtaking. "You're sure we should be here?"

"I have a key, don't I?" Bea snapped. She walked deeper into the house, each painting on the wall triggering a memory of the friend she'd just lost. She took a few minutes to run her hands over a few of the sculptures meticulously placed throughout, still in disbelief.

A thirty-two-by-forty-inch oil painting with large swaths of green and black dominated the living room. As with all of his paintings, the piece had a central element to ground it. This particular canvas had hung in the Guggenheim for many years. Entitled *Greene Street, 1972,* it was named after the location of the gallery they had once owned together.

"Follow me to the guest suites."

How long had it been since she was at the house? She had forgotten the tranquillity of the space, with its white oak floors and ceilings, the flat-panel doors with hidden fixtures. Everything was perfectly designed and seamless. Every inch was Henry.

The news reports speculated that Henry had suffered a massive heart attack, but Bea needed to get the facts from official channels. She'd left a message for Henry's attorney Victor Bonivent but had not heard back from him. Now she wondered if he had still retained Victor. How much did she really know about Henry's life in recent years?

The stairs to the upper level gave the illusion of floating along a white wall. Bea briefly considered going up to Henry's room but decided against it. She wasn't emotionally prepared for that; she would instead take a room in the guest suite.

For a few years after Henry built the house, Bea had declined his invitations to visit. Windsong had been the mistress who stole him away from Manhattan, away from her. Their rift had not been caused by the house, but it had coincided with the construction of Windsong, and so the place had seemed, for a time, to be the embodiment of their lost friendship.

"Do you want me to unpack your bag now?" Kyle asked in the doorway of a glass-walled room with a view of the bay.

Bea waved him off dismissively. "Tomorrow."

"Um, Bea, how long will we be staying here? Through the weekend?"

How long. How long indeed! How long did it take to honor the past? How long to stop feeling like she was staring into the churning waters of her own obsolescence? Of course there was no sense trying to explain this to a thirty-two-year-old, a man who no doubt believed he had all the time in the world. Bea remembered that feeling. And it was indelibly intertwined with her memories of meeting Henry.

"Kyle, Henry Wyatt was my oldest friend. And I was essentially his family — the only family he had." She couldn't change the past. She couldn't bring Henry back. But, filled with a sense of purpose she hadn't experienced for a very long time, she said, "I must settle his estate. I know he'd want me to take care of Windsong. We will be here indefinitely."

"Sorry my mom had to call you," Penny said to Angus.

He barely glanced at her. Angus had white hair and wore frameless round glasses. He wasn't fat but he had broad shoulders and he was big, like a former football player. Angus was a retired high-school history teacher, and as far as Penny was concerned, he needed to go back to work. He clearly missed it, since he was constantly subjecting her to impromptu lessons about Sag Harbor. He was a nonstop trivia machine, and although her mother found this endlessly fascinating, Penny didn't like feeling as if she should be taking notes over her breakfast cereal.

Penny's mother had told her that when she moved into the house on Mount Misery, shortly after Penny was born, she had immediately bonded with two of her new neighbors, Angus Sinclair and his wife, Celia. Unlike the waves of newcomers who'd been snapping up property for the past decade or so, and also very unlike the summer people, Emma Mapson had deep roots in Sag Harbor. The Sinclairs did as well; Angus's family had been one of the first African-American families to buy a vacation house in Ninevah Beach. This was in the 1940s, a time when African-Americans weren't allowed to buy homes in many other parts of the country.

"I wasn't asleep yet," Angus said, pulling up to their house on Mount Misery Drive. "I was watching the news." His voice was so deep, it made everything he said sound important. Tonight, maybe because she felt guilty about the party, it also made him sound angry.

Once inside the house, Penny tried to creep up the stairs without any more conversation, but Angus wasn't letting her off the hook.

"I just hope you're not getting yourself into trouble, Penelope Bay Mapson," he said.

41

Angus's late wife, Celia, had always used Penny's full given name when she was babysitting and got serious about something. *Bay* had been chosen by Penny's father. Her parents had met when her father was in town one summer performing in a play at the Bay Street Theater. He'd long since left, but Penny was still stuck with the weird name.

Penny went into the kitchen. "No trouble at all," she told Angus. *Lies, lies, lies.*

At the party, alcohol was everywhere and in whatever form anyone could possibly want — kegs, Jell-O shots, bottles of vodka and tequila. By the time Penny had arrived, empty red Solo cups were scattered over every surface, inside the house and out on the wide deck right on the water.

Penny didn't dare drink. Her mother would kill her. And unlike a lot of kids' parents, Emma worked around drunk people all the time and would notice the slightest sign of it. So while everyone was having fun, Penny was not. No one was talking to her. No one was even looking at her. And in her mind, she could still hear those sirens outside the hotel.

She couldn't be sure it was Mr. Wyatt who had died. But somehow, she just knew. All she would have to do was borrow someone's phone and Google it, but she was afraid to make it all real. At the same time, she couldn't stop thinking about him. Every ten minutes she'd gone to the bathroom and washed her hands, lathering and lathering to calm herself and then standing over the sink and letting them drip-dry. She couldn't bring herself to touch the towel hanging on the rack. And so, when Robin finally came over to talk to her and offered her a round white pill, as innocent-looking as aspirin, she took it. Anything to escape her own thoughts. "Don't worry, Mindy says her mother pops these like Tic Tacs," Robin had said.

At first, for maybe half an hour after Penny took the pill, she felt nothing. Then, out of nowhere, she was filled with a fuzzy happiness, like being wrapped in a magic blanket. She was still sitting on the couch, and she was still being ignored by basically everyone, but she felt the distinct absence of worry. It was incredible.

And then Mindy's older sister, Jordan, yelled: "The cops are here!"

Thank God she hadn't had that drink.

Now Angus harrumphed, settled into a cushioned chair next to the sofa, and turned on the television with a flick of the remote. In the kitchen, Penny rummaged through cabinets as a cable news show played in the background. She poured popcorn into a bowl, went into the living room, and offered it to Angus, who was busy mumbling his disapproval about current events.

That's when she noticed the news scroll at the bottom of the screen: ARTIST HENRY WYATT DEAD AT 83.

It was real. Mr. Wyatt was gone. And even the little white pill couldn't change that.

CHAPTER FOUR

Saturday mornings at the hotel were the busiest times of the week.

Typically, Emma did not take a break, did not check her phone, and was lucky to find a moment to use the bathroom. That was part of the deal when you worked in hospitality. But Penny's therapist, Dr. Alice Wang, would be out of town for their regularly scheduled appointment later this week, and today at noon was the only slot she had available. Emma didn't want Penny missing a session, especially in light of everything that had happened last night.

"I'll pick you up at eleven thirty," Emma had said to Penny on her way out the door that morning.

"I can just ride my bike over and meet you," Penny said. That would actually be much easier for Emma, but Penny was grounded.

"You're not to leave this house until I get

home," Emma said.

Again, Penny apologized for not telling her mother she was going to a party — a party where, it turned out, people were using drugs and alcohol.

"I only went because I was upset about Mr. Wyatt and I didn't want to be alone," she said.

Here, Emma blamed herself for not taking the time to call Penny and break the news. Now she had to both console her and punish her, and all before leaving for work.

Sometimes, she wished she had a mother she could ask for advice about Penny. But she was on her own when it came to her hopes for and worries about her daughter. And Penny, through no fault of her own, had given her plenty to worry about.

The OCD had started at around age eight; the anxiety, age ten.

When Penny was in fifth grade, Emma started her in CBT, cognitive-behavioral therapy, although Penny hated it. For a long time, there was very little improvement, and Emma was frustrated.

Then, over the past year or so, Penny had gotten noticeably better, and Emma couldn't help but think it had something to do with Henry Wyatt's drawing lessons. The drawing kept Penny's mind occupied.

Maybe there was something meditative about it. Maybe it was the sense of accomplishment after a contained task.

She had been surprised when Penny and the old man hit it off. Wary, to be honest.

It was a shame you had to think cynically, but in today's world? With a young daughter? But it was clear the old artist was just entertained by Penny's interest in drawing. And Penny, in her typical way, connected more naturally with an octogenarian painter than with a kid her own age. Henry Wyatt, for all his fame and money, was alone. Maybe lonely. So he and Penny were good for each other. She just hoped his death wouldn't set Penny back too much.

The desk phone rang.

"The American Hotel, Emma speaking."

"Em, it's Sean. I'm at the dock with a woman who's booked at the hotel. She needs help with her luggage. Can you send someone down?"

Sean Pine operated a water taxi and he also rented moorings to a lot of the seasonal boaters. Like Emma, he was a Sag Harbor native who had never left and had figured out how to make a living in town. His wife, Alexis, had grown up in nearby Southampton and now owned the bookstore.

Emma sighed. "I'm totally shorthanded."

"I'd bring the bags myself but I have another pickup."

Emma checked her watch. She had fifteen minutes before she had to go get Penny.

"I'll be right there," she said.

Outside, she shielded her eyes from the bright, late-morning sun, breathing in the smell of fresh coffee from the full patio tables. A jitney pulled up in front of the hotel and unloaded another pack of vacationers. She turned and walked to the wharf, passing the perfume shop and the upscale restaurant Wölffer Kitchen, where a friend was outside writing the day's specials on a chalkboard. Emma waved but kept moving; there was no time to chat.

The air smelled briny and fresh as she got closer to the water. She crossed Bay Street, where a family of ducks had halted traffic. She passed the theater and a seafood restaurant called the Dock House, then found shade in the shadow of the town's historic windmill. From there, she surveyed Long Wharf. The dock was filled with boats of every size and variety: yachts and elegant sailboats and small skiffs. In the distance, Emma saw local captain Cole Hopkins sail by on his signature turquoise catamaran. At the edge of the dock, a couple stood taking pictures of each other, the shimmering, still water in the background.

She spotted Sean's water taxi just pulling into a slip with one passenger on board, a woman who looked to be about eight months pregnant.

"Sorry to trouble you," the woman said as Sean helped her off the boat. "I'm not supposed to be lifting anything."

Sean's dog, a Jack Russell terrier named Melville, barked from the deck at a low-flying seagull.

"Not a problem," Emma said, hoisting the strap of the woman's stuffed Vera Bradley bag over her shoulder and taking hold of her roller suitcase. "It's just a few blocks to the hotel."

Sean called Emma aside. "Meet us for drinks tonight at Murf's? Alexis is done at nine."

"I can't go out. Penny's acting up."

Sean shook his head. "You need to live a little."

Sometimes Penny zoned out during her therapy sessions. Instead of listening, she marveled at Dr. Wang's endless array of shift dresses and matching accessories — gold trinkets, high-heeled and trendy footwear, intricately knotted silk scarves.

Basically, a dose of high fashion was the

only thing that Penny got out of the weekly visits. Two years and counting, and Penny felt no closer to being able to "boss it back." That was what Dr. Wang called not listening to her obsessive and compulsive thoughts.

Penny had admitted this to her mother, who must have repeated it to Dr. Wang. At their previous session, Dr. Wang said, "Penny, OCD is an illness and if you want to get better, you have to work at it. If a person had heart disease, the doctor would tell him to exercise and adjust his diet. You need to do the work so we can retrain your brain."

Penny was all for retraining her brain. It was just that none of Dr. Wang's advice helped.

"Remember, your OCD is not *you.* It's separate and something you can control."

So far, Penny had seen no evidence of that.

And the worksheets weren't helping. Every week, Penny was supposed to keep a log of things that triggered her anxiety — what had happened, what was she thinking, what was she feeling? Then she had to rate her level of worry on a scale of 1 to 10.

The concept of rating her worry was just so frustrating. She didn't want to admit that she never felt *degrees* of worry. She was worried, or she wasn't. Whether the scale was 1 to 10 or 1 to 100 meant nothing. Worry was worry, and when she felt it, it took over. That's when the compulsions kicked in.

And this brought Penny to the worst part of seeing Dr. Wang: Exposures. Yes, Penny washed her hands too much. Yes, she thought excessively about germs and getting a stomach virus. But it felt like torture to have to come to Dr. Wang's office and, for example, touch the light switch and then touch her mouth.

"How are you doing, Penny?"

Today, Dr. Wang was wearing a lavender dress with silver jewelry. Or maybe it was white gold? Contemplating this, Penny realized she'd forgotten to do her worksheet that week. Maybe Dr. Wang would forget about it too.

"Do you have your worksheet?"

Penny shook her head.

"Can you remember for next week? It's important, Penny."

"I'm sorry," she said. But really, who cared about a stupid worksheet? A worksheet wasn't going to help her. The one person who had helped her was gone. She felt tears in her eyes but blinked them away. No need to get Dr. Wang all excited. Drawing with

Henry helped her more than anything she'd ever done in therapy. When she was drawing, her mind was blank. She was free.

Dr. Wang handed her a tissue. "I know you suffered a loss last night. I'm sorry about Henry Wyatt." She asked Penny if she wanted to talk about it, but Penny shook her head. Still, Dr. Wang went on and on about death being a part of life and that she was lucky she had met him and all sorts of other true, positive things. But none of it changed the fact that Mr. Wyatt was gone. And none of it acknowledged the thing that Penny knew would sound crazy: Mr. Wyatt had been her best friend. Her only friend.

What did it say about her that her best friend was an eighty-year-old man? And what was she going to do now that he was gone?

CHAPTER FIVE

For two weeks after the death of Henry Wyatt, Bea Winstead barely left the great house called Windsong. The house made her feel connected to Henry, and it was painful to leave it even for a few hours.

She surfaced only to attend the memorial service back in Manhattan, at the Frank E. Campbell Funeral Home on Madison Avenue, where she had spoken to few people. One of those few had been Henry's longtime attorney Victor Bonivent.

"I'll call you," Victor had said.

But Victor had not called her. Bea realized, waking with a start in the middle of the night in Henry's guest room, that the probate process must be well under way.

In the morning, she left a terse message at his office. By noon, no one had returned her call, so she left another. And then, impatient and unable to lie around grieving any longer, she decided it was time to

53

get to work.

Bea paced in front of the floor-to-ceiling window overlooking a sprawling green lawn. Her eyes fell on a sculpture on the back lawn, a twelve-foot-by-twelve-foot hollow steel cube. Part of the second phase of Henry Wyatt's legendary career. First, the painting. Then sculpture. Then — the house.

He designed the house during a period when the two of them were, if not estranged, then certainly less connected than they had once been. For a few painful years, Bea had felt she was losing her biggest client and dearest friend.

She learned about the completion of Henry's modern masterpiece of a house from a magazine. She heard rumors that he was designing a building, that he was painting, that the State of Texas had commissioned him to do a sculpture for a public square. None of it was true. None of it except for the great house.

She wanted to get him back to painting. She wanted to get him back to New York City. She wanted the two of them to be what they had once been.

The night of her first visit to Windsong, they sat on terrace lounge chairs, drinking wine and looking out at the bay. A far cry from their early days in the East Village cooking on a hot plate.

"I think your heart is still in painting," she'd said.

He said no. His days of creating art were behind him. Looking forward, he wanted to turn the place into a museum someday. A permanent installation of his work. And he wanted her to be in charge of it.

The suggestion took her by surprise. She wasn't ready to let go of the idea of Henry returning to Manhattan and re-creating the magic of the old days. After the visit, back in the city, she all but forgot about the Henry Wyatt Museum. There was plenty of time for that later. And then time ran out.

Bea sat down and called for Kyle.

"Send for my clothes in New York. Clear my calendar for the next six weeks. Postpone all my events until the fall. We need to catalog all the art in this house, and I want a list of the private collectors who have his work so we can buy some back."

The sound of the front door clicking open and then closed startled them both.

"Are you expecting someone?" Kyle said.

"Certainly not!" Bea jumped up. "And the alarm was set."

Bea rounded the table and peeked into the hallway, caught between irritation and fear. She turned and waved for Kyle to follow her, then put her finger to her lips in a *shh* gesture. Kyle nodded, then picked up a heavy, decorative ceramic plate from a table. To use as a weapon? Finally, some proactive thinking!

They crept along until they reached the entrance foyer, where Bea realized a weapon would not be needed after all.

A gray-haired man in a jacket and tie looked up, startled, clearly as surprised to see them as they were to see him. "Bea! What are you doing here?"

Bea squared her shoulders. "If you'd returned any of my *many* phone calls, Victor, you would know what I'm doing here."

He sighed. "Bea, I've had my hands full."

"Indeed. Let's talk in the dining room," Bea said briskly. "Kyle, put on a fresh pot of coffee."

Victor did not move. "Bea, I'm sorry. I know this is a difficult time for you, but you cannot be here in this house."

"Don't be absurd, Victor. Where better for me to manage his estate than in the house with the work?"

Victor glanced at Kyle, then back at her. "Can we speak alone for a moment?"

Bea sighed impatiently but reminded

herself that dealing with Victor was just a temporary annoyance and soon she'd officially take the reins.

"My assistant can hear whatever you have to say. He's helping me catalog the estate. He's more helpful than you at this point, Victor."

"There's nothing for you to catalog, Bea. You have no claim to Henry's estate. He left it to another party."

"Excuse me?" she said, although she had heard him perfectly well. She needed to stall, needed a moment to process the unthinkable. He repeated the noxious statement and she reached for the wall to steady herself. "That's not possible!" Bea said. "There must be some mistake."

"The probate process has been very thorough. I have it all here in black-and-white. You need to vacate the premises immediately."

Emma had set the morning aside for pruning her rose garden.

She knew some people saw the annual task as a chore, but for her, any excuse to be down in the soil was welcome.

Her hybrid teas and floribundas had fared well over the winter; luckily, it had been mild enough not to test their hardiness too severely. Still, on close inspection, she saw that some of the canes were brown and shriveled. She pulled on her gloves, picked up her lopper, and set to work paring back the branches to reveal the fresh, white inside.

The usual peacefulness settled over her as she worked, although she still had the nagging feeling that she should have insisted Penny come outside and, if not help her, at least get some fresh air. An hour earlier, she'd found Penny in her room with a bunch of Henry Wyatt drawings spread out on her bed.

"Hon, you can't just stare at Mr. Wyatt's drawings all the time. It's upsetting you."

"The *drawings* aren't upsetting me. His *death* upsets me. I didn't even get to say good-bye. Why does life have to suck all the time?"

"Penny, life doesn't suck all the time. I wish you didn't feel that way. Sometimes good things happen."

"When's the last time something good happened?"

Emma had reached out to ruffle her hair. "Hmm. Well, maybe the day you were born. That was a good day."

"Fourteen years ago? That's sad, Mom. Really pathetic."

Emma hated to hear Penny being so negative, so fatalistic. It reminded her of her own mother, someone whom Emma certainly didn't want Penny to end up like.

Her mother, Vivian, was the one who taught her to garden. It was one of the few things that had brought her joy in life after they'd lost Emma's father suddenly when he was in his early forties.

"Life offers so little beauty," her mother had said. "The least we can do is try to grow our own."

Vivian was more ambitious with her roses than Emma. She didn't shy away from the finicky varieties and had a real focus on the most fragrant blooms, which were generally the darker and more heavily petaled flowers.

Every Saturday morning, her mother made blueberry pancakes, and then the two of them would work in the garden for hours. By her mother's side, Emma learned everything about soil and planting, how to harden off the roses in preparation for the winter, how to protect them from pests in the summer, and, her favorite part, how to cut the flowers. Her mother was a master at artfully arranging the blooms in vases all over the house.

But gradually, in the years following her

husband's death, Vivian Kirkland became less and less functional. Growing up, Emma accepted her mother's constant headaches and days spent in a dark room as normal. Vivian lost nearly every job she managed to get except for one, and that was because she'd quit before they could fire her. At least, that's what she told Emma.

When Emma was in high school, the last of her father's life-insurance money ran out. Vivian seemed to lose her already tenuous hold on normal thinking and behavior. She became very accident-prone — fender benders, slips on ice in the winter. Emma began to suspect that these "accidents" were deliberate, sources of lawsuits and, therefore, money. They also had the side benefit of getting doctors to prescribe painkillers, to which her mother had developed a nasty addiction.

By the time Emma was a senior in high school, her mother gave up on the garden. Emma took over, tending to the roses until the day the bank foreclosed on the house.

Vivian suffered a fatal overdose when Emma was three months pregnant. But when Emma was in the garden, her mother was still with her. To this day, the smell of roses, even in someone's perfume, brought back Vivian Kirkland.

"Mom?" Penny leaned against the back door and called to Emma in the garden. She was dressed in cutoff jeans and a Bleachers T-shirt, and Emma observed, not for the first time, that Penny's face was changing; she was starting to look like a young woman, not a child. With her height, her curly dark hair, and her dark eyes, she also looked strikingly like her father. It was a cosmic test, surely, to make the daughter she loved so much look like the man who'd hurt her so badly.

"Some guy is at the front door," Penny said.

"Some guy?"

"An old dude wearing a tie."

"He must have the wrong address. I'm coming."

Emma pulled off her gloves and wiped her moist hands on her jeans. Penny trailed her into the house and stood by the stairs.

Emma looked out the dining-room window and saw a short older man, silver-haired and wearing horn-rims. He carried a black leather briefcase. Strange.

The man rang the bell yet again and Emma opened the door warily. "Can I help you?"

"I'm looking for Emma Mapson."

"That's me. And you are?"

He extended his hand. "I'm Victor Bonivent, attorney with Smythe, Bonivent, Worth."

"What can I do for you?"

"May I come in?"

"I'm on my way to work, so if you can just tell me what this is about."

"Mrs. Mapson, trust me, this is worth a few minutes of your time."

Emma stepped aside and let the man walk into the house. Only then did she remember Penny lingering behind her. "Penny, go to your room for a few minutes."

Penny sighed dramatically and retreated up the stairs.

Emma asked the man to follow her to the kitchen, but she found Angus at the table reading the paper, so she turned around and led Mr. Bonivent back to the living room. The small house suddenly felt much smaller.

Emma sat in Angus's armchair and the lawyer sat on the couch and set his briefcase on the scarred wooden trunk that served as a coffee table. He opened it and pulled out a sheaf of papers.

"I'm sorry to bother you at home, but I only had this address. No e-mail, no phone number. You're the parent and legal guardian of Penelope Mapson?"

Emma squared her shoulders. "What exactly is this about, Mr. Bonivent?"

"My client was a man named Henry Wyatt. Did you know Mr. Wyatt?"

Emma leaned forward. "He was a regular at the hotel where I work."

The lawyer glanced down at the papers, then up at Emma. "Are you aware that Mr. Wyatt died recently?"

Emma nodded. "I am. I was at the hotel when it happened. A shame."

"Indeed." The man adjusted his glasses and handed the papers to Emma. "This is a copy of Mr. Wyatt's last will and testament. When you read it, you will see that he left his house on Actors Colony Road to your minor child, Penelope Mapson."

"I'm sorry, what?" Emma didn't bother looking at the papers.

Actors Colony Road was a private stretch of homes on the waterfront. She remembered reading in the paper last summer that the actor Richard Gere had sold his home there for thirty-six million dollars.

The lawyer repeated the bit about the house, and Emma knew that no matter how many times the man said the words, they still wouldn't make sense.

"There's been a mistake," Emma said. "I mean, he gave her art lessons and they had a nice little friendship, but this is . . . this is crazy!"

The lawyer, clearly unmoved by Emma's declaration, nodded toward the paperwork. "It's all spelled out in the documents."

Emma shook her head. "This doesn't make any sense. Do I need a lawyer?"

"You do not need a lawyer to take possession of the house."

"Do I pay taxes on this? I can't afford it. I can't even afford the utilities on a house like that."

"You don't pay taxes on the house unless you sell it. But the house is not yours to sell. As the child's legal guardian, you will hold the property until she reaches the age of majority. At that time, she can decide to sell it."

Emma's mind raced. Maybe Penny had mentioned to the old man that they had money problems? But no, she was grasping at straws here. There was no way that this made sense.

"Like I said, I can't afford the upkeep of the house."

"Money has been set aside for the care of the house and property. Just come to me when you need funds to manage lawn care, pool maintenance, that sort of thing. Mr. Wyatt also left your daughter the contents of the house."

"You mean the furniture?"

"The furniture, the books, his wine collection. But, most significant, his artwork. Aside from a few paintings he bequeathed to a museum in Texas." Mr. Bonivent flipped through his copy of the paperwork he'd handed her. "Again, the works of art in the house cannot be sold until the beneficiary reaches majority, and even then, there are some stipulations."

Emma nervously pulled her hair into a ponytail and then released it. She would have to talk to someone about this. Were any of the happy-hour regulars at the bar attorneys?

"Look, I'm sure Mr. Wyatt's family will contest this." But even as Emma said it, she realized that Henry Wyatt had never spoken of family. He'd never even spoken of friends. The guy was a loner.

"There is no family." Mr. Bonivent handed Emma a document and his business card. "This spells out the handling of his artwork. I'll need your signature in a few places. I'd be happy to answer any questions that arise."

"Wait — I've never even seen this house. This is just . . . you're kind of throwing me for a loop here."

The lawyer looked around the room, and Emma saw it through his eyes. For the first time in a long while, she mentally kicked herself for not doing more with the place. She spent her free time out back in the garden. When she was inside, she barely saw the cracks in the paint, the water damage on her bedroom ceiling that she hadn't gotten around to fixing. The area rugs were worn out, but they were functional. Why throw money away?

Mr. Bonivent handed her a set of keys. "We'll be in touch," he said.

Walking him to the door, she knew there was something she should say or ask but for the life of her, she couldn't think of what that would be.

Chapter Six

Bea knew she had crossed a line in grabbing the ceramic plate from Kyle and throwing it at Victor. In her defense, it had missed him by a good foot.

Kyle knelt on the floor and swept the shards into a dustpan. She paced a safe distance away, contemplating her next move. There was only one place to go.

"When you're finished with that, I need you to make a reservation."

"Where?"

"The American Hotel, the only civilized place in town. No — forget calling. We'll just pack and go there straightaway."

He looked up at her. "Bea, I can't stay out here any longer. I have a life back in New York."

She knew this was not true. His life was managing her life.

It had started out simple; Kyle had framed paintings, put together art installations, done the odd touch-up job on her floors. He oversaw her kitchen remodeling.

Bea started to rely on him more. She taught Kyle how to manage the catering for parties. For a time, there was art business in the Hamptons or Connecticut, and Kyle would be dispatched to handle issues if Bea did not feel like making the trip. And she never felt like making the trip. Kyle was spending so much time at 720 Park Avenue, she offered him a room in the guest wing when he worked late, which saved him the hour-long subway ride back to Brooklyn. After a while it seemed like a waste of money for him to keep paying the rent on his twenty-five-hundred-dollar-a-month studio, so he let it go.

Bea did occasionally wonder why a young, attractive, capable young man like Kyle was so willing to let his life be swept up in her own. She'd asked him once, only half joking, if he was hiding from something.

"Am I going to flip through the television channels and see you on *America's Most Wanted* one night?" she said.

"I'm not hiding from anything, Bea. The truth is, I lost the one thing I wanted to do with my life, and I haven't figured out a good alternative. I guess until I do, working for you is a pretty interesting distraction."

So the job she had handed him and for which she paid him so handsomely had served as a useful distraction, but now that *she* needed something, he was balking. People were so selfish! "Kyle, the whole reason we work so well together is that you are happy to let my life be *your* life. So stop with this nonsense. Have the car out front in twenty minutes."

She marched back to her room, her pulse racing from the exertion and from her deep indignation at what was taking place. In the hallway, a splash of blue caught her eye and she stopped to look at the painting. Henry's work always spoke to Bea, and this was true even in her current state. *Untitled Blue,* oil on canvas, 1960. It was the first painting Henry had ever shown her.

She hesitated only a second before removing it from the wall and marching it out to her car.

Emma could barely focus on the staff meeting.

Jack Blake had assembled everyone in the piano room. The staff pulled chairs around the Steinway, and Jack sat on the bench where a musician performed six nights a week all summer long.

Over and over, Emma mentally replayed

the conversation with the lawyer, certain there had to be some mistake. How could Henry Wyatt have left his house to Penny?

"This will take only a few minutes," said Jack. He wore a mint-green polo shirt, khaki pants, and one of the baseball hats emblazoned with the Sag Harbor zip code that they sold at the hotel. Jack was not very tall but he was distinguished-looking, with a year-round tan, deep-set blue eyes, and a thick head of white hair.

Jack Blake had bought the hotel in 1972 when he was just twenty-four years old. The Youngs family had owned the property and operated the hotel for ninety-four years. By the time Jack bought the place, it had been on the market for two years. No one but Jack had a vision of what the hotel could become.

In those early days, Jack didn't have a chef for the restaurant. He did all the cooking — fish and chips and burgers — himself. He did a lot of the repair work himself too, and what he couldn't do, he hired local plumbers and electricians to take care of. He'd spend days at wallpaper places looking for high-quality reams he could buy in bulk. He scoured antique stores for furniture. He was so consumed with his vision for the hotel, his young wife left him. Jack forged on, hiring a staff of people he wanted to surround himself with day in and day out. One of those first hires was Emma's father, Tom, also twenty-four and tasked to run the new bar.

Now, as Jack sat at the piano, he told the staff, "I wanted to make sure you all know about the fund-raiser to rebuild the movie theater. This is a cause close to my heart, since I'd say that, second only to live music, a good movie is vital to the soul — the soul of a person and the soul of a town. I think we all miss walking down the street and meeting our friends and family to watch a movie together. And I want that back."

Emma discreetly checked her phone. The visit from the lawyer was so unbelievable, she half expected someone to text her with *Just kidding!*

"So we're going to have a food table at the fund-raiser and we need volunteers for that. And if you can get on any other committee to make the night a success, let me know and I'll jigger your schedule here accordingly. Thanks, all."

The staff members all filed slowly back to their posts. Emma thought that even more than the movie theater, she missed SagTown Coffee and a few of the other shops in the adjacent building that had also been de-

71

stroyed. She couldn't remember the last time she'd seen a movie — or done anything else for fun, really. But she'd picked up chocolate chip cookies from SagTown a few times a week. She could go for one right now.

Back behind the front desk, she took a call from a guest who needed a blow-dryer. Apparently, room 8 was missing one. Emma called housekeeping to bring one up and then she checked the ledger to see who had checked out yesterday. People walked away with the strangest things.

"Miss, I need your assistance."

Emma looked up. The woman had asked for help politely, but there was a shrillness to her voice that told Emma she had about four seconds to respond before things got ugly. "What can I do for you?" Emma asked with a smile.

"I'm Bea Winstead," the woman said, as if that should mean something to Emma. She had coiffed white hair and wore gumball-size pearl earrings and a matching necklace. Her white blouse was embroidered with small green frogs, and one arm was laden with enamel Hermès bracelets. Her mouth had the telltale creases of a smoker or a former smoker. "I need two rooms for the next thirty days."

Was this a joke? Emma glanced down at the full reservation book, columns and columns of her own handwriting.

The woman in front of her mused aloud that maybe she actually needed three rooms, one for their luggage and other "operational needs."

Emma braced herself. "I'm afraid we are fully booked at the moment."

"How is that possible?" The woman pressed her hand to her chest and turned to look at a man who was standing next to her holding luggage. Her son? Tough to say. He appeared to be around Emma's age and she couldn't help but notice his all-American good looks. Hopefully, he would be the voice of reason.

"Well, we have only eight rooms. And we get quite busy this time of year. If you'd like, I can give you the names of some —"

"Where is Jack? I want to speak to him immediately."

It wasn't uncommon for people who knew Jack from around town or from Palm Beach, where he spent his winters, to ask to speak to him when they wanted something at the hotel. But it was Emma's job to be a buffer. Jack always told her that if there was someone at the hotel he wanted to hear from, she would know about it in advance. Before she could launch into her scripted response — Jack was away from the premises but Emma would be happy to call the general manager, blah-blah-blah — the man intervened.

"Bea, I'm sure this woman can direct us to another place to stay."

"This is the only suitable hotel in this backwater!"

Emma bristled at the slight to her hometown. She was used to visitors not fully appreciating its charm and history, but she'd never heard it outright insulted before.

The man looked at her with an apologetic smile. "If you have any cancellations, will you let me know?" He had dimples.

"Certainly," Emma said, taking his phone number.

And then Emma remembered that a couple who had reserved a room for two nights had found out that Baron's Cove had a pool and checked out a day early. She leaned over the reservation book to see a faint line in blue ink crossing out the second day of the booking. She should have made a bolder note. She had probably been doing three other things at once.

"Actually," she said, "we do have a cancellation. You're in luck. We have one room available."

"Young lady, I need *two* rooms," the woman said indignantly, as if Emma's insufficient solution to the problem were a personal affront.

Emma smiled. "Honestly, it's a miracle we have one."

"We'll take it," said Mr. All-American.

The woman slid her credit card across the desk.

Bea had really expected better service from the venerable hotel. The woman at the front desk practically had to be begged to take Bea's money. Very disappointing. Nonetheless, she followed her up the stairs to the third floor. Kyle followed close behind with their bags.

The hallways were narrow and lined with heavy wooden furniture, potted plants, and gilt-framed mirrors; the walls were covered in floral-print wallpaper.

"We call this room the Apartment," the desk woman said, turning her key in the door.

The room was a duplex. It had a small living area with an exposed-brick wall and a fireplace, next to which was a heavy antique wooden desk and a large potted plant. Across the room was a large couch covered in brocade cushions. Behind it, a framed painting of a sailboat. The plaid carpeting continued up narrow stairs that led to what Bea supposed was the bedroom.

"*More* stairs?" Bea asked, hands on her hips.

The woman, clearly at the end of her patience, headed out. "My name is Emma. Please call the front desk if you need anything further." With that, she left, closing the door behind her.

"That woman is very rude."

"No, Bea, she isn't."

Bea looked at him in surprise. This insubordination was not typical and certainly not acceptable. But she would give him the benefit of the doubt and assume it was due to the stress of their present circumstances.

"You're just saying that because she's attractive. Really, Kyle, I expect more from you. At least while you're on the clock." Men were all the same; when they saw a pretty face, their brains melted. She eyed the stairs. "Kyle, follow close behind me with my bag. If I take a tumble, I hope you have the presence of mind and physical fortitude to break my fall."

She made her way slowly to the upper level of the duplex, holding on to the wooden railing. The wall to her right was lined with books. She felt like she was slipping into a library attic hideaway. It was oddly delightful.

The room had a queen bed covered in a white duvet and a wooden cabinet by the bed with an old-fashioned phone on top. The wood-beamed ceiling was slanted low on both sides.

"See, they don't make rooms like this anymore," Bea said, turning to make sure Kyle was behind her. He hovered near the steps.

"So I guess I'll be sleeping on the couch?"

"We all have to make sacrifices, Kyle. We're here for a very important purpose, not a vacation."

"I know it's not a vacation," Kyle said. "But since I have absolutely nothing to do, I'm heading down to the bar. That's where you can find me if you need me."

Bea had a strict no-cocktails-before-five rule. But she supposed a glass of wine at this juncture couldn't hurt. "Fine. If you insist. I will join you."

The bar was just a few steps beyond the lobby. There was a working fireplace, half a dozen tables for dining, and eclectic odds and ends everywhere. On the mantel, an elephant candelabra, and on one wall, a mounted moose head with . . . was that a cigarette in its mouth? And everywhere, nautical paintings in gilt frames.

They found seats in the middle of the bar, which was set with little silver bowls filled with roasted almonds. A row of framed *Wine Spectator* awards lined one wall, and overhead were the same Tiffany lamps that could be found throughout the hotel.

Not a thing had changed in the thirty years since Bea had had a drink in that very spot.

She could still remember, like it was yesterday, the way Henry had looked sitting just about where Kyle was now. He had been in his forties at the time, his thick dark hair just starting to gray. Like all men, he'd grown more distinguished and handsome as the years passed, and like most women, Bea had become less physically alluring. It hardly mattered; she had never been a beauty, and she'd built her life and self-worth around her career. By the time they'd taken the fateful trip to Sag Harbor, all she'd cared about was work. It was her guiding principle in life — focus on success. Work was the one thing that never let her down. That was true to this day.

"Have you considered," Kyle said, "that maybe Henry really did simply leave his house to someone else?"

Case in point — her own assistant was

undermining her. "Really, Kyle? Whose side are you on?" Bea ordered a glass of sauvignon blanc, and Kyle asked for a shot of whiskey.

"Whiskey? Do you think that's appropriate?" she said.

He looked around. "We're sitting at a bar."

With a huff, she picked up the happy-hour food menu. Pâté de foie de canard. Free-range-rabbit confit with mustard. Pickerell's Hog's Neck oysters. "Young man, I'll have a shrimp cocktail," she called to the bartender. "I haven't had a thing to eat all day. Who could at a time like this?" Bea said, turning to Kyle. "Do you want something?"

He shook his head.

Bea noticed she was the only woman in the room. The men around them spoke in groups of three and four. There was talk of golf games and boats, of travel, wives, and children.

Bea turned to Kyle. "You know, Henry was alone out here. Vulnerable. We have to get to the bottom of this."

Their drinks arrived, and Kyle tossed his back and promptly ordered another. Bea felt a twinge of alarm. This was, perhaps, not the best environment for her assistant. He wasn't acting like himself.

She sipped her wine, and the thought

struck her that Henry had died sitting at that very bar. Of course, she had known this, but she had somehow been able to compartmentalize the detail until that moment. Now it felt like a punch in the gut. Tears filled her eyes. She had never felt more alone. At least she had Kyle.

The bartender appeared with her shrimp.

"Bea," Kyle said. "Listen. I really appreciate the opportunity you've given me these past five years. I've learned a lot. But I think it's time that —"

"I simply cannot eat," Bea said, slowly easing her way off the bar stool. "Now, if you'll excuse me, I'm going to retire to the room. I need to save my energy for the battle ahead."

CHAPTER SEVEN

Penny stood at the bathroom sink lathering up the soap, rolling it around and around in her hands until it frothed and bubbled like something breathing. The tap was running, and she knew she was both wasting water *and* exceeding Dr. Wang's thirty-second limit on hand-washing, but she couldn't stop herself.

Something was going on, and wondering what it was made her nervous. She'd tried to eavesdrop from the stairs when the man in the tie showed up at the house, but Angus had caught her and sent her back to her room. Angus! And tomorrow she was supposed to spend the day with him helping out at the Sag Harbor Historical Society. She hated that musty old building and there was nothing for her to do. She'd spent entire afternoons there during which only one person showed up to look at the archives.

Still, she had to admit she needed something to distract her. She missed drawing. She couldn't even look at a blank sheet of paper. It made her too sad. What was the point anymore?

People left you. That was the reality. They died, or they just left. Like her dad. She couldn't remember the last time she'd seen him. Well, she remembered it, but it felt more like a dream than like something that really happened. He'd called her on her birthday two years ago but he'd missed it this year. She hadn't thought too much about it, but now that everything else was going wrong, why not just throw him into the mix?

At least she still had the drawings. She'd saved every sketch Henry had made for her since the first one he'd done on a cocktail napkin two years ago. It was of a man fishing. "You draw so fast," she had said in amazement. His hand seemed to fly across the surface of the napkin, the image forming underneath as if dropped whole and not pieced together line by line.

Penny eyed the hand towel hanging on the rack but didn't use it. Germs! Instead, she held her hands up in front of her like a surgeon going into the operating room and trotted down the stairs to get a paper towel from the kitchen. Just as she turned the corner, she heard the back door open.

"Hey, you," her mother said, dropping a takeout container from the hotel onto the kitchen table. Another salad. "Did you eat?"

"Yeah. Angus made burgers." Penny dried her hands on the paper towel and then tossed it in the garbage, careful not to touch the rim.

"Penny, sit here for a minute," her mother said. She poured herself a glass of wine and sat down at the table.

Penny sat and looked across the table at her mother. Her shiny auburn hair was pulled back in a ponytail, and mascara flaked around her bright green eyes. Her mother was beautiful even when she was tired after a long day. Penny thought for the millionth time how unfair it was that she looked nothing like her.

Her mother started to speak, then stopped.

"What?" Penny said.

"Did Mr. Wyatt ever mention his house to you?"

Mr. Wyatt? Why was her mom asking about Mr. Wyatt? "No. What about his house?"

"Did you ever talk to him about money — about feeling like we don't have enough money or about wishing we lived somewhere else? I won't be mad at you. I'm just trying to figure something out."

"No. We only talked about art." Mr. Wyatt wasn't a big talker. She'd liked that about him.

"Penny, something very strange has happened. I hope you can help me understand it."

"Is this about the man coming to the house earlier?" Penny's heart raced a little. She had a feeling that something big was going to happen; she just didn't know if it was good big or bad big. Her hand instinctively went through her hair, and she tugged out a few strands. Another nervous habit.

"Yes. That man was a lawyer. He had been Mr. Wyatt's lawyer. And he told me that Mr. Wyatt left his house — his very big, expensive house on the water — to you."

Penny sat back against her chair. "He what?"

Her mother repeated what she'd said.

"Why did he do that?"

Her mother shook her head, eyes wide. "I have no idea. I was hoping you had some clue."

Penny blinked fast, her mind racing. Mr. Wyatt had left them a house! On the water! Their neighborhood was inland, south of town. From the time she was little, she had known she was approaching her street when she started seeing pickup trucks parked roadside and collections of tires on her neighbors' lawns. If she went too far and passed her house, she hit the railroad tracks. Their house was small and old, and she felt embarrassed to have kids over. But maybe this new house would be nicer than Mindy's. One day, she could have a party at this house on the water and all the kids would keep checking their phones to see if they were invited. She would finally belong.

"Will I have a bigger room?" she said.

Her mother didn't answer; she was busy responding to a text. Hypocrite. She was the one who was always telling Penny to be more "present."

"What? Oh, Penny — I'm not sure this is really happening. This whole thing is crazy. I'm just trying to make sense of it at the moment."

Her mother said Penny overthought everything, but the truth was, *she* thought too much. Like right now. What was there to make sense of? They could move away from Mount Misery and live on the water. A no-brainer. "Can we see it?"

Her mother looked at her and finally smiled. "I guess we should go see it." She stood and kissed Penny on the forehead.

"Maybe in the morning. I'm going to run out and meet Sean and Alexis for dessert. You go to bed. Have sweet dreams."

For the first time in a long time, Penny thought she just might.

Murf's Backstreet Tavern, tucked away on Division Street in a building that dated back to 1792, was a down-and-dirty bar; it had a crumbling brick fireplace and cheap beer on tap, and drinks were served in plastic cups. Murf's also had a jukebox, a dartboard, and one-dollar Jägermeister shots on Tuesdays.

Emma spotted Sean sitting at the bar; Alexis was playing the ring game. The original owner, Tom Murphy, had hung a small steel ring from the ceiling with a piece of fishing line and the idea was to swing it so it caught the hook protruding from a nearby post. In the spring, the fire department and the sanitation department organized teams and had a regular competition going.

"There she is! What're you having?" Sean said.

"Red Stripe. Hey, I meant to ask you earlier, what's with the beard?" she said. Sean had sun-bleached hair and bright blue eyes. But his Scottish good looks were being sorely tested by his overgrown hipster facial hair.

"Don't start with me. I got an earful from Alexis earlier."

Alexis tossed the ring one last time, then bounded over to kiss Emma on the cheek. They climbed onto bar stools and Alexis passed her a Harbor Books bag with a paperback inside. "It's an advance copy of a novel Penny might like," she said.

"That's so sweet of you!"

The bartender that night, Katie Cleary, slid Emma's beer across the bar. Katie, the daughter of Hal Cleary, who owned the hardware store, was barely twenty-one. Emma had been working behind that very bar at her age.

It was how she'd met Penny's father.

One early-summer night, a large, boisterous group had flooded the bar. They took over the table between the hanging moose head and the framed photo of Frank Sinatra. A delegate was dispatched to the bar for drinks.

He was tall with thick, wavy dark hair and dark brown eyes. He wore jeans and a black T-shirt and was extremely cute. He looked familiar, and she realized she'd seen his picture on posters outside the Bay Street Theater.

"Hey there," he said, smiling. "Three pitchers of whatever you have on tap and four gin and tonics." He slid a credit card across the bar.

Filling the pitchers, she looked closer at the group and spotted the actress Mercedes Ruehl, who was starring in the Bay Street Theater production of a play called *Dinner.*

"Is this some kind of cast party?" Emma asked.

He nodded. "Informal, but yeah, we're heading into our opening weekend. We did two preview shows this week."

"Very cool."

"I'm Mark," he said.

"Emma."

"You don't look old enough to be drinking here, let alone working here."

She smiled. "Everyone tells me that."

"Ouch. Sorry for being unoriginal."

There was something big about him — the way he talked, the way he gestured. Later, she'd see similar qualities in his actor friends, but in the moment, it made him seem special.

Mark Mapson. Emma remembered how it felt the first time she'd said that name aloud; it crackled like candy in her mouth.

She learned he was from Maine, that he'd graduated from the University of Pennsylvania, and that now he was dealing with very disapproving parents as he pursued an acting career. He seemed fascinated by the fact that she'd grown up in the village and never left. "Not even for college?" he'd asked, and she had to say no twice. She told him she didn't have money for school, and besides, she really just wanted to open a flower shop in town someday. "I like that," he'd said. "So simple . . . so real."

Sometime after midnight, his group dispersed and he asked for her number. She wrote it on a bar napkin. She watched him slip it into his pocket, certain he would never call. To her surprise, he did, and she didn't even have to wait twenty-four hours. They met for coffee the following day, and by the time he asked for the check, she was in love.

Six weeks later, she was pregnant. They married at city hall a month before Penny was born. A year after that, he left.

"Earth to Emma," Sean said, bringing her back to the present.

"Sorry. I'm a little distracted." Should she tell them about the Henry Wyatt house? They were going to find out sooner or later. And why should she feel embarrassed about it? For some reason, she did. Maybe talking it over with Sean and Alexis would normalize it a little. "Something kind of crazy happened today."

Before she could get into it, Chris Vincenzi walked in.

"Chris V. in the house!" Sean called out.

"You're off early," Emma said when he took the stool next to hers.

"Things got quiet." He signaled for Katie and ordered a shot of Tito's. "And I am moving on to job number two." He waved his key ring in front of them.

"What's that? Janitor?" Sean said.

"No, smart-ass." He separated out one key. "This opens the cabin on Bob Anderson's thirty-five-foot Chris-Craft. I'm taking care of it for two weeks. What do you say we take this party onto the water?"

"First of all, no," said Alexis. "Second of all, Emma was just about to tell us something. So what happened today?"

The three of them looked at her expectantly.

"Um, well, before I left for work, this guy showed up at the house. A lawyer."

The rest of the story came out in a rush, sounding even more unbelievable as she related it than it had felt as it happened.

Sean let out a low whistle. "Next round is on you," he said.

"Very funny," Emma said.

"Have you seen it yet?" Alexis said.

She shook her head. "Maybe tomorrow. I'm curious but . . ."

"Does Jack know?" said Chris.

"Jack? Why would I tell Jack?"

"I mean, are you going to keep working?"

This conversation was getting absurd. "You guys, the point is there's no way this is actually happening. And even if it is, there are weird constraints on the whole thing. It's Penny's house, not mine. I can't sell it or anything. It doesn't really change my financial situation today."

"But you get to live in a mansion on the water for free," said Sean.

"Well, yeah. There's that. I'm totally freaked out."

"Look at it this way," said Alexis. "This summer, you'll get a taste of how the other half lives."

They raised their glasses.

Bea, wearing her nightgown and a quilted robe, rested on top of the white comforter, staring at the wooden ceiling beams. The great charm of the room was its simplicity. No television, no placards with a Wi-Fi password. The phone next to the bed was a black rotary. The hotel harked back to a better time.

A time when she did not have one of Henry Wyatt's paintings hidden in the trunk of her car.

Oh, how could it have come to this? After all she had done for his career, after all their years together, she was reduced to smuggling his work out of his house like a common criminal. She couldn't leave it in the trunk, but she also couldn't carry it up the stairs by herself. Securing it in the room would have to involve Kyle. His attitude had already turned so sour, she didn't relish the idea of enlisting him in her questionable endeavor.

And yet, she felt justified in her action. The thought of leaving that painting behind, of letting some stranger do heavens knew what with all of Henry's precious work, was stomach-turning. If taking one of the paintings helped get her through the night, then so be it. Bea had always done things her own way — even when she made life harder for herself.

She'd moved to New York City in the fall of 1960. Just a year earlier, she'd made the shocking decision not to enroll at Vassar College, and as a result, she left Newport on terrible terms with her parents. It was a choice they saw as rebellious, as a rejection of all they had raised her to value in the world and what they had raised her to do with her life. What they didn't realize was that the seeds for her life-changing decision had been planted years earlier.

It happened when Bea was twelve, the summer the town hosted the first Newport Jazz Festival. Her parents were among several residents who were appalled by the prospect, certain it would bring an "undesirable" crowd into town. Her mother stopped speaking to her friend Elaine Lorillard, who organized the event, even though just the September before Elaine had wangled the Winsteads an invitation to the social event of the season: the wedding of Jacqueline Bouvier to Jack Kennedy.

After months of hearing whispers about the festival and seeing posters all around town, Bea was obsessed. The Saturday night of the event, after telling her parents she was babysitting for a neighbor, Bea sneaked off to the grounds of the Newport Casino. She took a moment to pray to God that she wouldn't get caught. Then she looked up and saw the glorious full moon. Decades and decades later, she could remember the feeling she'd had then, the sense that her life was really beginning.

The casino lawn seemed to be filled with

a million people. It wasn't just the vastness of the audience that astounded her; it was the mix of black people and white, sailors and schoolgirls. And the music! Eddie Condon. Dizzy Gillespie. Ella Fitzgerald. Jazz was unlike anything she'd heard before. The songs broke all the rules, and the musicians looked like they were from another planet. But, as she learned that night, they were not from another planet or even another country. They were from New York City.

It was the place Bea wanted to live when she grew up.

She never forgot it, not even when she held the Vassar acceptance letter in her hand. Especially when she held the Vassar acceptance letter in her hand. She saw Robert Frost's diverging roads ahead of her.

Bea didn't want to waste four years at Vassar and then return to Newport to make a "good" marriage. She had no interest in that kind of life. And the only escape she could imagine was New York City.

Her parents wouldn't hear one word about the move, wouldn't give her a dime, and so she landed in New York City broke and very much on her own. A *Village Voice* ad led to an apartment share on the Lower East Side with an NYU student who worked a few hours a week at an art collective on the Bowery. The scene captivated Bea.

When she wasn't hanging around one of the artist-run galleries on East Tenth Street, she was crashing any party where there was a chance that a gallery owner or up-and-coming artist might show up. She needed a job, but no one was handing out positions in galleries. She had to find a way to make a name for herself. This was her all-consuming thought the night she managed to get herself invited to a party at a massive Spring Street loft.

The hostess was a friend of Lois Dodd, one of the founders of the Tanager Gallery on East Tenth Street. Bea wanted an in with Tanager because it was one of the few spaces that seemed open to work beyond abstract expressionism, a movement that was already heavily represented. In order to break out, Bea needed to discover the next big thing.

She worked the party methodically, all business. But that changed the minute she spotted a tall, lanky, dark-haired young man at the center of a conversation near the makeshift bar. His hair was long enough that it would have drawn disapproving stares on the streets of Newport; his clothes were bohemian bordering on homelessness. But with his strong jaw and enviably symmetrical features, he seemed aristocratic. Bea moved closer, and her heart fluttered when she noticed his large hands were those of an artist, with tapered fingers and paint under his nails.

At one point, the handsome stranger fixed his blue eyes on her, and Bea forgot everyone else in the room. She hovered around the edges of that group until she was able to talk to him one-on-one. Later, she wasn't sure what, exactly, she'd said to him. He might have made some vague mention of his painting, but for the first time since Bea had arrived in New York City fifteen months earlier, art was the last thing on her mind.

She learned his name was Henry Wyatt, that he was from Texas, and that, like herself, he was a recent transplant to New York City.

There was some discussion of his painting, but mostly they drank too much gin and gossiped about everyone in their striving little circle. At some point when night had become morning, she stumbled home with him to his apartment above a deli on Greenwich Avenue that smelled of turpentine. They kissed and clawed at each other with drunken abandon, fumbling to remove their clothes. It was just after the birth control pill arrived on the market. Hugh

Hefner's new Playboy Club had recently opened its doors. And that night, on Henry Wyatt's bare mattress on the floor, another watershed moment: Bea Winstead lost her virginity.

In the morning, her personal milestone was forgotten the minute she set eyes on a painting propped up in the corner: The image was simple: symmetrical blocks of cobalt blue bisected by white lines. It was a stark and refreshing departure from abstract expressionism.

"Henry, my God. This is good." She moved from the bed to examine it closer and from different angles. "What's it called?"

He shrugged. "I don't name my paintings."

In her mind she was already calling it *Untitled Blue,* oil on canvas.

He reached for her, but she pulled away. Sleeping with him had been a moment of weakness. She had not come to New York to find a man. She'd come to find a career, to be independent.

She couldn't let herself become Henry Wyatt's lover. They would eventually fight and break up. And no one would take her seriously. No, the only possible direction for their relationship now that she'd seen his work was professional. There was no doubt in her mind she could make him famous and that he in turn would make her a fortune.

And she had been right.

The cozy hotel room suddenly felt small and claustrophobic. Bea pulled her quilted robe tighter around her. She would not lie there ruminating, alternating between feeling like a victim and feeling like a criminal. She put on her Belgian slippers and turned on the lights so she could see her way down the stairs to the lower level.

Kyle snored gently on the couch. She flipped on the end-table lamp and stood over him. She hesitated for a moment, then reached out and shook his shoulder.

"Kyle," she said. "I need to talk to you."

He barely stirred.

"Kyle, I need your help."

He sat up with a start. "Bea? What are you doing?"

"I'm sorry to wake you, but I need help getting something out of the car and into this room."

"Now?" He checked his phone. "It's one in the morning."

"It's important."

"What did you leave in the car?"

"One of Henry's paintings."

"From the house?"

She nodded.

"Bea, that's . . . I think that's stealing. You're going to get yourself into a lot of trouble."

"Let me be the one to worry about that. In the meantime, I can't leave it in the car overnight."

Kyle sank back against his pillow. "You're going to have to. I'm not getting involved in this."

"You don't understand!" she said.

"You're right. I don't," he said, his voice gravelly with sleep.

"I felt so rushed to get out of the house today, so blindsided. Taking the painting was just my attempt to have some control over the situation. But all of his other work is there, just waiting to be pillaged by whatever philistine has hijacked his estate. I need to catalog everything that's there or it could be lost!"

"Okay." Kyle sat up, rubbing his eyes. When he finally focused on her, she didn't recognize his expression at first. And then she realized he was looking at her with pity. Pity! "Bea, I feel for you. I do. I know what it's like to want something and have it taken away from you. It's not easy to recover from that. So I'll drive you back tomorrow. You return the painting, and then you can do whatever last-minute stuff you need to do to make yourself feel better. But then, Bea, that's it. I'm going back to Manhattan with or without you."

CHAPTER EIGHT

Early-morning clouds rolled in, and Bea tried not to take it as a sign. She slammed the trunk of the car closed and strode into Windsong's side entrance with a sense of resolve. Kyle trailed behind her, carrying the painting.

In the light of day, the words *trespassing* and *theft* nagged at her in a way they had not late last night. But the new "owner" of the house was illegitimate — of that she was certain. And so she was doing nothing wrong.

Just a few hours ago, she'd had the surprisingly belated idea to contact her own attorney, Richard Fadden. He knew Victor Bonivent, and he knew Henry — he could connect the dots and fix this problem. She got him on his cell just as the sun was coming up.

"It's a lengthy and complicated process to contest a will," he told her. "It will cost you." She said she'd give him a blank check.

Kyle was clearly in a hurry to get *Untitled Blue* back on the wall. He nearly tripped over a sculpture in the hallway.

"Be careful!" she said.

He ignored her. "Where does this belong?"

She directed him to the corridor leading to the guest suite. When he had secured it back in place, he said, "Okay. Now let's go."

So impatient! "Not yet. I told you I need to catalog the art. If you want to help things go faster, then walk through with me and I'll call out the titles of the work for you to write down."

"And then you'll leave?"

"Yes, then I'll leave."

They climbed the stairs to the library. Until this month, it had been years since she'd seen the room, and it had impressed her all over again with its sheer volume of books. Henry was a reader, yes, but there was a collector's mentality to the accumulation of hundreds and hundreds of novels, biographies, coffee-table books, and works on art history, art theory, and literary criticism. She pulled a few random hardcovers from the shelves but then a framed picture on the wall caught her eye. She replaced the books and walked over to get a better look.

Bea felt certain she knew all of Henry's

work. But there, between two of the book-shelves, was a drawing she'd never seen before. She inched closer to it, her stomach tightening. Sure enough, in the lower right corner was the loopy scrawl of his initials and a date — just eleven months earlier. Had Henry changed artistic direction in the past year or two of his life? What else did she not know about him? But no, she could not let herself think there were pockets of his life, creative or otherwise, to which she was not privy, because to admit that would be to allow a sliver of possibility that he had left his house and his work to a stranger for valid reasons.

"These drawings are new. Write them down as . . . sketches one, two, and three."

Kyle peeked out into the hallway.

"Am I boring you?" Bea snapped.

He turned back to her, pressed his forefinger to his lips, then whispered, "I hate to break it to you, but I hear people downstairs."

It looked more like a sculpture than a house, a monument carved from stone and glass and steel. Emma had the nerve to turn the key in the front door only because of the palpable excitement of her daughter standing next to her.

"It's exactly how I imagined it!" Penny said once she, Emma, and Angus were inside.

How could her daughter have imagined this?

It was bright and spacious with shining wood floors and floor-to-ceiling windows and sleek furniture. It was a house out of a magazine or a movie. It was a dream house.

This was real. This was happening.

"It's amazing how much space rich folks think they need for themselves," Angus said.

"Maybe he wanted someone to share it with but couldn't find anyone," Penny said. "So he gave it to us."

Angus shook his head. Last night, when Emma told him what was going on, he'd said the whole thing seemed fishy. Emma had agreed with him then, but all that was forgotten now that she was standing in the space that she realized was going to change her life. For the first time in a very long while, she didn't feel like she was treading water. Her daughter would have a beautiful place to grow up. And when she was an adult, Penny could sell it and have financial security.

Penny ran from room to room, practically jumping up and down with excitement. Emma followed close behind, her own joy barely any more contained.

"We should have brought bathing suits," Penny said, gazing out the window at an infinity pool. Beyond it, a stretch of beach along the bay. Angus moved to stand next to her. "What do you think?" Penny said to him.

"I do not swim."

"Well, now that we live here, you'll have to learn."

Emma smiled. And then she heard a noise from upstairs.

She was probably imagining it, or maybe the house was settling in a way she wasn't used to. The house on Mount Misery made all sorts of creaks and groans that she hardly noticed anymore. A few strange noises were the least of what she'd have to get used to in this sprawling home.

Could she live in this kind of luxury? She didn't know. Why not try? Maybe life didn't always have to be a slog. Maybe sometimes good things did just happen.

Bea stood at the top of the stairs, her heart pounding.

Could the interlopers be moving in already? She supposed if they were con artists — and, really, what else could they be? — they were well prepared for their scheme to come to fruition. Well, they hadn't factored one thing into their plan: her.

"We're going to confront them," she whispered to Kyle.

"Absolutely not. We're not even supposed to be here."

"What kind of attitude is that?" Bea descended the stairs slowly, holding the railing. She moved briskly through the central living space, following the sound of voices. There, in the dining room, she found three people standing side by side staring out at the pool.

"Excuse me," Bea said, her voice gratifyingly steady.

The trio looked around, startled. Then it was Bea's turn to be surprised. She knew that woman from somewhere. Her brain struggled to piece together discordant information, and finally the outrageous reality hit her: The American Hotel's desk manager. *"You?"* she said. Bea turned to look at Kyle. He shook his head and walked out of the room. When the front door slammed shut, she barely registered the sound.

"I'm sorry. We didn't expect anyone to be here today," the woman said. A young girl with wild curls stood by her side, and next to her was a gray-haired, African-American man dressed in khaki pants, a collared shirt, and a lightweight sweater-vest. What connection could this odd bunch have to Henry?

"You're staying at the hotel. Ms. Winstead, right?" the woman said.

The hotel, yes — now it made sense. Henry had spent a great deal of time in his final years sitting at that bar. He had drunk too much. He had said too much. This woman had wormed her way into Henry's life just to take everything upon his death. Had he slept with her? At his age?

So. The situation was so simple, it was practically a cliché.

"Who are you?" Bea said.

"I'm Emma Mapson. This is my daughter, Penny, and —"

"What are you *doing* here?" Bea said, moving to lean against the table. She'd barely slept. She was exhausted. The stress of it all.

"I could ask the same of you, Ms. Winstead."

The nerve! "This house belonged to my very dear, recently deceased friend Henry Wyatt. *That's* what I'm doing here. Now, since I knew Mr. Wyatt for fifty years and he never mentioned your name, I'd love to hear your excuse."

"First, I'm sorry for your loss. Mr. Wyatt was a very nice man. My daughter here had come to know him pretty well the past year or so. He gave her drawing lessons."

"Drawing lessons," Bea said, spitting the words.

"Yes. And he was a regular at the bar."

"None of that explains your presence in this house."

The woman turned to her daughter and suggested she sit out on the deck with the older man who was with them. Bea looked around for Kyle. Where on earth had he run off to?

Emma Mapson suggested they sit; she pulled out a chair from the dining-room table and offered it to Bea. Bea wanted to refuse, to say she preferred to stand, but her hip was bothering her. It was the damn stairs at the hotel. She had enough pride, however, to choose her own seat.

Emma sat across from her. "The truth is, Ms. Winstead, I just learned yesterday that my daughter has inherited this house."

"Inherited this house. An astonishing turn of fortune, wouldn't you say?" Bea leaned forward, bracing herself with her elbows on the table.

"It's come as a shock, yes."

"Oh, save it! A shock? You expect me —

108

you expect anyone — to believe you weren't a party to this? That you didn't actively scheme to get Henry Wyatt's estate?"

The woman shook her head. "I understand you're upset. You've suffered a loss. But I had nothing to do with this house situation."

"I don't believe you. Not for one minute. And I'm not leaving town until I get to the bottom of this. Just so you know, I've gone through all the art that is in this house. If any of it goes missing, I will see you in court."

It took some effort to stand up without shaking. She was more upset than she had realized, and it required all the strength she could muster just to maintain the illusion of calm and control as she walked away.

Now if she could just find Kyle.

CHAPTER NINE

Penny hadn't wanted to leave Henry's house. It was beyond beautiful, perfect in all the ways she'd expect a house that Henry had lived in would be. She saw him everywhere in the smooth pale wood and the stone and the massive windows. So much natural light! Henry was all about good light.

The best part was the pool. It was so narrow and smooth, it looked like a sliver of sky. It seemed like something designed for people to admire, not swim in. But she wanted to swim in it. And Henry must have wanted her to swim in it, because for some amazing reason he'd left the house to her. Finally, finally, something in her life was good. Something was special.

But then the old lady in the tweed jacket and giant pearls showed up.

Penny didn't know what the old lady said to upset her mother but as soon as the two of them were done talking, her mother made Penny get back in the car and they left Henry's house.

"Who was that?" she'd asked her mom in the car.

"She said she was an old friend of Henry's."

"Is she angry that he left us the house?"

"That appears to be the case."

End of conversation. Now, alone in her bedroom, Penny opened the hutch under her desk, pulled out her drawing board and paper, and carried the supplies to her bed. She rested the drawing board on her lap, ran her hand over the surface. For the first time since hearing about Henry's death, she had the urge to draw.

The board was one of the first art supplies Henry had given her. He'd gotten it for her after he'd found her sitting on the hotel-lobby couch and sketching on a piece of paper resting on her crossed legs.

"We create the lights and darks in drawing by varying the pressure applied to the pencil, right?" he'd said, looming over her. "So we need an even, hard surface underneath the paper."

The next day, her mother came home from work with the drawing board. "A little something from your art fairy godfather," she said with a smile. A week later, her mother came back with graphite pencils in 4H, HB, and 4B. She'd made Penny write a thank-you note.

"I don't have his address," Penny said.

"Just hand it to him the next time you see him."

Penny dutifully wrote the note and sealed it in an envelope. A few days later, when she was sitting in the lobby doing her homework, he ambled in and took his usual spot at the end of the bar. She felt awkward going up to him, but he'd seen her — acknowledged her with a little wave — so there was no avoiding it.

"Thank you so much for the pencils. I love them," she said, handing him the note.

"What's this?" he said.

"A thank-you note."

"But you just thanked me."

Penny felt herself turn red.

Henry placed the envelope on the bar. "I considered adding an eight B to your collection — the eight B creates wonderful darks. But I suspect you won't keep up with the sharpening maintenance."

A few months ago, he had presented her with a pack of 8Bs.

Penny bit her lip, fighting tears. Dr. Wang had told her she needed to learn the difference between things to really be upset about and things that were just getting caught in a loop in her mind. Was this one of those things? She didn't know.

She'd told Henry once about what Dr. Wang said, that she shouldn't think about what was bothering her over and over and over again, that she needed to let such worries float away. Henry didn't look up from his drawing but said after a minute or so, "Do you know what happens when an irritant works its way into an oyster? As a defense mechanism, the oyster coats it with fluid, layer after layer. Over and over and over again. And in the end, a beautiful pearl is formed."

Thinking about it now, Penny sobbed, her tears soaking the blank piece of paper in front of her. Another thing Henry always said was that a blank piece of paper was just a drawing waiting to be completed. But it was so hard to draw now that he was gone.

"Knock, knock," her mother said, rapping once before opening the bedroom door. Penny quickly wiped her eyes but it was no use trying to hide anything from her mother. "Are you crying?"

Her mother sat on the edge of her bed and reached out to hug her, but Penny pulled away.

"What's wrong, hon?"

Penny shrugged, and she saw her mother's face tense. It was her *I don't have time to deal with your nervous breakdown* look.

"Angus is leaving soon for the historical society. You're supposed to start helping out there this week."

"Ugh! It's so boring."

"Penny, our family has been part of this town for hundreds of years. Your ancestors helped defend Sag Harbor against the British during the Revolutionary War. We're lucky the history of this town is being preserved. When you're old enough to get a paying job, you can find another way to spend your summers. But for now, this is what you're doing."

"What about the house?"

Her mother inhaled deeply. "Nothing is changing for now. We need to just continue with our normal lives. Let me worry about the house."

"I want to live there."

Emma shook her head. "Big and fancy isn't always better, you know. We're lucky to have this place so close to town. We've been here since you were three."

"Yeah, but we rent it. It's not ours."

"No, the property technically is not ours. But it is our home. And it upsets me to

114

think you feel it somehow isn't good enough. That . . . mansion has nothing to do with normal people like us."

"Is this because of the old woman? Is she telling you we can't live there?"

"This has nothing to do with anyone, Penny. It's my feeling about what's best for our family and how we live our lives."

"Henry wanted me to have it. Why are you getting in the way? You always say no to things, and then you wonder why I'm so unhappy!" She looked down at the blank sheet of paper on her lap, warped and ruined by her tears.

Emma preferred to cut flowers late in the day — it was one of the small things that extended their vase life. But she wanted to bring a bunch to the hotel to set in the lobby. It made her happy to look across the room and see her own yellow New Day hybrid teas and her white Iceberg floribunda. Jack appreciated it too. He said her flowers lasted days longer than the blooms he bought weekly from the florist. Again, her mother's expertise guided her. It was all in the attention to detail: selecting the flowers at the right stage, clipping at the optimal time of day, when the stem had food reserves, cutting at a forty-five-degree angle, and then immediately putting them in water.

Emma set a bucket of fresh water on the ground and cut the flowers whose petals were unfolding. She placed each stem in the bucket. When she ran out of open blooms, she felt around the closed buds, squeezing a few to see if any were soft enough that they would open in the vase.

The sound of a buzz saw next door irritated her. She glanced over the hedge into her neighbor Ken Cutty's backyard. It had been Angus and Celia's home before Celia died, and they had been much better neighbors. Lately, Ken had been piling a lot of lumber in the yard. A discarded refrigerator was out there too, along with a few iron drums whose purpose she couldn't identify. The place was an eyesore.

Angus came out onto the back porch. "Is Penny coming with me to work?"

"She's going to bike over."

"I can drive her. Leaving in an hour."

"I think she wants to be able to come and go on her own," Emma said apologetically.

Emma wondered for the millionth time why Angus turned her into an approval-seeking adolescent. She knew that, from a psychology standpoint, it was because she'd lost her father at such a young age. From any older male figure Emma knew, she

116

found herself looking for either guidance or validation. It had been this way her entire life.

She was also painfully aware that, just as she had been raised by a single mother, history was now repeating itself. Though in some ways, she felt her daughter's situation was worse than her own had been. Her father's sudden death when she was still in elementary school had been devastating. But up until that point, Tom Kirkland had been a pretty great dad to Emma. Penny had never experienced a normal, day-to-day life with her father.

That was partly why she liked having Angus around. Aside from the logistics of having another adult to help out, she wanted some sort of male figure for Penny.

"This house thing is complicated," Emma said, moving her bucket of clipped roses out of the sun. She looked at him. "You haven't really weighed in. Why?"

"Celia always said I had a way of not talking to her when she wanted to talk, then trying to press her into talking when she needed space. I try to correct that whenever I can."

Angus had a sonorous voice, and it made everything he said seem wise. Emma nodded. "I'd like your opinion."

"Well, I think the situation is peculiar."

"That is it, Angus. It is most definitely peculiar. And I'm not sure what to do about it."

"What are the options?"

Emma leaned back on her heels, wiping her brow with the back of her arm. "I could just leave the house alone and let Penny deal with it when she turns eighteen."

"Or?"

"Or I could move in. But that woman is going to fight me in court. I don't have the resources to fight back."

"What if she doesn't bother taking you to court?"

"Okay, so, another thing is I guess a part of me can't imagine living in that big fancy space. Can you?"

Angus laughed. "I'm not living in that crazy house."

She looked at him, startled. "What? Oh, Angus. Of course you will. We need you around."

He smiled. "I didn't say I'm going to disappear. But maybe this is a sign it's time for me to live on my own."

Emma dropped her clippers onto the grass and stood up.

"No, it's not. And you know Celia would agree with me. There was a reason she made both of us promise that you would move in with us. She didn't want you living alone." In her final days, Celia had been thinking only about Angus. She told Emma, "I'm not afraid to go. I'm just afraid to leave him behind."

Angus shook his head. "I have to say, though I never admitted this to Celia, it was a mistake to have sold the Ninevah Beach house. I've never felt quite at home since."

Angus, like many of his generation, had faced a real estate dilemma. The former African-American enclaves of Ninevah Beach, Azurest, and Sag Harbor Hills had become appealing to a wider number of home buyers when the entire Hamptons area exploded in popularity. By the early 2000s, Angus's family home had increased to nearly ten times the amount it had been purchased for. And as he and Celia faced retirement, the ballooning property taxes combined with the potential payday of selling had made holding on to the house impractical.

"Angus, I understand that the idea of moving from here might trigger complicated feelings. But whatever decision is made, I want us to make it as a family."

Across the lawn, the buzz saw started up again. Angus waved her closer to the house.

When she reached the porch, he said, "Emma, this really isn't about what you want or what I want. There's only one thing to think about here: What's best for the child? The rest of it is just noise."

It wasn't just the deep voice; Angus *was* wise.

CHAPTER TEN

On the southern end of Main Street, quaint, historic clapboard houses merged seamlessly with the commercial storefronts. Penny's favorite yogurt shop, BuddhaBerry, was a two-story house with wide stone steps and white pillars. If it weren't for the chalkboard sign outside that read ARTISAN-QUALITY FROZEN YOGURT! WAFFLES! CREPES! BUBBLE TEAS!, it would be easy to miss.

BuddhaBerry had colorful mosaic-tiled tables, bright orange walls, and lots of Asian lanterns. It was just the medicine Penny needed before starting her sentence — sorry, her shift — at the historical society. Considering what time it was, she should have taken her pomegranate yogurt topped with shaved coconut and chocolate chunks to go, but she couldn't resist stalling at a table.

God, she hated the historical society. It

was just across the street but it might as well have been in another universe. The museum was formerly the Annie Cooper Boyd House, an eighteenth-century shack. Angus always tried to make it sound interesting but failed miserably.

"The house was once thought to be the place where David Frothingham first published the *Long Island Herald*. That was Long Island's first newspaper in the 1790s," Angus had told her.

"Okay," Penny had said politely.

"But in fact, research has proven this untrue. It's more likely that Frothingham ran the business from a building across the street."

Thanks to Angus, Penny knew enough trivia about Sag Harbor to make her a useful volunteer. But, as she told her mother, *it was so friggin' boring!*

Penny pulled a book out of her bag, *The Unbeatable Squirrel Girl: Squirrel Meets World*. This was a reread for her, but she needed something light after *This One Summer*. This old favorite was way less depressing. It was about a girl her age named Doreen Green who moves from California to New Jersey and totally doesn't fit in. But she has superpowers. All the books Penny liked best were about underdogs who finally got their day.

Squirrel Girl was the first graphic novel she'd shown to Henry. When she'd pulled it out of her bag, he was initially dismissive.

"I've never been a fan of comics," he'd said.

"It's a graphic novel."

He flipped through the pages. "Are they very popular with kids your age?"

"Graphic novels? Yeah. Totally."

"Why not just read a novel? There's something to be said for just a good, old-fashioned book."

"Henry, this is a great story *and* great art. I mean, you of all people should get that."

He smiled at her. "You certainly know how to sell it. Although I don't like the term *graphic novel.*"

"What would you call it?" she asked him.

"Sequential art."

"A sequential-art novel? That definitely does not sound as good."

He asked to see more, and she brought him her copies of *Coraline, The Graveyard Book, Awkward.* She showed him *Ms. Marvel* and *Roller Girl.* He took them home and read them all.

Henry appreciated the underdog element of the stories. He told her that someday she would find her own superpower. She just had to be patient. In that moment, she had believed him. But now that he was gone, she wasn't so sure.

She tossed her empty yogurt container in the garbage and packed her book away. Hopefully Angus would be busy and wouldn't notice if she sneaked off to the back room to read for an hour or two.

Penny walked down the BuddhaBerry steps just as Robin and Mindy were coming up. Everything about Penny that was wrong, Mindy got right: her hair (straight), her clothes (new), her jewelry (real), her phone (the latest). It was like she didn't even have to try.

She had every intention of slipping by with just a wave; the last thing she wanted to do was talk about her nonexistent summer-vacation plans.

"OMG, Penny, I was *just* talking about you," Mindy said, grabbing her by the arm.

"You were?" It was unimaginable that she would ever cross Mindy's mind, let alone be the topic of conversation. She could barely believe she was speaking to her.

"Is it true?" Mindy asked.

Penny stood mute and clueless. Was this a joke? What was she missing?

"My mom read in the paper that you inherited a major house on Actors Colony

Road," Robin said.

Henry's house was in the newspaper? "Um, yeah — it's true," Penny said.

Mindy and Robin looked at each other, then at her.

"That is *amazing,*" Mindy said. She touched Penny's arm again. "And you are *so* having a party." She smiled conspiratorially, then added, "Actually, I'm having some people over tonight. You should totally come."

"Okay. Sure. Great."

Mindy's phone pinged. She showed her screen to Robin, who giggled. Mindy hunched over and started tapping away furiously.

"Okay, well, I guess I'll see you later," Penny said, brushing past them quickly, dazed by the encounter.

The house was changing her life and she hadn't even moved in yet.

If there was anything Bea loathed, it was people who felt sorry for themselves. But walking up and down Main Street, invisible among the couples and young families, she fought that particular emotion with limited success.

Abandoned in her hour of need.

I told you I was leaving for New York today,

125

with or without you.

How could Kyle just quit? Half a decade of employment and he didn't give so much as one day's notice. It was profoundly disappointing that after all the time he'd spent with Bea, he hadn't learned the first thing about doing things the proper way. This was why she'd never had children — she wouldn't have been able to stand the disappointment.

Henry hadn't wanted children either. He'd never even married. Which made the idea that he would leave his estate to some random girl all the more outrageous.

Bea wandered in and out of a few art galleries. Every twenty feet she found another storefront filled with paintings.

She turned off Main and onto a side street, then walked toward the old Bulova watchcase factory that had been converted into luxury apartments. On Washington Street, she spotted yet another small gallery tucked between two furniture stores. The window display featured three bold, vivid portraits. She walked inside and appraised the work, surprisingly impressed with a few pieces done in oil on aluminum.

A young woman approached her. "Welcome," she said.

"Are you the owner?" Bea asked.

"No, the owner is Carol Amsterdam and she will be here tomorrow. I'm Julia and I'm happy to help you with anything you need."

Julia went on to tell Bea that the gallery specialized in contemporary art with a focus on narrative portraiture and magical realism by emerging artists.

"This artist is a woman?" Bea asked of the oil on aluminum.

"Yes. I'll show you her catalog."

Bea followed Julia to a back office. Her hip hurt and she pulled out a chair for herself but froze when she noticed a series of framed drawings on the wall — drawings just like the ones in Henry's library. She leaned in, pulling her glasses out of her handbag.

The work reminded her of David Hockney's drawings, not anything Henry had ever done in his career. But Henry's initials and the date were in the lower right corner, just like in the others.

"Are these . . ."

"Original Henry Wyatts. Remarkable, aren't they?"

Bea didn't bother responding. She moved close to the drawings, recognizing the first as their old building on Spring Street. Another was the scene of a crowded party.

One showed a man fishing. But the sketch that took her breath away depicted *her,* sixty years earlier, sitting next to Henry on a bench in Washington Square Park. The details brought her back to the exact moment — the thirty-cent can of beef ravioli in his hand, the knee-length thrift-store coat she wore. It had been one of their earliest days together, a time when their shared vision for the future was hatched. She'd made her official pitch to be his manager, convincing him that with his talent and her ambition, they could be major players in the art world. He said, and she remembered it like it was yesterday, *I trust you, Bea.*

And for the rest of his career, he did. Henry created, Bea managed. Even when he changed direction, even when he knew she didn't approve his choices, he couldn't resist calling her out to Long Island to see his work. And yet he had never mentioned these drawings.

What was going on here?

A temporary wall surrounded the charred grounds of the former movie theater. It had big red lettering thanking the first responders who'd battled the fire that scarred the "beloved Main Street," and it had two round windows so people could peer in and view the wreckage. Penny couldn't resist looking every single time she walked to the historical society or the whaling museum.

She stared at the burned ground now, seeing it as a perfect reflection of her mood.

Around her, people started lining up for the jitney. Penny thought it was strange that the company hadn't moved the pickup location after the fire. Now, instead of standing in front of a nice theater, people had to gather in front of that wall.

But they didn't seem to mind. Or notice, really. Penny watched them stand right in front of the burned-out pit and just check their phones, not giving it a second glance. They were just visitors, she guessed. People who lived in town knew exactly what was missing.

Only one guy peered through the windows, just like she always did. He wore a gray T-shirt and faded jeans and had a suitcase by his feet. Even from her side view, she realized she recognized him. He was hard to miss because he looked like that actor from the movie *Jurassic World,* Chris Pratt.

"Hey — you were at the house earlier," she said. "With the old lady."

He looked down at her, surprised. "Yeah. That's right."

She asked him his name.

"Kyle," he said, then he turned back to the wall. "What happened here?"

"A fire. Last December. It sucks."

"Well, it looks like they're going to re-build."

Penny shrugged. "I'll believe it when I see it."

The guy — Kyle — looked at her again. "That's pretty cynical for someone your age."

And then, before she realized what she was doing, she reached out her hand and leaned on the bus-stop sign. Gross! Immediately, she wiped her fingers on her denim shorts, but that wasn't going to do the job. "Do you have any Purell?"

Kyle shook his head. "Sorry."

She bent down to rummage through her backpack but knew she wouldn't find any hand sanitizer. She'd followed Dr. Wang's instructions not to carry it, and now she regretted her decision. She looked up at Kyle.

"So, is that old woman your grand-mother?" she asked.

He looked confused. After a beat, he said, "Uh, no. I work for her. *Worked* for her, actually." He glanced down the street, checking for the jitney.

"It's late a lot," she said. "So, listen, can you tell her to leave us alone? The house has nothing to do with her. Mr. Wyatt wanted us to have it. My mom isn't good with change, and your boss saying all that stuff is making it harder for her."

"What's your name?"

"Penny."

"Penny, I don't really know what's going on with that house. But I do know that Ms. Winstead was very good friends, longtime friends, with the owner. This is nothing against you or your mother. Ms. Winstead has just lost a friend, and as a friend she wants to look after his house and his art."

"He was my friend too. *I'm* upset too." Her eyes filled with tears. "I don't know exactly why he left me the house. Maybe it's because I like to draw and he gave me art lessons and he told me it was the happiest he'd been in years. He *told* me that. Maybe it's because he was rich and he knew my mom works really hard but we don't have a lot. I mean, not compared to most of the people around here. I don't know *why* he did it, okay? The point is, he *did* it, and no matter how long that lady hangs around here, she won't change that."

The bus pulled up and the waiting crowd moved into an orderly line. Kyle slipped the

131

adjustable handle down in his suitcase.

"Did you hear what I just said? About Mr. Wyatt?" Penny said.

He didn't answer her. But the weird thing was, he didn't get on the bus either.

CHAPTER ELEVEN

"Can you tell me how the owner acquired these drawings?" Bea asked the gallery assistant.

The woman looked up from sifting through catalogs. "The Wyatts? The artist gave them to Carol Amsterdam this past fall. Aren't they spectacular? So stark and emotional."

Indeed. "Was the owner of this gallery very friendly with Mr. Wyatt?"

"Everyone knew Henry."

"And did he just give his drawings to everyone?" Bea pressed, irritated.

The young woman, confused by the shift in tone, paused and then answered, "I don't really know."

How long had he been in this new phase of his career? But the more pressing question was why, after always being so protective of his work — of having Bea act as the steward of everything he created — had he started giving it away?

Bea was the one who'd convinced Henry to walk away from the downtown scene and aim for something bigger. It was 1961. John F. Kennedy had just been inaugurated. The country had a new heroine in First Lady Jackie. Bea, remembering the Newport frenzy over the Kennedy wedding seven years earlier, felt like it was a sign, confirmation somehow that, like Jackie, she could emerge from Newport and shine in a bigger arena. This was her moment, and she had to make it happen.

"We need to get you into one of the new galleries on Fifty-Seventh Street," she told him.

Henry protested; his friend was putting together a show for him in a space just a few blocks away.

"You can do better," she said, generations of entitled Newport breeding coursing through her veins. As much as she loved the romance of the artists' collectives, she sensed something bigger was around the corner, and if she didn't become a part of it, she would be left behind.

The era leading up to this moment had been the time of the Tenth Street galleries, run by the artists themselves. But Bea believed things were starting to change. Those closest to the scene would not or could not see it, but Bea was just outside enough and sharp enough to see that new power players were entering the game.

How did she know this? The same way Henry knew that the blue and black in the configuration of his painting would work. It was what she was hardwired to do. As much as she was attracted to the art world, she didn't have one moment of delusion that she herself was an artist. But she felt confident she could succeed on the business end of things. She didn't know exactly what her job would be or how long it would take to make something happen. She would just put one foot in front of the other until she got there. And she would take Henry Wyatt along with her.

Bea had her eye on the Green Gallery. Unlike the pop-ups and collectives on Tenth Street, the Green Gallery had financial backing and a wealthy, uptown clientele. Bea, unlike her new friends, was very comfortable around money. She spoke the language. She belonged.

Bea convinced Richard Bellamy, the gallery director, to visit Henry's apartment and view his work. After seeing Henry's paintings, Bellamy didn't waste time being coy.

"How soon can you be ready for a show?" he asked the artist.

Bea didn't let Henry answer; she walked Richard down the murky building stairs and, on the second-floor landing, told him that if he wanted Henry's work, he had to pay her part of the gallery's 50 percent commission.

"You're just a kid," he said dismissively. It was true, and she felt it sometimes — especially in that moment talking to him. He had experience and influence. Who was she to make demands? But she knew that if she let that cow her, *she* would never get to be the person with experience and influence.

"We're all just kids," she said, glancing pointedly up the stairs. Henry, several years older than her, was an adult, of course. But he looked much younger than his age, and she doubted Richard Bellamy cared about such fine distinctions anyway. "And we don't trust adults. So if you want Henry to let you be the one to sell his work, you're going to have to go through me. To be perfectly honest," she added, and this part was true, "he's happy to keep his work this side of Fourteenth Street."

"If he wants to make real money, I highly doubt that."

"He wants to be an artist. I'm the one who cares about money." Again, the truth. Bellamy appraised her, rubbed his jaw, glanced up the stairs, and said, "When can he be ready?"

The Green Gallery at 15 West Fifty-Seventh Street hosted the first show of Henry Wyatt's work on February 21, 1962. After that success, she brought Bellamy three more painters, all "minimalists," as Bellamy called them. Henry hated being shoved into any category, let alone one that was as "contextually meaningless" as minimalism.

By this time, Bea had informally moved into Henry's place on Greenwich Avenue. He holed himself up painting all day and she made the rounds of the studios of their ever-widening circle of friends, prospecting for new talent to add to her roster. Every night there was another party, sometimes two or three. On rooftops in the Lower East Side, in garden apartments in the West Village, in giant lofts in SoHo (one place was so big, the hosts had a roller-skating party). It felt like they owned downtown.

The one thing that nagged at Bea was how very much it felt like a boys' club. Most of the artists getting the big sales were men, as were most of the people running the galleries.

It was the glaring, astonishing talent of artist Anja Borsok, a chain-smoking blonde from Vienna, that inspired Bea to take a leap professionally. Anja, obsessed with Judy Garland, created paint-and-paper collages on canvas with incongruous references to *The Wizard of Oz,* gangsters, and Russian leader Nikita Khrushchev — sometimes all within the same work. Bea knew Anja could be her second big client.

Richard refused to visit her studio.

"It has to be because she's a woman," Bea said to Henry, walking fast to keep up with him. They were late for a party in SoHo, another sprawling loft, this one on Prince Street. Bea was falling in love with the cast-iron buildings with their impossibly high ceilings and faded grandeur.

"So take her somewhere else," Henry said. "There are other galleries."

They turned onto a cobblestone street somewhere near Lafayette. Bea stopped walking and grabbed Henry's arm. "Why should I have to beg a gallery to take work I know is good, work I know is going to sell? We should open our own gallery. Right down here."

A month later, Bea and Henry pooled

their money to buy a five-story cast-iron building on Spring Street for sixty thousand dollars. They turned the top floor into Henry's studio, the third and fourth floors into their living space, the second floor into an office, and the ground floor into the gallery.

The Winstead-Wyatt Gallery opened its doors in the fall of 1963. The press anointed them art's new power couple. Everyone, but everyone, assumed they were together. Bea never bothered correcting people.

As Bea was talking to Julia, the gallery assistant, her phone rang. She looked at the screen. Kyle, the turncoat. Bea had half a mind to send it to voice mail. But curiosity got the better of her.

"I need to talk to you," he said when she answered.

"Hence the phone call," she said drily.

"Where can we meet?"

"The hotel bar. Where else?"

She hung up the phone, opened the camera app, and snapped photos of the drawings against the protests of the gallery assistant.

"My dear, I assure you," Bea said, "it is taking all of my willpower not to simply pull these from the walls."

The young daughter of one of the housekeepers waited on the lobby couch for her
mother to finish her shift. She was about six
years old, and the sight of her made Emma
smile. The girl had big eyes and dark hair
bunched in pigtails, and she wore the type
of simple, pastel sundress Emma used to
put Penny in at that age. Like Penny, the
girl shifted impatiently and eyed the backgammon board.

Emma remembered sitting on that same
couch herself as a young girl, sometimes for
as long as a few hours while her mother ran
errands and her father worked at the bar.
When he finished, he would give her a lol-
lipop from the stash behind the front desk
before taking her by the hand to go home.

Emma reached down to a knee-level shelf
and pulled out the decades-old tin pail she
still kept filled with candy.

"Jasmine," she called to the girl. "Come
pick out a treat. But ask your mom before
you eat it."

The desk phone rang.

"The American Hotel, Emma speaking."

"Emma, it's Jack. I'm in the office. Can
you come see me for a minute?"

The back office was a tight space with just a desk, two chairs, and two filing cabinets. The walls were covered with postcards from around the world, yellowed newspaper clippings of articles about the hotel, and sports memorabilia.

"Take a seat," Jack said, standing in front of the filing cabinets.

She perched on the edge of the desk chair, reminding herself to finish e-mailing reservation confirmations to customers when they were done.

"So, I just wanted to discuss the elephant in the room, so to speak," Jack said.

She looked at him, confused. "Okay," she said nervously.

"The house," he prompted.

The house? "Oh, yes. *The house.* I guess Chris mentioned it to you?"

He looked at her strangely. "Emma, it's in the *Sag Harbor Express.*"

She was surprised, but then she realized she shouldn't be. It was enough of a local-interest story, she supposed. And real estate was always covered in the town papers. After all, that's how she'd learned about the sale of Richard Gere's house last summer. Amazing how the topic that used to be fun to gossip about was suddenly not so fun. "I'm sorry I didn't say anything. This all

just happened so suddenly. I'm still process-
ing it."

Jack held up one hand. "You don't owe
me any explanations. I just wanted to know
if this would affect your work schedule in
any way. Obviously, this is a dramatic
change in your circumstances. I don't want
any last-minute surprises with the summer
season starting. I need all hands on deck."

"Oh, nothing will change, Jack. I will be
here, ready to work."

He smiled. "Well, I'm happy to hear that,
Emma."

She couldn't imagine quitting her job.
Aside from the financial necessity of working here, the hotel was really Emma's
touchstone. She treasured the fact that she
worked at the same place where her father
had worked until the day he died. Every day
she looked at the same bar he'd tended, the
same couch they'd sat on together, the same
backgammon set they'd played. No, she
could inherit a dozen houses, and she
wouldn't change a thing about her work.

Back at the front desk, she e-mailed the
reservation confirmations and made a note
for the head of housekeeping that the
L'Occitane bath products needed to be
restocked upstairs.

"Are you Emma?" a blond, fit, forty-something woman sitting on the couch called out. She wore a white blouse knotted at her waist and black yoga pants.

"Yes, I am," Emma said.

The woman waved her over. Emma reluctantly left the desk. She always felt better with a barrier between herself and a person who might be about to start aggressively complaining. But this woman looked pleasant enough.

"I'm Cheryl Meister," she said, holding out her hand to shake Emma's. "I'm heading up the art-auction committee for the Sag Harbor Cinema fund-raiser."

"Oh, yes. Nice to meet you. You have a large party with us for lunch today, correct?"

"Yes, it's the committee. Do you have a moment to sit?"

Emma eyed the desk. "Sure. Just for a minute."

The woman moved over, making space for Emma on the couch. Across the room, Chris gave her a look, and she shrugged.

"Emma, I don't mean to intrude, but I heard all about your extraordinary circumstances of late," Cheryl said. "I know it's asking a lot, but I also know you are a town native and surely you care as much about restoring Main Street as any of us on the fund-raising committee, maybe more. If there is any way you can donate a piece of work from the Henry Wyatt estate, it would mean the world. Henry was such a beloved figure here and I imagine he would want to contribute to the effort."

Emma didn't know how to respond. The truth was that the art wasn't hers to give away — it belonged to her daughter. But that wasn't the point, and it wasn't this woman's business.

"You're right," she said slowly. "Mr. Wyatt would want to support the rebuilding of the theater. And, of course, I want to also. But it's too soon for me to make decisions about specific pieces of art. I hope you can under-stand."

Cheryl nodded, placing a manicured and bejeweled hand on Emma's arm. "I do. Absolutely. But as you sort it all out, please keep us in mind."

Then, as if struck by something obvious, she added, "You and your daughter should come to my house sometime. I have twelve-year-old twins."

"Oh, that's very generous of you. I'd like that." Emma couldn't think of anything that would be more awkward.

"And while you're figuring out the art situation, there are definitely other ways you can help. The committee meets Tuesdays at my house. I'll give you my address before I leave." She stood, smiled, and said with a wink, "I'm going to have one of Chris's famous martinis before the other ladies get here."

Emma watched her walk to the bar, feeling momentarily disconnected from her life. One minute she was logging a bulk order of bath products, the next she was being invited to lunch with a wealthy weekender.

So much for her promise to Jack that nothing would change.

CHAPTER TWELVE

Bea's seat at The American Hotel bar gave her an unfortunate view of Emma Mapson manning the front desk. Bea tried not to look in her direction, but she couldn't help sneaking curious glances. The woman was very pretty, and not in the brash, obvious way that was usual these days. She had a throwback kind of daintiness, a sweet Audrey Hepburn quality. Clearly, looks could be deceiving. The woman was a snake.

Kyle, sitting next to her, said, "Are you sure this is the best place to talk?"

"I will not be driven to substandard accommodations because of that woman," Bea replied, sipping her iced tea. "Besides, she won't be here for much longer. I already have a call in to Jack, the owner. I'm sure he won't be too happy to hear he's employing a con artist who's preying on his customers."

Kyle sighed. "Bea, that's what I wanted to

discuss with you. I ran into Emma's daughter and ended up talking to her for a few minutes. She seemed to know and genuinely care about Henry Wyatt."

"I'm sure a lot of people in this town knew and cared about Henry. But few are as attractive as that Emma Mapson. I shudder to think of how she leveraged that. Can you imagine?" She glanced over at the beautiful young woman, her heart suddenly beating fast.

"Bea, I think this whole thing might be legit."

"You're taking their side? That's disappointing, to say the least." She waved for the bartender.

"No, I'm on your side. That's why I'm warning you that this situation might not be what you think it is. When we lose something, when things go badly, we want to blame someone, but it's not always that person's fault."

"What do you know about loss? The only things you seem to lose are the phone numbers of the women you date."

Kyle shook his head.

"I haven't had much time for dating, Bea. Let's leave my personal life out of this."

"Fine. Then spare me the condescending advice."

147

"Bea, do you think I grew up thinking, *God, I hope someday I can spend my life running around doing the bidding for a demanding old lady?* That I thought, *If only I could figure out how to achieve that dream job!*" The bartender appeared. "Shot of whiskey, please."

So now everything was her fault? "I was unaware you had a problem with this job, Kyle. At least, not until you left me in the lurch."

"I never had a problem with this job. I've always been grateful for this job and grateful to you for showing up in my life at a time when I was pretty lost. Remember when you asked me if I was an aspiring actor and I told you no, I was happy to be a handyman?"

Oh, for heaven's sake. After all these years, he was going to confess his dreams of being a star. Had it taken all this time for him to get up the nerve to ask her to pull some strings for him?

"I make art careers, Kyle. Not acting careers."

He shook his head. "I don't want to be an actor."

Bea sighed impatiently. "So what, then?"

"Ever hear of the condition osteochondritis dissecans?"

"No. But now you're making me nervous. Are you trying to tell me you are ill? Truly, I cannot take any more drama!"

"I'm not ill. This is something I dealt with years ago. Osteochondritis dissecans is a condition where the bone just under the cartilage of a joint starts to die. In my case, it was the left knee. Ruined my soccer career."

"You were a professional soccer player?"

"No, I never got that far. I was forced to stop playing halfway through college. Lost my scholarship. Dropped out and had no idea what to do. I didn't have a degree, had no interest in anything. I went from a life of competition and world travel to, well, something far from that. I worked as a handyman. And then you offered me a job. I took it, and not just for the money. Like you said the other day at the house, my life became running your life. It was a welcome distraction for a time."

"And suddenly it's not anymore? Do you understand how incredibly selfish of you that is? I would like to know, just out of curiosity, why you would choose this moment to quit. I think you owe me that after all these years."

The bartender arrived with the whiskey. Kyle fidgeted with the shot glass, turning it around a few times.

"Sneaking around with all of this house stuff made me realize I need to move on. I've been avoiding dealing with my own life long enough. If this is what you want to do, I can't stop you. But I don't want to be a part of it."

"Then why are you sitting here right now?"

He shook his head. "Talking to that girl earlier . . . I know this is not going to end well for you, Bea. And I don't want to ditch you when you need someone. You were there when I needed someone even though you didn't realize it." He downed his drink.

"I don't want your pity, Kyle." Unbelievable. This conversation was going to drive *her* to afternoon whiskey.

"It's not pity. I know how much doing things the right way means to you. I didn't handle leaving this job in the right way, so I came back to apologize and offer two weeks' notice. I'll help you wrap things up around here."

She barely heard him. There, behind the bar, were a series of framed drawings she hadn't noticed before. Could they be . . . she eased her way off the chair and walked around the edge of the bar to the wall. On closer inspection, she saw that the sketches had been done on . . . cocktail napkins? Men fishing off the wharf. A piano player. A close-up of the backgammon table from the lobby, a male hand rolling dice.

"I'll be damned," she said.

"Bea, did you hear what I said?"

She turned to him, pointing at the drawings. "These are Henry's! Like the ones at the house. And I saw others like them in a gallery on Washington Street. He spent the last year or so, I don't know how long, giving his work away. Just giving it away!"

"I'm concerned about you, Bea," said Kyle.

"Be concerned about yourself," she snapped. "You're the one who is unemployed." She grabbed her phone and began taking photos of the sketches.

She wanted to tell Kyle to go to hell — she didn't need his charity. And then Emma Mapson walked by leading a group to one of the tables near the fireplace. Bea quickly looked away, her eyes falling again on Henry's framed drawings.

What, what, *what* was going on? Could Kyle be right? That this terrible turn of events was somehow legitimate?

She'd never felt more alone.

"Fine," she said to Kyle. "I'll take you up on the two weeks. Frankly, it's the least you

151

can do."

Kyle ordered another whiskey.

The painted sign out front was white with blue lettering and read MUSEUM: SAG HARBOR HISTORICAL SOCIETY. THE 1796 HOME OF ANNIE COOPER BOYD.

Penny followed Angus up the gravel path to the old house. Someone had stuck little American flags in the grass over Memorial Day weekend and they were still there. Penny knew they would remain there until the wind uprooted them and carried them away in the winter. Once something made an appearance at the historical society, it stayed at the historical society. On the front porch, exhibit A: An ancient carriage or sled of some sort that seemed to be made of wood and bones. It looked like it had been dropped there by Father Time himself.

Nothing ever changed at that place. It was a museum, so she supposed that was the point. But it wasn't like a museum that was shiny and new with all the old stuff in glass cabinets or framed on the walls. *Everything* was old. It had low, wood-beamed ceilings and a fireplace, above which hung a big portrait of a guy who looked like Abraham Lincoln but was some local doctor from the 1800s named Edgar Miles.

Random Christmas decorations hung year-round. One table in front of a window featured antique medicine bowls and pharmacy equipment; the window ledge was filled with antique glass bottles. These were from the exhibit called *Pills, Plants, and Poultices,* about the pioneering doctor who brought herbal medicine to the town in the mid- to late 1800s.

A framed illustrated guide to the history of the village whalers hung next to a strange but informative collage of images and trivia with the label *Dr. E. Miles headache or stomach pills.* Below, it posed a question: *What was in those pills?* And then a bunch of cards with various plants and flowers.

"When are you putting together a new exhibition?" Penny asked Angus. She hoped he could find something more interesting for her to look at every day. Maybe a costume show? Surely there had been someone in town who embroidered dresses or made hats or something.

"Maybe at the end of the summer," Angus said, turning on the lights and walking to the back room. He called for her to follow him.

"So, if you're not changing the exhibition, what am I going to do here every day?"

"Very good question! Come this way and

I'll show you."

Angus seemed way too excited. Penny followed him to the small back office tucked behind a wooden door hung with a colorful wreath. One shelf was filled with copies of a thick hardcover book called *Sag Harbor: The Story of an American Beauty,* by Dorothy Ingersoll Zaykowski. Penny's mom had a copy in her bedroom.

"Elizabeth invested in a new computer system," he said, booting up a laptop.

"Who's Elizabeth?"

"Elizabeth Tripp Gregory, head of the board of directors. She's a relative of Joan Bates Tripp." Penny knew that name. It was on a plaque outside the front door; she'd founded the museum in 1985. "Now, my eyesight isn't what it used to be and I can't be staring at this screen all day. But I know you kids just love your screens, so it shouldn't be a problem for you."

Penny felt a surge of hope. A computer! Suddenly, the entire spectrum of her day changed. She had six blissful hours of YouTube videos ahead of her.

"Now, what we have to do is get the museum archives logged in the system. The new program will make everything searchable by name and subject matter. Amazing, right?" he said, mistaking her smile as enthusiasm for the task at hand.

He sat in the desk chair and pulled up a screen that was filled with fields for data. He explained that there were different sections for different types of artifacts; books and diaries were logged in one section, postcards and other documents in another section. There was one whole section for maps, one for furniture, another for portraits. "I don't expect you to get this all done in one week or even one month," he said. "But every day, just chip away at it. That's how something gets accomplished."

Angus set a box of books and papers on the desk and left her to get to work.

She waited a minute, checked to make sure he was gone, and then scurried over to the computer and found the internet browser. She clicked on it. No connection. She went to settings and searched for Wi-Fi networks, but there was nothing except locked accounts from nearby businesses. No way. It couldn't be; even the whaling museum had Wi-Fi!

"Oh my God." The stretch of hours ahead of her seemed like a lifetime. She felt like the walls of the small office were moving even closer together.

Fighting a sense of panic, her anxiety rising like a fever, she considered running to the hotel to beg her mom to just let her sit in the lobby until she got off work. But she hadn't been to the hotel since Henry died. The sight of their usual spot at the couch would be too awful.

Her heart began to pound. She felt trapped — trapped in that museum, trapped in that town. Trapped in her life.

Palms sweating, she walked back to the main room of the house, where Angus was busy talking to visitors, a young family asking questions about an old map. Penny stood unnoticed in the corner, wondering what to do. There was no way to sneak past them.

She looked up at the portrait of Dr. Edgar Miles. He seemed so stately, so tough. Like an army general, not like someone who spent all day turning plants into medicine. *What was in those pills?*

And then she thought of one way to feel better. She slunk out of the room, hoping not to be noticed, then pulled her phone out of her pocket and texted Mindy: Do you have any more of those pills?

Mindy texted back, You are bad!

Penny responded, Is that a yes?

Come over tonight, Mindy texted.

I can't wait until tonight. Can you meet me

at BuddhaBerry at noon? I will owe you big time, I know!

Mindy wrote back that yes, she would meet her, and yes, Penny totally owed her. She used some emoticon that Penny's outdated phone couldn't translate.

Penny typed back Thanks while an alarm bell sounded somewhere inside of her, just faint enough to ignore.

CHAPTER THIRTEEN

Across the hotel lobby, in Emma's direct line of sight, a couple sat entwined on the couch. The man had a thick head of silver hair, a deep tan, and horn-rim glasses that made him look even more handsome and distinguished. The younger woman next to him, in a Tory Burch shift dress and strappy sandals, wore her blond hair in a high ponytail. She rested her head on the man's shoulder. He reached for her hand, and the gesture almost made Emma gasp.

She was starting to feel like she would never have a man in her life. It wasn't something she thought about every day or every week. It wasn't even something she was sure she wanted. There were just certain moments when it hit her, the same way thoughts about mortality or about paying for Penny's college or about any of life's other heavy and undeniable realities did.

In the years since her divorce, there had

been boyfriends. Like Eric McSweeney, who worked at the fire station. Eric was a good guy, a sweet guy. But he had a hard time dealing with Penny, who had been nine then and really a handful with her OCD. Eric was married now, to a woman who worked at the health-food shop on Bay Street. They had twins. Then there had been the banker from Manhattan who was only out on weekends and, Emma came to suspect, possibly married. There had been the occasional one-night stands, men she met at the hotel. She thought of those episodes as her weaker moments, and they always left her feeling depressed the next day. And really, it wasn't the sex she missed. It was having a partner.

When was the last time something good happened? Penny had asked her the other day. Well, it had been a while. But now, the house.

The phone rang. "The American Hotel, Emma speaking. How may I assist you?"

In front of the desk, a couple huffed and puffed impatiently to be seated for dinner, the woman leaning on the countertop as if proximity to Emma would magically make something open up sooner.

"Mom, it's me. You're not answering your cell."

159

Emma glanced under the desk to see if she even had her phone, then checked the time. Close to nine. "It's been nonstop, hon. Where are you?" Even over the din of the lobby and bar, Emma could hear that Penny was someplace loud herself.

"I'm at a friend's house. I'm going to sleep over."

"What friend?"

"Mindy Banks." Before Emma could protest, Penny said, "Robin's here and I really want to spend time with her."

Emma bit her lip. Robin was a sweet kid — at least, she had been a sweet kid before whatever metamorphosis this year had led her to ditch Penny for those fast girls. How could Penny think it was okay to sleep over Mindy's house?

"Penny, the last time you were at that house you left with a police escort. You're not sleeping there. And I don't want you biking home this late. I'm calling a cab to pick you up."

"It's only nine!"

"Text me the address and be outside the house in half an hour. Don't make me call Angus because I will send him inside to pull you out of there." An idle threat. There was no way she'd wake Angus up for that task. She'd have to leave work.

"Come on, Mom. I need a life!" Penny hung up.

Yeah, you and me both, kid, Emma thought. A waiter signaled to her that a two-top was open. "Your table is ready," she said to a couple hovering near the desk. Emma was relieved to lead them to a spot in the back of the bar. Maybe the night would finally shift into autopilot, and she could look forward to getting home. Home to deal with her recalcitrant daughter. Yes, that would be a lovely way to cap off the day.

Back at the desk, she checked her cell phone to see if Penny texted back to confirm that she would take the cab in half an hour. Nothing.

"You know, this hotel *is not big enough.*"

Emma looked up to find the old woman — Ms. Winstead. She was dressed in all black, a diamond brooch on her jacket. Her lipstick was a bright reddish orange, and the Hermès scarf around her neck featured the identical shade. She was probably only five foot five or so but something about her seemed towering.

She was the last person Emma wanted to see.

"Good evening, Ms. Winstead. Do you need something in your room?"

"I was saying, young lady, that this hotel

is not big enough for the two of us. How do you expect me to sleep under this roof knowing there is a thief at the helm?"

Oh, for heaven's sake. Was she for real? Sadly, the answer seemed to be yes. "I'm sorry you feel that way, Ms. Winstead. But this is my place of employment and I'm happy to assist you if you need something."

Across the room, the handsome couple disentangled themselves, stood from the couch, and walked arm in arm to the front door. Emma felt a pang.

Ms. Winstead leaned closer. "This will not be your place of employment for long."

"Excuse me?" Emma said.

"I'm having a little chat with your boss tomorrow morning to make sure he knows he has a fox guarding the henhouse. I don't think he'll be pleased. Do you?"

"My mom sucks! She says I can't sleep over. She's sending a cab for me." Penny rolled her eyes at Robin, who laughed on cue. They sat on the deck of Mindy's house overlooking the harbor filled with yachts and sailboats. Penny couldn't believe she had to leave when she was finally having fun.

"When?" Robin asked, as horrified as if Penny had said her mother was sending her off to do hard labor.

"At this point? A half an hour or so."

"You can't go! It's so early."

Penny nodded. She didn't want to leave, despite the weird thing that had happened downstairs earlier in the night. For the first time, she felt like she fit in. It was so different than Memorial Day weekend. She'd felt bad that night, inferior, because she couldn't help comparing Mindy's place to her own ramshackle house by the railroad tracks. But thanks to Henry, everything had changed.

Well, almost everything. As much as Penny tried to enjoy herself, to let go and be like everyone else at the party, she couldn't quiet her mind. The party was just Robin, Mindy, Mindy's lapdog friend Jess, and a few boys from Pierson High, including one kid, Mateo, whose family was from Spain and whose older brother Nick was infamous for wrecking the Porsche convertible he'd gotten on his sixteenth birthday.

Penny joined everyone playing beer pong in the rec room on the third floor, but she kept leaving to wash her hands. She'd accidentally touched the bottom of one of her shoes when she'd taken them off to sit by the pool, and she couldn't stop thinking about it. When she came out of the bathroom the third time, she found Mateo waiting for her.

"Hey, you don't like to share?" he said with a smile. He had very dark eyes, and there was a certain thrill to seeing them focused on her.

"Share what?" She hid her hands behind her back. They were dripping wet, because her OCD made it impossible for her to use the same towel all the other guests used.

Mateo put one hand against the wall and leaned his body in close to hers. "Whatever it is you're doing in there. You have blow?"

She told him no, she absolutely did not. She didn't have anything. Then he leaned in even closer and kissed her. She opened her mouth — was it to protest? And his tongue pressed inside. She jumped back, ducked under his arm, ran up the stairs to the first floor, and rushed out to the deck.

She was still trying to process it when Robin came looking for her.

"The taxi is here, but you still have time for this." She handed her one of the white pills. "You might have to leave the party, but the party doesn't have to leave you."

"Thanks," Penny said, pocketing it for her next dismal stint at the historical society. "You're such a good friend."

Emma had been working out her frustrations on Murf's black-and-red dartboard since the summer she'd spent behind the bar there. It had once been a reliable cure for all that ailed her, as the original owner put it. Tonight, distracted by Bea Winstead's threats, she was completely off her game.

The idea of Bea actually going after her job! And, worse, going after what belonged to Penny. She thought of Penny's face the day she'd said, "Why does life have to suck all the time?" And what had Emma told her? That sometimes good things happened. Well, something incredible had happened. Now it was Emma's job to protect it. And she would — no matter what it took.

Her previous two darts had lodged in the wall. She tossed a third. Total crap. She didn't bother keeping score on the cracked green slate propped up against the wall on a bench. Someone else's game was still etched in chalk underneath a logo that read THE CRICKETEER.

A crowd of people walked in and she waited for them to go past her before tossing her next three darts. On the jukebox, Amy Winehouse's "Back to Black" played. The door opened again, bringing in a rush of hot air. And an unwelcome face.

Please don't see me.

He saw her.

"Hey. Emma, right?"

"What are you doing here?" she said to Bea Winstead's friend. Or relative? She had no idea why the guy was with Bea. Nor did she really care. She just didn't want him in *her* bar.

"Drinking, like everyone else."

"Can't you do that at the hotel?"

"I'd like to get drunk away from my employer."

Employer? "What do you do for that woman, exactly? Never mind — I don't want to know. And I don't want to spend time with Bea Winstead's evil henchman. So, please, find someplace else to drink."

"No offense, but I think you're overreacting," he said. "Let me buy you a beer."

"I already have a beer," she said, retrieving it from the bench where she had all but forgotten it. She took a long swig.

"I'm Kyle Dunlap, by the way. Evil Henchman is just my stage name." He held out his hand. She ignored it.

"She's trying to get me fired, you know."

"She doesn't want to get you fired. She just wants the house. Actually, what she really wants is the art. She worked with Henry Wyatt his entire career. She's known him for, like, fifty years. This whole thing doesn't make sense to her."

166

Emma set down the bottle and said, "You know, I see people like you and that woman every summer. You waltz into town with your sense of entitlement, your greedy need to make this place your playground. And the second something takes a little too long or doesn't go right, you attack."

"First of all, I don't know why you're lumping me in with Bea Winstead. I just work for her." He looked around the bar. "I'm basically the same as you."

"Oh, is that right?" she said. "Do you have a kid?"

Kyle shook his head. "No. No kid. But I did get an earful from yours earlier today."

That got her attention. "You saw Penny? Where?"

"I was waiting at the — it's a long story. I was on the street and she came up to me. She said you weren't going to take the house because Bea Winstead was hassling you and she wanted me to tell her to back off."

"Penny said that?"

Kyle nodded.

Emma bit back a smile. *She has more nerve than her mother, that's for sure.* Maybe it was time to change that. "I'm not backing down," Emma said. "Bea Winstead is wasting her time."

"Look, I can see things from your point of

view, okay? One minute you're busting your ass catering to these rich assholes, and the next minute, you've got a multimillion-dollar waterfront house. What a windfall."

"I never asked for this," she said. "But it could be life-changing. I'm a single mother. I work seventy hours a week to support my daughter, save for college, and pay rent on a house I'll never be able to afford to buy."

"So you're not married?" he said.

She narrowed her eyes at him. "That's none of your business. But no, I'm divorced. Long divorced."

"Yeah. I've never been married."

Emma shook her head. She couldn't care less about his marital status. Was he missing the point of this conversation? "Do you have any idea what even a tiny house costs in this town these days? This used to be an affordable place to live. I was born here. My parents were born here. But it's like . . . you know the old story about putting a frog in boiling water?"

"Can't say I do."

"If you put a frog in boiling water, he'll jump out. But if you put him in tepid water and slowly turn up the heat, he won't realize what's happening and he'll be cooked to death."

"Why are we talking about frogs?" Kyle

said, picking up a dart.

"Because I am the frog! All of us who have lived here a long time are the frogs."

He tossed the dart and hit the bull's-eye. She hated him.

"Emma, I hear you. I've been working for Bea for five years now, and believe me, I put up with a lot of shit. But let's say she pulls a Henry Wyatt and drops dead at the bar tomorrow over her glass of sauvignon blanc. And then let's say it turns out that she left everything to me. Here's the headline: 'Park Avenue Socialite and Art Patron Leaves Multimillion-Dollar Estate to Assistant.' Do you honestly think that wouldn't be questioned?"

"That's a paranoid way to look at things."

"I'm just saying Bea isn't the only one asking questions. She's just the only person close enough to the situation to get involved."

"So you're defending her?"

"I'm telling you she's not a bad person. She can be a pain in the ass, but she's not malicious. She's acting in her own self-interest and I guess in the interest of her friend. This isn't really about you."

"No, it's not about me. It's about my daughter, because you're forgetting Henry Wyatt left the house to *her*. I know it looks crazy, okay? It seemed crazy to me when I heard it. But it's legitimate. I never asked for it, I never imagined it, but it happened. And I'm not going to let some woman swoop in from Park Avenue and take it away from her." Emma downed the rest of her beer, set the empty bottle on the bar, and walked out. The air was soupy with humidity, more like August than June. She breathed deeply as she followed Division to the water. How dare he come into her bar and try to justify Bea Winstead's behavior?

"Emma, wait up," he called from behind her. She ignored him, crossed the street, passed the Bay Street Theater, and walked by the shops leading to the pier. When she looked back, she saw he was following her.

She stepped over a low wooden plank and sat down on a bench at the edge of the water. Far offshore, dozens of lights winked from a cluster of boats.

She crossed her arms, staring off into the distance. "Go away," she said.

He sat on the far end of the bench, giving her some space.

"You seem like a nice woman," he said. "And your kid seems like a good kid. I'm not trying to upset you. I'm just trying to tell you what you're really up against. She's not some cartoon villain. This is complicated."

She turned to him. "It's not complicated. It's very, very simple. My daughter inherited the estate. This is all legit. So don't patronize me."

Sean's water taxi skimmed slowly to a stop in front of the dock, and she jumped up. "Sean!" she called. "Can you give me a lift?"

"You got it. Where to?" She pointed across the bay.

Kyle followed her to the landing steps. "Where are you going?" he said.

"To my daughter's house," Emma said. It was an impulse, but she wanted to make a point. What was the saying? Possession was nine-tenths of the law? "The house that your boss isn't going to scare me away from. Go back to New York, Kyle. Just leave. You don't belong here."

Sean's dog yipped loudly.

She moved to the helm of the small launch and held on to the metal rail, comforted by the rumble of the engine. Melville settled by her feet as the boat took off. Motion was good. Move forward. *Don't look back.* But she did — just one glance.

Kyle Dunlap was there in the distance, watching her leave.

CHAPTER FOURTEEN

Bea had always been a firm believer in rising early. There was nothing like Park Avenue when the only souls stirring were the doormen hosing down the sidewalks. The American Hotel at eight in the morning, she found, had a similar tranquillity. There was not a sound from a single guest room, and in the lobby, the only movement was a handful of workers stuffing tea roses into silver vases. And in this quiet, when all seemed ordered and as it should be, she felt overcome by the charm of the place.

She found Jack Blake waiting for her at a table in the dining room where they served a continental breakfast. The space was narrow but bright thanks to the skylight. One wall was exposed brick, the other wood-paneled with long mirrors. The potted plants reached the ceiling, and some hung down, giving the place an airy, garden feeling. The tables were dressed with white linens and set with floral-patterned china.

Jack stood and pulled out a wicker chair for her.

"What a lovely place you have, Jack. I haven't been here in many, many years but I'm pleased to see it hasn't changed a bit."

"Thank you, Bea. That's the idea."

"How much time do you spend in Sag Harbor?"

"Winters in Palm Beach, summers here. Sometimes Christmas too, but it depends on my wife."

"I think it was the holidays when I met you in Palm Beach. Isn't that right?"

He nodded. A waitress poured them coffee and set the carafe on the table. "Angela, bring us some croissants and the fruit salad, please." He turned back to Bea. "So, what brings you out here and what can I do for you?"

Direct. She respected that. Small talk was overrated. "Well, Jack, unfortunately, I came out here under rather unhappy circumstances. Henry Wyatt was a dear friend of mine."

Jack nodded. "He was a treasure in this town. A real shame to see him go."

He was too good for this town, Bea thought. But she shook that away. She needed to stay focused.

173

"Henry and I go back fifty years. We built his entire career together. We were quite inseparable for a time."

"I'm sorry for your loss."

"Well, thank you. Now, I'm telling you this because for the past year or two, Henry was a bit reclusive. And I'm afraid one of your employees preyed on his loneliness for her own gain."

Jack seemed to mull over Bea's accusation as the waitress set pastries and a bowl of fruit on the table.

"Are you referring to Emma Mapson?" he said.

She wasn't surprised to hear him identify her. Of course he would know about the house. Everyone knew about the house. The thing he did not know was how out of character this was for Henry and how all personal history and logic dictated that Bea should be the beneficiary of his estate. "Yes. Emma Mapson. She claims Henry left his estate to her daughter."

"Well, it's more than a claim. I understand there's a will."

Bea swallowed her frustration and took a deep breath. "Jack, you have to understand that Henry did not even like children. He never married. He was devoted to his art. Frankly, the closest thing he had to a wife in his entire life was myself, and his career *was* our child. As difficult as it was to think of it, we discussed what would happen to his work after his death. He had the idea of establishing a museum. Nothing was formalized, but at our age these conversations are more than idle chitchat. So you can imagine my surprise to hear that, out of the blue, he left everything to the daughter of one of your hotel employees. By her own admission, this woman barely knew Henry."

"A surprising turn of events."

It was a relief to hear him affirming her own feelings about the matter. Jack Blake had tremendous standing in the community. "It's not just surprising, Jack. It's suspicious. Frankly, I'm certain it's borderline criminal."

Jack nodded. "And you're proposing I do what?"

"Well, for starters, I'm sure you don't want grifters running your hotel. I think for your own good you should let her go."

"I see," Jack said. He poured himself more coffee. Across the room, the waitstaff began setting up the breakfast buffet. "The thing is, Emma might not have known Henry very well, but *I* know *Emma.* I've known Emma Mapson since she was this high. Her father was an employee of mine. A good man."

"I don't see what that has to do with any of this."

"Let's put it this way, Bea — if you're implying that Emma Mapson is some sort of scam artist or thief, it's best if you find yourself another place to stay."

Emma waited impatiently in the small corridor outside Dr. Wang's office, yawning and trying not to worry about getting to work. She sipped her takeout coffee and mentally kicked herself for staying out so late.

What had she been thinking last night? The drinks at Murf's, the boat ride out to Henry Wyatt's house. She'd stood in the dining room staring out at the shimmering pool, going over and over in her mind everything that had happened since the minute that lawyer showed up on her doorstep.

Henry Wyatt didn't have any living family. He'd never married, so there wasn't even an ex-wife to worry about. Okay, so this Bea Winstead had known the guy for fifty years, but Henry Wyatt had chosen not to leave his house and his art to her. And going by the internet search Emma had done, it wasn't like the old bird was hurting for cash. A *New York Times* article featured photos of her palatial Park Avenue apartment. So what did she care about the Sag Harbor house? That was the thing about the wealthy — they never had enough. She saw it all the time with the summer people, their unbelievable sense of entitlement.

When she finally got home, she was so adrenalized she couldn't sleep. She tossed and turned thinking about the house, wondering if Bea was going to get Jack to fire her over it.

Dr. Wang poked her head out of the office. "Emma, let's speak for a minute," she said, stepping out and closing the door behind her.

"Everything okay?"

"I'm afraid Penny is backsliding a bit. I want to bring up, again, the option of putting her on an SSRI. They can be very effective in getting baseline OCD and anxiety under control, and that would give her the breathing room to employ the cognitive techniques we're practicing here."

Emma had been afraid she'd say that. "I'd rather give this more time. Unless Penny really feels she can't get better without medication."

"I'll discuss it with her. I just wanted to make sure you're open to the idea."

Emma's experience with her mother's prescription-pill addiction made her especially wary of drug treatment. It was irrational, she knew; the type of medication Dr. Wang was proposing was nothing like the kind that had led to her mother's downward spiral. Still, she couldn't bring herself to agree to it. At least, not yet. "Penny has suffered a loss and I think that set her back. But I don't want that to change our whole game plan."

"Sometimes these things are beyond our control."

It seemed that went for just about everything lately.

Chapter Fifteen

Main Street hummed with activity. Shop owners opened their doors, café workers set out chalkboards announcing the day's lunch specials, mothers pushed strollers, and couples strolled hand in hand, sipping takeout coffee. It was all so picturesque, so lovely, Bea could almost forget the most recent indignity leveled on her by this town: *If you're implying that Emma Mapson is some sort of scam artist or thief, it's best if you find yourself another place to stay.*

Was that any way to talk to a customer? Eighty miles from New York City, and all common decency was lost. Obviously, she couldn't spend another night under Jack Blake's roof. She packed up her things but Kyle was nowhere to be found. She was already rolling her smallest suitcase to the car when he returned her call.

"Where in heaven's name are you?" she said, her voice shrill.

"I'm just down the street. On the wharf."

"I need you! Come back to the hotel immediately."

He muttered something and then the connection was lost. She waited and waited in front of the flower boxes framing the hotel porch and still no Kyle. She called, but again, he didn't answer his phone. Furious, she dragged her bag to the wharf.

She found him talking to someone on the dock, a fair-haired young man with an unfortunate scruffy beard.

"Kyle!" she yelled, walking to him as quickly as she could manage while maneuvering her bag on the uneven surface of the dock. *Bump, bump, bump.* She was certain the bottom was being destroyed. Her irritation gained strength, like a gathering storm. "What are you doing out here?"

"Bea, this is Sean Pine. He runs the water taxi out here."

Bea nodded at the man, then turned to glare at Kyle. Did she look like she was in the mood to play meet-the-locals?

"He's been doing this for nine years," Kyle said. "Before that, he was in the Coast Guard."

"Fascinating. Can I speak to you alone for a moment? Preferably in the shade?"

The only shelter was under the roof of the

dockmaster's office a few dozen feet behind her. Kyle took her bag.

"Why are you carrying this?" he asked.

"That's what I wanted to talk to you about. I've checked out of that horrid hotel. You'll have to go back for the rest of the luggage."

"I thought you said it was the only civilized place in town."

"Don't be smart with me, Kyle."

"So where are you going to stay?"

"*We* are going to stay at Windsong."

"I don't think that's a good idea right now."

"And why is that?"

"That guy back there, Sean? He gave Emma Mapson a ride to the house last night."

"He told you this?"

Kyle started to say something, then stopped. "Not exactly."

"Let's go. We'll take the boat there ourselves."

"That's kind of aggressive, Bea. I just told you that Emma might be there."

"She's probably on her way to work. Besides, isn't that a fundamental principle of war? To meet aggression with aggression? Really, Kyle. I know you've given notice, but during the two weeks you have remaining, please try to get with the program."

She walked briskly to the edge of the dock. "Young man," she called out.

Kyle ran up behind her. "Bea, let me handle this."

He asked the water-taxi captain to take Bea to the same place that Emma Mapson had gone last night.

"Aren't you coming?" Bea said.

He hesitated, then said, "You know what? I will. Just in case Emma is there and I need to act as a referee for you two."

"So now it's *Emma*? You're on a first-name basis suddenly?"

Kyle's face turned red.

Men! They were all the same.

He placed her bag on the boat and helped her step aboard. There was a padded bench in front of the controls and he kept hold of her arm until she was situated.

Bea held the metal rail and looked out at the open water. The launch went only about five miles an hour, but with the rumble of the engine and the wind in her face, she felt like they were really moving. She felt a sudden lightness, almost a happiness, despite the aggravating morning.

Kyle chatted to Sean the entire ride, telling him about his childhood at the Jersey Shore and about how his father had had a boat and about how he hadn't realized how much he missed the water. Kyle had been in Bea's employ for five years, but she was only now learning all this. Perhaps it was more than she needed to know, considering he was leaving her.

"I hear that a lot from people visiting out here," Sean said. "They spend a day on the water and it's like they never left it."

A small dog jumped up onto the bench beside her.

"Is this your animal?" she called out to Sean. Kyle shot her a look that said, *Don't complain.* The dog rested its head in her lap.

The house came into view and took her breath away. The vantage point you got from the water was much more dramatic than what you saw when you approached it from the street. She was sure Henry had planned it that way, and she felt a pang. How she missed him. How adrift she felt. Why had he muddled this situation with his estate?

When they reached the dock, she counted out some bills from her wallet, handed them to Sean, and told him to keep the change.

"Well, that was refreshing," she said as Kyle helped her off the boat.

"Glad you liked it," he said. He followed her to the sliding glass doors at the back of the house.

Inside, it was steaming hot. None of the shades over the large windows had been drawn, and the sunlight poured through the skylights. If Emma Mapson had been there last night, she certainly hadn't stayed very long.

"Put my bag in the master suite," Bea said.

"Not the guest room?"

"No. Because I am not a guest. I am *moving in.*"

Penny shifted in her chair, sitting on her hands so Dr. Wang wouldn't see them. The backs of her hands were cracked and bleeding from overwashing, and they were also glistening with the Aquaphor Penny had slathered on before her appointment in an attempt to hide the fact that they were a mess.

"Penny, it doesn't look like you're sticking to the thirty-second rule," Dr. Wang said. Eagle eye!

"I'm trying to," Penny said. Actually, she wasn't trying one bit. Lathering up the soap was one of the few ways to release the pressure she felt. It wasn't pressure as in the pressure to perform or do anything. It was more like a psychic weight that rested on her. Drawing used to give her some relief, but now she couldn't even enjoy that. She kept trying to sketch, but the second a stroke of her pencil strayed from her intention, when the lines didn't cooperate, she couldn't erase them and keep going. She had to throw the whole thing away no matter how far along she was. She knew it was wrong, she knew it was a compulsion, but she couldn't help herself.

She told this to Dr. Wang, who then leaned back in her chair, wrote something on her notepad, and looked at Penny with a warm smile.

"It sounds like you're having a tough time. A little bit of a setback."

Penny nodded, her eyes tearing up.

"I spoke to Mom about the option of adding medication to our program," Dr. Wang said. She always referred to Emma as "Mom." It was kind of weird.

Penny knew her mother was against medication. Penny could only imagine how her mom would feel if she found out about the little white pills from Mindy. She had to stop with that.

"Would that mean I don't have to come to therapy anymore?"

"No," Dr. Wang said quickly. "Medication and therapy work together. Penny, why are you so averse to therapy?"

She shrugged. "I guess I just want to be

normal. Coming here makes me feel like I'm not."

"What's normal? You're an artist. Some would say that's not normal. But you wouldn't change that, would you?"

Of course she wouldn't. But sometimes she wondered what good it did her.

CHAPTER SIXTEEN

"Emma, two things," Jack Blake said, appearing in front of the desk. "I need a bar table, party of four, for dinner in an hour. We'll need a bottle of the 2010 Lucien le Moine Chevalier-Montrachet from downstairs."

"Got it," she said, jotting down the name of the wine.

"Also, Emma, I had a conversation with Bea Winstead this morning. Seems she's less than happy about this turn of events with the Wyatt house."

So Bea had spoken to him after all. Her heart beat faster. "Yes, I know. I'm sorry. I'm not sure what to do about that."

"Just keep the drama out of the hotel, okay?"

"Of course. No drama — I promise."

That should be easier now that Bea Winstead had checked out. Thank goodness! Hopefully, she was on her way back to New

York City at that very moment. Or, at the very least, checking into another hotel.

Jack smiled, tapped the desktop, and said, "Make that two bottles of the Montrachet."

Emma blocked off his table in the reservation book, shaking her head. That woman had some nerve, making trouble for her at work. But what was Emma supposed to do about it? She could only hope Bea would get tired of arguing over a house that she had absolutely no legal claim to.

"Emma, hello!" said Mrs. Fleishman, a regular who always booked room number 8 for a week in June with her husband.

"Hi, Mrs. Fleishman. Wonderful to see you again. Let me just check to see if your table is ready."

"We're in no rush, dear. We're going to have a drink first. But I had to ask — is this you?"

Mrs. Fleishman slid a copy of the *New York Post* across the desk. Emma followed the woman's finger as she pointed to the words *daughter of the desk manager of The American Hotel in Sag Harbor.*

Her name. In the *New York Post.*

Her eyes scanned upward for the headline: "Battle Lines Drawn over the Estate of Artist Henry Wyatt."

188

Society maven and art patron Bea Winstead is using her considerable clout to mount a legal challenge to the will of the late artist Henry Wyatt in a bid to preserve his art for the public.

Winstead has hired the firm Smythe, Bonivent, Worth to look into the will filed by the legendary painter and sculptor, which leaves his Hamptons home and the bulk of his estate to the daughter of the desk manager of The American Hotel in Sag Harbor.

The article went on to chronicle the significance of Henry's body of work and suggested that Emma would somehow damage the legacy by selling it off piecemeal and not making the works available to museums. It said that the house, "designed by Wyatt, a piece of museum-quality art in itself," should be a public space.

It concluded with a quote from an anonymous source: "We are investigating all avenues, including the possibility this will is a forgery."

A forgery! This was absurd. Who would have forged it? *Her?*

She looked up to find Mrs. Fleishman beaming at her, as if Emma had just been profiled in *Time* magazine as its Person of the Year.

"Yep," she said, handing the newspaper back to her. "That's me."

Bea tossed and turned in the darkness of her old friend's bedroom.

The silence of the house on that remote, waterfront road was absolute. She would have liked to hear the stir of New York City outside her window, a distant car honking, the pipes of her upstairs neighbor. Anything to root her in the present, to assure her that she was tethered to the earth. Henry was gone, but she was still there.

Focus on the art. It had been the guiding principle of her entire adult life.

The thing that nagged at her most was the shift in style. Why the line drawings? The portraiture? She stared at the ceiling, growing increasingly certain that she was onto something, that if she could figure out the meaning of the last stage of Henry's artistic career, she could decipher the mystery of his inexplicable will.

When it was finally light outside, she padded down the floating stairs. She desperately wanted someone to talk to about all of this. Sadly, Kyle was all she had.

She knocked on the closed guest-bedroom door. Kyle opened it, wrapped in the bed comforter. His thick head of golden-brown hair was mussed and he looked startlingly young. She thought how very ancient she must seem to him. Sometimes, she saw this on his face. And then she wanted to shake him, to say, *Just you wait — it happens in an instant!*

"Bea, it's the middle of the night," he said, scratching his head.

"No, it's first thing in the morning. Meet me in the kitchen. I'll put the coffee on."

Some rooms of the house reminded her of Henry more than others. The kitchen was a sharp reflection of his personal taste, with its concrete countertops in dove gray, industrial-like metal islands, black-granite sink, and ultramodern acrylic bar stools. There were odd eclectic touches, like the scuffed brown Hamilton coffeemaker that had to be thirty years old. Kyle had taken one look at it, declared it unusable, and gone out to buy a sleek new Cuisinart programmable brewer (she'd warned him not to come back with one of those god-awful pod devices). In the kitchen cabinet she discovered Henry's collection of vintage ceramic Russel Wright plates.

She scooped the coffee into the stainless-steel brewer, poured the water, and got it started, ignoring most of the many buttons.

She looked wistfully at its old neighbor sitting neglected a few inches away on the counter. She reached out and touched the beige handle of the glass pot, wondering if Henry had used it his last morning in the house.

"Okay, what's so important?" Kyle said, now dressed in cargo shorts and a hoodie. He pulled two mugs out of the cabinet.

The coffee bubbled and hissed its way into the glass carafe. Bea leaned against the counter, too excited to sit at the table. "I think the drawings in town are clues. They mean something."

Kyle nodded, eyeing the machine. When it was finished he filled the two mugs, handed one to Bea, and took a long sip of his own. "Bea, I hope you take this in the right way, because I'm trying to help you here: I think that's wishful thinking."

"Kyle, you can take this however *you* want: You don't know what you're talking about! Why would he spend his final year or so drawing pieces and giving them away? Essentially scattering them around town?"

"How do you know they are that recent?"

"They're dated."

Kyle seemed to consider this. He walked from the kitchen to the dining room and stared at the dining table that was perfectly aligned with the infinity pool on the other side of the glass wall, the two symmetrical and perfect in a stunning example of grand design. "So what do you want to do, Bea?"

"I want to find every drawing that's out there. I need your help scouring this town."

Chapter Seventeen

In the early days of motherhood, Emma had wanted nothing more than sleep. Now all she wanted was more time with her daughter.

Emma missed the mornings when Penny was just a little girl and climbed into Emma's bed before it was light out. Penny would tuck her warm little body against hers, and once she was settled, her breathing would become slow and steady while Emma, fully awake, counted the few hours she had until she had to leave for work.

Now it was impossible to see Penny before work unless Emma woke her, risking her potent adolescent wrath in the process. But today she had to do just that.

If her own mother had been around, she might have warned Emma that the hardest stage of being a working parent wasn't when your child was small, although it had felt that way at the time. The reality was that at that point, any responsible adult's supervision would do. For years, knowing that Celia and then, when Celia was gone, Angus was with Penny was enough to give Emma peace of mind and her daughter a sense of security. The tricky part was when a kid hit middle school and high school, and that adult supervision wasn't needed. Well, it was needed, but not in the same way. Someone had to keep track of Penny's friends, her moods, the overall temperature of her life. Emma should be that person, and lately, she felt she simply wasn't doing a great job.

She stood outside Penny's closed bedroom door, rapped lightly twice, and opened it. "Pen?" she said, coming in and sitting on the edge of the bed. Penny was curled up on her side. When awake, Penny was starting to look like a young woman. But when she was asleep, her profile, the delicate slant of her arched nose, was the same face of her infancy. Emma remembered looking down at the tiny bundle in her arms, just six pounds, six ounces, for the first time. She had a little pink cap on, and her eyes were closed tight. Emma had never seen such perfection.

She touched Penny's shoulder, then shook it gently. "Pen, come downstairs and have breakfast."

Penny groaned, pulled the covers over her ears. "I hate working at the historical society. It's the summer and I'm in a windowless room staring at a computer screen all day. Why can't I just stay here while you're at work? I won't get into any trouble."

"It's not that I think you'll get into trouble, Penny. It's not good for you to sit around with nothing to do. You know that only makes your anxiety worse."

"Honestly, Mom — being there feels like a punishment."

"It's not a punishment. And Penny, helping out at a nonprofit organization is important. Come on. Remember what I said about trying to stay positive. Find one thing each day to make yourself happy."

Penny sat up and pulled the comforter over her knees. "Okay, this would make me happy — Robin wants to see the house. So does Mindy."

The house? Oh. Of course other kids had found out. People talked. She was in the newspaper, for heaven's sake.

"Well, no one is coming to the house yet."

Penny crossed her arms. "Why not? It's our house. *My* house. Why can't I show my friends?"

Emma sighed. "Penny, I don't have time

to think about the house right now."

"You never have time for anything — ever." Her eyes blazed with defiance.

"You're right, Penny," Emma said softly. "I don't. Least of all myself. But you don't see me complaining. Now, come on — enough with the attitude."

"I'm sick of this place!" Penny said. "I don't know why so many people come here. It's so boring. How can you live here your whole life?"

Emma, shocked, pulled back like she'd been physically struck. She said the first thing that came into her mind. "I love it here."

"Well, I don't."

Where was this coming from? "You need some perspective, Penny. I want you to do a good job today. When you act better, you'll feel better. Trust me."

It was good advice; Emma knew it was. And yet Penny rolled her eyes. *She'll come around*, Emma told herself. Maybe she needed to follow her own advice. If she acted like Penny's outlook was bound to improve, if she believed it to be true, things would take a turn for the better.

At least, she hoped they would. Beyond that, she didn't know what more she could do.

CHAPTER EIGHTEEN

Penny stared at the pile of old maps Angus had left for her to log in the computer system. It would take her hours and hours.

She was actually glad there was no window in the office. She didn't want to be reminded that outside it was a perfect summer day. Regardless of what her mother said about the job not being a punishment, it felt like one, and that's what mattered.

But today she was not alone in her exile; she had her new copy of the graphic novel *Anya's Ghost* in her backpack. It had been published a few years ago but she'd asked Alexis at the bookstore to order it for her. She'd read online that Neil Gaiman had called it "a masterpiece," so she'd added it to her must-read list. And from the description, it sounded like it definitely belonged in her preferred genre of misfit lit. Although, lately, Penny had to admit she didn't feel so very much like a misfit.

She dug into her stuffed bag and pulled out her phone. It was ten in the morning. She wondered what Robin was doing, if she was even awake yet. She shot off a quick text and was surprised by the immediate response.

Heading to the beach soon. Wanna come?
What beach?
Coopers.

Coopers Beach was in Southampton, a half-hour drive. It was a really nice beach with a great snack bar.

How are you getting there?
Mateo's brother's driving us.

Did she dare?

There was one major obstacle to accepting this invitation: Angus. Penny would have to sneak past him. She knew that once she was out of the building, she would be in the clear because yesterday, after setting her up at the computer, he hadn't checked on her again, and at one point, flying a little off the white pill, she'd abandoned her post in the office, wandered into the front room, and found Angus asleep in one of the antique rocking chairs.

So as long as she got out without him

noticing, he'd never figure out she was gone. Later, around the time he'd start thinking about going to the back of the museum to get her, she'd text him that she'd just left to meet a friend on Main Street for dinner or something. As for her mother, she'd be at work until eight and would never know the difference.

Great! Pick me up in front of BuddhaBerry.

It was close to lunch when Chris ambled over from the bar and called Emma into the hallway.

All morning, she'd been plagued by an unsettled feeling. She tried to chalk it up to the conversation with Penny, but then Chris said, "A woman at the bar is asking a lot of questions about you."

Her first thought was that Bea Winstead had returned, but Emma would have noticed her. No, this was something else.

"I think she's a reporter," Chris said. "And I have to let Jack know."

She nodded, uncomfortable. Of course he had to. Jack was sensitive about press at the hotel. He took their clientele's privacy very seriously, and he didn't like reporters nosing around or taking photographs without his permission. Jack put a lot of effort into making the place feel casual and open, especially for the celebrity clients who wanted to just hang out and be part of the crowd.

Back at the front desk, Emma eyed the customers at the bar, trying to pick out the interloper. It wasn't difficult; there were only three women, and two were regulars. The stranger appeared to be around her age, and, as if sensing Emma's gaze, she turned and looked right at her.

Then the woman stood and made her way over to the front desk. "Emma Mapson?" she said.

"Yes, how can I help you?"

"I'm Micki Leder from the *Observer,*" she said. "I'm writing an article about the battle over Henry Wyatt's estate."

One spoiled, pushy woman complaining wasn't exactly a battle. Still, every night Emma sifted through the mail, half expecting a legal notice from Bea's attorneys. So far, nothing had happened. She wondered how long she would have to wait for the other shoe to drop.

But she said none of this, knowing better than to get pulled into trying to tell her side of the story.

"I have no comment," she said.

The house phone rang.

"Emma, it's Jack. Come to the office for a minute?"

Emma said nothing further to the reporter; she just slipped out the door behind the front desk.

Chris, a serious look on his face, walked out of Jack's office.

"You were right," Emma said.

"Yeah, I know. Apparently, she's not the only one sniffing around."

"Really?"

Chris nodded his head toward the back room. "Talk to Jack."

Inside, Jack was unpacking a crate of the cigars they displayed and sold in the glass case under the front desk.

"Emma, I need you to please set these in the case on your way out," he said, handing her a box of San Lotano Churchills.

"My way out?"

He nodded, opened a box of Ashton Très Mystiques, and unwrapped one for himself.

"I got reporters at the bar, reporters calling on my cell phone. I can ignore them, but as long as you're standing in the middle of the lobby, they're going to show up."

Her stomach knotted.

"Oh my God. Jack, I'm so sorry. I just don't understand why people care."

"I'm hoping this will be old news soon."

Emma nodded, trying to quell her panic. In over a dozen years of employment, she had never had so much as one sick day. Leaving in the middle of her shift felt like a failure. Losing a workday tomorrow was unthinkable. Paid, unpaid — it didn't matter. This was just not a good road to go down.

"I understand today, but I really think beyond that would be overkill."

Jack tapped a pen against his desk. "Cheryl Meister told me she invited you to her fundraiser committee meeting tomorrow."

Emma had forgotten all about that.

"You should go, help out. It's a good cause."

Emma swallowed hard. Okay, so she guessed that was that. He didn't want her at the hotel. "Okay," she said. "But just so you know, I'm not talking to the press, and there's no story here. It's going to be fine."

He looked at her with his direct, sharp blue eyes. "I hope you're right."

CHAPTER NINETEEN

Bea and Kyle divided up the town and set out separately on their hunt for Henry's drawings. Her first stop: the Sag Harbor Historical Society at 174 Main Street.

Bea followed a gravel path, stopping to admire a large metal bell planted near the front of the house. The plaque below it read HISTORIC BELL: UNION FREE SCHOOL, 1871. She reached out and tapped the antique metal.

Then she made her way up the steps to a dark porch. The house, with its wood shingles and peeling paint and layers of dust, seemed to be a building that time forgot. How intriguing!

"Welcome, come on in," said a booming voice as the front door opened. The ceilings were low, the interior light dim. It took a moment for her eyes to adjust and still more time for her to place the man standing in front of her. He was decidedly familiar. And then she realized: she'd seen him at the house!

"*You,*" she said, walking deeper into the room. She stood by a fireplace and crossed her arms. "What are you people? Some sort of cabal?"

"Nice to see you again too, Ms. Winstead," the man said, seeming somehow amused.

"I wish I could say the same. Who are you, exactly?"

"Angus Sinclair. We weren't properly introduced at the house. At any rate, I'm in charge of day-to-day operations here at the historical society and museum. What brings you here this morning?"

"Wouldn't you like to know," she snapped. "I assume, since you were with *that woman* at *my* house, that you are a party to this attempted theft?"

He smiled, maddeningly, and shook his head. "I don't know anything about a theft, Ms. Winstead. But Emma Mapson was kind enough to take me in a few years ago when I became a widower. So, yes, I have been around to witness the events that have recently transpired. If that makes me a party to the situation, then I'm guilty as charged."

These people had an answer to everything, she thought. She had half a mind to walk right back out the door. But if this man was close with Emma Mapson, he must have known Henry. And if he knew Henry, there was a very good chance there were drawings on the premises.

She walked around, taking in the odd assortment of bric-a-brac. To a casual observer, most of it would look like junk. But she had a trained eye and knew valuable furniture when she saw it.

"Is that a Dominy chair?" she said.

Mr. Sinclair nodded. "That's correct. And over in that corner is an original Tinker chair. Dating back to 1850."

"I'm not familiar with Tinker furniture."

"Really?"

Why did he seem so surprised? "Yes, really. I'm in the art business; I'm not a furniture dealer."

"Nathan Tinker built the original brick building that today houses The American Hotel. This was back in 1824. He was a wholesale furniture dealer and made his own furniture as well. He lived in the top area of the building, and his workshop and storefront were on the ground floor."

Bea hated to take the bait, but she loved history. There were many times over the years when she'd felt insecure about not having a college degree, and she seized every opportunity she had to learn something.

"So when, exactly, did he turn it into a hotel?"

Mr. Sinclair moved the Tinker chair across from his rocking chair, invited her to sit, and settled in himself. One of the many upsides to spending time with people her own age, she thought as she sat down, was that they understood the body had its limits.

"In the 1840s, he operated a boarding-house for men working in the whale trade," Angus said. "The American Hotel as we know it today didn't come until later. There was a fire in town around 1877 that destroyed most of the houses, but the Tinker building was left standing because it was brick. By this time, Nathan Tinker had died, and his son had had enough of the building. It was purchased by a man named Addison Youngs and his father-in-law, Captain William Freeman, for the hefty sum of two thousand dollars. They decided to turn it into an inn: The American Hotel."

She shook her head. "Amazing. For two thousand dollars. *Now* that gets you, what, a weeklong stay there?"

"Well, they took out a loan of another two thousand dollars from Riverhead Savings and Loan. We have the paperwork here in the archives. Then Youngs and Freeman went about the work of installing gas, electricity, and indoor plumbing in the building."

"What do you think the hotel would sell for today?" Sitting there, she had the impulse to buy it. Take that, Jack Blake! She could fire Emma Mapson herself.

Mr. Sinclair shook his head. "We'll never know. Not as long as Jack Blake is alive, anyway. When he bought the place in 1972, it was in total disrepair. Everything you see today — that's Jack's vision. It's his baby."

Bea cared not one whit about Jack and his baby. She had her own baby to worry about. She stood slowly, stretching her back, and wandered the room.

"I'm looking for any Henry Wyatt drawings. I've learned he gifted some of his work around town during the past year, and I'm wondering if your little organization here was the beneficiary of his largesse."

"As a matter of fact, Henry did donate some of his work to us over the years."

"Great. I'd love to see them. Please, lead the way." She tried not to sound impatient but was aware she failed utterly.

"We don't keep them here."

"Why on earth not? If he donated them to this museum, as you call it."

"We run this place on a volunteer basis and don't have the security to keep original Henry Wyatts in the on-site archives."

"So where are they?"

"The library. Just across the street."

"Very well." She headed for the door.

"Ms. Winstead? One more thing. We're a nonprofit, so if you're ever inclined to consider a donation, it would be appreciated."

Bea raised her eyebrows.

"This has been a surprisingly painless conversation, Mr. Sinclair. Let's not push it."

Emma's first impulse after being dismissed from work was to run home and hide. If reporters were sniffing around the hotel, they might show up anywhere. But as soon as she walked into the house, she thought, *Why not make the best of a bad situation?* She had a free afternoon — two free afternoons. She could swing by the historical society and surprise Penny with a trip to the beach.

She packed bathing suits and towels in a bag and picked up sandwiches at the Golden Pear for a picnic lunch. She considered texting Angus that she was coming to get Penny, but she didn't want to risk him spoiling the surprise. She couldn't wait to see the look on her daughter's face!

But Emma's joy was tempered the minute she rounded the corner of the Annie Cooper Boyd House and spotted Bea Winstead heading out.

The old woman noticed her at the same moment.

Emma squared her shoulders. She wasn't entirely sorry to be running into Bea.

"Just so you know, you're not going to intimidate me by planting articles in the newspaper," Emma said.

"Oh, my dear, it's not about intimidation. But the court of public opinion *does* matter."

"What gossips in New York City think means nothing. The house is in this town, and in *this* town, no one will take your side. No one believes you."

"My dear, the small minds of this backwater town do not concern me."

"If you think that way about this place, then why do you even care about the house? You're rich — everyone knows who you are. Everyone knows what you have. Why are you bothering with this fight?"

"It's not about money. It's about right and wrong. At least it is for me. Clearly, that is not the case for you." Bea smiled pleasantly and crossed the street.

Emma shook her head. She could not, would not let Bea Winstead spoil her day.

Inside the museum she found Angus and a young couple standing at the portrait of Dr. Miles. Angus was mid-lecture, and Emma didn't want to interrupt him, so she slipped quietly into the back of the building.

"Penny?" she called, stepping over a box of books to reach the office. She knocked once on the closed door, not wanting to startle her. When she didn't get a response, she opened it. The light was on and the computer was on but Penny was gone. Emma looked around for her backpack but didn't see it.

Maybe she should have given her a heads-up after all. She'd probably gone out to lunch on her own.

Emma would just have to wait for her to return.

Chapter Twenty

"Penny, come on! We're starving," Mindy called from her beach towel. She wore a black bikini with a gold ring suspended between her breasts. She'd brought a bathing suit for Penny to borrow. "Last season's," she'd declared, tossing it at Penny when she climbed into the back of Nick's Jeep. Penny was just relieved it was a one-piece.

"Um, just a sec," Penny said now.

She stood at the edge of the ocean, the warm salt water lapping at her feet. The beach was crowded but the roar of the ocean swallowed up the sound of other people. A breeze blew over her, and she inhaled deeply. She waited to feel happy, but she was overwhelmed by unease. Was it because she'd sneaked off? She told herself it would be fine, that her mother would never know. *Stop worrying,* she told herself. *Boss it back.*

The water looked so perfect, but she couldn't wade in. Not yet. The tide washed over her toes, and she counted. *Two . . . three . . . four.* The water receded before she reached ten. She waited for the next wave: *Five . . . six.* Almost there! But then, a miss; the water trickled just to the tip of her big toe. *One . . . two . . .*

The ride to Southampton had given Penny an exhilarating taste of pure freedom. Nick Alcaldo drove fast, played the music loud, and tossed a pack of cigarettes to his brother with what seemed to Penny a shocking casualness. Mateo, sitting in front of her, turned to offer her one.

"I'm good," she said.

"Oh my God, you're a total pill-head but you won't have a cigarette? Spare me," Mindy said, lighting up.

A pill-head? She'd taken them a few times. It wasn't like she was addicted or anything. And she wasn't going to do it again. At least, not for a while. Especially not if Mindy was going to throw it in her face like that. But then Mateo told her she was too pretty to smoke, and that eased the sting of Mindy's bitchiness.

That was the first and last thing Mateo said to her all day, but the comment stayed with her, as bright and hot as the sun.

Pretty.

The water receded, then rolled toward her again. She was at nine. Almost there! She could feel Mindy's and Robin's impatience, their negative energy as tangible as the wet sand under her feet. They were going to abandon her and go eat without her — she just knew it. But there was nothing she could do about it. The water missed her toes.

One . . . two . . . three . . .

So Mateo thought she was pretty. That was just because on the outside, wearing a borrowed bathing suit, hanging out with her former best friend, she looked like one of them. But she didn't really fit in. If she forgot that for even one minute, her OCD was always there to remind her.

Four . . . five . . . six . . .

It was late in the afternoon, and the heat had settled around the back lawn like a blanket. Emma set down her bucket of water and knelt in front of her deep yellow Celebrity hybrid teas. They were her favorites. Sometimes, a lovely red blush would shade the yellow color. The flower had lush petals and the loveliest fruity aroma.

None of that was any comfort at the moment.

For the past few hours, she'd alternated between panic and fury. Jim DiMartino at the police station had assured her this was not the first time a teenager had gone "missing" on a beautiful day in the summer. "If she's not back by dark, call me on my cell." Dark? That would be after eight at night. She couldn't wait that long.

Emma drove around to all the local beaches. The prime ones in East Hampton and Southampton were so crowded, it was a needle-in-a-haystack scenario. Penny's hair usually stood out in a crowd, but today, Emma had no luck finding her. She checked the snack bars, then headed down to the water, knowing it was likely the minute she left the snack bar, Penny would walk in. Murphy's Law.

Emma clipped a flower, dropped it in the bucket, and burst into tears. Then she heard a car door slam out front. She jumped up and rushed around the side of the house just in time to see a Jeep pulling out of the driveway and taking off down the street. Penny stood there blinking at her in surprise.

"Where on earth have you been?" Emma yelled. "Do you have any idea how worried I was?"

Penny walked past her without a word and

went into the house. Unbelievable!

Emma grabbed her arm before she could run up the stairs to her room. "Sit on the couch, young lady."

By this time, Angus had appeared, and Emma was thankful for the backup. She was shaking with anger. She shared a quick glance with Angus and they sat opposite Penny in armchairs.

No one said anything for a minute, and then Penny cracked under the silence. "Don't freak out, okay? I was at the beach."

"You just ran off? Without telling Angus? Without a text or call to me? What were you thinking?"

"What are you even doing here?"

"For your information, I left work early. I came to get you from the historical society to take you to the beach!" The more she thought about it, the more furious she became. This motherhood gig was so unbelievably thankless. And she hadn't expected thanks. But she also hadn't expected this.

Penny seemed unmoved by this declaration. "I need some water." She jumped up and headed into the kitchen.

Emma looked helplessly at Angus. He waved toward the kitchen: *Go.*

Penny was searching through the refrigerator, and Emma was forced to talk to her back.

"You owe me an apology, Penny. And you're going to be punished."

Penny slammed the refrigerator door and turned around with tears in her eyes. "I hate you, I hate this town, I hate my life!"

She ran upstairs. Emma pressed her hand to her head and jumped at the loud slamming of Penny's bedroom door. And then, despite her best efforts, she began to cry.

"It's just the age," Angus said, appearing in the doorway.

"I wish I could believe that," Emma said. "I'm so sorry, Angus. This is more than you signed up for when you moved in here."

"It's no trouble," he said.

She barely heard him. "I'm not going to send her to work with you tomorrow. This is beyond what you should have to be responsible for."

"Emma, stop worrying about me. Go talk to her."

Emma, shaking, hugged herself. "I can't talk to her. I'm too upset. We're just going to end up shouting at each other."

"You should at least go up and have the final word. Make sure she knows this is unacceptable."

Emma looked at him. "You're right. I have

217

to ground her." Maybe the day off tomorrow was a blessing in disguise. "I have to go to this committee meeting around eleven. Is there any way you can be here until I get back?"

"Not a problem. It's slow at the museum midweek. And I'm behind on my crossword puzzles. I haven't finished one since Memorial Day."

Emma smiled at him gratefully. "If Celia were here, she'd straighten everything out."

"Yes, she would. She'd have that child turned around in no time."

"Oh, Angus. Is this my fault? Am I dropping the ball?"

"Looking back at myself at fourteen?" He whistled. "This child is like an angel."

"I don't believe it."

He smiled and pulled a pizza from the freezer. "I guess you'll have to take my word for it. Now go up there and put the fear of God in that girl."

"Angus, the only person full of fear right now is me. And I don't see that changing anytime soon."

Bea walked to the edge of Windsong's private dock, surrounded by the clicking and humming of nocturnal insects in the nearby grass.

Whenever she spent time away from Manhattan, she was amazed by all the stars that were visible. Places that were just moderately impressive in the daytime could turn quite majestic at night. She grudgingly felt this about the harbor as she stood at the edge of the bay under the dazzling constellations above.

But the natural beauty of the town was still not enough to give her one ounce of understanding of what Henry had done. In all the years since he'd left Manhattan, she'd never given up hope that he would tire of country living and return. But her disapproval over his move and his decision to stop painting paled in comparison to the distress she felt over what he'd done with his estate.

The day of searching through town had yielded nothing useful. She was so disheartened, she retreated back to the house for a nap before she even checked the library. As for Kyle, he seemed to do little more with his afternoon than work on his tan. He showed up at dinnertime with nonsensical chatter about boats.

"Do you expect to find Henry's drawings at the marina?" she had asked him.

Perhaps she should have just let him leave when he'd decided to quit. He was now a lame-duck assistant.

Her phone rang, and she recognized the incoming number: her lawyer's office. "You're burning the midnight oil, Richard. I hope you're calling with some good news."

"Bea, did you plant that story in Page Six?" he said.

"I did not plant anything. I answered a reporter's questions honestly."

"I wish you'd left the firm's name out of it. Our phone hasn't stopped ringing. And Bea, frankly, it appears Wyatt's will is legitimate. There is no evidence he wasn't of sound mind. And even if he wasn't, you don't have the legal standing to contest the will."

"Of course I have a right to contest it!"

"It's not a matter of right, it's a matter of legality. You're not family, you were never married to Wyatt, and there's no indication that you were the beneficiary of his estate in any prior will."

Bea felt herself begin to shake. "After decades on retainer, this is what you bring me? You're not even worthy of Page Six!" She hung up the phone, resisting the impulse to toss it into the bay.

Her attorney was willing to give up because of technicalities? She supposed when you billed by the hour, your thinking became rather small. Luckily for her, she'd never been constrained by ordinary work or ordinary thinking.

It was tempting to wonder if Henry had suffered from some form of dementia over the past year or so. But Bea hated when an older person did something out of character or upsetting and everyone just chalked it up to that person losing his mind. It was lazy and condescending thinking. No, Bea would not stoop to that assumption. It might give her a basis for pushing forward with legal action, but deep down, she didn't believe it. And more than wanting the house, she wanted the truth about her oldest friend — the person who had given her the most important thing in her life: her career. In her heart, she knew there was a reason for what Henry had done with his work at the end of his life. And there was maybe even a reason for this business with the house. Now, that didn't mean it was right. That didn't mean she wouldn't fight it tooth and nail in court. But she needed to understand it.

Somewhere along the way, she had missed something. And she would find out what it was.

CHAPTER TWENTY-ONE

Penny woke up to the loud click of her bedroom door opening.

"You are not to leave this house today," her mother said from across the room. "Do you hear me?"

"Yes," Penny mumbled.

The sun peeked through her curtains, and it hurt to look at it. Her eyelids felt stuck together from all the crying. She'd sobbed herself to sleep last night, replaying over and over in her mind the hour she'd spent trapped by her OCD at the ocean's edge. By the time she was able to relax and return to the towels with Mindy and Robin and the boys, no one was talking to her. "You have to stop acting like such a weirdo," Robin had whispered to her. "Why do you do things like that?"

"I'm going to a quick meeting and then I'll be home," her mother said, adding, "I'm really disappointed in you, Penny."

Penny felt tears return to her already swollen eyes. She pulled the covers over her head. Did she feel bad that she'd upset her mom? Yes. But her mother didn't understand how desperate she felt. She needed to escape.

What had she done with all of her time last summer? She'd hung out with Mr. Wyatt a lot. When she was drawing, her mind was blank. Sometimes, she had felt nervous showing him a sketch after she finished, but it was worth it for the times when he praised her. Earning his approval was the best feeling in the world. But Henry was gone and every time she picked up a pencil, she thought, *What's the point?* Yes, she'd been drawing before she met him. But once they started working together, it became so much bigger. So much better. And now she'd never finish her graphic novel.

Last summer, Henry had had the idea for each of them to write one. The day she'd brought copies of *Coraline* and *The Graveyard Book* to show him, he'd suggested they walk to the library to find more.

"They have a bunch but I've read them all," Penny had told him.

"Well, I have not, so humor me," he'd said.

Henry and Penny sat at a table near the

circulation desk and he pulled out his sketch pad. He stared at it for a moment, then began drawing. Penny looked over his shoulder as the image took shape. It was the bar at the hotel.

"I'm going to create my own illustrated story, Penny."

"You mean graphic novel?"

"You know I don't think that term makes sense. And Penny, you should start one of your own. We can work on this endeavor together."

"Me? I don't know how," she said.

"No one ever knows how to do anything. Until they do it."

She had believed him. Around Mr. Wyatt, anything seemed possible. Now her world was small again.

When she was sure her mother was long gone from the house, Penny dragged herself out of bed to the kitchen, hoping she still had Cap'n Crunch. She'd bought it herself at Schiavoni's, sneaked it into the house, and tucked it away in the cabinet with the spices and other cooking staples her mother never used. Penny was trying to make the sugary cereal last because she didn't know when she'd get to buy it again. She couldn't wait to be old enough to have a real job so she could get some freedom — freedom in what she ate, freedom to come and go as she wanted. Fourteen sucked. Fourteen was too young to get away with doing nothing but not old enough to do something worthwhile.

"Good morning," Angus said, looking up from his crossword puzzle.

Penny shook the last cupful of cereal into a bowl and drowned it in milk.

"Penny, you know your mother doesn't want you eating that junk. I'll make you some eggs."

The doorbell rang. Saved by the bell! "I'll get it," Penny said. She carried the bowl with her to the door, shoveling spoonfuls into her mouth along the way. "Who is it?" she asked dutifully, though looking out the peephole gave her the answer.

She couldn't believe what she saw.

She put the cereal on the floor, unlocked the door, and swung it open.

"Dad?" she said.

"Hey, kiddo," her father said.

How could this be? Her father was there, standing right in front of her. She couldn't even remember the last time she'd spoken to him on the phone. But the weird thing was, no matter how long she went without seeing him, she always felt an instant connection when she did. Part of it was that she looked so much more like him than like her mother. She had his height, his dark eyes, and his curly brown hair — although his was now threaded with silver at the temples. The one difference was that he had the olive complexion of the Italian side of his family, and it was even darker at the moment with his deep tan.

She flung herself into his arms.

He laughed, and she stayed like that for a long minute, the midmorning sun beating down on the back of her neck.

"What are you doing here?" she said.

He walked inside, looked around. Then he smiled at her. "You've gotten so grown up. Is your mom here?"

Penny shook her head. "This is so crazy! What are you doing here?" she repeated.

"I had some business in East Hampton."

"An acting job?"

"Ah, no. I'm producing a play. Well, trying to produce. Working on the fund-raising part just now. Anyway, I was going to head back to LA tonight but then I thought, *Why not take a detour and see Penny?* It's been too long, kiddo. What do you say you and I go to the beach and catch up?"

"Ahem." Angus stood in the archway between the dining room and the small foyer. His arms were crossed, his face stern.

226

"No one is going anywhere until her mother gets home."

Cheryl Meister's "cottage" was a cedar-shingled Southampton mansion with tennis courts, two swimming pools, and sweeping views of the Atlantic.

A member of the household staff showed Emma through the cavernous house to the kitchen. It was all white marble with a massive skylight and wide French doors that opened up to one of the pools. Beyond the pool, a low hedgerow and the ocean beach. If it weren't for her recent experience with the Henry Wyatt house, Emma would have been intimidated.

Cheryl sat curled on a stool at the island in the center of the room. She was barefoot, and she sipped from a small bottle of Pellegrino and chatted with a group of half a dozen women gathered around her.

"Emma, come in! Don't be shy." Cheryl made the introductions and Emma tried to remember everyone's name but all the women looked the same. They were uniformly attractive, with light tans and tight bodies in Lululemon pants and tops, as if they were all on their way to the same yoga class. The only real variation in their style was that some wore gold jewelry while others had trendy Buddhist trinkets around their necks and wrists.

The women all knew one another. Most lived in Manhattan full-time, reserving their Hampton homes for summers and weekends. They spoke of restaurants Emma had never been to; they commiserated over the politics of their kids' private schools; they expressed their irritation at the increasing number of social events all the way out in Brooklyn.

Emma checked her phone and realized it was dead. How quickly could she make her exit and get back to the house? This situation with Penny was deeply upsetting, and she realized the day off from work was a godsend. She had to find a way to get more quality time with her daughter.

"Diane is here!" Cheryl announced as a tall, slightly horse-faced brunette swept into the kitchen. She looked to be about half a decade older than the rest of the group. Her dark hair was cut in a sharp chin-length bob, and she wore a putty-colored linen suit and a large statement necklace.

The chatter slowed just enough for polite greetings.

Cheryl took Emma's hand as if they were girlhood friends. "Emma, this is Diane Knight. She's the director of the Sag Harbor

Cinema fund-raiser."

"Nice to meet you," Emma said. The woman smiled vacantly until Cheryl prompted her with "Emma is the new owner of the Henry Wyatt house."

Diane Knight's eyes sharpened with sudden interest.

"How fortunate we are that you've joined us," she said. "We would love to have a Henry Wyatt piece for the auction."

Emma, put on the spot, stammered out some reason why that wasn't possible at the moment. Before Diane could press further, the caterers called everyone to the back patio for lunch.

They filed outdoors to a long table overlooking the teardrop-shaped swimming pool. The water was the most vivid aquamarine Emma had ever seen. And she heard Alexis's voice from the night at Murf's: *You'll get a taste of how the other half lives.*

The table was set with name cards. Emma took her seat, and servers poured glasses of iced tea, white wine, and hard lemonade.

"Iced tea, please," Emma said when she was asked. A salad was slipped in front of her, arugula and frisée with walnuts and cranberries.

"Bread?" a server asked, holding a tray of thick, crusty sliced sourdough.

"Yes, thanks," Emma said, noting she was the only taker.

Cheryl stood at the head of the table next to where Diane was seated and tapped her glass with a spoon to get people's attention.

"Thank you, everyone, for taking time out of your busy schedules to be here. I know everyone has a million things to do, so let's get started. First, I want to remind you that any auction items accepted after next week won't make it into the printed catalog. The online version is already live — thank you, Kellianne and Susan, that was a lot of work."

Everyone clapped politely.

"I've locked down the auctioneer. He's fabulous. I've attended a few of his events in the city and he really knows how to excite the audience and drive up the bidding. So the real items of business today are setting the ticket price for the auction and finding a venue. On that note, I'm going to turn the floor over to Diane."

More clapping. Diane stood from her seat.

"So, as you know, the majority of the fund-raiser events will take place under the tent on Long Wharf. I had hoped to find a way to include the art auction at this location, but for insurance purposes, we cannot have it on the water."

The guests all murmured their disappointment.

"I'm sorry to be the bearer of bad news, but I'm sure this group can come up with an exciting alternative. And in the meantime, to incorporate our beautiful bay into the evening, I'd like to suggest chartering a yacht to transport guests to our venue, if that's feasible. Ideally, we will find a property right on the water."

Was Emma imagining things or had Diane directed that last comment at her? Maybe she was supposed to jump in and offer to do something constructive.

"I can talk to someone at the marina about getting a boat for the event," Emma said.

"Excellent," Diane said. "But again, before we can commit to that, we really need to nail down the venue."

The table erupted in conversation. Various restaurants and museums were floated as possibilities. Diane and Cheryl dismissed them one by one: Unavailable. Too small. Boring.

And then: "I have the perfect place!" Cheryl said, clapping her hands. "Where better to hold an art auction than at the home of Sag Harbor's most famous artist?"

This time, Emma knew she wasn't imagining it; the comment was directed at her. Everyone turned toward her. She was sure there was a deer-in-the-headlights expression on her face. "Oh, I don't know . . ."

"Brilliant idea!" said Diane. And from the way she and Cheryl looked at each other, Emma could see that this had been discussed — and no doubt decided on — before she had even walked in the door. "Emma, I know it's a lot of work," Diane continued, "but Cheryl and I are here to do the heavy lifting. It would be a huge draw and bring in that much more for this cause."

Emma's gut response, given her cautious, protective nature, was to say no. But then she thought about Penny wanting to spend more time at the house, and she thought about Bea Winstead laying claim to it. It was time for Emma to stop being so hesitant, so apologetic, about the good fortune that had come their way. She had to just step up and own it. Maybe Penny would want to help out with the auction — it could be something for the two of them to bond over.

"Okay," Emma said. "I'm in."

CHAPTER TWENTY-TWO

As soon as Bea saw the town library, a stately Classical Revival building just steps from Main Street, she felt heartened. If the John Jermain Memorial Library did, in fact, house some of Henry's drawings — as Angus had suggested yesterday — at least they had a distinguished home.

At the circulation desk, Bea found a young woman with cascading strawberry-blond hair and thick bangs.

"Excuse me," Bea said. "It's my understanding that this library is holding some original Henry Wyatt drawings."

"Drawings?" the young woman repeated.

"Yes," said Bea. "Are you the librarian?"

"I'm the assistant librarian." She tapped something into her computer. "I'm not sure about the drawings. Let's check the archives room. It's upstairs."

Bea followed her up a winding marble staircase to a third-floor rotunda, an impressive space with a sixty-foot-high domed ceiling of herringbone brick and stained glass. The room had wall-to-wall red carpeting, arched pediments, Tiffany lamps, and carved wood furniture. It was tranquil and elegant, and Bea decided that some things in that town weren't half bad.

The librarian led her across the expanse of red carpet, past the tables and desks, and through an opening framed by pillars. A stained-glass window dominated the room, which had little furniture, just some wooden shelves filled with books and several oversize editions stacked in piles. In the far corner stood a floor-to-ceiling metal filing cabinet. The librarian unlocked it and, after a few minutes of searching, pulled out papers protected by plastic sleeves.

"These are filed under Henry Wyatt," the woman said, passing them to her. "Is this what you're looking for?"

Bea's hands shook as she took them.

"You can only view them up here in the reading room. They cannot be checked out," the librarian said.

Bea bristled at being told what she could or could not do with Henry's work. But he had indeed left them in the stewardship of this town, so what choice did she have?

She waited until the woman retreated

234

down the stairs before carefully reaching inside the plastic. Holding the new drawings was different than simply spotting them on the wall. It felt intimate, like a final communication between them.

The first drawing was a self-portrait of Henry playing the guitar. He appeared to be roughly in his thirties in the sketch, and the sight of the young Henry at the height of his career gave her a pang. With her forefinger, she traced the arc of his cheekbone, the stretch of his refined neck. Somehow, his drawings were more immediate and intimate than photographs. The mark of a great artist was the ability to make something more visceral and real than reality.

How, oh, how could he be gone?

After a long while, she flipped to the next sheet of paper to find her own face etched in lines of black and gray. She was young in the drawing, and Henry had been kind. It was the best version of her, almost pretty. And yet her expression was tense, her posture defensive. A memory began to take shape.

If there was any doubt in Bea's mind about the context of the first two drawings, the next sketch erased it. It was an old barn. These pictures all stemmed from the same night, one of the more uncomfortable moments in their long friendship. She'd all but forgotten about it, and she'd thought Henry had as well — until he named his house Windsong. Even then, she'd told herself it was a coincidence, that there was no subtext. Now she wasn't so sure.

What are you doing, Henry?

He was speaking to her from the grave. Of that she was certain. But what was he trying to say?

Think, think. She closed her eyes, trying to put herself back into that long-ago night.

By the mid-1970s, Bea was so busy with her roster of artists and the Spring Street gallery that she rarely had time to scout for new talent. Henry, increasingly bored with painting and tired of the competitive scene in New York, was frequently away. He sought out the company of artists who worked in other media and who lived in other places. "There's a purity to their work that is impossible to maintain here," he'd told her. "This city is all about money."

And what was wrong with money?

With space between herself and Henry, she filled her time with her other clients. There was no shortage of people begging for her eye, her opinion, her validation. She was also in demand socially, and she had recently started dating a banker named

236

Shelby York.

Bea liked dating men outside of the art scene. They found her exotic and thought her world was glamorous, and this fed her ego. In return, she brought some excitement into their conventional lives. (Nothing like the appearance of Andy Warhol to spice up a dinner party.)

When Henry suggested a road trip to visit an unknown sculptor's Pennsylvania farmhouse, she didn't, as she so often had in the past, jump at the chance to travel with him. She was too busy and she didn't want to deal with his moods.

"This guy is talented," Henry insisted. "You'll kick yourself if someone else snatches him up. Trust me."

She could tell from his urgency that Henry had already promised the artist a visit.

"You owe me one," she said.

It was a four-hour drive, and by the time they reached the Pennsylvania Turnpike, Bea had all but forgotten the appointments she'd had to cancel and the theater tickets Shelby had bought. Henry seemed lighthearted, more like his old self, and they fell into an easy rhythm of gossiping about everyone in their circle, about whose star was on the rise and whose had fallen, about who was sleeping with whom. They both wondered why the entire scene felt suddenly bloodless.

"Everyone's playing it safe," Henry said.

"You're just cynical."

"I'm serious, Bea. That whole world has lost its luster for me."

She didn't take this seriously. He was having a midlife crisis. If he'd been married, he would've been looking to have an affair. "You're an artist, Henry. You can criticize the Manhattan art scene all you want, but it's where we both belong. And it's rewarded us greatly. What's this really about? Are you frustrated creatively?"

"Not at all. I feel incredibly inspired, in fact. Just in a different way." He told her he'd been learning to play the guitar. "I brought it with me," he said. "I think you'll be impressed with my repertoire."

"I'd be impressed with a little more painting from you," she replied.

It was dusk when they reached the farmhouse of Jed Rellner. Jed, tall and ruddy with prematurely white hair, was clearly nervous in her presence. It was agreed that she would look at his work in the morning, in natural light. Jed's wife served dinner outdoors. It was warm for October, and the foursome ate and drank bottle after bottle of red wine under the stars at a picnic table.

When Jed finally showed them to a single guest room, a loft above the barn, he said, "I know the room is probably more rustic than you're used to . . ."

"Don't be silly. It's absolutely charming," Bea said. And she meant it.

The room had two twin beds dressed with patchwork quilts, a bureau in unfinished wood, and that was about it. The bathroom was outside.

"A far cry from your accommodations when you're traveling with Mr. Finance, I would imagine," Henry said. "What do you see in him?"

She sat on one of the small beds and gave him a look. "Shelby's a very nice person, which you would know if you spent any time with him. Besides, it's nothing serious."

"You're never serious about anyone," he said. "Ever think that might be a problem?"

"You're never serious about anyone either."

"I'm open to it. I'm looking for something outside of work. I know there's more to life."

"Let's not start with this again," she said.

He opened his guitar case, took out the guitar, then sat beside her. "Case in point — my new hobby."

He began strumming but she didn't recog-

239

nize the song.

"It's the new John Denver," he told her. " 'Windsong.' " Henry loved John Denver, even though all their friends were into the Beatles and the Rolling Stones. He'd made her listen to the album *Poems, Prayers, and Promises* about a hundred times. "I don't know all the words yet. Just the music."

She listened and watched his hands manipulate the guitar strings, amazed at his obvious ease with the instrument she'd had no idea he could play.

"Henry, you're quite good! I admit it — I'm impressed."

"It's saving my sanity to have an outlet outside of art."

"What happened to *art* saving your sanity?"

"It became business. It became work. Seriously, Bea, I worry about you. You need to broaden your horizons."

"I'm very happy with my narrow horizons, thank you."

He switched to a different melody. Another John Denver song, this time one she recognized.

" 'Let me give my life to you,' " Henry sang. " 'Let me die in your arms . . .' "

He trailed off, strumming without singing

240

for a few seconds before putting down the guitar.

"Why'd you stop?"

And there, sitting in that barn loft, he did something he hadn't done since the night of that first party a decade earlier — he leaned forward and kissed her.

Bea pulled away with a swift, emphatic movement. "Henry, I'm sorry. We can't."

The rejection should not have been a surprise to him. And yet he looked stricken.

"Henry," she said in the darkness. "I'm glad this happened. Let's get this out in the open so it loses its power. We need to move forward and be best friends and business partners. Our creative relationship is something few people ever experience. We can't risk messing that up."

He shook his head. "You see things all wrong, Bea. You think this is going to get in the way of the important thing, work. I think you're letting work get in the way of the important thing."

She allowed him to embrace her, and she held him tight, telling herself he was wrong.

All these years later, she still believed she'd done the only rational thing given the situation. But Henry was just as stubborn as she was, and now, considering all that had happened, she had to wonder if he'd denied her the house and his art as some kind of punishment, a final rebuke. No; she refused to believe it. It was too cruel. If that had been his reasoning, it meant he'd never truly cared for her in the first place. She could not accept that.

She would keep digging.

Emma didn't recognize the Jeep parked in front of her house. In fact, she almost didn't recognize her house. It looked so . . . run-down after her lunch at Cheryl Meister's. And her time at Windsong probably didn't help either.

She couldn't let this stuff mess with her head.

She pulled her car into the driveway, second-guessing the promise she'd just made to the auction committee. Somehow, in addition to allowing them to use Windsong for the auction venue, she'd been talked into hosting the next meeting there. The way she saw it, this project was going to be either a lot of fun or a complete disaster. There was no middle ground.

Once she was inside the house, she heard voices in the living room. She followed them.

"Hello?" she called out, then she stopped short, blinking to make sure she was really seeing what she thought she was seeing. It couldn't be.

"Mark? What are you doing here?"

Her ex-husband jumped up from the couch while her daughter beamed at her from across the room.

"Mom! Look who's here!"

Yeah, I see.

How long had it been? At least two years since he'd visited. And, aside from his sporadic and paltry child-support payments, she hadn't had any contact with him in nearly as long. As far as she knew, neither had their daughter. Why on earth was he in her house?

She felt a hand on her shoulder.

"I've been calling you," Angus said quietly.

"My phone died." She turned back to Mark. "Can we talk outside?" she said.

Mark followed her out to the garden. The sun was getting high overhead so she moved to the shade of her poplar tree, swatting aside a yellow jacket.

"I see you're keeping up with the flowers," he said.

She was in no mood for small talk. "What are you *doing* here?"

He crossed his arms and smiled at her. "You look great, Emma. Really terrific."

She hated to admit how good the compliment from him made her feel. Why did she even care what he thought? Thirteen years, and she still wasn't over the sting of his abandonment. "Mark, I asked you a question."

He sighed as if she were being a drag for not acting like they were old pals. "I had some business in East Hampton and I couldn't leave without trying to see Penny."

"So you just suddenly had the urge to see your daughter?"

"It wasn't sudden. This was just the first practical opportunity."

Emma raked her hand through her hair. "Why didn't you call me? You can't just show up like this after all this time, Mark. It's not right. It's going to confuse Penny." It was confusing *her.*

"She's a great kid. You're doing a good job, Em."

The flattery hit her right where she was most vulnerable, and it was as strong as a rush of dopamine. "Thank you. Look, I'm glad you want to see her. I'm sure she wants to see you too. But there's a right way to go about things, Mark."

"I know, I know. Sorry, I just got carried away. You know I'm not much of a planner."

Yes, she did. He wasn't much on follow-through either. "So how long are you here for?"

He glanced up at the sky and exhaled. "I'm going to play it by ear. There's always a chance things will heat up on this project I'm working on and I'll have to see people in East Hampton again. So I'm going to stay local for a week or two."

A week or two? He hadn't spent more than a night in town since the summer he'd left for good. Somewhere deep down, an alarm bell sounded. But it was silenced — or at least muffled — when he pulled a check out of the pocket of his cargo shorts and handed it to her.

"Sorry I've been behind. So what do you say I take our kid to the beach for the day?"

Our kid. Powerful, powerful words.

Emma opened her mouth to tell him that Penny had run off yesterday and was grounded, but then she decided that was more information than he needed to have.

"Let's give this a day to settle," she said instead. "Why don't you let Penny go about her normal schedule today and you can pick her up tomorrow morning?"

He seemed about to protest, but then he stopped himself, smiled, and said, "You're the boss."

Yes, she was. So why did she suddenly not feel like it?

"Ma'am, we're closing in twenty minutes. I'm going to need to return those documents to the archives room."

Bea looked up in annoyance. *Documents* — as if she were perusing old housing records. "They're not documents," she muttered. Oh, Henry's work did not belong stuffed away in the library. For the hundredth time, she wondered what he had been thinking.

She waited for the librarian to leave, then quickly snapped photos of the drawings. Knowing she had a copy of them in her phone made her feel a little bit better, but only for a moment. Returning them to the circulation desk felt like handing over her child. This was all so wrong!

Heart heavy, she walked outside. Day was turning to evening. She stood between two massive stone Doric columns and called Kyle. Mercifully, he actually answered. She heard the distinctive rumbling of a boat motor.

"Don't tell me you're at the marina again," she said.

"Just spending some time with the locals," he said. "You never know what that will turn up. In fact, I did overhear an interesting conversation that I want to loop you in on."

"We can discuss it over dinner."

She told him to meet her down the street at Wölffer Kitchen. The restaurant was three doors away from the hotel, nestled between a sushi place and a Sotheby's real estate office. She'd read about it in the *Times*. The paper had given a glowing review of the restaurant's baby lamb chops, though she understood the menu was seasonal.

"They don't take reservations," she told Kyle. While that was a policy she found vexing, she had a grudging respect for it. Fortunately, it was early enough that they were seated immediately.

The Wölffer Kitchen dining room had a burnished, elegant feeling. The design touches were fanciful — lots of mirrored surfaces and whimsical hanging light sconces. From her seat on the banquette, Bea had a full view of the bar across the room, the liquor bottles shelved in a wall of textured glass.

"This restaurant is owned by the Wölffer Estate Vineyard family," she told Kyle. "You should have wine tonight instead of that dreadful whiskey."

"I like my dreadful whiskey. Thanks, though."

She ordered a bottle of rosé with the ambitious name of Summer in a Bottle.

"For fifty dollars, it had better be a damned good summer," she said, turning to the menu. "Do you know what you're having?" she asked Kyle. His face was sun-kissed, his brown hair tinged with gold. Two young women seated nearby glanced at him appreciatively. *They probably think I'm his mother,* Bea thought. *If they even notice my existence.* The invisibility of old age never failed to irk her. At least in New York City, people occasionally recognized her as *somebody.*

She ordered a watermelon salad with arugula, feta, and pickled onions and a grilled shrimp dinner with farro, artichoke, and baby chard.

"I'll have the local oysters," said Kyle, handing his menu to their server.

"So, don't keep me in suspense," Bea said. "What is this conversation I need to know about?"

"I was hanging out with Sean and he got a call for a pickup so I rode with him. He had to deliver fuel to a boat that rents a mooring from him —"

"You're not going to find Henry's drawings on a water taxi! Honestly, Kyle. If you can't make yourself useful, you might as well go back to Manhattan."

"I am trying to help you, Bea. If you would let me talk for one minute. So we get to this yacht and the woman who owns it was going on and on about a fund-raiser to rebuild the movie theater that burned down. You've seen that temporary wall around it, right?"

She nodded with impatience.

"Part of the fund-raiser is an art auction. I think you should donate something to the auction. Something big."

"And why should I do that? To impress your new friends?"

He sighed. "Bea, you're fighting to take a local house away from a local woman. I think it's a bad idea, but obviously your mind is made up. So the point is, you can't just take from this place without giving something in return. Everyone here is going to be against you."

Bea nodded slowly, thinking about her encounter earlier that day with Emma Mapson. *What gossips in New York City think means nothing. The house is in this town, and in this town, no one will take your side. No one believes you.*

Bea looked at Kyle with, she had to admit, a new appreciation. "You are absolutely right," she said. "In fact, I want to do more

249

than donate some work. I'm going to get on that committee to rebuild that theater. By the end of this summer, Sag Harbor will never want me to leave."

CHAPTER TWENTY-THREE

Early morning at Long Wharf was Emma's favorite time to be by the water. The sun was bright but gentle; the boats were empty and rocked gently on their moorings. The shops and restaurants weren't yet open, and the primary sounds were the seagulls calling to one another, undisturbed by people.

Cole Hopkins waved to her from the deck of his boat. Everyone in town knew Cole Hopkins and his signature turquoise-blue sixty-three-foot catamaran the *Louise.* Emma had met Cole and his wife, Louise, their first summer in Sag Harbor, the same year Emma started working at the hotel. Cole had spent thirty-six years as a commercial fisherman on crab boats in the Bering Sea before starting his luxury charter business. He was booked months in advance and did more than a hundred and twenty charters a summer. But Emma was still hoping there was a way he could help her out the night of the Sag Harbor Cinema fund-raiser.

"Thanks for meeting with me," she said. "I've got only a few minutes before I have to get to work." She had hoped they could just discuss it on the phone but he'd told her, "I'm not much of a phone guy."

They sat on white beanbag chairs on the stern of the boat. Louise, who worked with her husband on board as hostess and first mate, offered Emma a bottle of sparkling water.

"So, Emma, what can I do for you?" Cole said.

"You know about the cinema fund-raiser and that most of the events that night are here on Long Wharf?"

He nodded. "Great idea. It's going to be a big night."

"It is. I'm actually hosting an art auction off-site. At a house on Actors Colony Road." She still couldn't bring herself to say "my house," and anyway, she was trying to be discreet. "One of my committee members had the idea to provide transportation to the house by boat. I was talking to Sean about it and he said you have another boat, a dinner yacht, that you also charter."

Cole leaned forward. "I'd love to help you out but I have a sunset cruise booked for that night. I could put some feelers out, see who else might be around."

Emma was disappointed. She wanted to work with someone she knew was a pro, someone who had strong ties to the town.

"Let me ask you," he said. "The house on Actors Colony Road that you mentioned — is it the one that famous artist left to your daughter?"

So much for discretion.

"Um, yes," she said.

"We read about it," Louise said, joining them. "How incredible. It's like something out of a movie."

"Must be an interesting story there," Cole said, raising an eyebrow.

"I don't know about that." Emma shifted uncomfortably in her seat. "But I am hoping to at least put it to good use with the art auction."

Louise's phone buzzed; she checked it and then told Cole that the person he was meeting with at one o'clock was waiting on the dock.

"Ah, yes. Another friend of Sean's," he said to Emma. "Looking to buy a boat. Excuse me for a minute."

While he was gone, Louise asked about Penny and spoke of their own grown children. "We see them more in the off-season."

The Hopkinses spent October through April in the Virgin Islands, where they ran a winter charter business.

"I should be going," Emma said, though she didn't want to leave. Even docked, the *Louise* felt like a getaway. She could only imagine the serenity of sailing on the Peconic at sunset. Someday, she would like to see Sag Harbor through a tourist's eyes.

Louise walked her starboard to the steps, where Cole was talking to his visitor.

Emma stopped in her tracks.

"*You're* the friend of Sean's?" Emma said.

Kyle Dunlap smiled at her. "Emma! What a surprise. It really is a small world out here. I love it," he said.

She crossed her arms.

Kyle looked around and let out a low whistle. "This boat is a beauty."

"She was designed by Chris White," said Cole. "Intended for private use for a family to sail around the world. But by the time I got my hands on her, she'd been sitting idle for years. It took my wife and me three long years to convert her from a recreational yacht to a U.S. Coast Guard inspected vessel."

"Impressive. And Sean said you do more than a hundred and twenty charters a season?"

"That's right. Up to three a day."

"Since when are you a friend of Sean's?" Emma asked Kyle. She couldn't let it go. What the hell? Cole looked at her like she was a little off.

"I've been spending some time helping out on the launch," Kyle said.

She didn't know why this irritated her so much, but it did. "And you're buying a boat? Yeah, you're *really* more like me than Bea Winstead."

"Nothing like this," he said. "A fixer-upper. Right, Cole?"

"That's the plan. So my guy at Coecles Marina has two things for you to look at."

"You should ride over with us," Kyle said to Emma.

"To Shelter Island?"

"Why not? It's a beautiful day."

"Yeah, and I have to get to work. For some of us, this town isn't just a playground."

Penny couldn't remember the last time she'd felt so happy. Sitting in the passenger seat of her father's rented Jeep, she waited while he paid for the day pass for Coopers Beach, and then they drove up and parked. She could already feel the breeze off the ocean.

It was sunny and cloudless, an even better

255

day than when she'd gone there with her friends. Up ahead, the beach was dotted with blue umbrellas; a few kids about her age tossed around a Frisbee. The whiteboard at the entrance to the beach announced that the water temperature was sixty-five degrees and the surf was one to three feet. This time, she wasn't going to let her OCD ruin things for her. Nothing could ruin today. Her father had come back for her!

Talking to her dad was so much fun. She loved hearing about his life in Los Angeles. He was still doing some acting here and there, but he said he was transitioning to producing.

"It just takes money," he said.

"That's why you went to East Hampton?"

He nodded. "Yeah. Met with a guy who has deep pockets. There are some people in New York I've spoken to also. We'll see. Fingers crossed."

New York. Everything interesting in the world seemed to happen in New York City. She'd said this to Henry once and he said, "Can't really argue with you. My life certainly changed when I moved there."

"Can you take me to see New York City one day?" she asked her father.

He smiled at her. "You are just the cutest

thing I've ever laid eyes on."

Around him, she felt cute. It was different with her mom; her mom was her mom. She had to love her. But when her dad was around, he was making a choice to be with her, and every moment he continued to make that choice affirmed her sense of worth. But she also felt the need to be on her best behavior so as not to scare him off.

It had been so long since she'd seen him — sometime between Thanksgiving and Christmas during sixth grade. He'd taken her to eat at LT Burger, and she spent the whole time struggling not to rearrange the silverware or sip from her glass six times and put it down and then sip from it six times again. She'd done a really good job that night — he hadn't suspected a thing. And still, it had been years before he'd come back.

That's why there'd be no OCD today. She would boss it back if it killed her.

They put their blankets close to the water but not close enough to get wet when the tide rolled in. Her dad pulled a baseball hat out of his bag and handed it to her. "Wear that. Your mother won't be happy if I bring you home sunburned."

"I'm fine. I was just here a few days ago and I didn't need a hat."

"I guess your mom must bring you here a lot."

"Not really," Penny said.

"No? Why not?"

"I mean, she works all the time. And then she's tired and there's grocery shopping and all that stuff."

"Sorry about that, kiddo."

She shook her head. She wasn't trying to make her mom look bad. It was just the truth. "It's fine. I mean, I came with my friends the other day. It was fun."

"Your friends are old enough to drive?"

"Um, one of their brothers is."

"And your mom was okay with that?"

So many questions! She guessed, after all the time they'd spent apart, he wanted to catch up. "Um, she didn't exactly know," Penny said.

"What do you mean?"

She shrugged. "I don't always tell her where I am or what I'm doing. But don't say that to her, okay?" She didn't know why she'd admitted that. Maybe she wanted her father to see her as more grown up, to remind him that she wasn't a baby anymore. Maybe he liked teenagers more than little kids, and that was why he was willing to hang around for a little while.

"Well, I don't want you getting into any

trouble. You have to be safe."

"I am. Come on, Dad. Look at this place. Nothing ever happens here." And then she thought of something. Had her mother told him about the house? She hoped not. She wanted to tell him the news herself. "Do you know about the house?"

Her dad looked out at the waves. "What house?"

"I inherited a house! A big, amazing, gorgeous house on the water. The terrible part is that my friend died. But then the house thing happened and in some ways, it's like he's still here. Or like he's looking out for me in some way. I don't know."

She told him everything, including the part about the crazy old lady and how her mom was nervous about the whole thing.

"Wow. That's quite a story," her dad said.

"You have to come see it," she said.

"I'd like that, kiddo. I'd like that very much."

Emma made certain she was home in time for dinner. All day long, she'd been thinking of Penny out with Mark, and it had set her on edge. She knew she should be happy that her daughter's father was spending time with her, but for some reason, she just couldn't be. Maybe it was because her own relationship with Penny was strained. Or maybe it was because Mark had given her plenty of reasons over the years not to feel positive about him.

She wanted to discuss it with Angus, but she'd gotten home so late last night, he was already asleep. That morning, while Penny ate breakfast and talked excitedly about the day ahead with her father, Angus had given Emma a look that told her she wasn't alone in her concern. But all she had time to say to either of them was "I'm picking up dinner from Cavaniola's on my way home. I'll be back by six."

Now, sitting at the table, eating roasted lemon chicken and baby kale salad with Gouda (Cavaniola's was famous for its cheese), Emma didn't feel much better. Penny went on and on about Mark: Dad was going to produce a play, Dad was going to take her to New York one day, Dad was going to rent a place out there to spend more time with her.

Where was Mark's sudden interest in Penny coming from?

"Can I be excused?" Penny asked when she was finished eating. Her phone vibrated with a text and she ran upstairs.

Emma began clearing the table. Angus stood close to her at the kitchen sink and whispered beneath the sound of the running water, "This is all about the house, you know."

Emma turned off the faucet. "What do you mean?"

"You think it's a coincidence that Penny inherits a multimillion-dollar house and suddenly her father shows up after years of absence?"

The house had crossed her mind, but she doubted Mark knew about it. It was a local story. He was a West Coast person and, frankly, not big on current events. Although she was sure Penny had told him about it by now.

"Look, I'm the first one to be cynical about Mark, believe me. But I think the timing really is a coincidence."

"Be careful," Angus said.

"I'm trying to be." She was so unnerved, she was taking the next day off to spend it with Penny. And no, it wasn't lost on Emma that Penny's punishment for running off the other day had fallen by the wayside. "I've got it under control," Emma said.

Angus took a plate from her hand. "I'll finish these. Go talk to her."

Upstairs, Emma hesitated outside of Penny's closed bedroom door before knocking once sharply.

"Come in."

Penny sat cross-legged on her bed, hunched over her phone.

"Who are you texting?" Emma said.

"My friends."

"Put that down, please."

Penny complied but not without a sigh of annoyance.

"You were supposed to be grounded for a week, and you got out of that because your father showed up. But we're not done talking about what you did the other day. It's inexcusable, Penny. I'm taking your phone away for a few days."

"You can't! I have a right to talk to people. You can't cut me off from the world."

"I'm not cutting you off from the world. We have a landline in the house. You're free to make calls."

"What about emergencies? I can't walk around tomorrow without a phone."

"I didn't have a cell phone growing up and I survived. Besides, you'll be with me tomorrow. Now hand it over."

"What if Dad texts me? I can't just ignore him."

Emma felt like screaming. Now all of a sudden Mark had to be accommodated? "I'll let him know that if he wants to talk to you, he can call on the landline."

"This isn't fair."

"Why can't you look on the bright side? I just said I'm going to spend the day with you tomorrow. You don't have to go to the historical society. We'll do something fun."

"I don't want to spend the day with you."

"Penny, I'm really trying here. I need you to meet me halfway. Come on. What do you want to do?"

Penny looked up at her. "I want to go to the house. And I want to move in."

Bea rested on top of the bed, pushing aside her *New Yorker* and her reading glasses. She couldn't stop thinking about the drawings.

Why had Henry left them scattered around town? Surely he would have known that she would make the trip to Sag Harbor after his death. He knew she would notice the drawings, and he must have understood that she would not stop until she'd seen them all.

Up until today, the ones she'd found had been innocuous. But those drawings of that uncomfortable night? It was a provocation. Was he trying to remind her that she'd rejected him romantically and she'd rejected his move to the country, so she shouldn't expect to inherit his estate? Or were the drawings confirmation of his intention to leave her the house and his art, reinforcing that while their relationship had always been simply professional, at least in the end he'd left his legacy in her hands?

It was maddening.

The house had to yield more clues. She stepped out of bed; the bones of her feet felt fragile against the hardwood floors, and she put on her slippers.

She knew everyone thought she was crazy. This whole business with the house had even driven Kyle to quit! But then, none of these people had known Henry. If they had, they would've understood that Henry Wyatt was not a man to leave his entire life's work to a virtual stranger.

There must be something in that house that would help her case. But what? And where could it be? She'd already searched his desk. Henry, with his devotion to the spare and the aesthetically pleasing, had nothing as pedestrian as a filing cabinet. His paperwork was minimal. Bea had decades' worth of business documents pertaining to his work in her own office in Manhattan, and he'd never had an interest in having his own copies. Victor had been in possession of the damn will.

She made her way down the hall to the office and rechecked the room, but she was confident she'd been thorough the first time, and she found nothing new.

Downstairs, she wandered aimlessly. Funny; Bea had been called the architect of Henry Wyatt's career, but no one understood that Henry had been calling the shots all along. And was still calling them.

In the living room, shelves were embedded in the stone walls behind nearly invisible cabinets that were spring-activated and took only the lightest touch to open. She'd gone through these her first week in the house, but perhaps less carefully than the office and the bedrooms at this point. She checked them again, but they yielded nothing useful.

Frustrated, she walked back up the stairs to the bedroom. She sat on the bed, trying to think like Henry. What were his principles of design? Minimalism. Form follows function.

In Windsong, nothing looked like what it actually was; walls were windows, stairs floated, cabinets were invisible. But then, wasn't that function following form? Oh, it was maddening, the whole thing. If she were a different type of person she would simply retreat back to Park Avenue. But she'd never given up on Henry.

She paced the room and then paused at

the foot of the bed. The form always came first. Nothing was exactly as it appeared.

The wood base of the bed was thick and blockish, a few feet off the ground. Slowly, her back protesting with every inch, she lowered herself down, got onto her hands and knees, and examined the bed frame. Sure enough, she found two long, thin horizontal seams inches apart. She gingerly pressed the wood between them and jumped when a drawer slid out.

The drawer was shallow but functional enough to hold a few used Day-Minder calendars, blank sketch pads, and graphite pencils. In the back, she found a thick comic book of some sort, *The Unbeatable Squirrel Girl,* volume 1. Strange.

She pulled out the book and flipped through it. Why was it tucked away here and not in Henry's library? And since when did he read such juvenile material?

And then, a folded sheet of paper stuck between the last two pages. She shook it loose and spread it out on the floor. There, in Henry's neat cursive writing, the words she'd been looking for: *Last Will and Testament of Henry Wyatt.*

I, Henry Joseph Wyatt, being of sound mind, leave my artwork and my house on

Actors Colony Road, Sag Harbor, New York, to Bea Winstead of 720 Park Avenue, New York City, New York. It is my wish that the house at Actors Colony Road be turned into a permanent installation of my work and a public museum. The exception to this are the pieces noted below, which are to be donated to the Ellen Noel Art Museum in my hometown of Odessa, Texas. I also name Bea Winstead as executor of my estate.

Bea could scarcely breathe. It was dated May of 2000. It was old, but it was something! She closed her eyes, clutching the paper to her chest.

"Thank you," she whispered.

CHAPTER TWENTY-FOUR

While Emma waited for Penny to get dressed, she watched Angus sprinkle brown sugar over thick slices of bacon. He lined them up a few inches apart on the baking sheet and slipped it into the oven.

"No good can come from that house," he said, peeking through the oven window.

"Please don't say that around Penny. She's excited about it."

Emma had been thinking long and hard about how to let Penny "have" her house without turning their entire lives upside down, and she'd decided they would use it the way other people used a vacation house.

"It's our stay-cation house," Penny had said gleefully.

"Exactly," Emma said.

"Can I pack some things to bring over?"

Emma considered this. "Okay. But just enough for a few days. We'll go on weekends or some nights to swim and be on the water.

But our *home* home is still the house we live in."

She repeated this at the table in front of Angus, and he nodded his approval.

"Are you sure you don't want to come with us?" Penny asked him when she came down for breakfast.

"Young lady, I am going to work."

During the fifteen-minute ride to the house, Penny chatted to Emma more than she had the entire past month. No matter the strangeness of the situation, no matter Angus's misgivings or her own, Emma was relieved to see Penny so happy and animated.

Emma hadn't been to the house since she'd taken the impulsive water-taxi ride late at night, but when she walked into the kitchen, she realized something was different.

The sink had two used coffee mugs in it.

"Penny, wait a second," Emma said. "I need to look around. Someone has been here."

And she was sure she knew who that someone was.

Emma walked to the airy breakfast room just off the kitchen, the space with sliding glass doors to a patio and where the floating stairs led to the north wing of the house, the wing with the master suite. She climbed the stairs.

"Hello?" she called out. Nothing.

She passed the library and office and found the door to the master bedroom open. The room was pristine, but on the bedside table, a pair of reading glasses. A cashmere wrap was folded on top of the dresser.

Emma slid open the closet door and found a collection of Chanel, St. John, and Lilly Pulitzer that could only belong to one person.

"The nerve of that woman!"

Emma ran back down the stairs and found Penny outside on the deck.

"All right. We need to move into our bedrooms," she said.

Emma knew from her late-night exploration of the place that there were three guest rooms located on the side of the house opposite the wing with the master suite. The two parts of the house were connected by the central living space: kitchen, dining room, and living room. The guest rooms on the first floor each had its own full bath.

Furious, she swung open the first bedroom door and found large men's sneakers by the foot of the neatly made bed. An empty beer bottle rested on the nightstand.

Emma closed the door.

"What's going on?" Penny said.

"Those people are living here. The old woman."

"Why?"

Emma sighed. "Because she's a stubborn pain in the butt, that's why. Come on. Let's just put some things in the other two bedrooms. I'll deal with her later. This shouldn't spoil our day."

She let Penny choose her room of the two that were left. One had a four-poster bed of dark wood made up with stark white linens and half a dozen white pillows. The bedside table was glass and chrome, and each wall featured one of Henry Wyatt's paintings.

The final room had a softer feel to it, with a blue ceramic lamp, block prints on the bedspread, and, at the foot of the bed, a tufted blue bench with Lucite legs. On one wall, a gilded mirror, and next to it, a metal sculpture.

"I like the other room best. That bed is huge!" Penny said.

"Go for it," Emma said, sitting on the blue bench and dropping her bag. "And when you're done unpacking, meet me out by the pool."

Emma changed into her bathing suit, a white two-piece she'd bought on sale at the end of last summer. She was relieved to see that she was still in decent shape, considering her only exercise was biking to and from work and running up and down the stairs of the hotel. Apparently, that was enough for now. Still, every morning she saw women walking along Main Street in their yoga pants, carrying their rolled-up mats. She sometimes wondered what she was missing. But then, that was how she felt about most things in life.

God, she was pale. They were weeks into the summer, but anyone who looked at her skin tone would guess it was February.

Outside, Penny sat on the edge of the pool with her legs dangling in the water. "It's freezing!"

"I have to figure out the heater." And then Emma thought of the electric bill and decided Penny would have to get used to cold swims or wait for later in the summer when it would heat naturally. Or was heating the pool something she could pay for through the maintenance account the lawyer had mentioned? It was all so complicated.

She settled onto one of the four chaise longues lined up beside the pool and pulled a paperback out of her tote bag. Something felt really odd. Oh yeah — she was actually about to relax.

Penny let out a squeal as she submerged herself in the water.

Emma opened her book and tried to read but realized after turning a page that she wasn't absorbing a single word. The strangeness of sitting by the pool, looking out at the bay, was having a paradoxical effect. Not only couldn't she relax, she was flooded with tension.

How had this situation happened? Why had it happened? No matter how many times she told herself to just accept the circumstances, she couldn't stop feeling like she had to apologize. Last week, an old friend from high school called. She worked as a personal chef to a hedge funder and his wife in East Hampton and had heard the news about the house through the gossip mill. By way of explanation, Emma found herself saying, "I don't really know why he left Penny the house. Rich people are eccentric. You know that as well as I do."

On one level, Emma did believe that. Not everything that happened in life made sense, and often the inexplicable things that happened were bad. This, at least, was a positive turn. It was something that could make Penny's life better and her own too — if she could stop analyzing it long enough to enjoy it.

But then there was the Mark thing. *Was it the house that had lured him back, as Angus so cynically suggested?* Penny admitted to Emma that she'd told her father about the house and that he had "seemed really surprised." Emma felt like saying, *Your father is an actor.* But she held back. Despite all of her disappointment and frustration with Mark, no matter how negative her thoughts, Emma had promised herself she would not talk badly about him to Penny. It just wasn't right, and ultimately it wasn't good for Penny to hear her mother say bad things about her father.

And so what if it was curiosity about the house that had inspired his visit? The important thing was that he was there spending time with his daughter. Yes, it was frustrating to hear Penny talk about him with such glowing adoration when all Emma got was attitude and push-back. But it wasn't a competition. She was the only real parent, the one who did the hard work day in and day out. Penny might not appreciate that now, but she would understand when she was older. In the meantime, she should have fun with her father. It was harmless.

Emma watched Penny backstroke the length of the pool. Even though Penny was a strong swimmer, Emma felt a compulsion to keep an eye on her, as if she were still a toddler wearing floaties on her arms. But after a few minutes, she allowed herself to close her eyes. How long had it been since she'd really relaxed? Since she had taken a half hour to do absolutely nothing? She heard the gentle lapping of the water, a seagull calling out.

And a loud, grinding sound in the distance.

What *was* that?

It was coming from the direction of the bay.

"I'll be right back," she called out to Penny, slipping back into her flip-flops. She followed the stone pathway down to the beachfront. As soon as the dock came into view, the source of the noise was immediately clear. A dilapidated, thirty-foot wooden cabin cruiser was tied to the end, and standing at its helm was a sweaty Kyle Dunlap wielding an electric sander. He wore a T-shirt with a whale logo, cargo shorts, and some sort of shoe that was a cross between a sneaker and a boot. She almost didn't recognize him without his city pallor, his tan accentuated by the fact that his brown hair had turned golden from the sun.

She hurried to the edge of the dock, stepping around planks of wood and scattered tools.

"What is this?" she said, hands on her hips.

Kyle silenced the sander, looked down at the pile of wood at her feet, and said, "That's teak."

"No, I mean what is *all of this.* What are you doing?"

He wiped his brow with his forearm. "I'm fixing this boat."

"What are you doing *here*?"

Kyle put down his sander and walked closer to the edge. "Come on board for a minute so we don't have to yell back and forth?"

Fine! She stepped onto the boat and he reached for her arm to steady her.

"I'm okay," she said, pulling away from him. The floor of the boat was a ripped-up mess. They were no longer shouting back and forth, but she was going to end up with splinters. "Kyle, why are you here?"

He glanced back at the house. "Emma, I'm sorry. Bea is convinced the will is invalid. She's not giving up."

Emma shook her head. "I'm not going to go around in circles on this. I don't care what Bea thinks. This is trespassing."

The boat swayed, and a small metal

scraper slid near her feet.

"You're right," he said. "I mean, I guess you could just call the cops."

Yes, she could get Jim DiMartino on the phone right that minute. And he would . . . what? Arrest Bea when she showed up? Emma could already see the headlines in the local papers. The last thing she needed was more attention. No, she would have to handle this quietly. With a lawyer. How much would that cost her? Too much.

She folded her arms, looking around. "I guess my one consolation is that karma is a bitch — clearly, Cole Hopkins sold you a junker."

Kyle laughed. "Looks can be deceiving. This boat's a beauty. Trust me."

"Whatever, Kyle. I really don't care."

"Come check out the galley."

"I'll pass."

"Why not have a look? You can take sadistic pleasure in the job I have ahead of me."

She actually was curious about what kind of mess this Manhattan carpetbagger had gotten himself into. It would be good fodder for a few laughs with Sean and Alexis over drinks.

Emma followed him down a short ladder. She thought of her father, his love of old boats and his treasured long afternoons fishing. Oh, how she'd dreaded the days her father went out on the boat because she knew what would be for dinner that night: Fluke. Or flounder. Or whatever he caught. The appeal of fresh-caught fish was completely lost on her until later in life.

"She'll appreciate the food more if she sees how much work goes into it," her mother had told her father.

The next week, Emma was out on her dad's boat. He taught her how to bait a hook, and he stood behind her with his strong arms helping to steady her line. She never forgot the thrill of feeling her first tug on the other end and the excitement of her father reeling in her catch. But when the fish was on board, flopping helplessly on the hook, she burst into tears. Her father promptly removed the hook and threw it back into the water.

"Will it be okay?" she asked, sobbing. He assured her that it would. And when her father told her something would be okay, she always believed him.

Kyle's cabin was in even worse shape than the deck. The wood was largely eroded, wires snaked out of the side boards, and the floor was missing planks. Rolls of paper towels and industrial tape were scattered underfoot.

"I see that look on your face," Kyle said. "But you'd be surprised what a little varnish and paint will do."

"This is way beyond anything you can accomplish with a paintbrush," she said. And yet the raw condition of the old boat reminded her of Jack's stories of the hotel's state of disrepair when he first took ownership, and his hard work had paid off: The American Hotel was now the gem of Main Street.

Kyle shook his head. "So little faith. I'm going to redo the galley and the head and put some cabinets in here so it's fit to live aboard."

"Yeah, good luck with all that." She climbed up the ladder and at the top, she turned around to add, "Just keep the noise down, okay?"

She was halfway back to the pool when the grinding sound of Kyle's electric sander started up again.

Penny stepped out of the pool and wrapped herself in one of Mr. Wyatt's plush towels. Everything he had was nice. Everything seemed new. It was like being in one of those rich people's houses on an E! television show.

Except rich people usually didn't have a bunch of strangers squatting in their mansion. What was with the old lady and Kyle? That's how she thought of them: the Old Lady and Kyle. Just two more adults to make things complicated and annoying on top of her mother and Angus. When she told her dad about the Old Lady, he seemed really surprised and asked a lot of questions she didn't know the answers to, like whether her mother had a lawyer. "No way," Penny said. "Do you think Mom would ever pay for a lawyer?"

She wanted her dad to see the house. And she wanted Mindy and Robin to see it too. She still felt bad about how things had gone down that day at the beach and needed a way to get back on track with them.

Her mother's tote bag rested next to her abandoned lounge chair. Penny glanced up at the house, then quickly rummaged through the bag to find her mom's iPhone. She glanced around one more time, and when she was certain she was alone, she snapped photos of the pool and the house and the view of the bay. She grabbed her own beach bag, took out her crappy Motorola (that her mother had never bothered taking away after all), and found Mindy's and Robin's numbers. She sent them a series of photos showing off her new house. DNR to this number — not my phone, she warned. Then she erased the threads and put her mom's phone back.

She couldn't understand why her mother was so strict about things like screen time. It was the only way to communicate. It was hard enough to keep up with her friends without being in tech jail.

Walking back to the pool, she had the thought that maybe she hadn't put the phone back. So she turned around and went back to check. And she checked again. And again.

"Penny — what are you doing in my bag?" her mother said.

Busted! "Looking for sunblock," Penny said.

She didn't know who was a tougher warden, her mother or her own mind.

CHAPTER TWENTY-FIVE

Bea's lawyer returned her call just as she was settling into a chair at the Salon Xavier on Bay Street for her weekly blowout. What a relief it had been to find a temporary stand-in for her beloved John Barrett Salon.

She cupped her hand around her phone and said quietly, "Richard, I can't say too much because I don't have privacy at the moment. But you got my message?"

"I did. An interesting development. And to answer your question, yes — this does give you the standing to contest the most recent will. But it doesn't overturn it, you understand."

"I know, I know. Obviously, it's eighteen years old. But you said as long as I was the beneficiary of a prior will —"

"Send it to me. I'll start the paperwork. But Bea, this is a long shot. The current will was executed properly, so we can't invalidate it on a technicality. That leaves three other avenues: The decedent lacked the mental capacity to make the will. The decedent was unduly influenced to make the will. Or the will was procured by fraud. Any of these grounds are very difficult to prove."

"Well, then you have your work cut out for you. Let's not waste time chitchatting," she said and ended the call. She smiled into the mirror at the stylist poised behind her. Her phone buzzed again: Kyle. She ignored him and waited until her snow-white hair was as straight as a pin, the edges of her hair just grazing her jawline, before reading the texts that followed.

Emma Mapson at the house. With daughter. Just FYI. Let's not have a scene?

Twenty-four hours ago, this would have been bad news. Now it was more than welcome.

She canceled her manicure appointment and called for a cab. For a fleeting moment she thought of the water taxi — it had been surprisingly quick the other afternoon — but then decided against it since she'd just had her hair done. Instead, she sat in the cab as it moved slowly through the traffic in town, crossed over the bridge, and took her down the winding, secluded streets to Wind-song. It gave her plenty of time to think of what she would say to Emma Mapson.

Emma sat in the dining room eating from a takeout pint of BuddhaBerry frozen yogurt and watching Penny in the pool. She was still irked by Kyle and the boat, but something about the house had a calming effect on her. She didn't know if it was all of the natural light or the lack of clutter, but it felt like a big exhale just sitting inside. Her one issue with the house was that some of the rooms felt a little impersonal. She could remedy that with a few well-placed bunches of roses.

The front door slammed shut.

"Hello?" Emma called out, standing.

Bea Winstead swept into the room like she owned the place. She wore a light cashmere cape despite the fact that it was eighty degrees outside. Dropping her keys on the table, she said, "I see you've made yourself right at home."

She clearly wasn't surprised to find Emma there; Kyle must have tipped her off. Jerk!

"Yeah, I actually could say the same to you," Emma said, sticking her spoon in the plastic container. "This is trespassing. I could call the police and end this right now."

"So why don't you? Why haven't you?"

"I didn't know you'd moved in here until a few hours ago."

"Really? Or maybe it's because you know that *you're* the one who is trespassing."

Oh, for heaven's sake. Not this again. "Ms. Winstead, I don't want to make a scene. This is a small town. I don't want to be in the papers any more than I have been already. But more than anything, I want to protect my daughter's privacy. So I'm willing to ask you, politely, to leave. If you need a few days, we can work something out."

"How generous of you," Bea said. "But if *I'm* forced to leave, *you* will be forced to leave."

Emma pressed her hands to her temples. "I don't have the energy to play these games with you."

"I assure you, my dear, I am not playing." Bea set her Hermès purse on the table, opened it, pulled out a sheet of paper, and waved it in Emma's face.

"Henry's original will — naming me the executor of his estate. Expressing his wishes that this house be a museum of his work, not a playground for a hotel manager and her child."

Emma reached for the paper but Bea snatched it away. "Henry did everything by

285

design — everything. There's no way he'd make a random decision to just leave his entire estate to virtual strangers."

"Well, he did."

"The courts will have to see about that; I'm contesting your inheritance. In case there's any doubt, please be assured I have the best lawyers money can buy. So don't get too comfortable. And if you push the issue about who gets to reside here, chances are we'll both be asked to vacate while things get settled."

Emma looked outside to Penny happily splashing around in the pool.

"Ms. Mapson, do you understand me?"

Emma nodded, still looking out the window at her daughter.

There was no way around it. She needed a lawyer. The "free" house was already costing her.

Her mother didn't say much during the ride back to their own house. Penny could tell she was in a bad mood and so she didn't want to push, but she was frustrated they'd left early. The plan had been to have dinner at the house, maybe to sleep over for the first time. But then, the Old Lady.

Why did her mother always back down? Penny knew her mother tried to do the right thing, but she was so cautious all the time and the result was their boring life. The worst part was that she was trying to make Penny be the same way. And even more frustrating than that, every time Penny tried to be bold and daring, her OCD got in the way.

"Do you want to go out for dinner?" Emma said as they headed over the bridge.

"Sure."

"LT Burger?"

Penny nodded. At least her mom was trying to make it up to her. LT Burger, with its waffle fries and milk shakes, was her favorite. Her phone buzzed in her hand — a text from her father.

"Dad wants to take me to the beach tomorrow," she said.

Emma glanced at her. "What happened to helping at the historical society? You made a commitment to Angus, Penny. It's not right to just bail on him."

It struck Penny as funny when her mother used words like *bail.* It reminded her that her mother had been young once. Maybe she'd bailed on a few things in her time. Maybe she could still remember what that was like.

"Mom, I said okay to helping out at the historical society because no one wants to hire a fourteen-year-old for a real job."

"Did you even try?"

"Yes! A few places. I really wanted to work at BuddhaBerry. The owner said next summer. And fine, I know you said I can't sit around the house alone all day. But things changed. Dad is here for now, but who knows how much time I'll get to have with him? The historical society isn't going anywhere."

Emma pulled into a parking spot. They walked to the burger place in silence.

Penny's phone buzzed again, this time with Mindy's response to the photos she texted of the house.

That place is sick!

Penny contemplated what to write back. *Thanks* seemed weird; *I know,* obnoxious. Was she overthinking it? God, she hated how hard she tried. But the sting of the other day at the beach was still with her. She just had to move past it.

Inside, LT Burger was all white subway tile, funky lamps, chalkboard menus, and wire ceiling fans. They sat at a table near the orange-topped wraparound bar. Penny didn't need a menu. She always ordered the standard burger, waffle fries, and, for dessert, the Death by Oreo milk shake.

"Penny," her mother said. "I need you to stop fighting me on everything. Do you think I like always having to be the bad guy? I don't. But I'm trying to do what's best for you even when that makes you upset with me. It's important in life to do the right thing even when it's hard. Especially when it's hard. Do you understand?"

Penny nodded. She thought she did. Basically, her mom was as tired of arguing about everything as she was. And, really, she didn't want to add to her mom's stress.

"I'm sorry," Penny said.

Emma shook her head. "I'm not complaining. I love you. I just want you to know that I'm not trying to make you miserable. But I'm the adult and I see the big picture in a way that you can't. You have to trust me and not view every decision as me taking something away from you."

"But when you tell me I have to work at the historical society instead of spending the day with my dad, that is taking something away from me."

Her mother leaned back and sighed. "You know what? How about a compromise? Work at the historical society for a few hours in the morning and early afternoon, then your dad can pick you up for the beach and dinner."

Penny smiled. "Good deal."

The waitress took their order. Her mom must have felt better after the talk because she ordered their milk shakes as appetizers instead of dessert.

And then Penny's phone buzzed in her lap with a new text from Mindy.

Party at my place Friday nite.

Penny glanced at her mother.

Okay, maybe what her mother didn't know wouldn't hurt her. Penny didn't need to debate every little thing she wanted to do.

She just needed to be more careful not to get caught.

Chapter Twenty-Six

Bea was heartened by the discovery of the old will, but she knew it wasn't necessarily a smoking gun. She had no intention of sitting back and waiting for lawyers to get the job done. There were still drawings to be found, and so her destination that afternoon was the whaling museum.

The Sag Harbor Whaling Museum was a white Greek Revival mansion with a temple-front portico bearing, in gold letters, the words MASONIC TEMPLE. Two enormous whale jawbones framed the doorway.

The building had double-height ceilings and a magnificent oval staircase. The only blight on an otherwise noble interior was a gift-shop counter. And it was there that she found Angus, ringing up souvenirs for a family with small children.

"Do you work at *every* museum in this town?" she said.

"Ah, Ms. Winstead. We meet again," he

said. There was something very calming about his voice. As rankled as she felt by his association with Emma Mapson, Bea found him to be quite pleasant.

It was probably time to dispense with the formalities, although she and Mr. Sinclair were both from an era when manners were ingrained. Oh, she'd shed all that like a second skin when she'd moved to Greenwich Village in the sixties. But she found that as she got older, she instinctively reverted back to the habits of her conventional upbringing.

"Please, call me Bea," she said.

"Bea, what brings you here today? Interested in the town's rich whaling history? I'm happy to give you a tour."

She knew he was teasing her. "As fascinating as that might be, I think you know I am here looking for significantly more recent artifacts."

"You're very goal-oriented, aren't you? Has anyone ever told you to stop and smell the roses every once in a while?"

"Mr. Sinclair, I am in no mood."

"Angus. Since we're on a first-name basis." He walked around to the front of the souvenir case. "I'll show you to the archives room. But you'll have to humor me if I point out a few treasures along the way."

She followed him to a room just to the right of the entrance hall and winding central staircase.

"Look at this beauty," he said, pausing in front of a book enclosed in a glass case. "An illustrated limited edition of *Moby-Dick*. The preface is by Jacques Cousteau and the book is signed by him."

Bea peered at the volume, opened to pages somewhere in the middle.

"Very nice," she said impatiently.

"Read the plaque there."

She skimmed the information about the display, details of the lithograph illustrations by LeRoy Neiman and some quotes from Jacques Cousteau. And then she read *Donated to the Sag Harbor Whaling Museum by Henry Wyatt.*

She looked up at Angus in surprise, and he smiled.

Oh, Henry. He did love his books. She made a mental note to go through his library more carefully. If she found other books that might be worth contributing to one of the local museums, she would show them to Angus. And then she remembered she had no legal right to do anything with the estate. That's why she was there. To find a clue, a way to reverse the travesty of the will.

Passing through several rooms, moving toward the back of the building, Bea took more notice of the crown molding, intricate plaster ceiling, and Corinthian columns than she did of the exhibits. "This was once a private home?" she said to Angus.

"Indeed. It was built in 1845 as the home of Benjamin Huntting the Second and his family. Huntting made his fortune in the whale-oil business."

"Who designed the house? Anyone of note?"

"A very prominent nineteenth-century architect. Minard Lafever."

"I'm familiar. But why the Masonic signage out front?"

"After Huntting passed in 1867 the house changed hands a few times. It was unoccupied until 1907, when a well-known philanthropist, Mrs. Russell Sage, took ownership. It was her summer cottage until her death in 1918. Two years later, the Freemasons bought the building. Shortly after that, the historical society began exhibiting some artifacts on the ground floor. That was the beginning of the space becoming a museum, although that didn't happen officially until 1936."

"You are just a font of knowledge," Bea said.

"I used to be a history teacher at the high school," he said.

"When did you retire?"

"Ten years ago."

"And you miss it."

"Every day."

"Well, I suppose now you can think of yourself as teaching adults."

They reached a room with a long table and heavy wood cabinets. Angus made a sweeping gesture with his arm. "You have arrived."

Penny's dad picked her up in a different car this time, a black convertible.

"What a perfect day, right?" her dad said, pulling into the Coopers Beach parking lot.

It was hot but not too hot, just enough clouds to occasionally drift over the sun. The beach was as crowded as if it were a weekend.

Penny followed her father down the long rubber mat covering the hot sand to a spot near the ocean. She wanted to dash right into the water, but they'd picked up sandwiches from Bagel Buoy on the way over and if they didn't eat them, they'd go bad. Her dad hadn't thought to bring a cooler like her mom always did.

"Thanks for giving me an excuse to get

out of work," she said.

"Yeah, it should be against the law to work on a day like this," he said, passing her a bottle of Poland Spring.

Penny still didn't fully understand what her dad did for a living. He'd said the acting thing wasn't "panning out." He tried to explain producing, but to her it just sounded like hunting around for money, and how did you make money by asking people for money?

"So where are you staying?" Penny asked. That, too, had been vague during their last conversation.

"I found a great rental just off Division Street."

"How long are you going to be here?"

He smiled at her. "You sure like definitive answers, don't you?"

"Mom says I have a particularly low tolerance for gray areas."

That's why she wasn't looking forward to sneaking around later that night to go to the party. But she would do it. A part of her wanted to talk to her dad about the conflict she felt between trying to keep up with her friends and sticking to her mother's rules. But talking to her father about that somehow felt even more disloyal to her mother than lying about it in the first place.

They finished eating and headed to the ocean. Her dad waded in up to his waist while Penny stood at the edge, letting the water rush over her feet.

Don't think about it, she told herself. But another part of her brain, the stronger part, was already counting.

In the distance, her father waved her in. She held up her hand, one finger. *Just a sec.* Back to counting.

After a minute or so, her father made his way back to her. By that point, she was on the verge of tears.

"Hey, you don't want to come in?" he said.

"I do. But I can't!" And then the tears did come, hard and messy. She stood there sobbing like a baby. Surprised and clearly confused, her dad put his arm around her and led her back to the towels.

"What's going on?" he said, passing her one of the paper napkins from their lunch. She wiped her nose, realized the napkin had cream cheese on it, and started crying even harder. Her dad looked at her with alarm. She had to say something, to explain. It was hard to admit what was going on, but sitting there sobbing for the rest of the afternoon was clearly not an option.

"I have OCD," she said.

Her dad seemed to consider this for a few

seconds. "You mean you wash your hands all the time? That sort of thing?"

She nodded. "Yeah. That and other stuff."

"What other stuff?"

Again, she hesitated. She didn't want to scare him off. Visiting with her was supposed to be fun. But she realized, looking down at the soggy napkin in her lap, knowing her face was red and puffy, that it was too late for that. So she told him about the counting, the checking on things, the germ phobia.

Her dad nodded, and she could tell he was trying to play it off like this was totally not a big deal. But she could hear the urgency in his voice when he said, "What does your mother say about all this? Did you see a . . . therapist or something?"

"Yeah. Dr. Wang. She helps me try to manage my thoughts. It's a kind of therapy called CBT."

"But it's not working?"

Penny shrugged. "Maybe for a while. I felt better last year. I was drawing a lot — with the artist who left me the house. I don't know. When I was doing that, I felt a little better. My therapist says it takes time and not to get frustrated. But I feel like it's never going to go away. She said I could try taking Prozac."

298

"Okay, good. Sounds like a plan."

"Well, not exactly. Mom's nervous about it. She wants me to wait."

"But a doctor recommended it. Your mother isn't a doctor," he said.

Uh-oh. "It was just a suggestion," Penny said. "It's not a big deal. Most of the time I'm fine."

"Well, obviously not," he said in an irritated tone she hadn't heard before. He looked around the beach, then back at her. "Maybe we should get out of here. Try a different activity today. Is there somewhere else you want to go?"

Oh, how she wished she could rewind fifteen minutes, go stand at the water and boss it back. Her dad probably wanted to leave the beach so he could drop her off at home as soon as possible. She'd totally ruined everything. What could she do to turn things around?

"Do you want to see my new house?"

CHAPTER TWENTY-SEVEN

The Sag Harbor Whaling Museum archive room was windowless. Bea had no sense of how much time was passing, but once she found a folder of Henry's drawings, she did not care.

The collection included architectural plans for Windsong, dated 1989, and two sketches of a man tending bar. The American Hotel bar, clearly. His angular features looked familiar. It took her a few moments of staring at the page to realize it was the man who had been tending bar the first time she and Henry visited Sag Harbor, in the spring of 1988. Immediately, she recalled the sketch of the crowded party she'd seen in the art gallery on Washington Street; that wasn't just any party, it was the dinner party they'd gone to that same weekend.

The event had seemed important at the time. The host was a big art collector and on the board at the MoMA and the Guggenheim. Henry, with his typical disdain for any "scene," had had no intention of attending even though he was the guest of honor.

As his manager, Bea insisted they go. "Forget about the professional obligation. Look at it as an excuse to visit a new town." This reasoning got to Henry, as she'd known it would. He prided himself on his sense of curiosity. And while they had spent time in the Hamptons, they had never ventured far enough north to experience the village of Sag Harbor.

The American Hotel was the place to stay, people in the know assured them. Bea and Henry were not disappointed; they were immediately enchanted by the old-fashioned charm of the place. They checked into their rooms, dressed for the party, and met at the bar for a warm-up cocktail.

"Time seems to have stood still in this place," Henry said to the bartender, a man who looked to be in his thirties with bright green eyes and russet-colored hair.

"That's the idea," said the bartender.

Bea knew that Henry was not thrilled with the direction of the world. The 1980s had ushered in Ronald Reagan, new wave music, and, in the fine-art world, the rise of neo-expressionism.

The bartender was too young to be nostalgic for the sixties, but he and Henry seemed to hit it off anyway. Apparently, the bartender was a prizewinning fisherman in his spare time.

"Maybe that's what I should do," Henry said to Bea. "Give up painting and start fishing. Living off the sea."

"Ha-ha," Bea said, not amused. After an hour of the two men's boat talk, she told Henry that if they didn't leave right away, they were going to be late.

"Go without me."

"Henry," she said, fighting panic. "Don't be absurd. The whole reason we're here is for this party. You're the guest of honor!" Bea was tempted to remind Henry that he was lucky that the guest of honor at this party was him and not the new art-world darling Jean-Michel Basquiat. But provoking him wouldn't get her anywhere.

Henry, stubborn as always, refused to leave the hotel. Bea went to the party alone. When Henry finally showed up two hours later, he was clearly drunk. The host was simply delighted that he'd arrived at all, but Bea was furious.

In the morning, Bea handed in her room key to the front desk and was unhappy to find Henry once again seated at the bar, although this time he was drinking coffee.

"Are you ready to go?" she asked him.

The bartender, the same man as the night before, greeted her with a friendly smile and said, "Bloody Mary?"

"Certainly not," she snapped. She knew it wasn't the bartender's fault that Henry behaved badly last night, but she also didn't want him encouraging a repeat performance. Best to get on the road.

"Bea, Tom here's had family roots in this town since the Revolutionary War."

"Is that so?" she said, glancing at her watch.

"Yes," Henry said excitedly, more animated than she'd seen him in some time. "His great-great- . . . well, however-many-greats-grandfather was a member of the Eastern Regiment of 1776. He fought in the Battle of Long Island. Tell her, Tom."

"Really, there's no need. I'm far from a history buff," Bea said.

"As you probably know, it was not a successful battle," Tom said. Henry nodded vigorously. As she probably knew? Who on earth had ever heard of the Battle of Long Island? "Morale faded pretty quickly after that loss. The British took control of the island and held it for over half a dozen years. The townspeople of Sag Harbor were forced to house and feed the British army.

303

They had to pledge their allegiance to King George the Third or they would become prisoners of war."

"Can you imagine?" Henry said. "Right here!"

"Well, I doubt they sat at this bar, Henry."

"Actually, they did," said Tom. "Or at least, at this site. The British set up a naval blockade so that supplies couldn't be sent to the American army through the Port of Sag Harbor. Officers used this very spot as their lodging and tavern. Some of the original brick is still part of the facade."

"Imagine that!" Henry said, slamming his palm down on the bar. *"Imagine that!"*

"Henry, I'll pull the car around. We should get on the road."

Henry shook his head, finished his coffee, and set the cup down with a flourish. "I've decided to stay a few days."

"What? Why?"

"Tom is going to show me around. What am I rushing back to New York for? The banality of the now?"

The banality of the now? How was she supposed to argue with that? No, she knew better. She had learned, over the course of two decades, to accept his sometimes infuriating artistic and impulsive temperament. And yet leaving him in that hotel bar that morning gave her a feeling of deep trepidation.

Three days later, after not so much as a phone call from him, she finally swallowed her pride and left him a message at the front desk of the hotel. It was two more days until she heard back.

"I've decided to rent a house out here for the summer," he said.

Fine. Let Henry have his Sag Harbor adventure. Maybe it would inspire him to get back to work. He hadn't produced a substantial painting in months. He would return to Spring Street refreshed.

How could she have imagined that he would never again call New York City his home?

In the windowless archive room of the whaling museum, Bea looked up from the drawings at a mounted harpoon on the wall. Next to it, a display of maritime art. She thought of the book in the case in the front room, *Moby-Dick.* The greatest whaling story of all time.

What story are you trying to tell me, Henry?

"Now, this is the way to live!"

Penny was in the pool, and her dad sat in the same chair where her mother had lounged just a day before. But the house felt different with her dad there. Somehow it felt more like her own. "You've got the pool, a view of the bay. What more could you ask for?" he said.

When they'd first walked inside, he'd let out a low whistle. "This place has got to be worth a fortune," he said. "Explain to me again how you knew this guy?"

Penny told him about meeting Henry in the lobby of the hotel and how that had turned into weekly art lessons. She'd introduced Henry to the whole graphic-novel thing, and they decided to write their own. "But I haven't worked on it at all since he died. I just can't focus. And it doesn't feel the same. What's the point? There's no one to show it to when I'm done."

But by that time, it was clear her dad had tuned her out. He walked from room to room, examining the art and the furniture. She stood next to him in the dining room, staring out at the pool.

"What do you think?" she said. He'd turned very quiet.

After a pause, he'd looked down at her and said, "I think we should go swimming."

So now Penny was in the cold pool, waiting to warm up like she had yesterday. Her father was busy on his phone but said he'd jump in soon. Penny floated on her back, watching a cloud drift over the sun. She closed her eyes and tried to luxuriate in the perfection of the moment, but something wasn't right. When she let this feeling take shape, she recognized that it had something to do with her mom and the fact that her mom would not be happy to know she was at the house with her father. She didn't know why her mother would be upset, but she felt certain she would. It was another example of her not doing something truly wrong but still wrong enough that it put herself and her mother at odds.

"Dad," she called out, holding on to the edge of the pool.

"Be right there."

"Dad, I need to ask you something."

He looked up from his phone. "What's up?"

"Can you not tell Mom about coming here today?"

Her dad smiled. "It will be our little secret."

Penny didn't know if this made her feel better or worse. She tried to put it out of her mind, but of course she kept obsessing over it until, a short while later, her dad called out, "How's the water temp?"

"A little cold, but you get used to it."

He walked over. He didn't get into the

water like her mom, who dipped one toe in and then, wincing, slowly waded in until she was fully submerged. He just plunged right in.

"Wow. That'll wake you up," he said.

He swam a lap but climbed out right after. Penny paddled around a little more but got bored without company. The point of today was to spend time with her dad, right? She headed back to the chairs, but he was so busy texting he didn't notice her standing right next to him until she dripped onto the seat.

"Penny, back up. I'm trying to dry off."

She knew it was a reasonable request but something about it stung. She wrapped a towel around herself and settled into a chair. She watched her father bent over his phone, his jaw set, and something strange happened. That whole feeling of familiarity, of knowing him in this special and unspoken way, disappeared. It was like looking at a stranger.

She pulled her old iPod Touch out of her bag. It was so outdated she couldn't even get Snapchat on it, but that's why her mom let her keep it despite the whole social media and screen ban. It still played music.

Penny put in her earbuds and closed her eyes. She was almost asleep when her father tapped her arm.

"Penny, who the hell is that?" her dad said, pointing toward the steps leading to the beach.

She squinted in the distance and saw Kyle. He took off his aviator sunglasses and waved at her, then made his way quickly across the wide deck between the pool area and the slope to the shrubbery lining the beach-front.

"Oh. That's Kyle."

"Is he . . . is that your mom's boyfriend?"

"What? Oh — no. Remember that old lady I told you about? He works for her."

"Hey," Kyle said from the other side of the pool. "How's it going, Penny?"

Her dad stood up and Kyle walked over to him.

"Kyle Dunlap," he said. "And you are?"

"I'm Penny's father."

Kyle looked at Penny. "Your mom know you're here?"

"I don't see how that's any of your business," her dad said before she could answer. "And what are you doing on this property?"

Kyle gave her dad a smile that seemed just a little mocking. "The same thing you are, man."

"This is my daughter's house."

Kyle nodded. "That seems to be the case.

But who knows?" He walked up to the house.

Her dad stared after him, arms crossed, then turned to Penny, looking very pissed off. "What the hell is going on here?" he said.

"I told you about the old woman," she said. "He works for her."

"And your mother is just letting strangers live here with you?"

"Well, we're not living here yet. And it's not her fault. She can't get rid of them."

A strange expression crossed her father's face, and she instantly wanted to take back her words. Nothing she said was coming out right.

"Dry off and get dressed," her father said. "We're leaving."

CHAPTER TWENTY-EIGHT

At nine in the morning, the hotel was coming to life, with guests filling the airy breakfast room for the complimentary continental buffet. At the bar, Chris was setting up for lunch service, and in the lobby, a couple sat playing backgammon. Outside, the sun began peeking through the clouds.

Emma set a bucket of freshly cut roses from her garden on a table in the piano room. She lined up a few silver vases, filled them with fresh water, and treated the water with a few squeezes of lemon juice, some sugar, and a touch of bleach — another little trick, courtesy of her mother, to extend flower life. She placed the roses into the vases one by one, alternating white and yellow, gently removing the leaves that would fall beneath the waterline.

A waiter poked his head in. "Emma, someone's at the front desk for you."

She set the roses she was tending to back in the bucket, pulled off her gloves, and slipped through the narrow corridor to the lobby, where she found Mark sitting on the couch.

"What are you doing here?" she said, looking around.

"I want to talk to you about Penny."

Her stomach tightened. "What's wrong?"

"You tell me. I took the kid to the beach and she had a meltdown. What's with this OCD?"

Emma sighed, partly relieved that this was his concern, but also partly irritated.

"Come on, Mark. You scared me for a minute. I told you, years ago, about her anxiety and all of this. I'm dealing with it, okay? She has good days and bad."

"She said the shrink recommended meds and you said no."

"First of all, she sees a therapist who is helping her with cognitive-behavioral therapy. It's important that Penny develop the tools to deal with her OCD and not just rely on pills."

"So you know better than a doctor?"

"When it comes to my daughter, yes, I do."

"*Our* daughter," he said.

"Oh, so now it's *our* daughter? Where

312

were you the past five years when I was taking her to therapy appointments twice a week?" And where she'd be going later that day, leaving work when she shouldn't. "Where were you the times she was sobbing at the sink after twenty minutes of hand-washing and I had to drag her away? She's doing much better."

"Where were *you* when she rode to the beach with a bunch of older teenage boys the other day?"

Emma felt her face flush. Boys had been there that day? What boys was Penny even friends with?

"I was here, working! You think any of this is easy? Who are you to waltz in here and criticize me?"

"I'm her father."

"How nice of you to remember. And what interesting timing."

"What's that supposed to mean?"

Should she say it? "It means your daughter just inherited a house worth a fortune and suddenly you're Father of the Year."

Mark shook his head. "That's extremely cynical and unfair, Emma."

"Well, so is your attitude toward my parenting."

"But since you brought up the house, why the hell are you letting strangers live there?

313

Penny seems to feel these people want to take the house from her. You have to be smart, Emma. This is big-league stuff here."

"I can't believe you! This *is* about the house!"

"No, this is about the fact that you're obviously having problems with managing everything. That's not a criticism, Emma. I'm trying to help."

"Look me in the eye and tell me you had no idea about the house when you showed up last week."

"I had no idea. And I think you're deflecting because you know I'm right about things that are going on with Penny."

"What I think is that after all these years of hearing basically nothing from you, I don't need your input now!" she yelled.

"It's not about what you need. It's about what Penny needs. And I have a right to be in the loop."

Be careful what you wish for, Emma thought with a chill. How many times had she lamented being in this parenting thing alone? And now he was here. And it felt all wrong.

"Okay, Mark," she said evenly. "I'll keep you in the loop." *Just please leave. Leave this lobby, and leave this town.*

He smiled in a way that set her further on

314

edge. "I appreciate that, Emma. Let's talk later in the week." He headed for the door, but then he turned around and said, "You know I just want what's best for Penny, right?"

She nodded. But she didn't know that. Not at all.

Penny handed Dr. Wang her worksheet. It was a four-part chart logging triggering situations, the obsessions and compulsions that resulted, and her anxiety levels.

"So I see that the bathroom light switches are still a problem," Dr. Wang said. Her reading glasses were narrow rectangles framed in gold wire. Dr. Wang was such a style icon! And yet annoying.

"Yeah," Penny said. It was the top of her list. If she had to touch the bathroom light switch before lunch or dinner (trigger), she worried she'd get sick (obsession), and then she had to wash her hands for a full five minutes (compulsion), and her anxiety level was at 10.

"But this is a new one," she said, reading farther down Penny's chart. "Tell me what happened at the beach."

Penny had tried to forget about the compulsive counting at the ocean the day with her friends. But when it happened again with her father, she realized it wasn't going away.

"I don't know. I just had the feeling that if the water didn't touch my feet in a certain way a specific number of times, it would be bad luck."

"Okay. When you were in this situation, were you able to think at all about some of our bossing-back techniques?"

"I tried telling myself I didn't have to listen to the OCD, that it was lying to me. That I had to trust myself. That, okay, realistically there was no connection between the water and something bad happening. But it didn't help." Penny burst into tears. It was so frustrating!

Dr. Wang passed her a box of tissues. "Penny, I know it's hard. And you're going to have good days and bad days. I want you to also remember the floating-by strategy: Don't overthink it when it's too difficult. Don't try to shut the thought down. Just let it pass over you like a cloud without acting on it."

Penny nodded. In her back pocket, her phone vibrated with a text. "I need to use the bathroom," she said.

She went in, locked the door, and leaned against it, her heart pounding. As usual, the soap was missing. Dr. Wang never forgot to hide it from her.

Ru coming 2nite?

The party at Mindy's.

Yes. Telling my mom I'm sleeping at ur place.

Mindy's house, with the little white pills. Penny slipped her phone back into one pocket, pulled out her mini–emergency bottle of hand sanitizer from another, and slathered it on until her skin burned.

CHAPTER TWENTY-NINE

Printing out the photographs of Henry's drawings from her phone had been surprisingly easy. Well, easy after she tipped the young man at Walgreens to do it for her. It was amazing what modern technology and a little cash could accomplish. Of course, she would eventually buy all the originals. But that was a different project entirely. She had to prioritize.

Bea spread the images out on the dining-room table. She had drawings from several places: The American Hotel, the library, the art gallery, and the whaling museum — over a dozen prints altogether. The challenge was to organize them into some sort of narrative order. But where to begin?

She stood and paced, then stopped in front of a geometric cube in the corner of the room, one of Henry's earliest sculptures, done that first summer in Sag Harbor. When Henry refused to go back to Manhattan with her, Bea had thought for sure he would quickly grow stir-crazy and then appear one morning at the Spring Street office as if he'd never left. But that didn't happen.

In response, Bea filled her calendar, hitting the smaller galleries and underground shows like she hadn't in years. Every season brought a new crop of young artists to the city, so if Henry wanted to exile himself to the backwoods of Long Island, there were plenty of ambitious young people eager to take his place. Of course, this was no consolation. Henry Wyatt was a once-in-a-generation artist.

When he finally called and invited her to visit, her pride answered for her. "I'm busy," she said. But Henry knew how to get to her.

"I have some work to show you."

Fine. If there were paintings to see, she would go.

Henry's rented house had an untended lawn and was surrounded by trees. It was less a vacation house and more the abode of a budding recluse.

"What do you do out here?"

"I've started fishing," he told her excitedly. He was tan and trim, and there was a lightness to him.

"But this house . . . is this the best you

319

could find?" she asked.

"This is perfection! Come out back."

She followed him through tall grass and down a gravel path to a large shack in the backyard. The ground around it was littered with sheets of metal and blocks of wood. Her first thought was that the people he rented from really should have cleaned up the mess. She did not make the connection to Henry's work, not even when Henry swung open the door to the shack and she saw that it was empty of furniture. It was empty of anything except for three metal, five-foot-by-five-foot hollow cubes, each with a metal pole in its center.

"What do you think?" he said.

"I think you should get a refund on this rental."

"What do you think of my *work*?"

Oh.

She walked around the metal cubes, forcing herself to focus and not let the confusion about this change in medium get in the way of an honest assessment.

"They're interesting," she said. "Strong. I just . . . I had no idea you were interested in sculpture. Why didn't you mention it to me?"

"I know how you feel about my painting. You hate when I turn my attention elsewhere. But Bea, I'm done with it."

She looked at him sharply. "I'm sure that's not the case, Henry."

He laughed, a genuine merry outburst. "Oh, Bea. I wish, just for one minute, you could see things more expansively."

"And I wish you would stop making rash decisions!"

"It's not an intellectual decision," he said. "It's the way I feel. This is big-picture stuff, Bea. The past few weeks, spending time with Tom sailing and fishing and building fire pits for outdoor cooking, I've realized there's something to be said for getting your hands dirty — and not just with paint and varnish. When you really delve into the physical world, the natural world, you realize you're connected to everything. At this stage in my life, well, I need that. It's important to be part of something, Bea."

"You are a part of something," she said slowly. "You're one of the most important artists of your time. Perhaps of all time. We have a gallery together. Something we've built over many years. That's something, is it not?"

He smiled and shook his head as if she were a child who was simply not getting the wisdom being bestowed on her by an elder. Heart in her throat, she tried to steer the conversation onto more solid ground. She assessed the sculptures on autopilot, putting them in context and talking about their strengths and how he might build a cohesive body of work from this point.

"We'll ship these to the gallery when you're ready," she said.

"I'm not selling them," he said.

Well, that was a small relief. He couldn't be that serious about the sculptures if he was just going to leave them lying around like rejects of a yard sale.

They walked back outside and stood in silence for a minute, surrounded by insects humming in the grass.

"So what's the endgame here, Henry?"

He shook his head. "Always so goal-oriented, my friend." The sun was so bright, it was almost difficult to see color. Everything was washed out.

"Since you ask, I'm going to build a house out here. I'm designing it myself. It will serve as a permanent installation space for my work." His face flushed with excitement.

Bea did not panic. *This too shall pass.*

And yet she couldn't bring herself to stay in Sag Harbor overnight as she'd planned. Whatever was going on with Henry, there was clearly no place for her in the process. She wanted to get back to her beloved

Spring Street, even if Henry was temporarily turning away from their shared home. Was this just another of his small rebellions? Or something deeper — a fear of irrelevance? Of death? But no — she kept coming back to the undeniable joy in his countenance.

Around Christmas, he sent for his belongings to be moved out of Spring Street. Four months later, a year since their first trip to Sag Harbor, he did an interview with the *New York Times* announcing his retirement.

She heard rumors that he was designing a building, that he was painting, that the State of Texas had commissioned a sculpture for a public square. None of it was true. On the rare occasions when they spoke on the phone, they always discussed the past — it was as if the present didn't exist and there were no plans for the future.

Bea was trying to arrange the drawings on the dining-room table into some sort of order when the doorbell rang. Who the devil was bothering her now?

She made her way to the foyer, recalling with a small shudder the day Victor appeared with the unthinkable news about the house. That felt like months ago, not just weeks. And so little progress had been made.

There was no need for a peephole in the

door; the entrance was framed by glass on both sides. She could see a tall man with dark, silver-tinged hair. He wore khaki pants, a polo shirt, and a pair of those obnoxious mirrored sunglasses.

She opened the door. "What can I do for you?" she said in a tone that she hoped conveyed *Please leave.*

"Hi, Ms. Winstead. I'm Mark Mapson, Penny's father. I'd like to talk to you if you have a minute."

Oh, for heaven's sake. Who was going to come out of the woodwork next?

Mark Mapson had a slick look about him. His features were handsome, but there was just enough off about the way they all came together to prevent him from being truly attractive.

"I do not have a minute. Your daughter has taken up enough of my time and energy, and unless you are here to tell me that all of you have decided to relinquish claim to the house and estate that *clearly does not belong to you,* we have nothing to discuss."

He nodded and removed his sunglasses. His eyes, dark and sharp, met hers.

"I hear you, Ms. Winstead. And I assure you, we definitely have something to discuss."

He might be slick, but now he had her attention.

She opened the door wider.

"I hope you are quick to get to the point, Mr. Mapson. I am not a patient woman."

It took all of Emma's willpower not to lean on the horn. Damn this summer traffic!

Dr. Wang had spoken to Emma after Penny's appointment, as she always did, but she'd gone on longer than usual. Emma tried to pay attention while the doctor talked, but she kept checking the time. She appreciated Dr. Wang keeping her in the loop, showing her the exercises Penny was supposed to be doing that week, but all she could think was that it was close to three, and the happy-hour crowd would be arriving soon.

She dropped Penny off in front of the house on Mount Misery.

"Okay if I sleep at Robin's tonight?" Penny said.

Distracted, in a rush, Emma said fine.

By the time she was back behind the desk, the reservation book was covered with Post-it note messages for reservations, and the lobby was full of people waiting for spots to open up at the bar. Chris had left her a list of bottles of wine to pull from the cellar, one with the note that said *ASAP.*

"The American Hotel, Emma speaking," she said, wincing at how out of breath she sounded.

"Emma, it's Jack. Come see me in the office, please."

She knew the appointment had taken too long.

As she walked to the back of the first floor, her mind raced with apologies. When she sat down across from Jack, she was shaking.

"I'm sorry I took such a long break. I had to get Penny to her therapy appointment, which usually falls on my day off, but the schedule is different because you asked me to take those days off last week, so it was just not great timing. I'll take care of everything that needs to be done."

Jack squeezed the brim of his Delta Marine baseball hat with both hands and sighed deeply. His facial expression said, *This is going to hurt me more than it hurts you.* And that's when she knew she was in big trouble.

"I didn't call you in here because you left the desk this afternoon. I'm more troubled by complaints that you got into a loud personal argument in the lobby early this morning."

The conversation with Mark? Had it been

that noisy? She'd checked around, and the lobby had been empty. Had people heard them from their rooms? The bar?

"Oh, I'm sorry, Jack. My ex-husband showed up. I tried to get him to leave as quickly as possible."

Jack shook his head. "This is a place where people come to relax. To be taken care of and to feel a sense of privacy. I work very hard to cultivate and maintain that in every detail of this hotel. Emma, I care about you as a person, but my priority has to be my business. You're missing days at work, you're late for work, and, as I told you before, I don't want drama around here. And since you seem incapable of keeping the drama away, I'm going to have to ask you to leave."

"You mean for the day?"

"No, Emma. I mean that the recent changes in your personal life have made it problematic for you to act as a steward of this hotel. Regretfully, I need to let you go."

It struck Bea that Mark Mapson was quite the operator — the flattery, the obsequiousness, the soft-selling. If she hadn't been so interested in what he had to say, she would have gotten great pleasure in throwing him out as quickly as she'd let him in. But she was very, very interested.

At the kitchen table, she poured herself another cup of iced green tea. Mark Mapson had declined her offer of a beverage.

"I would be a much more effective executor of my daughter's estate than my ex-wife, who, let's face it, is a glorified hostess. This is serious business, and she is in way over her head. But at the same time, I'm obviously a less qualified representative for Henry Wyatt's art than *you* are."

"Indeed. So what is your point?"

"I'm thinking of how to remedy this situation. First, I need to gain some legal standing to take control of my daughter's inheritance, and once I do, and after Penny turns eighteen, I'm happy to work out a deal with you for the sale of this house and other pieces of his estate. Minus my commission."

"When Penny turns eighteen, she, not her parents, will have control over this estate. So I don't see how you can make any promises."

"Eighteen-year-olds don't want to be stuck in some big house in the middle of nowhere. They want to move on from the place where they were raised no matter how fancy the digs. And financial security for the rest of her life will be a big motivator to sell. My daughter is not stupid."

"And neither am I. Why are you coming

to me now? This conversation is four years down the road, the way I see it. *If* it even comes to that."

"In the short term, I need money to pay lawyers."

"Money from me?"

He nodded.

"Mr. Mapson, I'm paying my own lawyers, and they are busy working on the very strong possibility this will isn't valid."

"Well, in that case, look at this as insurance. If the will isn't valid, you've got your lawyers on the case. If the will *is* valid, I'll have my lawyer on it. Either way, you win."

Oh, he was an operator, all right. But this might be an easy way to fight the battle on an entirely new front.

"I need to think about this," she said, standing. "I'll see you out."

CHAPTER THIRTY

The party at Mindy's house was twice the size of the one on Memorial Day weekend, and Penny instantly knew she'd done the right thing by showing up. To miss it would have been social suicide.

All the usual suspects were there — Robin, Jess, and the other basics from her grade — but also Mindy's sister, Jordan, and Jordan's friends, who were rising seniors; Mateo and his friends; and Mateo's older brother.

"So you're the one who got the artist's house?"

Penny glanced around to make sure the superhot guy — maybe the best-looking guy she'd ever seen — was actually talking to *her.*

He was.

"I'm into art," the boy said. "Henry Wyatt was a legend. Are you related to him or something?"

"Um, no." And then, realizing he was

waiting for more, she said, "I'm into art too, and he gave me lessons. We were friends."

He seemed about to say something, but then Jordan Banks slid over and looped her arm through his. She then proceeded to yell at Mindy to get her friends outside or upstairs. "Out of my face!"

Mindy herded Penny, Robin, and Jess up the stairs and into her parents' room.

"There are so many people here," Penny said.

"Wait until the Fourth of July," Mindy said. "That will be epic."

Another party. A summer of parties!

"When are you having us over to your house?" Mindy said.

Uh-oh. "Soon," Penny said, wondering how she was going to pull that off.

"Maybe *you* should have a Fourth of July party," said Mindy. "That way we could have our own thing without Jordan ruining it by being a total bee-atch."

The master suite had a big terrace with a professional-looking telescope; there was a Jacuzzi in the bathroom and a nearly movie-theater-size TV screen on the wall. But Mindy wasn't interested in any of these entertainment options — she headed right for the medicine cabinet.

"Party favors," she said, passing around a

prescription bottle of Percocet. "Then we go outside. If Jordan's kicking us out of the house, we'll just take over the deck."

Penny swallowed one of the pills with a swig of her Diet Coke, then followed Mindy, Jess, and Robin downstairs to the back deck. She settled onto a chaise longue and waited for the warm buzz of the medication to wash through her. After a while, Penny looked up in the darkness to find Robin looming over her.

"Come on — we're going on the boat."

"I'm fine right here," Penny said. *Fine* was an understatement. She didn't know if it was the music (Rihanna, "Hate That I Love You"), the breeze off the bay, or the winking lights of all the party yachts in the distance, but it felt like maybe the best night of her life.

"You're not fine where you are. You're just high. Let's go."

Robin grabbed her hand and pulled her to her feet. "Come on — I don't want them to leave without us."

Penny ran alongside her to the short dock where the Bankses parked their speedboat. It was white with a navy canvas roof over the helm and *The Adventurer* written in navy-blue script on the stern. There were two seats at the controls, already filled by

Jordan and her boyfriend. Behind that was a curved, upholstered banquette that could seat maybe eight people. In the middle was a small white table with a drink holder in each corner.

"Design brilliance," someone said, sticking a beer bottle in one holder.

To the side there was a small sink and standing room for a few more people.

"Mindy, get your loser friends off. It's too crowded."

"Who made you the boss?" Mindy called from a corner of the banquette.

"The captain is, by definition, the boss! Ever hear of fucking maritime law?"

Penny laughed. Everything was funny. Everything was perfect. She looked up and saw a million stars in the sky. The universe was smiling at her.

The motor rumbled to life and someone cast off the lines. Penny grabbed the railing as the boat lurched out of the slip. Water sprayed her face and she laughed giddily.

A bunch of kids sitting around the table laughed and shouted back and forth. The only people Penny recognized were Mindy and Robin. Jess wasn't on board. Somehow, she hadn't made the cut and Penny had. Was this decision Robin's call or Mindy's? And, really, did it matter? No. She was there on the boat in that glorious moment. She wanted to memorize everything about it, to take a mental snapshot so that when she was stuck at home feeling miserable, she could pull it out and remember what it felt like to be happy. Was that the sort of thing Dr. Wang had been trying to teach her to do? To manage her thoughts? For once, everything made sense. When she was feeling bad, she could think about what this moment had felt like and then superimpose that positive feeling onto her bad ones. Like cutting and pasting emotions. As simple as that. Why hadn't she realized this before?

Music played on someone's phone but you could barely hear it over the motor. She watched someone from the banquette pass Jordan a beer and wondered if drinking while driving a boat was as bad as drinking while driving a car. But the worry was fleeting. How could she worry? She was free.

"Okay, we're going back and your friends are getting off so we can pick up more people. Next trip out is seniors only," Jordan called to Mindy. More squabbling ensued as the boat circled around and headed back to the house. The boat seemed to pick up speed even as the dock came in sight.

"Slow down!" someone yelled.

Penny felt the first trickle of alarm. She tried not to panic, telling herself there was plenty of time for Jordan to reduce the boat's speed before it reached the dock.

Until, very quickly, there wasn't.

Emma sat on a bench on the dock, staring out at the boats in the distance. Next to her, Alexis finished eating a cup of frozen yogurt and checked her phone.

"Sean texted he's just a minute away," she said.

Emma nodded morosely. Alexis reached over, the gesture made musical by the half a dozen silver bangle bracelets on her wrist clinking together. She was dressed in a flowing batik sundress and wore a straw hat over her long, pink-tinged blond hair. Alexis had an enviable millennial-flower-child look that was effortless and beautiful. And she had a personality to match. She was a decade younger than Emma but had become a close friend in the past year or so. And Emma knew Penny liked spending time in the bookstore and looked up to Alexis. Henry was gone, but at least there was someone still around for Penny to talk to about books and art.

Alexis moved the paper bag holding their six-packs from the ground onto the bench.

She pulled out a beer. "Do you want to start without him?"

"I wish that would help," Emma said.

"So what, exactly, did Jack say?"

"It was something like 'Your personal life has made it a problem for you to work at this hotel. I need to let you go.' "

Alexis put her arm around her. "He can't mean it. After all this time? You come in late a few times and have one argument in the lobby? He's just having a bad day."

"No," Emma said. "You know how he is. There's no margin for error this time of year. And he hates the press. He prides himself on the privacy of the place. I'm attracting the wrong kind of attention to it. I'm a liability."

"Okay, but all of this will die down. It's temporary."

"The damage is done. He doesn't trust me anymore."

The bright light of Sean's launch signaled his approach. When he pulled into the dock, a middle-aged couple disembarked before Emma and Alexis boarded.

"Do you have to bring those people back somewhere later?" Alexis asked.

"No, they're staying in town. I'm done for the night."

"In that case . . ." Alexis handed him a beer.

Emma popped open her beer, sat down in the boat, and looked up at the stars.

"We just have to wait for Kyle," Sean said.

"Kyle?" Emma turned around to look at him.

"Yeah. He's doing some woodwork across the dock for a guy who's going to fix his motor. I'm giving him a lift back to his boat."

"Ugh," Emma said. "The last person I need to see is him."

"What's the problem? He's a decent guy."

"Is he? You know that he's essentially squatting at my house along with Bea Winstead."

"Trust me — that guy isn't interested in some mansion. All he cares about is the water," Sean said.

"Great. Then he can go live with you." She chugged her beer.

Sean glanced at Alexis with a look that said, *What's with her?*

Emma, feeling bad that she was being cranky, started telling him about losing her job. But before she could get into it, someone shouted from the dock. Emma saw that it was the harbormaster, and he was running toward the boat.

"Sean! I was just about to radio. There's been an accident. Ride with me."

The harbormaster was bald with a trim white beard, tall, and broad-shouldered; he carried with him the air of authority and the faint whiff of cigar smoke.

"What happened?" Sean said.

"A bunch of people went joyriding and plowed into a private dock."

Sean looked apologetically at Alexis.

"It's fine, hon — go," she said. "I'll take a cab home."

Sean and the harbormaster jumped onto a speedboat and disappeared into the night. Alexis and Emma stood on the dock looking after them, Alexis holding the remaining beer.

"Summer people are so irresponsible," Alexis said. "Sean gets calls every day to help tow people off of rocks."

"Ridiculous," Emma said, shaking her head. "Well, it's still early. Do you want to grab a drink at Murf's?"

Alexis glanced at her phone. "I think I'm going to call it a night and just wait for Sean to get home. You going to be okay?"

"I'm fine," Emma said.

Alexis waved to someone over Emma's shoulder. "Here comes your favorite person."

Kyle crossed the dock carrying a toolbox and with a knapsack over his shoulder. He wore faded jeans and a T-shirt that hugged his torso. He had a sunburn.

"Hey," he said to Alexis with a quick nod to Emma. "Is Sean on his way? I've been texting him but haven't heard back."

"We were just with him but the dockmaster needed help with something. Sorry about that."

Alexis gave Emma a quick good-night hug before taking off. Emma stood awkwardly on the dock with Kyle. A cabin cruiser pulled in across the dock, music blasting. The moment was vexing enough without the added indignity of Katy Perry's "California Gurls."

"You heading back to the house?" Kyle said.

"No."

"Want to grab a drink?"

"With you? No, thanks."

CHAPTER THIRTY-ONE

Murf's was crowded. Emma took a corner stool under a string of pink and red Christmas lights. At the other end of the bar, Katie Cleary poured a row of Jaeger shots for three guys and knocked one back herself.

"What are you having?" Kyle said from the seat next to her. Despite her initial protests, she hadn't been ready to go home and deal with the reality of losing her job. She wanted company — even if that company was irksome Kyle Dunlap. And, frankly, she needed more than a beer.

"Shot of Tito's."

"Going for the hard stuff tonight?" he said.

"It's been that kinda day."

"Sorry to hear it. Does your less-than-stellar mood have anything to do with your ex being in town?"

She looked at him. "What do you know about that?"

"He was at the house the other day. With Penny."

Was that true? How could Penny have kept that from her? "Damn it," she muttered.

"Seems like a bit of a jerk, if you ask me," Kyle said.

"I didn't."

Katie passed Emma's shot and Kyle's beer across the bar.

"Bring me one more, Katie? Thanks," Emma said.

"Um, maybe the next one should be club soda?" Kyle said.

"Spare me. I'm fine." Emma watched Katie. The way she handled the bottles, the way she flicked her wrist to end a pour, triggered Emma's own muscle memory of her time behind the bar. "I've known the bartender since she was younger than my daughter."

"Oh, is she older than your daughter?" Kyle joked.

Emma didn't crack a smile. "I was tending this bar when I was her age. Nothing's changed in this place. And in ten years, it might be Penny back there." She shook her head. "Penny's right about this town. It's hard to leave, but it's hard to stay."

"It seems like a great place to raise a kid,"

he said, picking their drinks up off the bar. "Let's take these over there," he said, nodding to a table by the door.

"Why?"

"I'm in the mood to beat someone at darts," he said.

"Please. I've been playing darts here so long, I can hit the bull's-eye blindfolded." And then she remembered the first night she saw him at Murf's, the night her game was off, and the way his casual toss of the dart landed right on the mark.

"I am open to that handicap," he said.

Emma's phone rang. She squinted at the incoming number and answered it.

"Hello?"

"Emma, it's Jim DiMartino. Penny's been in an accident."

She jumped up, losing her balance.

Kyle reached for her arm. "Are you okay?"

She waved him off and ran outside to hear Jim DiMartino better. With her head cloudy from alcohol, it took an effort for her to process the details: A party. A boat. Drinking.

"I'll be right there," she told him and ended the call.

"What's wrong?" Kyle said, startling her. She hadn't realized he'd followed her outside.

"Oh my God," she said. "I need my keys. I need . . . damn it! I can't drive."

"I can drive," Kyle said. "Where do you need to go?"

"Southampton Hospital," she said.

There was no traffic at that hour of night. Emma was thankful Kyle didn't try to talk to her during the twenty-five-minute drive that felt like two hours. He did, however, pat her leg in some effort to comfort her as she sobbed.

"She's going to be fine," he said. And it was true; Jim had said Penny's injuries were not life-threatening, maybe a few broken bones. "She was very lucky."

Maybe a few broken bones!

Kyle pulled up to the entrance. "I'll meet you in there after I park," he said.

"No — no. I've got it from here. Please. You should go." She closed the door on his protests.

Inside, a woman at the information desk directed her to the emergency department, where a nurse sent her to a waiting room.

"A doctor will be out as soon as possible to speak with you."

A bunch of other people were in the waiting area, a large room with couches and tables filled with magazines and wide win-

343

dows facing the interior hallway. Emma spotted Robin McMaster's mother and father. Emma sat as far away from them as possible and grabbed a copy of *Time* magazine to hide behind. She didn't want to talk to anyone.

Sitting alone, she realized there was one person she couldn't avoid talking to; she had to call Mark and let him know that Penny was in the hospital. After all, he was — as he'd made such a big point of saying — her father. She'd told him she'd keep him in the loop. Now she had to make good on that promise.

She walked out of the waiting room for a more private spot in the hallway, dialed his number, and, thankfully, got his voice mail.

"Mark, I hate to leave a message like this but I wanted to let you know that Penny was in an accident. A . . . boating accident. She's going to be fine but she's at Southampton Hospital. I haven't seen her yet but when I do I'll call you with an update. Okay . . . bye." She looked up to see that Kyle, completely disregarding her instructions, was heading toward her.

"What are you doing here?"

"I'm not leaving you alone. You'll need a ride back. I drove you here in your car, remember?"

What a night to decide to get drunk.

He followed her to the waiting area. She sat in the same seat as before and he offered to go find a coffee machine.

"That would be great," she said.

She watched the door. A woman in a white coat opened it and called out a name; a couple jumped up and followed the doctor into the hallway.

Kyle returned with two Styrofoam cups filled with weak coffee.

"This waiting is impossible," she said.

"Do you want me to check and see what's going on?"

She shook her head. "I already asked."

"Ask again. The squeaky wheel gets the grease and all that."

Maybe he was right. Still, after years of working at the hotel front desk, Emma hated to hassle people while they were just doing their job. But this was about Penny, and she couldn't waste time being polite.

She went up to the nurses' station and said, "I'm sorry, but I need to check in again. Penny Mapson? Any word on her?"

The nurse looked up wearily and told her they were doing the best they could. "We're treating over a half a dozen patients from this incident, so please, just be patient. The doctors will speak to everyone."

Emma told herself that maybe the waiting was a good sign — that Penny was basically fine and the doctors were busy with more serious issues. Not that she wished anyone else's child harm. But she had to find some way to deal with the fact that her child was somewhere around here and she couldn't see her.

She returned to the waiting room. Time crawled by until a nurse finally called out, "Mrs. Mapson?"

Emma nearly jumped out of her skin. Kyle stood up with her.

"Please, just wait here," she told him.

In the hallway, she was met by a reed-thin man with dark olive skin and rimless glasses. His narrow face appeared young but his hair was threaded with gray.

"I'm Dr. Saroyen," he said, shaking her hand. "Your daughter is going to be fine. Her leg is broken, but luckily it's not an open fracture."

"Okay," Emma said, nodding. "A broken leg."

"A fractured tibia. She won't require surgery, and the orthopedist is splinting her leg now."

"Emma!"

She looked up. Mark was striding down the hallway, dressed in jeans and a sports jacket. *Talk about things going from bad to worse.*

"Mark, this is Dr. Saroyen. Doctor, this is Penny's father."

The doctor repeated the information to Mark. When he finished, Emma asked if she could see her.

"Yes, but before you do, there is one more thing. It was clear that several of the teenagers on the boat were intoxicated at the time of the accident. I asked your daughter before I administered pain medication if she had been drinking or taken any drugs. She admitted she had taken a Percocet earlier in the evening."

"A *what*?" Emma said. It was a rhetorical question, but the doctor went on to explain that it was an opioid. As if she didn't know — all too well. She pushed away thoughts of her mother.

"Where the hell did she get that?" Mark said, looking at Emma.

"Not in our house! You know how I feel about prescription drugs."

"Please," the doctor said. "This is an important issue but one that should wait for another time. I know Penny is anxious to see you."

They followed him down the bright corridor.

"You reek of alcohol," Mark said.

Oh, how she regretted calling him!

Dr. Saroyen opened the door into a room divided by a curtain. Penny was on the far side, sitting on a table, while a woman, presumably the orthopedist, wrapped her leg with a wet, bright pink bandage. Penny's hair was frizzy and wild, and she had a bruise on her cheek. Emma's heart ached. She hugged Penny, apologizing to the doctor, although she didn't care if she was interrupting the splinting. She began to cry.

"I'm okay, Mom," Penny said.

The doctor asked Emma to step aside so she could get the splint finished.

Mark paced in the room. Emma shot him a look, willing him not to get into the drug thing. Not now.

After the doctor finished the splint, she told them she would be back to check on Penny in fifteen or thirty minutes.

"And then I can go home?" Penny said.

"Yes, then you can go," the doctor said. "But you have to stop by the desk for the discharge paperwork. And, Mom, I'll put the cast on when the swelling goes down, so I'll need to see her again in a few days — this splint is temporary. Once she's got the cast on, no powder and no lotion on the leg. No sticking anything inside the cast,

348

even if it feels itchy. I'll give you written instructions for showering."

"How long will she be wearing the cast?" Mark asked.

"Six to eight weeks. Have you ever used crutches before?" she asked Penny. Penny shook her head. "You'll get the hang of it." The doctor turned to Emma and Mark. "The biggest adjustment will be inside the home. No stairs."

"How am I going to get to my room?" Penny said.

Maybe you should have thought of that before you took drugs and went joyriding, Emma thought, surprised at the flash of anger. Now that the immediate emergency was under control, she was flooded with conflicting emotions. "I'll be back in a minute, sweetheart," Emma said. "I'm just going to take care of the paperwork."

Mark followed her silently to the nurses' station.

Her mind turned to logistics. How was Penny going to get around all summer? What would she do all day? Angus would have to help her up and down the front steps of the historical society. She wouldn't even be able to get in and out of Buddha-Berry by herself. Now, instead of Penny helping Angus, Angus would have to babysit

Penny. It wasn't right.

Then Emma shifted the blame from Penny to herself. Maybe this was her own fault. From the way Mark was looking at her, she figured she wasn't the only one thinking that.

She ignored him, took a clipboard full of papers from the nurse, and signed everything. Kyle must have spotted her from the waiting room across the hall because he appeared holding the handbag she hadn't even realized she'd left behind.

"What's he doing here?" Mark said.

"He's a friend," Emma said.

Mark gave Kyle the side-eye, then said, "Penny should come home with me. My rental is a single level. Penny won't have to deal with stairs until she gets the hang of those crutches."

Emma's breath caught in her chest. "Don't be ridiculous. Penny is coming home with me. We'll figure it out."

"There's no need to be territorial here, Emma. I'm just trying to do what is best for Penny tonight."

"I think I know what's best for Penny," Emma said.

"You're hardly in any condition to make that call."

"Actually," Kyle said, stepping closer to

Emma, "Windsong has everything Penny needs on the first floor. So I'll drive you there."

Emma smiled at him gratefully. "That's a good idea." She didn't know if it was or it wasn't — the last thing she needed tonight was to deal with Bea Winstead on top of everything else. But at least it shut down Mark's case for taking Penny. And at that moment, all she wanted was to get her daughter out of the hospital and escape the judgmental glare of her ex-husband.

What could Bea Winstead do to her, anyway?

CHAPTER THIRTY-TWO

Bea awoke with a start to the sound of voices.

At first, she thought she'd imagined it, the patter of a dream seeping into her waking moments. But the conversation grew more distinct, and she sat up. Was she hearing what she thought she was hearing?

Kyle. And a woman.

Was he out of his mind? This was no place for his lady friends.

She put on her glasses, her silk robe, and her slippers and quietly slid open her bedroom door. From the top of the stairway landing, she heard the voices more clearly, and it was even worse than she'd thought. With her pulse racing in outrage, Bea rushed down the stairs to find Kyle and Emma Mapson in the kitchen. The woman seemed right at home and was making herself a pot of tea.

"What is going on here?" Bea said. "It's

the middle of the night!"

Emma calmly poured tea into one of Henry's vintage mugs, glancing at Kyle. "I'm sorry we woke you. We're all going to sleep now."

"All going to sleep now? Why are you even *here*?"

"Bea, come on," Kyle said. "Don't start."

"Penny had an accident. She broke her leg and we're staying here because she can't use the stairs at our other house. Again, I didn't mean to wake you. But this is our house now, and you should be leaving."

She should be leaving?

"I'm sorry to hear about your daughter's misfortune," Bea said. "But that does not give you license to barge in here at this hour."

"Emma, you've had a long night," Kyle said after glaring at Bea. "Try to get some sleep. I'm just down the hall if you need anything."

"I'll be fine. Thanks for everything." Emma shuffled out of the kitchen.

Bea watched the exchange incredulously. What was going on here?

Kyle opened the refrigerator and pulled out a beer. "Bea, enough is enough."

"Whose side are you on? This is outrageous. Did you give me two weeks' notice just so you could sabotage me? Is there no loyalty left in this world?"

The girl had had an accident, and that was unfortunate. But children got into all sorts of messes — again, she'd chosen not to deal with that in her life. And she wasn't about to start now. The bottom line was that broken bones would heal in a matter of weeks. If she lost Henry's legacy, it would be gone forever.

"I am not trying to sabotage you," Kyle said. "I was all for helping you recover the estate of Henry Wyatt. But come on. How long are you going to play this game? These are decent people. Emma barely has the energy to deal with her job and her kid. You think she masterminded some swindle? I can't believe you really think that."

"I showed you his will from 2000. That was a major breakthrough on this."

He shook his head. "I don't agree. The guy had a different will in 2017 than he did in 2000. He changed his mind. It happens all the time."

She expected this from strangers — from people in this myopic town who cared more about a burned-down movie theater than about the fate of a priceless estate. But she'd thought she could count on Kyle, if for no other reason than he was on her payroll!

Oh, the betrayal.

"I want you out of here tomorrow!"

The surprised expression on his face gave her a bit of satisfaction. But not enough. Not nearly enough.

She whirled around and headed up the stairs, wired with so much adrenaline she felt ten years younger. She'd never fall back to sleep.

Back in her room, with her door closed against the invasion, she paced with impotent rage. This fight was not over. But what more could she do?

And then, with a glance at her phone on her nightstand, she recognized her next move. She rummaged through her handbag and found the business card that he had handed her earlier that day.

Then she texted Mark Mapson that she would gladly write him a check for his legal fees.

The pain in her leg woke her up. *Ow,* that hurt!

It was still dark. Penny reached for the Advil and water her mother had left by the bed and swallowed two of the pills. Her mother said if she needed her during the night she should text her, but Penny didn't want to do that. It made her feel like a baby, and it would compound her already heaping pile of guilt.

Now she'd really done it. Why, oh, why hadn't she just stayed home last night? Or why, when Robin said to come on the boat, didn't she just say no?

She reached for the light and was startled to find herself in the strange room. She'd completely forgotten she was at Windsong. The details of the night came rushing back to her: The hospital. Her dad being there. How strange to have him around after all this time.

The room was big and there was so much distance between her bed and the bathroom that she was afraid to attempt the trip on her own. She'd have to text her mother after all. She turned on her phone and it chirped with a flood of texts, all from Jess. Mindy had a concussion. Robin had a broken wrist and a fractured collarbone. Jess wasn't injured, but she was grounded for the rest of the summer.

Penny was going to be grounded for the rest of her life, probably. And she deserved it. In any case, she had to be on crutches for six to eight weeks. That took her to the middle of August, at least. The summer was over.

Penny shook her head. What a friggin'

disaster. And then, feeling like the biggest loser in the world, she texted her mom for help going to the bathroom.

Emma appeared, still dressed in the clothes she'd worn the night before. Had she fallen asleep in them? Penny felt a flash of shame for giving her mom such a hard time lately.

"Are you in pain?" Emma asked, serving as a human crutch to help her hobble to the bathroom.

"Yeah," Penny said. "How long does it take for the Advil to work?"

"Maybe twenty minutes."

When Penny was settled back in bed, Emma eased next to her and sat down on the edge.

"I'm sorry, Mom," Penny said, her eyes filling with tears.

Emma hugged her. "Okay. It's going to be okay." When she pulled back, she took a deep breath and said, "Penny, where did you get the drugs? And how long have you been taking them?"

Penny hesitated at first but then it all spilled out in a rush, as if she'd been dying to confess all along. It had started Memorial Day weekend; Mindy said the pills were harmless, that her mother took them "like Tic Tacs." And Penny didn't even feel that weird on them, just happier, and she didn't get caught in any of her OCD loops. "It was just a few times," she said.

"Maybe Dr. Wang is right," her mother said.

"No! This has nothing to do with Dr. Wang. Honestly, I don't even see the point of therapy. It doesn't really help. I keep telling myself I'll get back into drawing soon. When I was really busy with that, I felt a lot better."

Emma sighed. "Well, you can't be drawing every minute of the day."

"Now I can," Penny said with a smile.

Her mom gave a little laugh. "Yeah, well, can't argue with that." Emma tucked the comforter around her and kissed her forehead. She turned off the light. "Try to get a few more hours of sleep."

"Mom," Penny said in the darkness before Emma reached the door.

"Yes?"

"I love you."

CHAPTER THIRTY-THREE

The hospital bill would be astronomical. Not a great time to be unemployed.

Emma stood in front of the glass wall overlooking the infinity pool. The irony of being surrounded by opulence at a time when she felt financially vulnerable was not lost on her. Now she really had no money to waste on lawyers to fight Bea Winstead. It crossed her mind that she could simply call Jim at the station and see if he could make Bea leave on the grounds that she was trespassing. Of course, if Bea was trespassing, then so was Kyle. And, really, he had been a lifesaver last night.

The doorbell sounded, a delicate, melodic ping that was as unique and pleasant as the rest of the house. Henry Wyatt had overlooked no detail. Again, the question nagged at her: Why had he chosen Penny as his beneficiary?

Angus stood on the front stoop.

"I come bearing gifts," he said, handing her a straw basket full of treats from Schiavoni's Market and two graphic novels Emma recognized from Penny's bookshelf. "I brought these just in case she needed something to read. How's she doing?"

"She's sleeping, thankfully. Oh, Angus. Can you believe this?"

"It's going to be fine," he said in his deep, commanding voice.

"I know. But I'm caught between relief that her injuries weren't more serious and fury that she acted so recklessly. She's going to be on crutches all summer."

"She'll do anything to get out of working at the historical society." He smiled.

Emma unwrapped the basket in the kitchen. Penny wouldn't mind her taking off the cellophane and bow — easier access to the brownies and chocolate chip cookies. Emma opened a tin. "You really shouldn't have bought all of this," she said. "But Penny will love it. And I'm starving. There's no food here. From what I can tell by looking in the fridge, Bea Winstead lives on sparkling water and organic blueberries."

"Is the grande dame here?"

"No, she flew off on her broom earlier this morning."

"Emma, you don't need this aggravation.

We can make up the couch for Penny at home. And you've been saying for months you have to get the first-floor bathroom fixed anyway."

Emma pulled out a few Bosc pears and rinsed them in the sink. "Angus, I can't have the bathroom fixed right now. I'm in a bit of a bind. I lost my job. And if I don't find a new one soon, I'm going to have to give up the Mount Misery house to save the rent money. At least we can live here for free. And 'we' includes you."

Angus pulled out one of the stools next to the island and sat down. "It's true, there's no need to pay rent on Mount Misery when you have this place. But as I told you when we first started discussing this, I'm not comfortable in this big, strange house. It doesn't feel right."

"Angus —"

"Don't worry about me! Whatever you decide to do, I'll be fine."

Emma wanted to say that *she* wouldn't be fine. But she didn't want to push him for her own selfish needs. But what about —

"And I'll always be here for Penny," Angus added. He knew her too well.

"I don't want you to make a rushed decision on this," she said, her hands gripping the tin of baked goods like it was the steering wheel of an out-of-control car.

Angus reached for one of the brownies, announced that he absolutely shouldn't be eating it, then popped the whole thing into his mouth.

"Angus," she said. "I'm really hoping you'll reconsider."

He looked up at the ceiling, steepling his fingers. "Emma, when I was faced with losing Celia, I was more than happy to promise her that I'd move in with you and Penny, that I wouldn't be alone. Because the truth was, I was afraid of it myself. She was the one dying, but I felt like my life was over too. I realize now she didn't just want me to have company. She wanted me to go on with my life. I wasn't ready five years ago, and I'm not sure I'm ready now. But I can't be afraid of change. And neither can you."

Emma had gained a house but she felt like everything else that mattered to her was slipping away. And she had no idea how to turn things around.

It had been an expensive day, and despite all her wealth, Bea hated expensive days. First, she'd written a check to that no-good Mark Mapson. Then, after a long negotiation, she'd bought the drawings from the art gallery on Washington Street. That, at

362

least, had been worth every cent. Because now that she had them set out on the glass coffee table in the living room, she noticed something on the back of each one. A number.

"I *knew* it!"

She had been right all along — there was sequential meaning to the sketches. Now she would have to go back to the library and the museums to see if there were numbers on those drawings as well.

The unmistakable sound of the girl's crutches against the hardwood floor distracted her. What was she doing wandering around? Shouldn't she be in her room? There had to be some boundaries in this undesirable situation. The living room and dining areas were her territory.

More noise.

Oh, for heaven's sake. Bea gathered up the drawings to take them to the privacy of her room. On her way to the stairs, she spotted Penny balancing on one foot, propping her crutches against the breakfast table. One crutch teetered over and then crashed to the ground.

"You are going to scuff these floors!" Bea said.

The girl had a book pinned underneath her chin; she'd been trying to carry it

363

without using her hands. She lifted her head, and the book fell onto the table with a thud.

"Young lady, you must treat this house with more respect. You can't knock about with no regard for —"

Bea recognized the book on the table. It was the same cartoonish tome she had found in Henry's hidden drawer. A co-incidence?

"Did Mr. Wyatt give you that book?"

"No. I'm the one who told *him* about graphic novels." Penny maneuvered herself into a chair.

"You . . . told him about graphic novels. In what way?"

"I read them all the time and I showed him my favorites," she said, looking up at her. "He got pretty into it."

Bea felt her pulse quicken. Standing there, she realized having the little urchin under her roof might be a blessing in disguise. This girl might be the most important link to Henry she could find.

"Penny, did Mr. Wyatt give you any drawings?"

"Sure," she said. "He drew stuff for me all the time."

Bea tried to keep her voice measured. "May I see them?"

"No," the girl said.

"What? Why on earth not?"

"Because you'll try to take them away from me, just like you're trying to take away this house."

Out of the mouths of babes! "I promise I will not try to take them from you. I just want to see them. Mr. Wyatt was my friend for almost my entire life. More years than you can imagine being on this earth, probably. His work is all I have left of him. Do you understand that?"

"Of course," the girl said, her dark eyes steady. "It's all I have left of him too."

CHAPTER THIRTY-FOUR

Emma closed the sliding glass door behind her and carried her glass of wine to a chair by the pool. At close to eight at night, the air was cooling. And she had survived day one of Penny's broken leg.

She lit a citronella candle and settled in, looking out at the water and trying to calm her nerves by telling herself that at least Penny was sleeping comfortably. She seemed, all things considered, to be in good spirits. Emma wished she could say the same for herself.

"Hey. Sorry to disturb," Kyle said, walking down the stone steps and hoisting a duffel bag over his shoulder.

"Going somewhere?"

He gestured toward the bay. She wasn't sure what that meant. An evening swim?

"How's Penny doing?" he asked.

"Um, pretty well," she said, sitting up straight, zipping her sweatshirt up over her tank top. "She's getting the hang of the crutches and she doesn't seem to mind being housebound. At least, not in this house. It's still a novelty to her."

Kyle glanced back at Windsong. "And what about your uninvited guest?"

"So you admit this is rightfully Penny's property?" Emma said.

"I never said it wasn't."

Emma nodded. "That's true."

"I have to say, as far as Bea goes, her bark is probably worse than her bite. She's not a bad person. I think she's actually very lonely," Kyle said. "However, she did kick me out. So I guess she's not that lonely."

"Kicked you out? It's not even her house!"

"Clearly, a technicality that has not slowed her down."

Emma looked at him. "Kyle, don't take this the wrong way, but . . . what are you *doing* working for her?"

Kyle put his bag down and ran one hand through his hair. "It's complicated. I started out fixing things in her apartment, then doing art installations for her parties. And it just sort of . . . evolved." He smiled and snapped his fingers. "It's like your frog-in-boiling-water story."

She smiled.

"Anyway, this whole thing with the house

367

made me realize enough was enough. I quit. Although I guess she just fired me. Either way, it seems I'm moving on."

"So where are you going to stay?"

"My boat."

"Is that . . . safe?"

He laughed. "That's right. You don't have much faith in my restoration abilities."

She felt her cheeks color. "Sorry about what I said the other day. I didn't mean to be rude."

"Yes, you did. It's okay."

"I just see a lot of weekend warriors out here. Most don't go the distance."

Her phone rang. Mark. His second call of the day. His last voice mail said they needed to "discuss Penny." She had a feeling she knew the direction that discussion would go in — namely, putting all the blame on Emma for what happened. It wasn't a conversation she wanted to have and it wasn't a conversation that would help anything.

"Bad news?" Kyle said.

Was her expression that easy to read? "It's just my ex calling. Speaking of weekend warriors."

Kyle sat on the edge of a chaise. He pulled it closer to hers.

"Let me ask you something. When you're

not working or taking care of your daughter or dealing with your ex-husband or fighting a Park Avenue socialite over an estate . . . what do you do for fun, Emma Mapson?"

What did she do for fun? Emma thought about it, unnerved for a minute that she didn't have an answer. But then it came to her.

"I grow roses," she said, as pleased as if she'd just answered a game-show trivia question.

"That's cool. But it sounds kind of solitary. What do you do to get out, let off steam?"

His focus on her was starting to get embarrassing. It struck her, as he sat in the moonlight, his big blue eyes on her, that he was very attractive. She recalled that that had been her initial impression but somehow, it had gotten lost in all the Bea conflict.

"Kyle, I don't know. I'm fine, okay?"

He leaned back, running his hand through his hair and smiling.

"When I was a teenager, sometimes we'd run around at night in the summer and go pool-hopping," he said.

She smiled. "We did that too. My friends got busted once. It wasn't pretty."

"I always wished my parents had a pool."

"Me too. And look — now I have one."

"But you're not using it." He stood up. "Come on. We're going swimming."

"What? No. I'm tired. It's late."

Kyle ignored her and headed to the pool. He pulled off his T-shirt and jumped in.

"Isn't it freezing?"

"No! It's perfect. Bea turned the heat on."

Maybe as long as Bea was claiming the house, she could also claim the utility bills.

"What are you waiting for?" he called from the shallow end.

"I told you, it's late."

"Do I have to come out there and throw you in?"

"I strongly advise you not to do that," she said.

"That sounds like a dare."

He pulled himself out of the water and headed for her.

"Kyle, seriously," she said, laughing nervously when he reached her chair.

"Last chance to do this the easy way," he said, holding out his hand.

"I'm not going in."

"Oh, you're going in." He leaned over and scooped her up. Water dripped onto her sweatshirt.

"Put me down!" she yelled.

"You're going to wake up the whole house," he said. It was true; she imagined

Bea dressed in some absurdly lavish night-gown running out to reprimand them.

"Come on, this isn't funny," she said as he held her over the deep end.

"Then why are you smiling?"

She didn't want to admit it, but she did feel the pull of the water, the sudden urge to let go for once. "Fine, maybe it's a little funny."

With that, Kyle dropped her into the water and jumped in after her.

The water was, as promised, the perfect temperature. It was cooler than the night air but not jarring. As she surfaced, she felt her heart pounding, her muscles contracting. She reached for the ledge and wiped water from her eyes. "Are you happy now?" she said.

"Are you?" he asked.

She glanced up and saw that he was being literal. Then she looked up higher, to the stars in the clear night sky. She slipped back under the water and glided to the shallow end. Her entire body groaned with unfamiliar effort, and it felt good. Kyle swam over to her.

"Race you back."

"You'll lose!"

He took off and she followed, kicking furiously.

Yes, she thought, pushing through the water in the moonlight. *For the moment, I'm happy.*

All day and into the evening, Bea burned with the news that Penny had Henry's drawings at her house. She tried to forget about it, tried to tell herself she could work on changing Penny's mind about sharing them with her. But alone in her bedroom, she knew she wouldn't sleep. The numbered sketches from the art gallery were set out on the dresser, and she itched to fill in the blanks with the others he had left behind.

She thought of Angus and then hesitated only a minute before calling him. "Sorry to bother you at this hour, but there's something I need to discuss."

He said it wasn't a bother and gave her his address. Mount Misery Drive? Who on earth would name a street that?

Without Kyle in her employ, she was forced to drive herself the twenty minutes to the dilapidated two-story house. It had worn wood siding and a mulch-covered driveway — not even paved. Above the front door, a blue wooden whale hung from small hooks, the only source of color in a rather barren tableau.

Angus appeared behind the screen door

before she rang the bell.

"I heard the car," he said by way of greeting. He held open the door and she stepped inside. "Is everything okay at the house?" he asked, concerned.

"I didn't mean to alarm you. There's no problem at all. It's more that I have an opportunity for you."

She walked into the living room and took in the worn couch and the local newspapers scattered on the scuffed wooden chest alongside it. And yet the small, rather dull room was accented with vases filled with remarkably vibrant yellow roses. They drew Bea deeper into the space, and she noticed an array of photos in handmade frames on the fireplace mantel. Some of the frames were made out of seashells; one had been constructed out of Popsicle sticks. Most of the photos were of Penny, but several featured a surprisingly familiar face — the man in Henry's drawings.

The bartender.

Bea picked up the frame and stared at the picture.

"Angus," she said slowly. "Why does Emma have a photo of the old American Hotel bartender?"

"That's Tom Kirkland. Emma's father."

Bea looked up sharply. *What?* Was that

what this was all about? The damn bartender he'd befriended all those decades ago?

Her impulse was to ask if the man was still in town, to try to talk to him. But then she recalled that the bartender had died suddenly many years ago. Thinking about it now, she could remember the phone call from a bereft Henry.

Bea placed the photo back on the mantel, trying to think. So what had happened? Henry made a friend, lost him shortly thereafter, and then, decades later, met his granddaughter and decided to leave her his entire estate? She refused to accept that. It couldn't be! No, this was just a red herring. She had come for the drawings, and she would not be side-tracked.

At least she knew she had come to the right place. There were answers to be found in this house.

"As you know, I've been scouring the town for any drawings Henry did in the year leading up to his death. Today I learned that Penny has some here in this house. I need to see them."

"She told you where she keeps them?" Angus said.

"No, not exactly."

"Well, I don't want to take it upon myself

to guess. I can call her in the morning and find out. I'm sorry you wasted a trip over here. This will just have to wait until tomorrow."

Bea put her hand on his arm. "Penny isn't being cooperative. But if you can just show me to her bedroom, I'm sure I can find them."

He looked at her in a way that was decidedly less congenial than seconds before. "I can't do that, Bea."

"Why on earth not? She's just a child. This is an adult matter and she's playing games. I can't believe you want to be a party to that."

"This is Emma's house, Bea. I can't let you go rooting around in it."

"And Windsong should be my house, but no one seems to care about that!" she said. "Really, Angus. I thought we were . . . on friendly terms."

"We are. And I've tried to stay neutral over this matter."

"You're not being neutral. You're being an obstructionist." She walked to the hallway and he blocked her path.

"Bea, I'm going to have to ask you to leave."

CHAPTER THIRTY-FIVE

Penny watched Bea with intense focus. She was such a great subject with her big jewelry and even bigger attitude. Penny moved the pencil in long strokes to establish Bea's body before attempting to sketch her facial features, willing herself not to give in to the voice in her head telling her the outline wasn't right, that she should start over.

"Didn't your mother ever tell you it's not polite to stare?" Bea said, moving around the kitchen, opening and closing the cabinet doors like she was searching for something.

"Artists have to observe. Right?" Penny said.

Bea looked at her. She started to say something, then stopped.

The idea to try to finish the graphic novel she'd started with Henry last summer came to her in the middle of the night. It was as if Henry himself had sat on the edge of her bed and whispered, *Do it!* But earlier that morning, when she looked through her old sketches, they'd seemed really childish and not at all what she wanted to say anymore. She didn't want to write about girls with superpowers. Now she had a real story to tell — the story of Henry, of the house, and of Bea Winstead trying to take it away.

"Young lady, just because you had the good fortune to meet the greatest artist of the past half century doesn't make *you* an artist. You're a child."

Penny switched pencils. "Henry said he started drawing when he was six. He always knew he was an artist."

"Indeed." Bea sniffed.

Kyle walked in and Penny felt the dark cloud of Bea's attention shift.

"Morning, Bea," he said.

"What are you still doing here?"

Penny observed Kyle reaching for the coffee. How old was he? Maybe her mom's age. Maybe younger? He wore a faded gray and blue T-shirt with a fire department logo on it and dark blue shorts. Penny would have to include him in her story too. She just wasn't sure how, exactly, he fit into it. Kyle had come to town with Bea; he lived with her at the house. But Bea was yelling at him to get out.

"I slept on the boat last night. Technically,

I'm not staying here. But frankly, I need coffee and I probably have about as much of a right to stand in this kitchen as you do."

"Oh, so now you're a lawyer? How dare you tell me what rights I do or don't have?" She turned to Penny. "And that also goes for you and your mother!"

Penny looked down at her sketch pad and drew a dialogue bubble. She filled it with *And that also goes for you and your mother!*

Yes, Penny had an awesome story to tell.

She just had no idea how it was going to end.

Emma was tired. She'd stayed up far too late, but her exhaustion was a small price to pay for such a delightful night.

The impromptu pool party had lasted well into the early hours of the morning. After she lost the first lap race, Kyle climbed out of the pool and mixed them both whiskey sours at Henry Wyatt's amply stocked bar.

They drank standing chest-deep in the pool, talking until Emma realized she'd be useless in the morning if she didn't get some sleep.

Yet why couldn't she let herself be useless for one day? Penny didn't have any appointments, and there was no job for Emma to get to. Yes, at some point she needed to start looking for one, but she wasn't ready to let go of her old job. The American Hotel was more than just a paycheck to her, always had been. There had to be a way to regain Jack's confidence, to prove to him she was still the reliable person he'd hired a dozen years earlier. When she'd told Sean about getting fired, he'd said Jack was loyal but he also got spooked easily. "You have to remember, the hotel always comes first."

There was nothing she could do immediately, and while it frustrated her, it forced her to think about what she could fix. For one thing, if they were going to live at Windsong for the foreseeable future, she needed a way to make it feel more like a home. She needed to put her stamp on it, and there was only one way she could think of to do that.

Outside, she stepped off the stone path leading to the pool and walked around the back lawn. The area was meticulously landscaped, with low-growing perennials and a bunch of blue-rug juniper — probably for deer control — surrounding a few blockish metal sculptures. She would have to carefully consider where a rose garden would fit in; she didn't want to ruin the balance of Henry's strong aesthetic. She was concerned, too, about the ground. This close to the beach, the soil would be sandier than what she was used to working with on Mount Misery. Sandy soil would drain before the roots of her roses could get hydrated.

"Emma?"

She turned, cupping her hands over her eyes and squinting against the late-morning sun. Kyle stood on the front walk, waving her over. The sight of him made her stomach jump in a funny way — a way she hadn't felt in a very long time. Was this a good thing? Bad? Maybe best not to overthink it.

"Hey," she said, going over to him. "How was your first night on the boat?"

"Slept like a baby. You?"

"I was a little restless."

They stared at each other for what felt like a long time before he glanced back at the house. "There's someone for you at the front door."

"Really? Who?"

"A man who seems very businesslike."

Who could it be? She wouldn't be surprised if it was Henry Wyatt's lawyer telling her there'd been a mistake after all.

The layout of Windsong made it quicker to reach the front door by walking through the house rather than around it. A quick peek out the window told her it was not Henry Wyatt's lawyer. She opened the door warily.

"Are you Emma Mapson?" the man said.

"Yes. How can I help you?"

He handed her a manila envelope and walked away. Strange. Closing the door, she examined the package. A stamp in the upper left corner read COUNTY CLERK'S OFFICE, SUFFOLK COUNTY.

Emma ripped open the envelope and pulled out a sheaf of papers. At the top of the first page were the words *Petition to Modify Custody Order.* She leaned against the door, heart pounding, reading as quickly as possible as she tried to absorb the information. It didn't make sense. She read and reread the words *Petitioner: Mark Mapson* and *Defendant: Emma Mapson.* It named the judge who had granted her sole physical custody of Penny thirteen years earlier. And then a paragraph detailing why *the best interests of the child(ren) will be served by the court in modifying the order.* There was technical wording like *material change of circumstances* and *child endangerment.*

Petitioner requests that the order be changed to provide as follows: Mark Mapson shall have sole legal custody of his minor child, Penelope Bay Mapson.

She must have let out a scream or a cry because Kyle came running from the other room, asking what was wrong. Shaking, she handed him the first page.

"Bastard," he muttered.

Emma started sobbing.

"I'm going to call Angus. Don't worry, it's going to be okay."

He put his arm around her and guided her to the living room. The space, with its skylight, a stone fireplace, and an entire wall of glass, usually felt very serene. It had a large Wyatt painting dominating one wall and a white oak floor, and at the foot of the couch there was a shag area rug and a set of floating bookshelves filled with hardcovers. But her anxiety level was so high, she might as well have been sitting in the middle of a four-lane highway.

"This can't be happening," she said. Kyle sat next to her. Mercifully, he didn't try to talk her out of being upset. He just let her sob quietly. She tried to pull it together but every time she calmed down for a second, the wording of the petition hit her fresh: *Material change of circumstance. Nonsupervision. Unstable home environment. Failure to follow the medical advice of mental-health pro-*

fessionals.

Bea walked into the room.

"So is this how it is? Everyone's just sitting around this house all day, living the life of leisure? Must be nice!"

"Bea, not now," Kyle said.

Undeterred, Bea sat in one of the structured chairs next to the asymmetric coffee table.

"Henry designed much of the furniture in this house," Bea said. "Not that I expect you to appreciate that." She got up and walked over to the large green and black painting. "Did you know that this piece, *Greene Street, 1972,* hung in the Guggenheim for several years?"

"I don't care about the art right now!" Emma snapped.

"Fine. Then let me say we need to discuss some boundaries around here. Your daughter seems to plant herself in whatever room I'm occupying and she's watching me like a hawk, doodling in that sketch pad of hers. It's unnerving and, frankly, quite rude."

The doorbell sounded.

"That must be Angus. I'll get it," Kyle said, going to the door.

"You invited that insufferable man to my house?"

Emma ignored her, wiping her eyes and

383

fighting fresh tears. Angus rushed into the room.

"I'm so sorry," he said, sitting next to her on the couch and patting her knee. His deep voice carried all the gravity of the situation.

"I can't believe it," she said, breaking down all over again.

"What on earth is going on here?" Bea said.

No one answered her, and when it was clear she wasn't going to take the hint and leave, Kyle finally said, "Her ex-husband is fighting her for custody of Penny."

Angus asked to see the petition.

"You're nobody until somebody sues you," Bea said.

"Bea, honestly. Not helpful," said Kyle. He turned to Emma. "None of what's in this petition will hold up."

"You don't know that," Emma said, shaking her head.

"It's just a landgrab," Angus said. "This is about the house."

"I can't prove that."

"He's been absent for over a decade, and now he's here a month after Penny inherits a multimillion-dollar estate," Angus said.

"A judge won't care about that. He's going to read these complaints against me — and they look really bad."

Bea sighed. "I've been around great wealth all my life. It attracts all sorts of ne'er-do-wells and prospectors. Such a burden."

"This house!" Emma put her head in her hands. "It's a curse. I don't want it." She looked at Bea. "You can have the damn house! Okay? Satisfied?"

"Well, I am sorry for the unfortunate circumstances, Emma. I don't wish to see anyone this upset," Bea said. "But I am relieved you've finally come to your senses about the house."

"It's not your house to give away, Emma," Angus said.

"Always the gatekeeper," Bea snapped.

Emma looked back and forth between the two of them and realized Angus was right. She was just the guardian of the house. Guardian of Penny equaled guardian of the house. As Mark was well aware.

"The bottom line is you need a lawyer," said Kyle. "Do you know anyone in town?"

Emma shook her head. "Years ago, I had someone handle my divorce. The mom of one of my high-school friends was a lawyer. She wasn't even a divorce lawyer — she just helped me because I needed help and had no money. And it wasn't that complicated because Mark didn't fight me. Maybe I

385

should call Mark. Try to reason with him
—"

They all interrupted with the unanimous opinion that that was a terrible idea.

"What's going on?" Penny said from across the room.

At the sight of her daughter, Emma broke down again. And then she ran to Penny, swept her into her arms, and held her tight.

CHAPTER THIRTY-SIX

Angus was so self-righteous! Refusing to show her the girl's collection of Henry's drawings, putting a damper on Emma's impulse to return the house to her, its rightful custodian.

Oh, a wolf in sheep's clothing, that's what he was. And he was a wolf sitting in the middle of her kitchen.

"Am I supposed to feed you now? This isn't an inn," she said, chopping kale on a cutting board. "All evidence to the contrary."

"Of course not. I'm just collecting my thoughts. This is very upsetting, obviously."

"I'm not offering counseling services either."

Though at that point, she had to admit that she wouldn't have minded some therapy for herself. She was still grappling with the discovery that the hotel bartender from all those years ago — the man who had dazzled Henry with his talk of fishing and living off the sea — was Emma Mapson's father. She chose to view this as an insignificant detail. Henry simply would not have left his entire estate to the granddaughter of a man he had befriended briefly forty years ago. The odd thing was that Emma had never mentioned this connection. Was it possible she didn't know? If so, Bea certainly wasn't going to be the one to tell her.

"Please don't be cross with me," Angus said. "I'm not trying to antagonize you and I wasn't trying to last night either. But Emma's like family and I have to look out for her."

Bea wondered what it would be like to have someone that devoted to her. Kyle had been ready to hightail it out of town without so much as a word to her. She didn't have a spouse, didn't have family. Not even someone "like" family, as Angus put it. Her sense of being alone in the world suddenly felt as sharp as the knife she was holding.

And if Angus knew that she had allied herself with the ex-husband — had in fact bankrolled today's calamity — he would not be speaking to her. She shook away the pang of guilt. She was fighting for the future of her lifelong friend's artistic legacy. It was not her job to look out for the woman who was taking it away! Still, seeing Angus's ashen, concerned face made her feel bad.

"Well, in that case, I suppose you might as well stay for lunch. I'm making a kale salad with red cabbage and mango."

Angus shook his head. "Thanks for the offer, but I'm a carnivore."

She raised an eyebrow. "And I'm sure you have the cholesterol levels to prove it."

He laughed. "Did you invite me to stay so you can punish me?"

"Don't be silly. I would never consider my company a punishment for anyone."

She turned her focus back to the counter and mixed the sesame dressing, smiling.

The adults in her life had officially gone crazy.

Penny washed her hands in her bathroom — she loved having her own bathroom — and started counting to sixty. But then, midway, she was able to stop herself. The more time she wasted in the bathroom, the less time she had to work on her book. And she really wanted to get another panel drawn before it was time to go to sleep.

Today's drama had given her another great scene to add, even though she didn't entirely understand what it had all been about.

She'd caught a little of what they were discussing in the living room but not enough to really make sense of it. Her mother was upset, maybe because her father was back in town and trying to be more involved in her life. But why would they have a whole group conversation about that? Whatever the reason, seeing her mother and Angus and Kyle sitting there like some sort of assembly of the Justice League talking to Bea was really bizarre. The Justice League didn't have joint meetings with its enemies. Wonder Woman didn't sit down for coffee with Lex Luthor.

Wasn't one of the Justice League's archenemies named Queen Bee?

Queen Bea. Ha!

Penny climbed back onto her bed and pulled the drawing board into her lap. She felt bad that her mother was upset, but if her mother wouldn't tell her what was happening, then Penny couldn't help. Really, Penny couldn't do much of anything except (a) try to boss back her OCD, (b) stay out of trouble (easier to do now that she was on crutches), and (c) draw. *Someday you will find your own superpower.*

Two summers ago, when she'd first started spending time with Henry, he'd told her that although the world was a place of chaos

390

and disorder, artists could impose order within the confines of their work. He said when he was painting or creating a sculpture, his mind was completely blank.

"It's important to be able to find that kind of quiet in your life," he said.

"My life is already quiet. Too quiet!"

"You feel that way now, but someday, you'll look back at this simple time and miss it terribly."

She doubted that.

"When you're young, your life, your perspective, has only one direction — forward, toward the future. But when you're old, you also have the past."

"But you don't move toward the past. The past is over."

He pointed at her and waved his finger. "The past is never over. The past informs the present and therefore shapes the future."

When they'd decided to create their own graphic novels, he said his story would be about his past. Penny said she didn't know what to write about, and he advised her to just make something up. She tried, but there was a problem — she was a decent artist, but she wasn't a great creative writer. That's why she'd never finished the superhero story. But now, with the real-life drama unfolding this summer, the story was writing itself.

It was weird; in some ways, the boat accident was the best thing that could have happened to her. Yeah, the cast was annoying, and when she got an itch it was enough to drive her crazy. But given her own physical limitations and the fact that her friends were grounded, she was free of the pressure she usually felt to run around with them and try to fit in. She felt calmer. And with not much else to do, she focused on creating. This made her feel closer to Henry, like, yes, he was gone, but a part of their friendship was still alive. Of course, she wished he were there to see it. Maybe this was what he meant about the past informing the present. For the first time, she was looking back at something. It made her feel sad but also a little more grown up.

With a few quick strokes of her pencil, she began sketching her mother into the scene with Queen Bea.

That's it! Penny thought excitedly, writing out the words. She had the title of her novel.

She reached for her laptop and opened her browser to a link she'd saved earlier in the week. It was a graphic-novel contest she'd found on an online art journal called *ArtHub.* Now that her story was really coming together, she was going to enter it.

It was amazing how things were turning around. Maybe Dr. Wang was right about thinking positively. For the first time all summer, she felt like things were going to be okay.

Emma paced in her bedroom and lit a cigarette, the first one she'd had since she'd been pregnant with Penny.

She opened the window and tried to wave the smoke toward it. Then she pulled out her phone and dialed. No one agreed with her on this, but she had to talk to Mark. Hand shaking, she tapped in his number. Her call went straight to voice mail.

Coward. She'd spent the last two hours Googling New York State child-custody law. She knew she should stop. It was like looking up symptoms on the internet when you felt sick; everything came back as cancer. Still, she couldn't stop herself.

Someone knocked on her door.

"Who is it?"

"It's me."

Kyle. "Just a minute." She flushed her cigarette down the toilet, wiped her tearstained face, and let him in.

"Hey," he said.

"Hey."

"You doing okay?"

"Fine," she said, closing the door behind him.

He sat on the edge of her bed. "You smoke?"

"No," she said, looking at the floor.

"Emma, it's going to be okay."

"You don't know that."

"The only thing you can do is fight back."

She nodded. "I realize that. I've been making calls. Sean referred me to a lawyer he knows in town. I have an appointment the day after tomorrow." She pressed her fingers to her temples. "I know I keep saying this, but I can't believe this is happening."

Her phone buzzed with a text.

I told you, I only want what's best for Penny.

Heart pounding, she wrote back, Bullshit.

Have you told her what's going on?

No. And I'm not going to. Mark, don't do this. She watched three dots form as he wrote his response, then they disappeared.

She paced in front of the bed, glancing at the phone again, knowing it was useless to appeal to Mark's decency. Kyle was right; the only thing she could do was fight back.

She would move money out of her meager savings account. Whatever it cost. She could give up the Mount Misery house and put what she would spend on rent toward this legal battle.

"Emma, sit for a minute." Kyle reached for her hand and guided her to the edge of the bed next to him. They sat inches apart, the space between vibrating with a strange energy, a tension she realized had nothing to do with her distress over the custody fight.

"You'll feel better after you talk to the lawyer," Kyle said. "I'll go with you."

"You don't have to do that."

"I want to."

"Why?"

"I think you know why."

His eyes focused on her with an intensity that made her look away. She could get lost in that blue. He squeezed her hand gently.

"Things are just so complicated right now," she said. "I'm not sure it's the best time to —"

"I get it," he said, nodding.

"Friends?" she said. He hugged her, and she thought maybe she was making a mistake. Here it was, the thing she'd longed for. And she was squashing it. She wasn't quite sure why. Maybe she was saving herself for the battle ahead.

Nonsupervision. Unstable home environment.

Or maybe she was punishing herself.

CHAPTER THIRTY-SEVEN

Dr. Wang smiled at Penny. "Well, I'm glad you're drawing again. It's important to have an outlet. But your mother told me about the pills. My concern isn't just that you're using dangerous drugs recreationally but also that perhaps you are self-medicating in an attempt to control your ruminations."

Her mother looked at her expectantly from across the room. Penny swallowed hard.

"I mean, yeah, when I took that stuff, it helped keep my thoughts from getting caught in loops. But I know that was a really bad thing to do and I'm done with that." She turned to her mother. "Really. I swear."

Dr. Wang leaned back in her chair and adjusted the scarf around her neck. "I want to work on the way you view things, Penny. Think of your negative perceptions as glasses you can take off if you choose to see things a different way. As an exercise to start retraining your thinking, I want you to create a positivity board in your bedroom. Every day, I want you to post three good things that happened. It could be a compliment someone gave you or something you accomplished . . ."

A compliment someone gave her? Did her therapist think that actually happened? Dr. Wang probably walked down the street and got compliments every day, so, yeah.

"And Mom," Dr. Wang said to Emma, "when Penny says something negative, I want you to challenge it with something positive."

Penny waited for her mom to respond, but she looked completely zoned out. *WTF?* "Mom?" Penny said.

Emma seemed startled, like she'd forgotten she was in the room with them. "I'm sorry," she said. "What was that?"

"I was just saying that when Penny veers to the negative, I need you to be the counterpoint. To show her that there is always a positive side."

And then, unbelievably, her mother burst into tears.

The law office of Andrew Port was located in a shingled two-story building on tree-lined Noyac Road. Emma barely made it to the appointment on time after the debacle at Dr. Wang's. How could she have lost control like that in the middle of Penny's therapy session? And it just added another ten minutes to the session, as the doctor had to address Emma's outburst and bring things back into calm focus on Penny.

Kyle had been waiting for her in the building's narrow entrance hall.

A paralegal sat them in a sunlit conference room, offered them coffee, and then asked Emma for information she knew she'd already given the lawyer over the phone. She patiently repeated the information, understanding this was just the beginning of what would be a long and stressful process.

By the time Andrew Port joined Emma and Kyle, Emma's stomach was in knots. She knew she wasn't thinking clearly, and she was thankful Kyle had followed through on his offer to come along with her.

"Ms. Mapson. A pleasure to meet you," Andrew Port said.

"Please, call me Emma. And this is my friend Kyle Dunlap."

Andrew Port was younger than she'd expected, with hair that was just starting to go gray at the temples. He was tan and wore a navy blue blazer over a white shirt and dark jeans.

He sat at the table and leafed through a pile of papers for a minute. When he looked up at Emma and Kyle, his expression was serious. "So I want to give you a sense of what to expect in this process. In a few weeks we'll have a court date. The judge will give you and your ex the chance to work out an amicable compromise. I will be talking to the opposing attorney to help facilitate that. If we cannot come to an agreement on that date, the court will most likely order a psychological evaluation of Penny to assess her needs. That costs a few thousand dollars and is usually paid by the petitioner. We have an adjournment for a few months while any court-ordered evaluations take place. Then we'll get a trial date."

"And if it goes to trial, then the judge just . . . decides? Then and there? He or she could just take my daughter away from me?"

"Emma, I'm going to do everything I can to prevent that from happening."

"Okay," she said, fighting tears. Kyle reached over and patted her leg.

"I reviewed your original divorce stip. Penny's father was granted a standard visitation schedule — every other weekend, alternating holidays, et cetera. But you said he rarely sees her?"

Emma nodded. "That's right." She told him that Mark had visited Penny fairly frequently in the early days of their divorce, but then his appearances slowed steadily, and eventually they stopped altogether.

"And his child-support payments?"

"Erratic. He'll pay it, and then four months will go by before he pays again. He usually catches up. It's just not regular."

"And you never considered going to court over this?"

"It would cost me more to go to court, so I just wait for him to catch up."

Andrew nodded and wrote something on a legal pad. "So when did he reestablish contact with your daughter?"

"At the beginning of this summer."

"And prior to that, he hadn't seen her in over a year?"

She nodded.

"Emma, I think you should tell him that Mark didn't even call you. He just showed up," Kyle said.

"Oh, that's a good point." She explained about Mark turning up at the house unannounced, expecting to take Penny to the beach. Again, Andrew Port wrote on his pad. "Like I said on the phone," Emma added, "Mark's appearance coincided with Penny inheriting the Henry Wyatt estate.

He claims he didn't know about it, that it has nothing to do with him suddenly wanting to be more involved in Penny's life. But I don't believe it."

"Either way, that doesn't change the grounds of his petition. A judge won't care *why* he came back if it appears he's acting in the best interests of his child. If this goes to trial, we'll have to answer to his claims that she's unsupervised and that this lack of supervision resulted in injury. There's also the question of whether or not her psychological health is being adequately taken care of, but that will be in part decided by the psych eval if this goes that far."

"My God," Emma said. "I can't believe this is happening."

"I know this is very upsetting," Andrew said in the understatement of the year. Emma looked at Kyle.

"I'm wondering," Kyle said, "does Emma have to allow her ex to see Penny during all of this?"

"That's a good question, and the answer is yes; you can't act punitively toward your ex because he filed this motion. Remember, he's saying he's acting in the best interests of the child. This isn't a personal attack against you."

"Of course it is!"

Andrew nodded. "I know it is. And I certainly know it feels that way. But it's important that you not act defensively or punitively. If you want to deny him extra time that he requests, that's fine. But his visitation weekends stand."

"Doesn't the fact that he's been absent for so long count against him in any way?" Kyle said.

"You mean if this goes to trial?" Andrew said.

"I mean now. Why does he even have visitation rights still?"

Emma was touched to see Kyle so worked up on her behalf. She looked at Andrew expectantly.

"Again, everything in family court comes down to the best interests of the child. A child benefits from having a relationship with both parents unless one parent is proven to be a danger or unfit. Mark Mapson's absence might not be ideal, but in cases like this the father usually says he was traveling for work, he had financial hardship, that sort of thing."

"It sounds like Mark gets the endless benefit of the doubt while Emma is being vilified," Kyle said.

"I'm just playing the devil's advocate here. I want you to have a realistic understanding of what we're dealing with."

Emma nodded. "I get it."

Andrew ran through a few more things, then said, "And how long have you two been together? I only ask because sometimes the issue of a significant other comes into play."

"We're just friends," Emma said quickly, nervously adding, "I don't have time to date. I haven't had a . . . significant other in years. Certainly no one who has had anything to do with Penny." For once, her pathetic personal life felt like a bonus.

When the meeting was almost over, Andrew asked if she had any other questions.

"Yes," she said. "What am I supposed to do now?"

"Just live your life as normally as possible. I'll let you know when we have a hearing date. And in the meantime, try not to worry. Think positive."

The second time that day she'd heard that advice. She realized, as her daughter had long been telling her, it wasn't so easy.

CHAPTER THIRTY-EIGHT

Bea was not usually swayed by the weather, but the morning was so flawless that it demanded at least some time outdoors. Still, the girl insisted on spending hour after hour at the dining-room table bent over her sketch pad.

"What is it you're working on so diligently?" Bea asked on her way to the pool.

"My graphic novel," Penny said, not bothering to look up.

"You're writing one?"

She nodded.

Bea peeked over Penny's shoulder and was surprised to see a very fine sketch of Emma, her brows knit together in anguish. Bea felt the visceral, pulse-racing response she always felt when she spotted talent. *Okay, Henry — so she can draw. But did you have to give her the house?*

"Penny," Bea said, pulling out the chair next to her and sitting. "It's wonderful that you get up every morning and draw. Henry was the same way. He created every day of his life —"

"I miss being able to show him my drawings," Penny said, turning to her, biting her lower lip, her eyes filled with emotion. Bea experienced a pang; how odd, how unlikely, that she and this girl should share even a sliver of the same grief.

"Well," Bea said slowly. "I suppose you could show *me* your work. Henry always did, you know." At least, he had for a time.

Penny wrinkled her nose as if Bea had suggested she drink sewage.

Very well, then — back to business. "As I was saying, Henry created every day of his life. But then he moved out here and something changed. It was difficult for me when this happened because his work and my work were so intertwined for many, many years. We had an art gallery together. Did he ever mention it?"

"No," Penny said.

"It was in SoHo, a very exciting neighborhood at the time. Unfortunately, it has now been reduced to an outdoor mall. Have you ever been to New York City?"

Penny shook her head. "I really want to go. Maybe even live there someday. I guess then I could see your gallery."

"Oh, the gallery is long gone. Shortly after Henry retired, I closed it down. Sold the building." It had been a practical but painful decision, one that sent her into a sort of mourning.

Shortly thereafter, Henry had suffered a loss of his own. He called her, his voice breaking, late one day nearly two years after his move to tell her that his good friend Tom, the bartender from the hotel, had died suddenly. This time, Bea did not hesitate to make the trip to Sag Harbor. How silly it seemed then to view the house as a threat, a rebuke. Life was too short. Her friend needed her.

"I'll stay for as long as you need me," she told him. The gesture was not altogether selfless; she wanted to reconnect with him, wanted for them to find their way back to what they'd once shared.

But a few weeks into her visit, she realized there was no going back. She was dealing with a different Henry Wyatt. Instead of talking about the latest issue of *Artforum* or gallery gossip, he went on and on about crab fishing. Instead of spending hours in his studio, the air filled with the smell of turpentine, he spent all afternoon prepping hearty meals, stews and roasts made from venison caught by a local hunter he had befriended down at the marina.

The last night of Bea's stay, Henry made a campfire and they huddled under blankets while finishing bottles of wine.

"So this is your life now," she said.

"Not bad, right?"

"It's not New York," she said.

"I never enjoyed the rat race as much as you did, Bea. I don't have your competitive spirit. But I always admired it."

"And I always admired your creative spirit. You know, when you built this place, I read all those articles speculating that the next phase of your career would be architecture. But I never believed it. I think your heart is still in painting."

"I'm done with painting but I'm also done with architecture. This place was a onetime burst of inspiration," he said.

The house had been built in his frenzy to escape the city, to create a new life for himself. Bea knew how it felt to be fueled by such passion. She'd built both of their careers on it. And she wasn't ready to give up.

"So come back to Manhattan. You're not done yet. I'm not done yet. We can create something bigger and better than the Winstead-Wyatt Gallery."

He shook his head. "Bea, don't you see

there's another way to live? I'm happy out here. I wish you could find the kind of peace I've found."

"I don't need peace! I need work. I need a reason to get up in the morning. And there was a time when you needed that too. I'll never understand why you walked away."

"And I'll never understand why you can't slow down. Experience something in life other than work." He reached into his pocket, pulled out a key, and pressed it into her hand. "I hope you'll spend more time out here. You have an open invitation."

"I appreciate that, Henry. But I have a very busy life in the city."

"You could be busy out here," he said.

"Doing what?"

"Someday I want to turn this place into a museum. A permanent installation of my work."

A museum in a small harbor town? That was his legacy? How could their visions be so different?

It wasn't until months later, alone in her Park Avenue apartment, that she'd warmed up to the idea of the Henry Wyatt Museum of Sag Harbor or whatever it would be called. It wasn't an eponymous gallery in SoHo, but it was better than nothing.

She'd called Henry and said, "Okay. I'm

in." But he'd never followed up with her.

Bea looked at Penny, who was huddled over her work, humming softly to herself. "Penny," Bea said. "I've been looking at a lot of drawings that Henry left around town. I wonder if they are intended to be pieced together, sort of a treasure hunt of art. That's why I wanted to take a look at the drawings he gave you, to see if they help make sense of things. To see if maybe, when they're all put together, they tell a story."

"Like his graphic novel?"

Bea's heart started to pound. "What graphic novel?"

"The one he wrote last summer. I was supposed to finish one too. But I just didn't have a story to tell."

"Henry wrote a graphic novel," Bea said slowly.

"Yes."

"What was it about?"

"I don't know for sure. I saw only a few pages of it here and there, never the whole thing. He said it was for adults."

Bea put her hand on Penny's shoulder. "Penny, where is the book?"

Penny looked at her and shrugged. "I have no idea."

It all made more sense now. Penny had shared her love of graphic novels, and it had inspired him, the way hanging around sculptors inspired him to sculpt and meeting fishermen inspired him to fish.

So where the hell was it? She'd already searched the house, the museums, the library. Where could the book be?

Henry, I still don't understand. But I'm getting closer!

At one in the afternoon, Emma knelt in the back lawn digging up soil when Penny hobbled out and called to her from the steps, "Some lady is here to see you."

"Who is it?" She scrambled to her feet, her stomach tightening. At that point, she felt that any news was bad news. Following Penny back into the house, she steeled herself for whatever and whoever awaited her on the front doorstep.

"Cheryl?"

"I'm a little early," Cheryl Meister said brightly, marching into the house and unabashedly examining every corner. "But I was just dying to take a peek in here."

Early? What was she talking about? And then it hit her: the auction committee meeting.

Minutes later, the doorbell rang again. Diane Knight brushed past Emma, looking for a place to plug in her MacBook and asking

411

for an iced tea.

What was she going to do? She was completely unprepared to host a dozen people for lunch. There was no food in the house except what she needed to make Penny's grilled cheese — that was about it. She didn't have so much as a bottle of sparkling water to offer the members of the group as they descended on Windsong wearing their Lululemon best and chattering about last night's dinner party.

"I'll be right back," Emma said, ushering everyone into the living room while she retreated into the kitchen to catch her breath.

She opened and closed the refrigerator as if that would make a tray of crudités and tea sandwiches magically appear. Did anyone deliver all the way out on Actors Colony Road? She did a quick search on her phone for options and came up with only pizza. That would not fly with the art-auction ladies.

"What, pray tell, is going on in the living room? It looks like the cast of *Real Housewives of God Knows Where* just invaded," Bea said, sweeping into the room wearing a crisp blouse and pale blue linen pants. Her straw hat sported a navy-blue ribbon with ducks on it.

Because Emma didn't have enough to deal with. "That's an auction committee. For the cinema fund-raiser? I don't know if you've heard about that. But they're having an art auction and —"

"Oh, yes. I spoke to Cheryl Meister on the phone about making a donation."

"You did?"

"I'll go introduce myself since you somehow failed to mention to me that we were hosting a meeting this afternoon."

We?

And then, for the first time since Bea had waltzed up to the front desk and demanded a room, Emma was thankful for her existence. "Bea, this is the thing — I totally forgot they were coming today. I have nothing here — no food, nothing to drink. I haven't given one thought to this auction since I left Cheryl's house after the last meeting."

"Why didn't you say something? Emma, this is *what I do.* You should have come to me in the first place!"

This woman was trying to snatch a house away from her daughter; what reasonable person would enlist that woman's help in planning a party? But clearly, all normal boundaries were gone from her life.

"Okay, well, if you can help, that would

be great. I need to get food here somehow and no one will deliver out here last minute. I should have picked up something from Schiavoni's this morning."

"Anyone will do anything for the right price. I'll have lunch here in no time." And she did. She also delighted the ladies with her appearance at the meeting. Cheryl introduced her as "a living legend" in the art world.

"My parents were big collectors," Diane said, fawning over her. "I visited your gallery when I was a teenager. What a thrill. I'll never forget it."

Seating arrangements. Catering options. Tickets. Bea had opinions about all of it, and the ladies of the auction committee ate them up faster than the remoulade crab cakes and baby kale salad delivered from Cavaniola's. Watching her in action, Emma saw for the first time the dynamo who had built an art dynasty, not just a crazy old woman battling her over a house. And it dawned on her that surely, Henry Wyatt must have known this woman would not take Penny's inheritance of his estate lightly. As someone who'd seen Bea Winstead operate for decades, he had probably known she would show up in town.

And Emma wondered, as she had that

very first day she learned about the house, what exactly Henry Wyatt had been thinking.

CHAPTER THIRTY-NINE

Penny usually loved the Fourth of July, but this year it felt different. Her mother seemed really down — and that wasn't negative thinking, it was a fact. Still, in an effort to prevent herself from going into a death spiral of worry, she pulled out a pad of hot-pink Post-it notes and tried to think of something for her positivity board.

She came up blank. All she could think about was the conversation she'd had last night with her mother when, just before going to sleep, she finally got up the nerve to ask what was bothering her.

Her mother didn't seem surprised by the question. She sat on the edge of Penny's bed and furrowed her brow in the way she did when she was maybe not telling Penny the absolute truth. The way she had years ago when Penny asked why she never saw her grandparents, and Emma explained that the Mapsons were "very busy people."

Penny later figured out this meant that her dad's parents just weren't all that interested in seeing her.

So when she saw that expression on her mom's face. she knew she was in for a nonanswer.

"Your father and I are just trying to work something out," she said.

"Like what?"

"Like . . . how much time you spend with him."

"Oh." She didn't know what she'd expected, but this wasn't it. "Do you mind that I spend time with him? I mean, he's not around that much."

"No, hon. Of course I don't mind that you spend time with him. It's just that we're trying to work out a schedule."

"So why are you so stressed out?"

Shockingly, her mother's eyes filled with tears. "I'm not," she said.

"Mom!" Penny leaned across the bed and hugged her mother, who sagged against her like a wilting plant.

"I'm just tired," her mother said. *Lie.*

"Come on, Mom. For real."

Her mother lowered her head and rubbed her brow. "Your father thinks maybe you'd be better off living with him more of the time. Maybe all of the time."

417

Penny blinked for a few seconds, absorbing this. "Okay, that's crazy. He doesn't even live here."

"Well, maybe he plans to."

"I don't want to live with him. I mean, it's fun to see him and hang out but . . ."

"I know it's unreasonable. But that's what we're discussing. So if I seem a little tense, it's because I'm trying to make him understand that it's not a good idea."

Her mom was clearly worked up, and Penny had a sudden and terrible thought.

"This is because of the boat accident, isn't it? He blames you."

Her mother shook her head. "No, I don't think it's because of that."

But Penny knew that this time, she really was lying.

So, all things considered, it was hard for Penny to be excited about the fireworks. Besides, she was okay with the crutches at home or on the Main Street sidewalk, but on the grass surrounded by crowds of people? She'd be lucky to hobble far enough to find a spot to sit down.

She wondered if any of the other kids would be out this year. She'd spoken to Robin once since the night of the accident, and that was enough for her. Every time she thought about Robin and Mindy, it just brought back all her guilt over lying to her mother and getting into trouble. And now, thinking that all of that might be the cause of the problems between her parents, she was even less interested in those girls.

Her mother knocked on the doorway of her bedroom. She had a stuffed bag over her shoulder, a beach blanket poking out.

"I'm not really in the mood for fireworks," Penny said.

"Neither am I. But we're going."

"Why?"

"Because it's tradition."

With everyone at the waterfront for the fireworks, Bea decided to make good use of her precious solitude by doing a little snooping.

The curiosity was just killing her. What was the girl drawing, day in and day out? After a lifetime of sniffing out talent, of homing in on art like a fly drawn to honey, Bea couldn't very well stop herself from looking now.

She crept down the hall slowly, quietly, even though no one was around to hear her. *Can't be too careful,* she told herself.

The bedroom door was open.

Penny was surprisingly neat. What had she expected? Clothes strewn everywhere.

419

Candy wrappers. Who knew? She'd never lived with a child before. But the room looked almost the way it had before the Mapsons moved in. The bed was made, the nightstand had only a few personal items on it — some scattered hairbands, a mini-bottle of hand sanitizer, a tube of lip gloss with a pink cap shaped like a cat's head, and a laptop computer.

Bea sat on the bed. Behind her, on the wall, was some sort of collage, a rainbow of Post-its scrawled with notes like *Made progress on the novel! Mom brought home BuddhaBerry!*

Oh, Bea hated being old. But fourteen — well, that hadn't been a picnic either. The whole world was *almost* open to you. How dazzling the possibilities; how frustrating the limitations! She would never forget the feeling on the casino lawn the night of the Newport Jazz Festival. She had been just shy of Penny's age when she'd decided she wanted to move to New York City someday. Funny, Penny expressed the same intense desire to get out of her hometown. Maybe that's why Bea felt a grudging affinity with the girl. That and, of course, the drawing.

Bea sighed and leaned against the pile of throw pillows. Under the small of her back, she felt something poking her, and she reached behind to find a graphite pencil. Well, the girl wasn't so meticulous after all. How could she leave a pencil in her white bedding? Very careless.

She walked the pencil over to the Lucite desk in the corner, where she found an open box of Faber-Castells. She slipped the offending object inside, then picked up a spiral drawing pad. Underneath, she found a pile of loose sketches.

The first was a detailed and rather flawlessly rendered black-and-white drawing of Windsong. She wasn't surprised to find a picture of the house; Windsong would inspire even a fledgling artist. But she didn't know quite what to make of the words on the top of the page written in bold strokes: *Queen Bea.*

She moved it aside for the next page, the drawings divided into panels. The top left corner featured another sketch of Windsong along with some text: *First came the house. Then came Bea.* Next, a cartoonish but undeniably accurate rendering of Penny and her mother sitting on a bed in an unfamiliar room. The drawing of Emma included a dialogue bubble: *Sometimes, good things do happen.* Another drawing of Windsong followed, the house as seen through a car window.

The bottom of the page featured the interior of the house. Penny, Emma, and Bea stood in the dining room, the infinity pool visible outside the window. Bea shook her head at Penny's depiction of her, the exaggerated pouf of her hair, her pin-striped pantsuit, and her pearls rendered absurdly large. In the drawing, Bea's arms were crossed, a stern expression on her lined face. Her bubble of dialogue read *Interlopers!*

Bea pored through the sketches, more than twenty of them, that pieced together the drama of the past few weeks. No one was spared Penny's savage pen; there was Kyle, Angus, her father, and a woman named Dr. Wang.

I'll be damned. How many times had newspapers and magazines asked Bea to explain how she knew when an artist had "it"? She always gave the same response: *The hairs on my arms stand on end.* Well, they were standing.

The doorbell sounded.

"Oh, for heaven's sake. Can I not have one moment of peace in this house?" So much for quiet country living. This place was like Grand Central Station! She put the pages back the way she'd found them and then went down the hall to deal with the disturbance.

When she saw that the disturbance was Angus, she felt slightly less irritated for some reason. "Well, hello there. You're about an hour late. Emma and Penny already left."

"I should have figured. I usually take Penny to the fireworks because Emma's working. I guess she didn't need me this year." His disappointment was palpable.

How thoughtless of Emma. Truly, the woman had no consideration for others. "In that case, I think you should be thankful you're off the hook. There are far more civilized ways to spend an evening. I have reservations at a delightful restaurant in town and I insist you join me. Dinner is on me."

"I appreciate the offer but —"

"It's the least I can do to thank you for educating me about the town."

"Hmm," he said. "And you don't consider this consorting with the enemy?"

"You know what they say," Bea said with a teasing smile. "Keep your friends close and your enemies closer."

Marine Park was alight with fireflies. Emma pointed them out to Penny, who sat next to her on a beach blanket.

"Yeah, Mom, I see," Penny said, shifting around and trying to get comfortable with her leg extended. "I hate this cast."

"Well, think about that the next time a kid asks you to get into a boat. Or a car, for that matter," she said. A few feet away, Penny's third-grade teacher waved at them. "Look, Penny — Ms. Lowen is over there."

The entire town had turned out and there was something about sitting next to her daughter, surrounded by people she'd known all her life, that comforted her. Nights like this gave her a sense of continuity. As much as things changed, some things never did.

She'd considered inviting Angus along or even Kyle when she spotted him working on his boat earlier. It had been steadying to have him by her side at the lawyer's office. But in the end, she decided to make it just a mother-daughter holiday.

"Mom?" Penny said. "I was thinking about our conversation last night."

Emma bit her lip. This was the last thing she wanted to talk about. But she also didn't want to shut down the lines of communication. If Penny wanted to talk about the situation with her father, so be it. "Oh? What are your thoughts?"

"Maybe he just wants me to visit him

more. Like in New York or LA or any of those cool places. That could work, right?"

Emma felt like Penny had slapped her. "I thought you said that you didn't want to live with him!"

"I *don't.* I said *visit.* Like, so I can get out of town sometimes. I'm bored, Mom." She looked around. "I'm not like you. I don't belong here. I don't even have any *friends* at this point."

The first fireworks burst overhead, ending the conversation. The crowd reacted with a collective, delighted gasp. Penny, completely oblivious about how much she had just rattled Emma, stared up at the sky, her face rapt.

Let it go, Emma told herself. She closed her eyes, choosing a memory over the kaleidoscope of lights in the sky. She thought about fireworks of long ago, a night when she sat on her father's shoulders in that very park, has big hands anchoring her while she looked up, up, up. Her mother had probably been by their side, but all she saw in her mind's eye was her dad. A few months later, he was gone.

It was a Sunday morning when she found out her father had died. She could still hear the hollow sound of her mother's voice calling her into her bedroom. Even at eight years old, Emma had the intuition to know something was terribly wrong. The words her mother used at the time felt vague and inadequate: *Sudden death. Painless. He didn't suffer.* Later, when she was older, the technical term *brain aneurysm* filled some of the gaps. But even now, as a grown woman — a parent herself — it was hard to understand how it could have happened, how she could have lost him in an instant. She hadn't felt a true sense of security since.

Pop!

She opened her eyes, willing herself to feel joy instead of sadness, to look at the lights instead of dwelling in the dark. Next to her, Penny had her eyes fixed on the sky, a big smile on her face. And Emma reminded herself that while the universe took, it also gave.

"Em!"

The voice came from somewhere a row or two back in the crowd. She looked around and spotted Sean and Alexis and . . . Kyle? When she saw him, something inside of her did a little flip. She ignored it. That was not why she'd thought about inviting him along. She'd felt bad about the idea of him spending the holiday alone. Apparently, she hadn't needed to; she should have guessed that Sean would invite him. The boat people

426

were such a club.

"I texted you an hour ago," Alexis said, looking relaxed and beachy in an orange sundress and matching flip-flops. "So glad we found you!"

They squeezed in around her. Sean's dog, Melville, jumped on Penny and licked her face. Penny inched sideways, moving closer to Alexis and away from her mother. Here Emma was, going out of her way to arrange a fun mother-daughter night, and the whole time Penny couldn't care less.

Kyle moved near her, so near their shoulders touched. She kept her eyes on the sky but was intensely aware of him.

"How's it going?" he said. She just smiled and nodded. There was enough noise from the fireworks that she didn't need to make real conversation. Still, she felt his eyes on her when he should have been looking at the sky.

She kept her gaze fixed overhead, even when it all started to feel too bright.

CHAPTER FORTY

The Dockside Bar and Grill was housed in the American Legion building on Bay Street just across from the marina. Bea had reserved an outdoor table, although she had failed to realize she would be subjected to a full view of the fireworks.

"I didn't expect to get to see the fireworks after all," Angus said.

"Well, I have to admit, that is an unintended consequence of this location. I'm not a fan of loud noises and bright lights."

He shook his head. "Try to be positive for a few minutes."

"I'll do my best."

She ordered a bottle of white wine and the Peconic Bay oysters to start, along with steamed artichokes. For her main course she chose the herb-crusted cod with lemon beurre blanc. Angus ordered the pulled-pork dish that was served with cheddar and black beans.

"You realize you found the only unhealthy thing on the entire menu," Bea said drily.

He nodded. "My wife used to keep me on track with my diet. She passed five years ago, and I'm afraid it's been a steady slide into bad habits ever since."

"I'm sorry you lost your wife."

"It seems to be that time in life. Were you ever married?"

"No, I was not."

"Well, that's a shame," Angus said. "May I ask why not?"

"I suppose I'm married to my work."

"That sounds lonely."

Bea shrugged and took a sip of her wine. A child from the table next to theirs ran to the lawn in front of the dining patio. Bea had a view of a large and eclectic assortment of buoys hanging from the shingled siding of a house.

"That's Billy Joel's house," Angus said, following her gaze.

"Is it really? How interesting that he would want to be in the middle of all this. I much prefer privacy."

"There's a fine line between privacy and isolation, wouldn't you say?"

"No," she said. "I wouldn't."

"I think the whole point of being in a town like this is for the community. My family left Brooklyn to spend summers here starting back in the 1940s and they got more than just a house on the beach. We had dirt roads and didn't even see streetlights go up until the eighties. I don't remember a single television set. It was all about parties and seafood picnics and us kids running around the private beach, in and out of everyone's house. I don't think the houses even had locks on the doors. If they did, they certainly weren't ever used."

"It sounds lovely."

"It was," he said wistfully. "It really was."

Their main courses arrived on brightly colored plates, the food artfully arranged.

They ate in companionable silence. There was something to be said for being with someone your own age at your own stage in life. Certain things were just unspoken. Even though the two of them had no shared history, there was the illusion of it. Spending eight or so decades on earth was a bit of a club. So was loss. And, though she wouldn't admit it, so was loneliness.

"So how is your treasure hunt going?" Angus asked. "Are you finding what you're looking for?"

"I don't know exactly what I'm looking for," she said. "I have a bit of a mystery on my hands."

"Have you considered the possibility that you are on a wild-goose chase? That Henry Wyatt left his house to Penny and that's the end of the story?"

"I know that would be quite convenient for you. But no. Henry did everything by design. He would not casually drop his work all around town; at the end of his career, he didn't even want to share his work with me. And I refuse to believe he'd make this decision about his estate. I'm missing something. But I'm going to find it."

He sighed, reaching for his glass of wine. "I wish this whole thing had never happened. I don't see the inheritance as a positive turn of events. I guarantee Emma's ex-husband would not be fighting for custody if it weren't for that house. Now she might lose the most important thing in the world to her. It's terrible."

Bea suddenly found it difficult to swallow. She placed her fork down on her plate, thankful for the distraction of the fireworks — an excuse to look away from Angus.

The sky erupted in a sequence of red, white, and blue hearts for the grand finale, and Kyle reached for Emma's hand. Surprised, Emma looked at him, and he smiled.

"That was amazing!" Penny said. Alexis

and Sean decided that was the best fireworks show yet, then admitted they said that every year.

Emma folded up the blanket and Kyle offered to carry it for her.

They all made their way slowly through the bottleneck of people heading for Main Street. Emma put an arm around Penny so she didn't get jostled and knocked over by the crowd.

"Can we go to BuddhaBerry?" Penny said.

"I don't know," Emma said. "It's late and the line is going to be out the door." With the way Penny hobbled along, especially with so many people around, it would take a half an hour just to get there.

"You and I could walk up ahead to get in line," Kyle suggested to Emma.

"Yes, you two go ahead. We'll catch up," Alexis said with a wink.

Kyle didn't give Emma a chance to say no. He took her by the hand and guided her through the throng streaming toward the shops and restaurants. She didn't know exactly what to do about the hand-holding situation, so she decided to just let it be. For half a minute, all was right with her universe. Then they got to the hotel.

The American Hotel's outdoor tables were full, the lobby crowd spilling out onto the patio. She could only imagine what a mob scene it was inside at the bar. The Fourth was one of their biggest nights of the year. Oh, how she missed everyone!

"Do you want to go in for a minute?" Kyle asked.

"I have such mixed feelings," she said. "I'd like to see everyone, but —"

Jack Blake appeared on the patio and spotted her at the same instant she saw him. There was no slinking away.

"Happy Fourth!" he called out jovially.

She introduced him to Kyle and they made small talk. With each breath she was tempted to blurt out, *I want my job back.* But she couldn't guarantee that she'd have the focus and calm he needed from her, not when Penny couldn't get around by herself, not with the legal battle ahead of her. It was bad enough that she'd let him down once. She didn't want to make promises she couldn't keep. She hoped there was a day when her life would be back to normal. When *she* would be back to normal. She couldn't imagine it.

"Come inside, have a drink," Jack said.

"Oh, thanks, but we have to —"

Kyle touched her arm. "I'll text Sean. It's fine," he said with a wink.

The energy in the lobby was heightened

in the way it was only three times a year, the other two being Christmas and New Year's. From behind the front desk — her desk! — the assistant manager gave a friendly wave. Fighting a sharp pang of regret, she let Kyle take her hand again as they threaded their way through the crowd toward the bar. They didn't get very far and ended up standing under the moose head. Someone had stuck a mini–American flag in its mouth.

"What're you having?" Kyle asked.

"Um, dirty martini. With Tito's. Thanks." She checked her phone. *Penny's fine. Relax.*

She probably should have been the one to order the drinks. It would have been easier for her to get Chris's attention on a night like this. She looked around for Kyle but couldn't see him.

"Emma?"

Diane Knight tugged on her handbag to get her attention, and before Emma could muster a "Happy Fourth," the woman began gushing about how fabulous Bea Winstead was and how much was getting done for the auction. "She is a godsend," Diane said.

Well, that was one way of putting it.

"And Emma, I'm aware that you know —"

The room went silent, filled with white

noise. Somehow, Mark was in front of her. Somehow, Diane Knight *was holding Mark's hand.*

"Hey," Mark said quickly.

"I love this town," said Diane. "It's such a small world."

"How . . . how do you two know each other?" Emma said.

"We met at the Bay Street Theater party last week. Mark performed there one summer. Oh, but you know that . . ."

"Mark," Emma said, struggling to keep her voice even. "Can I speak to you for a minute outside?"

She could see he was about to refuse, but then he reconsidered. He probably didn't want to risk a scene in front of his new friend.

Heart pounding, she pushed her way impatiently through the lobby, glancing back a few times to make sure Mark was following her. When they were on the sidewalk, he said, "This isn't the time or the place, Emma."

"I can't believe you're trying to take Penny from me!" she said.

"I'm not debating this with you now," he said. "Anything you have to say about this can go through your lawyer."

"Do you have any idea what it takes to

raise a child full-time? You take her to the beach for one day and think you've got the whole thing figured out? You're out of your mind!"

"Is anything I said untrue? Really, Emma. Look at it in black-and-white and tell me I'm the bad guy."

"You *are* the bad guy!" she yelled. People turned to look at her.

He shook his head. "I'll see you in court, Emma."

Somewhere in the distance, a single firecracker sounded. Emma started shaking, standing alone on the sidewalk.

CHAPTER FORTY-ONE

It was the party that would not die.

More than a month after Bea had abruptly walked out on the Frank Cuban showing in her apartment, Joyce Carrier-Jones was still pushing for her to reschedule.

"What are you doing out there all this time?" Joyce asked. "Taking the whole summer off?"

"Of course not," Bea said defensively. She hated how everyone was always waiting for her to start slowing down, to retire. But how to explain her continued self-exile in Sag Harbor? She did not want to admit she was still fighting over Henry Wyatt's house without a shred of progress. Her lawyer had not given her any good news since she'd found the old will. She herself was no closer to making sense of Henry's intentions. And as for her Hail Mary pass with Penny's father, who knew how long that would take to play out? The only positive spin she could put on her situation was to say "I happen to be organizing a big art auction. I'm hosting it at Henry's house."

"How fabulous! So you've rectified that whole mess with the hotel woman out there? What was *that* all about?"

Oh, how she regretted that Page Six article. She'd gotten absolutely nothing out of it except fake sympathy from members of her professional circle who were faux scandalized that Henry Wyatt had overlooked her.

"It's complicated," Bea said. And then, in an effort to deflect: "Why don't you send me one of Frank's pieces for the auction? It will be great publicity for him."

"Send it? I'll bring it myself!"

Bea considered how to extricate herself from this unwanted visit, then realized perhaps it wasn't so unwanted after all. She missed her Manhattan life, and if she couldn't be in New York City at the moment, why not let New York City come to her for an afternoon?

And yet, when Joyce Carrier-Jones arrived, Bea felt out of sorts. Emma was gone for the day, packing up the Mount Misery house and therefore one step closer to staking a permanent claim to Windsong.

"You're a sight for sore eyes," Joyce said,

giving her an air kiss on each cheek. But it was clear as soon as she walked into the entrance hall that the only thing she had eyes for was Windsong. Bea should have known she wasn't driving two and a half hours in Saturday traffic just to spend time with her.

Bea gave her the tour.

"The sculptures are amazing," Joyce said. "What a shame he never showed them anywhere."

"Yes, it was greatly frustrating."

"I can imagine. And then this business with his estate! Honestly, Bea. I'm just happy to see you ended up with this place after all."

Bea said nothing. Lunch arrived. It was too hot to eat outdoors, so they sat at the dining-room table looking out at the pool.

"Thank you again for including Frank's work in this auction. It's great exposure. You know, after all these years, it still gets me in the gut when I see real talent. I know you understand."

Bea immediately thought of the graphic novel in Penny's room. Finally, someone she could talk to about it!

"I want to show you something," she said. "I'll be right back."

Somehow, it felt a bit more like a violation

439

to go into Penny's room this time. Bea wasn't quite sure why, exactly. Still, she would not be deterred by an inconvenient pang of conscience.

Penny's manuscript was still on the desk. Bea flipped through the pages, looking for drawings that didn't include her. No need for Joyce to know the *whole* story. She chose a few pages and brought them to the dining room.

"Tell me what you think of these," she said, sliding them over to Joyce. As the dean of admissions for the Franklin School of Fine Arts, as someone who evaluated young people's work year after year, Joyce would be able to put Penny's artistic ability into context for her. Not that she had very much doubt.

Joyce put on her glasses. She took her time examining the sketches, laughing at a few bits of dialogue. She looked up at Bea. "Who's the artist?"

"She's a fourteen-year-old."

"Fourteen? That's extraordinary. Where is she in school?"

"Out here," Bea said. "She's a local."

Joyce turned back to the drawings. "What a shame. I'd love to have her at Franklin. I can only imagine what she'll be doing in high school if she keeps this up." She

440

adjusted her glasses so she could peek over them at Bea. "Leave it to you to discover the next Alison Bechdel. And everyone thought you were out here licking your wounds all this time."

Bea bristled. "Well, how fortunate that you can now go back to the city and set the record straight."

It was Saturday and Coopers Beach was packed. Penny's cast was sealed in a waterproof cover her mom ordered online, so her leg looked like it was wrapped in a blue tarp. It was hot, she was cranky, and her dad was talking to her like she was three instead of fourteen.

"Let us adults deal with the details, Penny," her dad said.

"I don't see why you have to fight with Mom about it," Penny said. "Besides, it's *my* life and I don't want anything to change."

"Sometimes change is good. Like, the new house — right?"

"That's different. Besides, when's the last time you lived in Sag Harbor?"

He was distracted, waving to someone. Penny spotted a tall woman wearing a black one-piece bathing suit and a sarong heading for them. She had short brown hair and wore a thick, ropy gold necklace that really didn't belong at the beach.

"Sorry I'm late," the woman said, kissing her dad on the cheek.

It was sort of awkward to be sitting when the two of them were looming over her and smiling, but it was too much effort to get up.

"Penny, this is my friend Diane. Diane, my daughter, Penny."

"So lovely to meet you, Penny. I've heard a lot about you."

Who was this woman? Her dad never mentioned someone else joining them today. And what, he was in town for a few weeks and already had a girlfriend that he had to introduce to Penny? She knew she should have bailed. She hadn't even wanted to go in the first place but she felt bad refusing, and her mom said if she didn't go he would think Emma was manipulating her. But if she'd known her dad would have been just as happy spending the day at the beach with his new "friend" Diane, she would definitely have stayed home.

He helped Diane open her collapsible beach chair and adjusted the umbrella to shade her completely. "Diane's in town for the summer helping out with that big fund-raiser for the movie theater. Isn't that great?"

"Great," Penny said dully. She reached for her crutches, making sure the special beach supports were secured on the bottoms. Her mom ordered those online, too.

Her dad helped her get to her feet, but once she had her crutches under her arms, she was independently mobile.

"Don't go into the water," he said.

"I'm just walking to the edge."

Penny hobbled to the ocean. Just a few feet away from the chairs, and the breeze felt stronger.

The water rolled in fast, over her good ankle. She watched it recede, and as it rolled toward her, she felt the urge to count, the voice in her head louder than the waves. *I'm not listening to you,* she told the impulse. *I'm tired of listening to you! I'm tired of everyone!* It felt good to be angry. Anger was preferable to helplessness. The water washed over her feet, and she repeated her mantra: *I'm not listening to you.* It seemed to be working. The only thing keeping her from running into the water was her broken leg. She was bossing it back, but she couldn't move forward. As usual, she was stuck.

She turned around, waved to get her father's attention. "I want to go home," she yelled. The wind carried her voice away.

The rosebush was a small victory.

Emma knew it might be folly to transplant an entire rosebush from the Mount Misery garden to Windsong, but she wanted to try. She'd prepared for this venture a week ahead of time, visiting the Mount Misery garden and watering the rosebush with a B_1 plant fertilizer to foster root development. Then, in the Windsong back lawn, she dug a hole that would give her about six inches of space around the root-ball. She'd tested the spot ahead of time to make sure it had adequate drainage.

It was a particularly hot day, and digging out the root-ball was challenging. But the physical work was a good way to keep her mind off the fact that Penny was with Mark. Emma cut into the ground with the sharp shovel and moved in a circle, sweating out her rage. Then, when the plant was loose, she quickly transferred it onto a tarp for the transport to Windsong.

"I'm sorry," she said to the plant, knowing it was traumatized and hoping the roots didn't dry out before she could secure the bush in its new home.

She pulled her car to the side of Windsong, not bothering to use the garage. Every minute felt precious. She opened the door and nearly collided with Bea, who was strolling the grounds with a woman Emma had never seen before.

"Emma, I want you to meet —"

There was no time to be polite; Emma, holding the tarp, rushed past them with the urgency of someone about to perform an organ transplant.

She put the tarp down next to the fresh hole in the ground, then treated the planting site with some well-aged cow manure, a cup of bonemeal, and some peat moss. The plant itself seemed to be holding up okay, and by the time she placed it into the soil, just above the crown, she felt confident it would be able to adjust and thrive. Success! This was why she loved gardening. A little planning and a little effort always paid off, unlike the rest of life.

In the distance, she heard the faint strains of music coming off the bay. Kyle playing something while working on his boat. She brushed the dirt off her jeans, wiped her brow, and sat back on her heels.

Maybe it was time to tend to herself as carefully as she tended to her roses.

Chapter Forty-Two

Penny didn't speak to her father the entire ride back to the house. When he pulled into the Windsong driveway, he turned off the ignition.

"Penny, I know there's a lot going on and you're confused. But I'm not the enemy here."

"You're not exactly a father either," she said, and she slammed the door the best she could without losing her balance.

Inside the house, she leaned against the front door to steady herself. Her whole body was shaking. Her father had been so busy with that woman, he'd barely spoken to her the entire day. Eventually, she'd given up and put on her sunglasses and her headphones. Except she didn't listen to music; instead, she eavesdropped on her father and Diane's conversation. Diane talked a lot, and most of it was about spending her ex-husband's seemingly endless money. "You should produce this play with me," her dad said. "We'll make a fortune."

"I already have a fortune," Diane said, laughing.

Then there was no more talking, just really gross PDA.

Thinking about it made Penny's head hurt.

"Did you enjoy your beach excursion? What a beautiful day!"

Bea. She was always around. If Penny hadn't known better, she might have thought her mother had actually invited Bea to stay at the house to help keep an eye on her.

"I did *not* enjoy my beach excursion," Penny said. Bea spoke in such a stilted, formal way sometimes. Penny liked taking her absurd phrases and repeating them back to her, and she knew Bea kind of liked it too because sometimes it made her smile. But today Penny did it out of irritation, not playfulness.

"I'm sorry to hear that," Bea said. "I suppose it was the company?"

That was another thing about Bea; she just said whatever she wanted. It was like she had no problem saying things that other people only thought.

"The company didn't help," Penny said,

hobbling to her room.

Bea followed, and Penny tried to think what she could say to get rid of her. She tossed her crutches against the bed and dropped her bag onto the floor. Bea immediately swooped in and brushed sand off the comforter. "You should take the crutches into the bathroom and deal with the sand, Penny. Not drop them in here."

Bea sat on the edge of the bed. Weird! What did she want?

"I'm really tired," Penny said.

Bea cleared her throat. "I read your graphic novel."

What? "Oh my God, were you snooping around in here?" She couldn't believe it. Even her mother at her most annoying didn't mess around with her stuff.

"I think that's an excessively negative characterization."

"That's an invasion of privacy! It's totally not okay!"

"Penny, sit down for a moment," Bea said. "The book is . . . quite brilliant."

Penny looked at her. "Really?"

"I apologize for, as you said, invading your privacy. But Penny, I love art. I love art the way Henry loved it; I just never had the ability to create myself. Because of this, when I'm around artists, I have a compulsion to see what they're doing. My role in the creative process is to nurture and facilitate great talent when I find it. And I see great talent in you."

Penny could only look at her in surprise. Was she for real? She had to admit, the compliment felt good. It felt like talking to Henry. "I just wish Henry were here to see it," Penny said, her voice breaking. She started to cry.

Bea, clearly taken aback, reached out and patted her shoulder. "I think Henry did see your talent. That was why he enjoyed spending time with you."

"And why he left me this house?"

Bea pulled her hand away like she'd touched something hot. "Let's not, Penny."

"When Henry died, I felt like my art went with him. I'm afraid of forgetting things he taught me, and I can't tell if what I'm doing is any good. I mean, I can show my mom, and of course she's going to like it because she's my mom. But she doesn't really get it."

"Penny, you're an artist. People can't take that away from you, not with their approval or disapproval, not with their presence or absence."

Penny thought about that for a minute. "But when Henry was around, I felt like drawing meant something. Like it could be my future. I know Henry liked it here, but he'd already lived in New York City and done everything he'd wanted to do."

"It's hard to be patient when you're young, waiting for life to happen. I know. I felt the same way."

"You did?"

"Yes. And as soon as I turned eighteen I moved to New York."

"That's four more years for me." Penny groaned. "I can't wait that long."

She grabbed her crutches, made her way over to her desk, and pulled the graphic novel from under her sketch pad. Flipping through the pages, she cringed a little at some of the harsher sketches of Bea. The Bea in the novel was the way she'd seen Bea in the beginning of the summer, not now. The Bea sitting on her bed, talking about life and art and Henry, would make for an entirely different book. Maybe her next book. But first, the contest.

"Can I ask you something?" she said, looking back at Bea.

"You may." Bea sat rod straight, as if steeling herself against what might come out of Penny's mouth.

"I'm entering a contest," Penny said. "But I can't send in the whole graphic novel. I just have to pick two drawings for the first round, and I can't decide which. Maybe you can tell me the ones you think are the best?"

Bea looked momentarily stunned before breaking into a smile. It was a completely unfamiliar expression on her face.

"I'd be delighted," Bea said.

Penny handed her the manuscript.

"It's not finished yet, by the way. But the contest deadline is next week."

"And what do you win?"

"First prize is two hundred dollars. If I win, I'm going to use the money to self-publish the book." She'd thought it all through — she'd print a bunch of copies and ask Alexis to sell them at the bookstore.

"And if you don't win?"

"I'm not sure. Maybe Pauline will put it in the local/indie section in the back of the library."

"What's the local/indie section?" Bea said.

"It's stuff that people in town write that doesn't really get published. Like if you just wrote a book and printed up copies for your friends. Or I guess I could photocopy these pages and bind it up. That sort of thing."

"Stuff that people in town write that doesn't get published?"

Penny nodded. "Yeah, you know, like —"

Bea stood up from the bed, grabbing one

of the posts like she was suddenly unsteady on her feet. Then she left without a word, taking the manuscript with her.

Emma had to admit, the progress on Kyle's boat was impressive. The gunwales, stripped and refinished, gleamed in the sunlight. The floor was restored and varnished; it was hard to envision the state it had been in the last time she'd stood on the deck.

"It looks great," she said, taking a seat on a narrow bench near the helm.

"Thanks. I've made a lot of progress but it's not done yet."

"And you're sure this thing is seaworthy?" Emma said when he started the engine, only half teasing.

"Sean's mechanic completely rebuilt the motor. I did some woodwork for him in return. The next major task is finding the right name."

"Ah, yes — the grand boating superstition."

"Tradition," Kyle corrected her, casting the lines.

"This one regular at the bar, Pete Hasting, named his boat after his wife. They had this horrendous, ugly divorce but he said he couldn't change the name because it was bad luck."

Kyle laughed. "That's a problem. But, yeah, I guess there's a fine line between tradition and superstition on the water. But I like that about it. Rules, ritual, camaraderie. It's like religion without all the guilt."

She smiled, looking up at the sky as they backed out of the slip. A gull soared overhead, and for that moment, she felt almost as free as the bird.

It was a perfect day to be on the water, and the bay was littered with boats. She recognized a few sailboats from the marina but she was sure a lot of the traffic was daytrippers sailing in from Connecticut or Rhode Island. She had no doubt that in a few hours, a lot of people from these boats would be calling Sean to pick them up and take them to Main Street for dinner. A month earlier, she would have been the one seating them in the hotel dining room.

Emma watched familiar landmarks pass. She breathed deeply. When they were beyond the breakwater, he picked up speed.

"We really should be doing this at sunset," Kyle said.

"Sunset? Hmm. That sounds pretty romantic," she said. "Maybe too romantic for just friends."

"You'd be surprised how much can fit under the heading of 'just friends,' " he said.

Emma smiled. "I probably shouldn't be."

He reached for her hand. Her phone rang.

"Sorry," she said, pulling it out of her bag. "I just need to check who it is —"

Andrew Port.

"Emma, is this a good time to talk?" he said.

She pressed the phone firmer against her ear, trying to hear him clearly. "Um, sure. Everything okay?" No, everything was not okay. That was why she had an attorney in the first place.

"We have our first court date. July twenty-eighth."

Hearing the word *court,* she tensed. It suddenly felt ridiculous to be out having fun when so much was at stake. "And what happens then?"

"This is the custody conference that I told you about when we first met. Ideally, you and Mark will come to a compromise or some kind of agreement on this date and avoid further litigation. If that doesn't happen, then we go to trial."

"Okay," she said, her voice sounding strange to her own ears.

"We'll talk before then. But let me ask you while we're on the phone — opposing counsel says you're living with your new boyfriend and some other woman you just met this summer?"

"What? No — he's not my boyfriend," Emma said, glancing at Kyle. Kyle, who was next to her on the deck of a boat in the middle of the afternoon. "We're just friends. I'm allowed to have friends, aren't I?"

"Of course you are. Just . . . try to keep a low profile until the court date. Maintain normalcy. At this stage of the game, everything is fodder, you know what I mean?"

She did.

After she put her phone away, Kyle said, "What was that all about?"

"It was Andrew Port. The court date is set for the end of next week." Kyle started to say something, but she cut him off. "I'm sorry, but I need to go back."

"Okay, but —"

"Now!" she snapped, instantly regretting her tone, if not the sentiment.

"I'm trying to be supportive, Emma. Don't keep pushing me away."

She shook her head. "I need some space. And I really need for you to take me home."

The woman at the circulation desk looked up at Bea, perplexed.

It was the same assistant librarian as the last time, the one with the long strawberry-blond hair and heavy bangs. The one who had not allowed her to take the drawings out of the library. The one who had somehow failed to mention that there was a Henry Wyatt graphic novel in the collection!

"Yes, ma'am. I do remember you being here last month and I do remember you asking to see the Henry Wyatt drawings. And I pulled all of the drawings for you."

"But you never thought to mention that he had *an entire graphic novel* here?"

The woman consulted her computer screen, then looked back at Bea. "It's actually listed here as nonfiction. It doesn't say anything about format."

"Oh, for heaven's sake, never mind! Just show me where to find it."

Bea followed the librarian up the winding marble staircase to the rotunda and into the same back room where the sketches were stored.

The woman consulted a Post-it note, then checked the spines of a row of books on one of the higher shelves. Finally, she pulled out a slim paperback volume.

"Here you go," she said, handing it to Bea. "Would you like to check it out?"

Bea stared at the cover, marveling at the parallel to Penny's. It was a drawing of the exterior of Windsong, so finely sketched, it was like she could reach out and feel the texture of the stone. At the bottom, his initials. There was no title.

"I'm going to check it out, yes," Bea said. "After I read it. If you'll excuse me."

The rotunda was quiet. Who else would be in the library on a flawless July afternoon? Bea switched on the Tiffany lamp at one of the tables even though sunlight flooded the room. She didn't want to miss a single detail, not even the faintest stroke of his pencil.

Henry, why did you make it so difficult for me? I suppose you wanted us to have one last adventure.

She turned the pages gingerly. Henry's final work. Who would have imagined this was the form it would take? Life was a strange road, but perhaps never stranger than in the path of an artist. These were the people she'd chosen to surround herself with, and she should have learned by now to embrace their vagaries.

The first drawings were all familiar images — their old gallery on Spring Street, his apartment on the top floor, and sketches of himself and Bea. His rendering of Bea was much more flattering than Penny's drawings. He'd captured Bea in her prime. How many people were left who remembered her like that? Now, thanks to Henry, that era was immortalized right there, in black and white. It felt like a love letter.

The images shifted from the industrial streets of 1980s SoHo to the two of them driving in the quiet backwoods of the South Fork of Long Island. The American Hotel's exterior appeared in one frame. On the following page, a replica of a drawing she'd seen at the whaling museum, the one of the hotel bartender. The man Bea now knew to be Emma Mapson's father.

The following pages depicted Henry's newfound love affair with country living: Henry in the woods, Henry fishing with the bartender, Henry grilling over an open flame in a backyard. In one frame, Henry meets a pigtailed little girl visiting the hotel. Emma Mapson. Emma *Kirkland*.

Tom Kirkland. Emma. Penny. Three generations of a family. Maybe the embodiment of some sort of ideal Henry had in his mind? Henry made sure there was no doubt about what this period in his life meant to him. Unlike the black, white, and gray sketches in the beginning of the book, these were in color.

Bea closed the volume. How foolish, how sappy, to have felt even for a moment that this book was any kind of tribute to their relationship. She had, in the end, been nothing more than a work partner to him. And then he'd decided midlife that work was no longer important.

Of course he had not left the house to her. She had rejected him romantically, and it did not matter that she did it to protect their working relationship, because in the end he himself rejected the work. Ultimately, his deepest happiness had come from the life he'd made without her.

Bea's breath caught in her throat and she suddenly felt more alone than she'd ever felt. Had she wasted the past few decades? What was art, in the end, if it didn't translate into something beautiful in real life?

She wanted to hurl the book across the rotunda. Perhaps she would. But first she had to finish it, no matter how painful.

In the last quarter of the book, Henry returned again to black-and-white images. Tom Kirkland died; his funeral was mapped out in somber, sparse panels. And then Bea's visit to Windsong.

Her heart began to pound. He had remembered, and rendered exactly, a Ralph Lauren dress she'd worn during the trip. The question was, had he remembered the conversation they had the night sitting by the fire? The answer, spelled out in the dialogue bubbles, was decidedly yes.

He re-created, almost word for word the way she remembered it, their discussion about a future Henry Wyatt museum. Here was proof about his intentions for the house, for his work!

Disappointingly, that scene was her last appearance in the book. It was followed by drawings of Henry in solitude and at the hotel bar, sketching on cocktail napkins. His work had literally become disposable to him. And then, meeting Penny: *Emma's kid. I see the resemblance.* Their drawing lessons: *Every blank piece of paper is just a drawing waiting to be completed.*

All she could think about was the dialogue about the museum. Impatient for more validation, she flipped impatiently to the end of the book. But instead of finding more evidence that Henry had intended Bea to act as the steward of his legacy, she was confronted with half a dozen blank pages. Well, not completely blank. They seemed to be rooms at Windsong, but without any people or furniture in them. And then a blank page.

She sat still, her heart pounding and her stomach tight. Slowly, she flipped back a few pages to a scene of Henry with Penny bent over a drawing board. *Every blank piece of paper is a drawing waiting to be completed.*

Was this book finished? Or had he left it for someone else to fill in the blanks?

Bea packed the memoir in her bag. It felt heavy as lead. She walked slowly down the winding stairs to the checkout desk.

Chapter Forty-Three

With the court date looming on her calendar, Emma saw the auction planning as a welcome distraction. Really, what she wouldn't have given for a twelve-hour shift at the hotel. But short of that, the endless details for the auction soaked up enough of her time to keep her sane. And yet, it was evident that Bea could easily have coordinated the entire event on her own. The woman's organization and imagination were tireless. Emma had to force herself to take charge of something.

"Fine," Bea said, relenting. "You deal with the party yacht. I don't care how the guests get here. I'll just make sure it all works when they arrive."

After wrangling over logistics with the dockmaster, Emma was finally able to hire Cole Hopkins to transport guests from the marina to Windsong in his 142-foot dinner yacht, the *Great Blue.* Cheryl Meister convinced the party who'd already booked him for that date to reschedule their plan for the boat, writing them a hefty check for their inconvenience. Now all Emma had to do was a quick walk-through with Cole.

"This looks so wonderful! The guests might not want to leave for the auction," Emma said, standing on the sundeck outside a glass-enclosed atrium. She was only half joking. She followed him down to the lower deck, which featured a swimming platform at the stern and housed the engine room and crew quarters. The main level had a sheltered exterior deck leading into the dining room and galley; the upper deck had an outdoor dining space and a sky lounge.

"My concern is making sure I have adequate crew," Cole said. "How many are you expecting?"

"I think we'll be at capacity. One hundred and fifty."

He nodded. "Aside from Louise, I'll have an engineer and a few deckhands. The catering staff is your hire."

"I'm working on that. I'll make sure you're well covered."

He led her back up to the sky lounge, and she mapped out where the guests would have drinks and hors d'oeuvres. She pulled out her phone to calculate some budget items, signed the last of the paperwork, and disembarked feeling pretty good about everything.

She stood on the dock for a minute, blinking against the bright sun, looking to see if Sean was around to give her a lift back to Windsong. Instead, she spotted Kyle working on someone's boat, sanding with a giant planer, his T-shirt soaked through with sweat. Totally focused on what he was doing, he didn't notice her until she was close enough to climb on board.

"Hey! How's it going?" she shouted over the grinding of the machine.

He looked up, nodded, then went back to what he was doing.

Okay. She pushed back her feelings of rejection. Hadn't she told him she needed space?

So why did it feel so bad?

Angus rang the doorbell at Windsong just after two in the afternoon to drop off the last of the boxes from Emma's Mount Misery house. He was thoughtful enough to call ahead so Bea was expecting him.

Bea found herself dressing with extra care. She wanted to look nice, but not too "done." Still, no matter how hard she tried, she would never fit in with the town's impossibly casual aesthetic; she would make it to her grave without ever having worn yoga pants or a sweatshirt. But she felt compelled to put forward a softer look. She chose a pair of navy slacks from Carolina Herrera's resort collection. They were embellished with birds. She paired the pants with a white, lightweight knit top and a gauzy wrap. It was as casual as she could get.

She told herself she was just trying to make her life simpler, to finally get into country living mode after all these weeks. That it had nothing to do with her visitor that afternoon.

"Hello there, Bea," said Angus, easing a large box into the foyer. "Where would you like these?"

Back at the other house. Oh, she was trying to be less negative. Really, she was. "Do you want me to see if Kyle is around to help?" she said. "You shouldn't be lifting all of this."

As soon as she made the offer, she remembered, yet again, that Kyle was no longer at her disposal. She had driven him off, perhaps prematurely. It was her way. And it was regrettable.

"I'm just going to leave them right here until Emma gets back," Angus said.

Great. Now the front hall was a cluttered

mess. "That's fine," said Bea.

"Is Penny here? I haven't seen her in a few days."

"Emma dropped her at the bookstore while she's doing her errands in town," Bea told him regretfully, not wanting him to leave. She didn't know what to make of the urgent feeling of wanting his company, but she listened to it. "I brewed some peach tea and it should be chilled by now. I bought it from that organic place on the corner of Bay Street. Come have some."

"I don't want to impose . . ."

"Angus," she said. "Please stop being polite with me. I'd like to think that we're friends."

He smiled, and something deep inside of her began to thaw. She could feel it, like a loosening muscle. And it struck her, faced with all the boxes, that Angus was about to become homeless.

"May I ask where you plan to move once you vacate your current house?"

"I'm working on a few options. Until I find something permanent, I'll be staying in one of the rooms upstairs at the whaling museum."

In the kitchen, she noted that he sat in the exact same spot at the island that he'd chosen the day Emma got served with the court papers. The thought made her shudder. If he ever found out about her role in that . . .

Shaking the thought away, she pulled two glasses from the cabinet and sliced a lemon, a lime, and an orange. When she set the pitcher of tea and the sliced fruit in front of him he said, "That's a lot of citrus."

"I got in the habit from the tea at the Golden Pear," she said. "The way they do it is quite lovely."

"I agree," he said.

They sat in congenial silence for a few moments. She felt an unusual pressing need for him to think kindly of her. She didn't understand it, but it prompted her to say, "Angus, you should consider moving in here. Kyle has left — there's plenty of room. And I'm sure it would make Emma happy."

He shook his head. "I think you moving out would make Emma happy."

"Yes, well, I have news for you. One person does not mind having me around: Penny. I've proven to be great fodder for her art."

"Fodder?" he said.

"Yes. Are you aware of her graphic novel?" The look on his face told her he'd had no idea. "Wait here. I'll be right back."

She took the stairs to her room. Last

night, she'd pored over Penny's drawings and selected a few pages for Penny to submit for her contest. But she was not ready to hand it all back over to her. Instead, she had placed it side by side with Henry's book, certain there was something she was missing. It nagged at her all night. At four in the morning, she began flipping through them both, and she'd kept at it until the sun came up.

She went back down the stairs. Her body ached but her mind, her spirit, felt lighter. Oh, to share this puzzle with someone else! What a relief.

She moved the tea pitcher out of the way and wiped condensation from the marble surface before setting down both manuscripts. "Penny has been working on this since she moved in," Bea said, sliding her work over to him. "Be careful, the pages are loose."

"Queen Bea," he said, raising an eyebrow.

"She has quite a sensibility," Bea said.

"I know she's constantly reading these graphic books, but I didn't realize she'd set out to write one of her own."

"I think Henry encouraged her. They were working on them last summer. In fact, he finished one himself. I found it at the library. And I want to show you something in it." She flipped to the back of the book where Henry had written their conversation about the house becoming a museum. "See? I didn't make this up. I'm not the villain here." *Except in Penny's novel, of course.*

"Bea," Angus said, his expression softening. "I never thought you were a villain. I just knew Emma wasn't at fault here. If anyone muddied the waters, it was Henry. He should have made his intentions clear to you."

It was true. And she knew it wasn't an oversight.

She turned to the last pages of the book and paused at the empty dining room of Windsong, the pool visible through the wall of glass.

Angus read through Penny's book, chuckling at some of her dialogue. He pulled aside one page, a drawing of the four of them facing off around the dining-room table. It was the day Bea had first discovered them at the house.

"Henry knew you for many years, right?" Angus said.

"Over fifty," she said.

"He might have guessed you would run out here, lay claim to the house. That you wouldn't give up so easily. He could have avoided that if he'd told you his wishes ahead of time. Okay, let's say he didn't want to argue with you, didn't want to debate it. He could have just left you a note with his will stating his intentions. And that could have prevented this scene." He slid the drawing over to her. "You told me once he did everything by design."

Bea took the paper from him. *Every blank piece of paper is just a drawing waiting to be completed.*

"What are you saying?"

Angus shrugged. "I didn't know the man very well. I met him a few times picking up Penny from the hotel. But I do know that when my wife was ill, she was thinking more about me than about herself. That's what you do when you love someone. She didn't want me to be alone and she made me promise to stay with the Mapsons. She said she couldn't rest in peace knowing I was alone."

Bea turned to the back of his book, the final empty pages. And she slid Penny's drawing of the four of them standing together in the dining room right into the end. She looked at it and shook her head.

"Henry would know I'd never want to live out here with some woman and her child. That's not who I am! No, this isn't the answer at all."

And yet her hand shook as she closed the book.

CHAPTER FORTY-FOUR

Her mother had sneaked off without saying good-bye that morning. She thought Penny didn't know about the court date, but Penny knew everything. How could she not? Her mom did a lot of talking, and really, most of the house was just one big open room. It had been a lot easier to keep secrets on Mount Misery. That's how Penny had gotten herself into trouble in the first place.

She didn't say any of this to Dr. Wang.

"Your mother's not here today?"

Penny shook her head. "Just me."

Angus was outside in the waiting room. He'd told her on the drive over that her mother had a "meeting." Secrets! Lies! The endless suckage of being a kid. This had to do with her life too. Didn't anyone care about that? Just thinking about it made her squirm in her seat.

She considered a trip to the bathroom, but then remembered she didn't have her

Purell. She was trying, really trying, not to give in to her compulsions. She'd left her hand sanitizer at home on her nightstand.

"How's the positivity board going?" Dr. Wang asked.

"I haven't worked on it very much," Penny said.

"And why is that?"

"I've been busy."

"Penny, if you don't do your exercises and follow my directions, then I can't help you."

Maybe not. But *something* was helping. She thought of the way she'd bossed it back at the ocean that day with her dad. She thought of the entire graphic novel she'd written without throwing away drawings to start over. She looked at the back of her hands, barely dry. No cracks. No bleeding. Didn't Dr. Wang notice?

Art was her positivity board. But Dr. Wang would never understand.

Emma thought she had mentally prepared herself for the court appearance. But she realized, sitting on a long wooden bench in the corridor of the courthouse, that all along she had been in some degree of denial. Accepting the full weight of the situation all these weeks would have crushed her. Now, seeing Andrew Port walk in wearing a suit

473

and carrying a briefcase, there was no avoiding what was happening, no glossing over what was at stake. Her insides felt like liquid, like the only thing holding her together was the external shell. Even that was about to crack.

"I'll be back in a few minutes. Just sit tight," Andrew said. She watched him walk down the hall to consult with Mark's lawyer, Carter Shift, a much older, stout man wearing a seersucker suit and a pink and silver tie. So far, she hadn't seen Mark. The sight of him should just about do her in entirely.

She fumbled through her bag for the paperback she'd brought with her. It was a reread — she couldn't focus on anything new. She opened the book and the words swam in front of her eyes, as impossible to process as if they'd been written in a foreign language.

Someone sat next to her. She glanced over, bracing for whatever update Andrew would give her. Instead, she found Kyle.

"Oh! Hi. What are you doing here?"

She hadn't seen him in days, not since the afternoon on Long Wharf when he'd barely nodded at her. She'd walked down to the Windsong dock every night, but he was never there. She knew she could find out where he was if she asked Sean and that she should reach out to him, but she didn't. It was like the situation with her job; she wasn't in a better place, and she wasn't capable of offering any more of herself now than she had been before. So she did nothing.

"I wanted to be here for support."

"Thank you," she said. "You really have been such a help and I'm sorry if I've seemed ungrateful."

He reached over and squeezed her hand. "It's okay, Emma. We're friends."

She squeezed back.

"Where's Andrew?" he said.

"He's down the hall somewhere. Talking to Mark's lawyer."

Kyle leaned forward, peering down the corridor. "I see him. He's heading back."

Andrew walked briskly, all business. Emma sensed he was keyed up, like an athlete before a big game. He nodded at Kyle and sat on Emma's other side.

"So we're just waiting for Mark to get here," he said. "Then I'm going to negotiate — with your input — with the opposing counsel to try to come to a compromise. The court wants us to work this out, and trust me, it's always better not to go before the judge."

She swallowed hard. "I just don't know

what the compromise would be. I don't think he should even have partial custody."

"I know you don't. But it might be better than the alternative."

Kyle put his arm around her. Andrew pulled a stack of papers from under his arm.

Minutes dragged by. Carter Shift strode over and signaled to Andrew. The two of them walked off, heads bent together.

"What's going on?" she said.

"Em, try not to freak out," Kyle said. "It's going to be a long day and you need to just trust Andrew to do his job. That's why you're paying him."

Kyle reached for her hand. For a moment, it was comforting. More waiting. When she finally saw Andrew walking back to them, she jumped up.

"Any news?"

"Mark is here. I've been negotiating with his attorney but we're not getting anywhere."

"So what does that mean?" Emma said.

Carter Shift walked toward them. He didn't so much as glance at Emma — not that she wanted to be forced to smile or talk to him. Still, it was dehumanizing. But maybe that was the point. His job was to take her child away from her.

"Can your client meet?" he said.

Andrew said something affirmative, and before she knew what was happening, she was following him down a hall that seemed to stretch on forever. Her uncomfortable heels, last worn at a funeral, made too much noise against the tile floor. Carter Shift walked a few feet ahead of them. No one said a word.

The sight of Mark inside the conference room was a punch to the gut.

He was tan, dressed in a sports jacket and khakis. He didn't look like an out-of-work actor. He looked like perfect casting for the role of Handsome Dad.

The room was bare, with just a long rectangular table surrounded by half a dozen wood chairs. The air-conditioning unit wheezed freezing air. She sat next to Andrew on the side of the table closest to the door. Mark sat directly opposite her. She glared at him. *I can't believe you're doing this.* He avoided her eyes. *Coward.*

"You want to open here, Andrew?" said Carter.

Andrew shuffled through some papers. "I'll reiterate: My client has been the sole custodial parent for the past thirteen years. There is no material change of circumstance and there is no cause for changing custody.

She is willing to consider expanded visitation."

Carter shook his head as if they'd been over this a dozen times already — which they probably had. He took off his glasses and looked at Emma.

"That's not going to cut it, Andrew. My client is not willing to leave his minor child unsupervised for twelve hours a day — a lack of parental control that resulted in an accident that left her with a broken leg. In addition to that is the fact that your client has ignored the advice of the child's psychiatrist to medicate in order to treat her obsessive-compulsive disorder, which leaves the child suffering unnecessarily. Your client has showed a reckless disregard for the child's safety and well-being."

Emma turned to Andrew. Reckless disregard? Was he serious?

Someone knocked on the door and before anyone could respond, an officer of the court poked his head in.

"Can I speak to counsel?"

Andrew and Mark's attorney conferred in the doorway. Emma glanced at Mark. His expression was wounded, as if *she* were the one doing this to *him*. How unbelievable that she had once loved this man. He had held her hand while she gave birth, and now he was trying to destroy her life. Because that is what it would do if she lost Penny. How had she gotten into this position? How had things gone so terribly off course?

The house.

She should have known the day Henry Wyatt's lawyer showed up that it was too good to be true. She was Cinderella and the clock was striking midnight.

The lawyers returned to the table and packed up their paperwork.

"The judge is calling us in," Andrew said to her.

She followed him back into the hallway, Mark and his lawyer a few feet behind them. Again, the long walk, the clacking of her heels. Andrew stopped in front of an elevator. Mark took the stairs.

"What does this mean?" she whispered to Andrew.

"The judge will want to make sure both parties understand what happens if we can't come to an agreement today. He's going to really stress how beneficial it would be — not just for you, but for the child — to get this settled."

"Can we?"

"Your ex isn't budging. So unless you want to give in — and obviously you don't — I'm afraid not."

Courtroom B was on the second floor. Outside the door, a list of cases being litigated that day. She spotted *Mapson v. Mapson.*

Inside, the room was smaller than she'd expected but otherwise exactly like the courtrooms she'd seen on television. Lots of wood paneling; long benches for seating. A wooden divide up front with a low swinging door and, beyond that, the elevated bench area for the judge. The only people in the room were a court officer and a stenographer.

Emma followed Andrew down the center aisle and sat next to him in the second row. Across the aisle, Mark took his place next to his attorney.

Andrew checked his phone. The gesture shocked her. How could he think of anything except what was about to happen in that room? She rubbed her hands together. They were like ice.

The court officer announced the Honorable Gerald K. Walker, and a man with brown hair threaded with silver and a ruddy complexion took to the bench. Judge Walker spoke to the court officer and then called Andrew and Mark's attorney to the front. They seemed to talk for a long time, though it was probably less than five minutes. Annoying phone habit aside, she felt better when Andrew was beside her and was relieved when he finally slid back into his seat.

"Ms. Mapson, Mr. Mapson. Your attorneys have advised me you are not reaching a settlement today. I encourage you to go back to conference and give it one last try. Otherwise, we will set a date for trial. We will have to establish home visits and I will assign a court psychologist to interview the minor child. The trial date will be roughly six months from now —"

Something captured the judge's attention. He narrowed his eyes, glaring at the back of the room.

"Ma'am, this is a closed hearing."

Everyone turned, and Emma gasped. Bea made her way down the aisle, dressed in a red, black, and white Chanel suit with ropes and ropes of pearls. She was a peacock in a roomful of pigeons. She marched forward like it was a royal court and she was queen.

"Your Honor, I do apologize. But I need to speak."

"You can wait outside and speak to counsel." He glanced at his desk, jotted something down, and then dismissed everyone. Bea turned on her heel and walked out of the room, followed by Mark and his lawyer.

481

"Who was that?" Andrew said to her.

"Bea Winstead. She was a longtime friend of the man who left my daughter the house. She's the one who has been staying there."

"What's this all about?"

Emma shook her head. "I have *no* idea."

They were about to find out.

Mark, his lawyer, and Bea were already huddled in the far corner of the hallway. Emma wanted to pull Bea aside and talk to her alone. Whatever this was, it wasn't something she wanted to deal with in front of Carter Shift, Mark, or even her own attorney.

Kyle spotted them and made his way down the hall. Carter tried to shoo him away but Emma said, "He's with me. I want him to stay."

Kyle gave her a *What's going on?* look. She shrugged.

"I'm Ms. Mapson's attorney, Andrew Port," Andrew said to Bea. "Can I help you with something?"

"Lovely to meet you, Mr. Port," she said, fanning herself with a silk scarf. "I was just asking Mr. Shift if he was aware of the agreement between his client and myself."

Emma looked at Mark, who stared at Bea with an expression she couldn't decipher. Surprise? It was more than that. It was fear.

"We should do this in a conference room," Carter said, picking up on Mark's unease.

"I cannot stand to move to another drab room," Bea said. "I don't know why legal quarters need to be so dreadful. It's as if you're found guilty just by walking through the door."

"Bea, what's going on?" Kyle said.

Bea ignored him and addressed Andrew and Carter. "In the hopes of all of us getting out of here as expediently as possible — or at least, in the hopes that *I* can get out of here expediently — let me bottom-line this for you. Last month, Mark Mapson came to me with promises to sell me his daughter's recently inherited mansion as soon as it was legally feasible to do so. In exchange for this transaction, he would get a fee upfront and a commission on the vast sum of money I would ultimately pay to acquire the house. Of course, in order to take control of the estate, he first needed legal guardianship of his daughter." She smiled. "He asked me for a check for his legal fees, which I gave him. I suppose that's where you come in, Mr. Shift."

Could this be true? Mark and Bea conspiring against her? And all this time she'd been letting the woman live under her roof! Emma wanted to scream.

"That's quite a story, Ms. Winstead," said Carter, glancing at Andrew. "I'm sure my client takes issue with your interpretation of any conversation that might have taken place between the two of you."

Emma stared at Mark and he looked away, his head bowed.

Bea was telling the truth.

"I need to speak with my client," Carter said. "Andrew, let's adjourn for the day. I'll be in touch."

Andrew signaled for Emma to follow him down the hall so they had some privacy. She glanced back over her shoulder and saw Bea had already left.

"This is unbelievable," Emma said.

"I have to admit, this is a new one for me." Andrew rubbed his jaw.

"Does this mean it's over?"

"No, but it certainly gives us a stronger negotiating position for a settlement. I'm hoping Mark is now nervous enough to compromise."

"But this makes it so obvious this isn't about Penny's best interests — that it's about money and an expensive house!" It took a lot of effort for her to keep her voice at just a loud whisper.

"Still, we don't want to end up before the

judge. You just never know what might happen."

Wasn't that the truth.

CHAPTER FORTY-FIVE

Penny stared at the pool, wishing for the thousandth time she hadn't gone out and broken her leg. Swimming would have let her burn off her nervous energy. Her mother had been out all afternoon, and there was still no mention from Angus about what was happening with her "meeting." With every hour that passed, the weight of what it could all mean grew heavier. And Bea wasn't even around to distract her with her bossiness and complaints.

She moved her pencil across the sketch pad in her lap, outlining the shape of the pool. Then she let herself just stare at the water. Henry always said if you want to draw something accurately, you have to really *see* it. What was the water doing? Was it still or moving slightly? Even Henry admitted that reflective surfaces were tough.

"An easy trick is to let the light do all the work," he said. It took her a while to understand what he meant by that, but that's where all the hours of drawing side by side with him came in. How would she keep getting better now that he was gone? She could find an art class, but that was hardly the same thing.

The sliding glass door to the house opened behind her. She turned around, expecting to see Angus checking up on her again. Instead, her mom headed down the path, dressed up in a skirt and blouse and high heels. She took off her shoes as she got closer to the pool, padded over to Penny, and gave her a hug.

"Sorry I didn't see you before I left this morning," Emma said. "How was therapy?" She pulled sunglasses out of her purse and rolled up her shirtsleeves.

Therapy? Who cared about therapy? Were they going to act like her mom hadn't spent the day with lawyers? She was dying to know what had happened, but something held her back from pushing. She didn't want to upset her mom — even if it meant having to wait a little longer for information.

"Um, therapy was okay. The usual."

She tried to read her mother's expression for clues about her day but her eyes were hidden behind sunglasses.

"Dr. Wang left me a message that you need to keep up with your positivity board and your worksheets."

Penny sighed and held up her drawing pad. "This is my positivity board."

Her mother looked at her skeptically. "Penny, it's really important that —"

"I'm serious. I've written almost a whole graphic novel. You know how I have a hard time sticking with things, not starting over. But I pushed through it for this and I feel so much better when I'm working. And I've been able to keep the same mind-set when I'm not drawing. See?"

She held out her unblemished hands, and her mother looked down. She reached for them and clasped them in her own.

"Mom," Penny said, swallowing hard. "Where did you go today?"

Her mother nodded, as if she'd been expecting the question. "I met with lawyers and your father about the custody issue."

"And?"

"And . . . I'm working on it. We'll see. Don't you worry."

From the tight set of her mother's mouth, Penny understood that she was absolutely worried.

"It'll be okay, Mom."

"I know," she said quietly. "I'm doing

488

everything I can to make sure nothing changes. Except, actually, one thing will be changing. Bea won't be living here."

Penny looked at her in surprise. "She said she's leaving?"

"It's not up to her," Emma snapped.

Had something happened to make her mother hyped up again about getting rid of Bea? She couldn't imagine why her mom was even thinking about that when she had the more serious stuff going on with her dad. Did everything have to do with the house?

"I heard you say once that Dad was only spending time with me for this house. Is that true?"

"Penny, you shouldn't eavesdrop."

"The house is all *open*, Mom."

Her mother sighed. "I don't know what goes on in your father's head."

Penny looked out at the pool. The sun was really dancing off the water. *Let the light do the work.*

"Where is Bea going to go? Back to New York City?"

"I really don't know, Penny. And frankly, I don't care."

Penny had been thinking a lot about Bea Winstead's story about leaving home as soon as she turned eighteen. Bea understood Penny's feelings about wanting to leave, but her mother never would.

"She's lucky she gets to go," Penny said.

Her mother looked at her sharply. "We live in this beautiful house now and you're still complaining?"

Penny shook her head. "No. I mean, not about the house. It's amazing. But I don't know. Someday I might not live here. You know what I mean?"

"I understand," Emma said slowly.

"So you'd be okay with that?"

"Penny, you could live on the moon and it wouldn't change the fact that I'm your mother, that I love you more than anything in the world. But for now, I'm so happy you're right here with me."

Her mother still had her sunglasses on, but Penny spotted a wet streak on her face. Penny leaned forward, bracing herself on her good leg, and hugged her. Her mother's arms felt like they'd never let go.

Emma vacillated between feeling that some of her rage toward Bea was misplaced and also thinking she wasn't angry enough.

She couldn't get her mind around the idea of Bea sitting down and writing Mark a check. How had that even happened? She had every intention of asking Bea the

490

minute she walked into the house. The opportunity to confront her was the only thing keeping Emma from changing the locks.

Emma paced in the kitchen. She poured herself a peach iced tea from a glass pitcher in the refrigerator, resisting the urge to turn it into a Long Island iced tea. As soon as she heard the click of the front door opening, she rushed to the entrance hall.

Bea's face was shiny with perspiration, her white hair frizzing slightly at the ends. She dropped her straw Chanel purse on the foyer side table with an uncharacteristic weariness.

"I want to talk to you," Emma said.

"I suspected you might," Bea said. "Perhaps we should go outside. For privacy."

"Privacy. Yeah, I'm sure you don't want anyone to hear what I have to say. Luckily for you, Angus already left and Penny's by the pool."

"Very well, then," Bea said. "Can we at least sit down?"

She strode ahead to the kitchen, Emma keeping pace right behind her. Why was Bea still acting like she was in charge, even in this interaction? It was infuriating!

Bea poured her own glass of the iced tea, then sat at the island. Emma stood directly opposite her, the width of the table between them.

"How could you give Mark money to take my child away? Actually, back up — how did you two even meet?"

"He came to the house," Bea said, twisting one of the ropes of pearls.

The audacity of it, the premeditation of it all, took her breath away. "When?"

"Before Penny's accident. I'm truly sorry, Emma. In my defense, I did not give him money to take Penny away from you. My motivation was simply to help him gain control of the estate. It was just a business decision."

"*Business* is not more important than family. And you almost ruined mine. You still might have!"

Bea shook her head so vigorously her large pearl earrings wobbled. "Mark's case is completely undermined."

"No, it's not! We still have to settle. And you don't know him. He's like a dog with a bone. You gave him this opening and he's not going to give up easily."

She knew, even as she said it, the court case was not entirely Bea's fault. Mark would have made his play with or without her. But she certainly made it easy for him.

"I'll give you any amount of money you

need to see it through —"

"I don't want your money! Did you ever think that maybe the reason Henry didn't leave you this house is that you're a bad person? All you care about is money and *things.* You have no idea what really matters."

Bea, looking stricken, pressed her hand to her chest. "I apologize for hurting you, Emma. I mean it sincerely."

"You need to get out."

"I understand, but —"

"No, Bea. This is over. Leave. Today."

"I would like to suggest, if you would consider it, that I stay until after the auction next week. There's work left to be done and I can at least take that off your hands and see this event through to the end."

Emma was so emotionally drained, she couldn't imagine even attending the auction, let alone managing the last-minute details. "Fine," she said. "But that's it. You're out of here the day after the auction. Not packing, not starting to leave — you're out of the house. Or the next time you're in court, it will be for trespassing."

Bea was not typically one to hide from her problems, but she was not above hiding from people who were angry with her.

During a solitary, early dinner at Wölffer Kitchen, she mentally replayed the conversation with Emma over and over. She sipped her rosé, picked absently at her cod, and had the realization that if Emma had such a horrible opinion of her, so must Angus.

Bea pushed her plate away, her stomach churning. She had to talk to him.

"Young lady, the check, please," Bea said, hailing the waitress impatiently.

"Would you like that to go?"

"No," Bea said. "I'm finished." But it gave her an idea.

She walked around the corner to Dockside Bar and Grill. A breeze blew off the water, the air particularly fragrant. The gulls squawked, couples walked by holding hands, and all the while Bea felt like a virtual criminal. She had made a mistake. Now she had to find a way to make it right.

The outside patio was already full, and she felt a pang to see the table where she had happily sat with Angus not that long ago.

After checking in with the hostess, she ordered the pulled-pork dish with cheddar and black beans to go. While she waited, she debated whether to call Angus first and tell him she was stopping by but decided against it. Why give him the opportunity to tell her not to come?

The food took quite some time, enough of a wait that she nearly lost the nerve to visit him. But once the hostess placed the package in her hands, the idea of simply retreating back to Windsong, sticking the food in the refrigerator to stand as a shameful reminder of her aborted mission, was equally as distressing. And then the task of apologizing to Angus would still be ahead of her.

She called a taxi to take her to Mount Misery. The sun was just beginning to set but it was still close to ninety degrees. The taxi driver somehow hadn't thought to put on the air-conditioning, so that unpleasant exchange added to her roiling nerves. At least when she was back in the city, she would have her regular driver. She would, of course, need to start looking for a new assistant. At the moment, her former assistant was probably yet another person who was angry with her. Well, that was one apology she had no intention of making. She might have made a mistake, but she still didn't answer to Kyle Dunlap.

The front of Angus and Emma's old house looked different. The decorations and trinkets that had once hung outside — had it been a whale above the door? — were gone.

She wondered if Angus had already moved out.

Holding the dinner package in the crook of one arm, she rang the bell. Long minutes passed before Angus opened the door.

"Oh, good! You *are* still here," she said.

"What are you doing here?" he said through the screen.

"I've come to apologize."

He hesitated. She hadn't considered the possibility that he might close the door in her face.

"I realize it's an imposition to show up at dinnertime but I've brought you food from Dockside. It would be a shame to let it get cold."

Angus shook his head but opened the door and stepped aside for her to enter.

The house was nearly empty. In the living room, the only remaining furniture was the couch and an end table. All of the picture frames, vases, magazines, and knickknacks that had cluttered the place during her last visit were gone.

"Have you decided where you're moving?" she said.

"Don't pretend to be my friend, Bea. That's over."

The comment hurt — a lot. "I'm not pretending," she said quietly. She handed him the bag from Dockside, and he took it from her, stone-faced. She followed him into the kitchen, standing awkwardly in the doorway while he shoved the food into the refrigerator. He turned to her, shaking his head.

"You think you can just show up here as if nothing has happened?" he said.

"Of course not. I've come to apologize. That's why I'm here."

"The part I can't get past is that during all of our talks, during all the time we spent together, you were secretly helping Emma's ex-husband. How could you even look me in the eye?"

She swallowed hard. "There were times when I couldn't. It bothered me — it did. I felt conflicted but I was looking at the transaction with Mark as a business decision. It took some time for me to see things through a different lens, but as soon as I did, I set out to make it right."

"Did it occur to you that it might be too little, too late?"

"No, because it's not. It's going to get fixed. I'll do whatever it takes."

Angus seemed not to have heard her. He pulled a chair from the kitchen table and sat down. When he finally spoke, it was while looking down at the braided cloth place mat in front of him.

"The worst part for me is that it had been such a long time since I enjoyed the company of a woman my own age. I had thought maybe . . ."

"Angus —"

"It's just very disappointing." He looked up at her, and their eyes met. "I need for you to leave."

Chapter Forty-Six

Bea woke before dawn and wandered the still house like a ghost.

For once, she took no pleasure in the quiet of the early hour. Days after the court hearing, she had never felt more alone. She moved from room to room, staring at the art, trying to find peace of mind standing in front of the relics of her past.

Back in the bedroom, sitting on Henry's bed, she read and reread the memoir, seeking comfort in the images of their time together but finding even that somehow hollow.

She flipped to the back and checked the due date at the library. It was unthinkable that she would return it to be exiled to that records room. She decided she would make a sizable donation to the library, and certainly after that, they would overlook an unreturned book.

With that settled in her mind, she placed

it on top of the pile of belongings she would begin to pack later that day and noticed Penny's drawing poking out of the book where she'd stuck it.

She picked it up again, but an inconvenient thought suddenly struck her: As much as she wanted to keep the book for herself, she knew there was someone else who should see it. Maybe even someone else who should have it.

She lowered herself to the floor and pushed the bed frame to release the hidden drawer. She took a drawing pencil and a sheet of paper from one of the notepads and began writing.

Dear Emma:

I know I hurt you and your family with my actions and I wanted, in a small way, to try and give something back. I don't know if you were aware that your father and Henry were friends. I made the connection myself only recently. He is remembered here, in this book by Henry. I thought you and Penny might like to have it.

Sincerely,
Bea

She wedged the note into the front of the

book, then paced uncertainly in the room. She wanted to make the gesture, but she didn't want to let the book go. She ultimately decided that it was more important to make the conciliatory gesture toward Emma than to keep the book. She hoped, desperately, to make things right.

Bea put on a linen pantsuit, her pearls, and a straw hat. It was always easier to face a difficult moment when one was well attired.

Again, she walked down the stairs, this time holding the book. The house was still quiet, but a quick look through the guest wing indicated that Emma had already left the house. Where could she have run off to so early? And then she thought about the flowers and realized she might be in the garden. The woman was always elbows-deep in dirt.

Outside, it was already humid. She swatted away a yellow jacket. All this nature was wearing on her. She spotted another Manhattan transplant over by the water — her former assistant waved at her from the bow of his little boat. She ignored him, but he shouted her name. Oh, for heaven's sake. She looked around for Emma and, not finding her, figured she might as well see what on earth Kyle wanted.

"I'm not setting foot on that thing, so if you want to talk you're going to have to get onto dry land," she said from the dock, and she huffed impatiently while he disembarked.

"You went on the water taxi," he said. He was tan; his hair was bleached shades lighter from the sun. He looked like a different person than the one who'd driven her out to the house two months ago.

"That man was a professional," she said.

"Well, so am I."

"You're a professional what?"

He nodded toward the boat. "I restored this boat. I'm living on it. Other people in town are hiring me to work on their boats."

"Well, good for you. So what can I do for you, Kyle? I'm quite busy."

"You were out here anyway."

"I'm looking for Emma."

"I don't think she wants to talk to you."

"Don't you start in on me too. I know it was not my finest hour, but I'll fix it."

He bent down to adjust a rope hanging off the dock. "I believe you will, Bea."

"Finally. At least one person who doesn't underestimate me."

"I definitely never underestimated you. I think, though, I underestimated myself the past few years in New York." He stood up, looking out at the water. "It was time for a change."

"Yes, well, I've always said, one has to be the architect of one's own life. And now I suppose if I ever need . . . boat renovation, I know whom to call. We all need to move forward." She felt perspiration around her neck. Very damaging to pearls. "I need to get indoors."

She walked back up the dock.

"Bea," Kyle called out. She turned, shading her eyes with her hand.

"Yes?"

"Make things right for Emma."

Hadn't she just said she would? How irritating. With a shake of her head, she continued making her way back to the house.

She checked the kitchen and the living room and the breakfast nook. Emma was nowhere to be found, nor was Penny. She supposed she wasn't the only one with the impulse to make herself scarce. It was going to be a long week for all of them.

Emma's bedroom door was open. She peeked inside, and when she was certain no one was there, she placed Henry's book on the bed.

Yes, they all had to move forward. She had hoped Henry's drawings would give her a clue how to do that. But they had raised more questions than they had answered.

She removed Penny's drawing from the back of the book so she could return it to where it belonged in the loose manuscript pages of her graphic novel. Penny, the budding artist.

With a sudden burst of clarity, she realized what Henry had wanted.

She stood very still, holding Penny's drawing of the four of them — Penny, Emma, Angus, and Bea — in the Windsong dining room. The scene of the absurd circumstance of their first meeting, the day she had learned that Henry had left his house to a child.

Outside, a woodpecker hammered away at a tree. Bea told herself to breathe.

Okay, Henry. I finally get what you want.

She just hoped it wasn't too late to make it happen.

It was part of Emma's new routine: Say good night to Penny, pour a glass of wine, and sit out by the pool until she felt like maybe, just maybe, she was tired enough to fall asleep. Tonight was a little different because, as she settled into one of the chaise longues, she had Henry Wyatt's book propped up on her knees.

Earlier that day, after Penny's appointment with Dr. Wang, she'd returned to the house to change into lighter clothes before she ran out again to do more errands. But then she found the book. At first, spotting it against her stark white comforter, she thought it was something Penny was reading and had left accidentally in her room. The note sticking out was the only thing that flagged her attention to take a closer look. And once she'd read Bea's words, she forgot about her errands.

At first, she considered simply marching Henry's book back to Bea's room and leaving it there unread. She did not want to let Bea get to her, did not want to be manipulated into forgiving Bea for what she'd pulled. But the opportunity to look at Henry's remembrance of her father, a friendship she almost could not believe had existed and that she had not known about, was too much to resist. And after she read the book, she was glad she hadn't resisted. Oh, the drawings!

Sketches of the two men fishing and boating and drinking at the bar at the hotel captured her father in ways she'd never witnessed. The true gift of an artist's eye was seeing things no one else saw — things that not even a camera could pick up. It warmed her heart to get a glimpse of the happiness her father had experienced the last year of his life as he shared his beloved town with an outsider. She'd always thought of her father as the ultimate local, someone who would never mix with the summer people. And yet a stranger from Manhattan had walked into his bar and inspired a true friendship. It said something about her father's generosity and openness that made her suffer the loss of him all over again. But it also made her think about the type of woman he'd want her to be.

It was impossible, too, not to see Penny's drawings in a whole new way. Her art wasn't just a hobby or good therapy for her. She could someday do work that touched other people. The significance of her talent, the responsibility of it, felt suddenly weighty.

She looked up at the sound of Kyle's boat, the motor rumbling in the distance. It was hard to tell if he was coming or going until the rustling of the tall, weedy grass bordering the stretch of beach beyond the pool clued her in that she was getting a visitor.

"Hey," he said, emerging from the shadows. "I hope this isn't too much of an intrusion."

"Not at all," she said, putting the book aside. The truth was, she'd been thinking about him. They hadn't crossed paths since the day at the courthouse. She didn't know if this was because she was running around getting things finalized for the auction party, because he was busy working, or because he was simply less interested in spending time with her now that they were firmly in the friend zone.

But she did know that something inside of her soared just a little as he moved closer.

"Have a seat," she said.

"I actually need your help on the water."

"My help?"

"Yeah. I'm ready to christen the boat. It's bad luck to do it alone," he said.

"You sailors and your superstitions. Isn't Sean around?" Why did she have to give him such a hard time? She was delighted to be asked. Would she ever stop being so defensive? One day she was going to push him too hard and he'd never come back.

"Sean is home with Alexis. But aside from that, a woman is supposed to do the honors."

Was that true? More important, did she care?

She slipped her sneakers on and fell into step beside him as they went down the stone path past the grassy patch to the gravelly sand. The ground was still wet from rain

507

the night before, and her feet sank into it. When they reached the dock, she stopped for a minute to shake the sand out of her sneakers. Kyle turned on a flashlight.

"It's okay. I can see," she said. The moon was nearly full and the reflection bounced off the water like the bay was lit from below. Still, he held out his hand and helped her aboard. It was peaceful and quiet, the only sound the water lapping gently against the sides of the boat.

In the moonlight, she could see the gleam of the refinished floor. "I guess I can understand how you'd fall asleep here," she said. "Though I don't think I'd ever be able to." Her words came out in a rush, and she realized she felt oddly nervous.

"I'll be right back," he said, and he retreated into the galley. When he came back, he handed her a bottle of Krug Grande Cuvée. She recognized the vintage from Jack Blake's collection.

"This is an expensive bottle of champagne to spill over a boat."

"It's a momentous occasion," he said. "Come on — we need to stand in the right spot." Again, he took her hand, and this time he led her to the bow. The boat just barely swayed underneath their feet. "So you're going to have to lean over this edge and swing down with the bottle to hit the bow. No pressure, but it's really bad luck if the bottle doesn't break."

"I told you I don't believe in superstition."

"They didn't christen the *Titanic.* I'm just saying . . ."

"Okay, okay — I got it. Make sure it breaks." She raised the bottle.

"Wait! You have to say something first."

"I'm really trying to be a good sport here but this feels ridiculous."

"We have to appease Neptune."

"Neptune? I thought the god of the sea was Poseidon."

"Neptune is the Roman name. Same god. Okay, I'll make it simple for you. Just say, 'I, Emma Mapson, christen thee' — then say the boat's name."

"Fine. It's your party. What's the boat's name?"

"Lucky Penny."

Had she heard him right? "You're naming the boat *Lucky Penny*?"

"Yes."

"As in Penny, my daughter's name?" She put the bottle down by her feet. "Kyle, that strikes me as a pretty large gesture."

"There is such a thing as a lucky penny, you know. And as we've established, I've never met a superstition I didn't completely

509

buy into. But I do think that Penny — your Penny — is lucky for me. If it weren't for her and the house she inherited, you and I would never have met."

She smiled, a warm feeling filling her chest. Kyle bent down, picked up the bottle, and handed it to her. His fingers grazed hers, and she felt the floor beneath her move, though she was certain the boat was completely still.

Chapter Forty-Seven

Penny couldn't get used to how freaky her leg looked now that it was out of the cast. It was shriveled and scaly and, most upsetting, covered in dark hair.

"Your skin is very sensitive right now. Wait a few days before you shave it," her mother told her.

Now she was out by the pool, hoping that getting some sun would help the situation. Ugh!

The weird thing was that she wasn't as happy about having the cast off as she'd thought she would be. The cast had been like an anchor, keeping her still and protecting her from all her worst impulses. She was able to really focus on bossing back her OCD and working every day on *Queen Bea*. She loved creating the drawings so much that she didn't want to finish it, but the final page rested in her lap.

Her phone pinged with a text. Her friends

seemed to be back in their old routines. Everyone's punishment was over. Bruises and broken bones had healed. It was like the night of the party had never happened. Except Penny didn't find Mindy and Mateo and the rest of them all that interesting anymore.

Ignoring her phone, she ran her pencil along the edge of the paper, shading the background of the final panel. The depth of gray wasn't coming through, and she realized that the sketch pad the page was resting on wasn't a hard enough surface. She thought of Henry and his early gift of a drawing board.

"Hey," her mother called as she came up from behind her. She was dressed in shorts and a bathing suit and had a canvas tote over her shoulder. "I thought you wanted to go to the beach."

"I can't go with my leg looking like this. I need another few days."

Her mother pulled up a chair.

"Mom," she said. "I'm kind of busy."

"Oh? What are you working on?"

"My graphic novel. I'm literally finishing the last page."

The story ended in a way Penny hadn't expected. She'd thought Queen Bea's leaving would feel like the vanquishing of a villain, but it felt like just another loss. The last image in the book was Bea's face in the window of a jitney that was pulling away from Main Street, and it almost made her cry. There had been moments this summer when she'd felt like her life was really beginning, that things had been set in motion with this house. But now everything was going back to the way it had been; she just lived in a fancier place.

One part of the summer she didn't include in the novel was the stuff with her father. It was too confusing. She hadn't heard from him very much since the day in court, just a text here or there checking in with *How's it going, kiddo?* She didn't even know if he was still in town. She tried not to care.

"You know," Penny said slowly, "when Dad first showed up this summer, I thought, *Okay, I'm going to have a father around.* But the more time I spent with him, the less he felt like one."

Her mother sighed loudly. "I'm sorry, hon. But try to look at it like this: There's the family you're born into, and the family you create along the way. Sometimes that second family is even better."

"Like Angus?"

"Yes. Exactly. Like Angus. And as you go forward in your life, there might be other people who play important roles. Would it be nice to have a perfect family? Sure. But it's also nice to have room for the other people."

Penny had never voiced it to herself that way, not exactly, but yes — there were times when she wished for a perfect family. Or at least a regular family. It was the same nagging feeling she had at therapy: *Why can't I be normal?* And then the house had happened, and she thought, *Okay, I might not have normal, but I can have special.* She understood now it was more complicated than that.

"So," her mom said with a smile, "when do I get to read that?"

"My graphic novel? Whenever you want. This is just the ending. You have to get the rest of it back from Bea."

Her mother looked surprised. "What's Bea doing with it?"

Penny told her about the contest and how she'd wanted Bea's opinion on what drawings she should submit. And then Bea kept asking to see more of the panels. "I have to get the rest of the book back from her anyway so I can add this part," Penny said.

"I'm really proud of you for starting and finishing such a big project. Just think, at the beginning of the summer, you were having trouble completing even one drawing. After Henry died, you felt like you wouldn't be able to draw again. And now look at you!"

Penny nodded, trying to muster the enthusiasm to match her mother's.

"You don't seem very excited about it."

Penny shrugged. "I thought getting the house and Bea leaving would be the happy ending. But now that it's here, it doesn't feel that way."

Emma climbed the stairs to the master bedroom Bea had so audaciously claimed for herself at the start of the summer. The truth was, Emma probably wouldn't have been comfortable sleeping so far from Penny, not after all the years of their bedrooms being just a few feet away from each other.

She'd barely explored this separate, more private wing of the house. She peeked into the office and the library and thought it really would be a perfect suite for Angus if he'd stop being so stubborn and agree to move in. "The house isn't the enemy," she'd told him. But she was starting to suspect it had nothing to do with the house. The house was just an excuse. Angus might simply be ready to move on.

The bedroom door was ajar. Bea had set a garment rack next to the bed, and it was packed with clothes from end to end. Emma rapped on the door frame.

"Bea? I need to talk to you for a minute."

She didn't wait for an invitation. Bea sat on the bed folding her scarf collection. Emma stepped around the garment rack, noting the half-filled suitcases on the floor. "Bea, I haven't had the chance to thank you for sharing Henry's book with me," Emma said. That wasn't exactly true; it wasn't so much a lack of opportunity as it was a hurdle to get over her anger at the Mark situation. "Those drawings of my father are priceless."

"Yes, well, I feel that way about all of Henry's work," Bea said. "But I imagined you might appreciate those images."

Emma's mind had turned to Henry Wyatt many times over the past few weeks; she was still grappling with the odd but incredible gesture he'd made in gifting the house to Penny. The memoir did little to make sense of any of it. It actually made her more perplexed. She hadn't known his years in Sag Harbor dated all the way back to her childhood. Why had he never mentioned that he'd spent time with her father? Why didn't he show her the drawings he'd done of him? Or, if not her, why didn't he at least show them to Penny? Was talking about his friendship with her father somehow too personal for Henry? It seemed, from the memoir, to have affected him deeply. Maybe Henry dealt with emotions only through his art.

"Why do you think he never showed me himself?" Emma asked. "Or at least said, 'Hey, I knew your dad'? Or even told Penny he knew her grandfather?"

"My dear, I've spent this entire summer trying to figure out Henry's perplexing choices. He didn't make it easy for me, so why should it be any different for you?"

She had a point.

"I'll admit, the part where he asked you to turn the house into a museum helped me understand why you were confused by his decision to leave it to Penny," Emma said. Yes, she'd felt some empathy for Bea after reading the book. But that didn't excuse her behavior.

"I *was* confused. But I'm not anymore," Bea said. "I finally have clarity."

Emma wasn't all that interested in Bea's "clarity." She wanted to see her daughter's book. "I actually came up here for Penny's graphic novel. She needs the pages back so she can add the ending."

517

"Ah, yes. The ending is missing," Bea said, a thoughtful expression on her face.

"I didn't know she'd asked you for help with her work. She just told me about the contest."

Bea smiled. "She asked me to pick out a few drawings. I have to say, it was difficult to choose just a few. She's very talented."

Emma shifted her feet uncomfortably. It was difficult not to feel cynical about any goodwill gesture from Bea after the stunt she had pulled with Mark. But Emma knew that whatever had transpired between Bea and Penny was genuine.

"Well, thank you for helping her," Emma said. "I appreciate it. I know she misses having Henry around to talk about art and it seems you stepped in." As she said it, a strange thought came into her mind — Bea's insistence that Henry did everything for a reason. She shook it away.

"Emma," Bea said. "There's something you should know. I hesitated to bring this to your attention because I understand you've been cross with me. But I showed a copy of Penny's graphic novel to a friend of mine. She's the dean of admissions of the best fine-arts high school in Manhattan. She loved Penny's work and has asked me if Penny would be interested in a spot in their incoming freshman class."

Had she heard her right? "Bea, that's impossible. I can't pick up and move to New York City."

Bea pushed the pile of silk and chiffon aside and gestured for Emma to have a seat. She perched uncomfortably on the very edge of the bed.

"I had a feeling you might say that," Bea said. "So I'm offering to take her back with me."

Now Emma knew that Bea was not just eccentric; she was truly out of her mind.

"Bea, I appreciate the interest you've taken in her. I do. But our life is here."

"*Your* life is here. Penny might have a different future in mind."

"I'm sorry, this is crazy talk." Emma tried not to think of her daughter's restlessness, of all the times Penny had expressed her desire to leave town. She tried not to think of Katie Cleary working at Murf's just as Emma had. As Emma hoped Penny would not. "She needs her mother. And she has a school here. And she's in therapy . . . that's very important." See? Bea's suggestion was impossible.

"Well, my dear, there isn't exactly a scarcity of therapists in New York City. I'd venture to say it's the psychiatry capital of the world. And before you say no again, I just want to add one more thing: I said a few moments ago that I'm not confused anymore. I came out here certain Henry would have wanted me to have his estate. I now see that he wanted me to spend time here, to get to know Penny. I think he knew I needed someone in my life. He didn't want me to be alone in the world. But I also think he knew Penny needed me too."

Emma stood up, crossing her arms in front of her chest. Really, this woman had some nerve. "I'd like my daughter's artwork, please."

Bea sighed and pushed herself up from the bed by bracing herself on the nightstand. She stood slowly, her hands on her lower back.

"You're going to have to help me out here. My sciatica is acting up. Press the lower part of the bed frame. A drawer will open. See — the seams in the wood?"

Emma bent down, found the spot Bea had described, and touched it gingerly. Nothing happened.

"Press quickly and firmly," Bea directed. Sure enough, a drawer slid out. Inside was a pile of drawings. Emma retrieved them, straightened up, and held the manuscript tightly against her chest.

"Thank you," she said briskly, and she started to leave the room.

"Emma," Bea called out. Emma paused but didn't turn around. "Won't you at least consider it?"

She kept walking.

CHAPTER FORTY-EIGHT

Emma sat on the edge of Penny's bed, zipping her into her dress, a petal-pink georgette sundress with a flared skirt that fell just above her knees.

At the store a few days earlier, Penny had balked at the color. She wanted something black. But Emma convinced her to try it on, and then she'd stood behind her at the store's full-length mirror outside the dressing room. The soft pastel against her dark hair and eyes was so breathtaking, Penny couldn't resist smiling at her reflection.

"You were right," she'd said. Could a mother ask for any more than those three little words?

Emma's dress was a white silk sheath that she'd splurged on at Calypso. She still wasn't entirely comfortable with her role as hostess for the evening but she had to get comfortable with it — fast. In an hour, one hundred and fifty guests were arriving for the auction via Cole Hopkins's yacht.

She was thankful she'd agreed to let Bea stay the extra week. With her cantankerous but super-organized housemate running the show, Emma didn't have to worry about the caterers, the tent constructed on the back lawn for the post-auction cocktail hour, the valet parkers for guests arriving by car, or the auctioneer and his staff. The only person she would be directly overseeing for the night was Chris, who'd agreed to work the pop-up martini bar. It had been Emma's idea.

"We're raising money to rebuild a Sag Harbor institution. I want the party to have the flavor of another town institution. The American Hotel martini bar will remind everyone what's at stake if we don't preserve the spirit of Main Street," she'd told Jack when she pitched him the idea.

She'd summoned the nerve to approach him after the Fourth of July, when he'd invited her into the hotel for a drink — a peace offering. And once Jack got involved, he was a great addition to the project. But midway through a logistics meeting that included Bea, Chris pulled Emma aside and said, "I cannot deal with that woman." She'd promised that if he would work the party, he wouldn't have to take orders from Bea.

Aside from making sure Chris was set up and had everything he needed, all Emma really had to worry about was her speech opening the evening. When was the last time she'd spoken in public? Maybe high school. She vaguely recalled a presentation in social studies class and the jitters she'd had beforehand followed by the thought that it was a waste of time — she'd never have to do this in real life. Now there she was.

She opened her small evening bag and slipped the notes for her speech inside. "Okay, I think it's almost showtime. Are you ready?" she said to Penny, who had closed herself in the bathroom with the water running. Emma sighed and knocked on the door. "Are you washing your hands?"

"No," Penny said, the water still running.

"Penny, open up."

The water was turned off and Penny cracked the door open. Emma glanced down at her wet hands.

"Why are you nervous?" Emma said.

Penny shrugged. "Who am I going to talk to all night? I'm bad at parties."

"Penny, don't overthink, okay? Just try to have fun. And I'm going to do the same."

■ ■ ■ ■

The air felt different in the hour just before the start of a party. There was a frisson, a tension. It was as if the molecules themselves changed.

Bea felt truly in her element for the first time all summer. She couldn't remember when she had gone this long without playing hostess for *something*. She'd almost forgotten the particular thrill of anticipation that drove her from room to room, checking every last detail.

Everything was coming together beautifully, except —

"Not this again!" Stemless wineglasses. Clearly, the new scourge of civilized society.

She complained to the catering director, who not only seemed unmoved by her distress but was clearly not inclined to replace hundreds of glasses as guests were arriving.

"I just don't understand why it's so difficult for things to be done the proper way," Bea huffed to an audience of no one.

The doorbell rang, and since the committee member who had been tasked to act as official greeter for people arriving by car had not yet arrived, Bea took it upon herself to answer the bell.

"Bea! It's a miracle I made it on time. The traffic from the city was a nightmare. I should have stayed over last night." Joyce Carrier-Jones swept in wearing an amethyst-colored, embroidered kimono-inspired dress, her wrists decorated with bright bangles.

"Well, you're not just on time, you're early. Come in. Have a glass of wine."

She flagged down a server in the living room and took two glasses of champagne from a tray that was headed outside. Most of the guests would be arriving by boat, a plan that proved to be more trouble than it was probably worth. Cole Hopkins's dinner yacht was too large to pull up to the existing dock, so Kyle and Sean had rigged a floating dock to connect to the boat's gangway. Bea tried not to envision the entire thing collapsing, the bay filled with women and men swimming to shore in their cocktail dresses and dinner jackets.

"Bea, forgive me," Joyce said, "but I have to ask again about the girl. I can't stop thinking about her work. Any luck talking to the mother?"

"Unfortunately, she isn't interested." Bea looked around the room. "Not another word because her mother is right over there.

Come, I'll introduce you."

Emma looked beautiful, her auburn hair swept into a loose knot at the nape of her neck, her trim figure accentuated by the lines of her chic little dress. Really, it was a shame Emma's generation didn't take the time to dress more during the day.

"Oh, Bea. I was looking for you. I'm going to head to the dock to make sure Sean and Kyle have everything under control."

"My dear, why don't you just text Kyle instead of traipsing all the way down there?" Bea knew why; she no doubt wanted an excuse to see him before the party started. Did Emma think their budding romance had gone unnoticed?

"I tried but he didn't answer. It's fine. I have plenty of time before the guests make their way up to the house."

"Emma, this is Joyce Carrier-Jones of the Franklin School of Fine Arts."

"Nice to meet you," Emma said, glancing at Bea.

"Your daughter is quite a talent," said Joyce. "Is she here?"

"She's around somewhere," Emma said.

The doorbell sounded again.

"Emma, perhaps show Joyce to the living room on your way out? I'll see you in a bit," Bea said.

She could see the wariness in Emma's expression, as if she thought Bea was somehow trying to manipulate the two of them into getting to know each other. Really, when would that woman stop thinking the worst of her?

Bea headed to the front hall to welcome the new arrivals, and in an instant Emma's feelings about Joyce Carrier-Jones became the least of her concerns.

"Diane," Bea said, frozen in the doorway. Diane was not alone.

Diane was with Mark Mapson.

"Bea!" Diane said, air-kissing her on each cheek. "Can you believe the big night is finally here?"

"I believe it," Bea said, glaring at Mark. Diane attempted to make an introduction, but Bea cut her off and asked her to check on the tables in the tent. "I told the caterers they were too close together but I haven't seen the rearrangement."

Bea grabbed Mark by the arm before he could walk off with Diane. "Not so fast," she whispered.

"Bea," he said. "Do you really want to make a scene at your own party?"

"I'm not making a scene. But I would like to know what you're doing here."

"Obviously, I'm a guest of Diane's," he

said smugly. "And I'd like to see my daughter."

"Don't play the father card with me," Bea said. "That's a bit tired, wouldn't you agree?"

Mark yanked his arm free of her grip and walked away.

Oh, this was not good. She had to warn Emma. And Emma might need backup. She sent off a text to Kyle.

The tented lawn was festooned with paper lanterns and aglow with hundreds of votive candles. Inside the entrance, Chris's martini bar was ready for service. Jack Blake sat at the end with a drink in one hand and a cigar in the other. He waved for Emma to join him. "There she is! The woman of the hour. Great job, Emma. This evening came together beautifully."

"The usual?" Chris asked Emma, tossing ice into a shaker.

"I shouldn't," she said. "I have to introduce the auction soon, and public speaking isn't exactly my thing." But she could already taste the brine of her dirty martini. "Okay — but make it weak." She'd have just a few sips.

"A weak martini? Blasphemy," Chris said. "This high-class living is making you soft."

"Yeah, right." She slid onto the stool next to Jack, looking around at the catering staff setting up the food stations. "Excuse me one minute."

She checked in with the woman directing the food service to make certain she knew that the guests wouldn't be arriving at the tent until the auction was finished. She didn't want the warm appetizers heated up or the cold ones set out too early.

When she returned to the bar, Jack said, "This new life seems to suit you."

"What new life?"

"This house. This party. Cheryl said the whole thing looks like it'll go off without a hitch . . . it's like you've planned a million fund-raisers."

"I can't take that much credit," Emma said. "Bea Winstead did a lot."

"Don't be modest."

His praise emboldened her. "Jack, the truth is, this whole scene isn't me. Of course, the house is spectacular. And I'm glad the night is turning out okay. I hope it raises a lot of money for the theater. But if I had my way, instead of spending this past month debating whether or not we need lanterns *and* candles or the merit of crab cakes over shot glasses of lobster bisque for the passed hors d'oeuvres, I would rather have spent it behind your front desk."

"Emma . . ."

"I loved my job. It was my home away from home. I know I dropped the ball. I let the messiness of my personal life interfere with the hotel. And you had to put the hotel first. I get it. But I just wanted to let you know, all that's behind me now. I'm really in control —"

Her phone buzzed with a text from Bea. Come back to the house. I need to talk to you.

"I'm sorry — I need to excuse myself," Emma said, fishing the olive out of her drink and popping it into her mouth. She set her glass on the bar. "I'll see you up there."

Sunset was turning to dusk. The grounds hummed with crickets. She breathed deeply, wondering if she'd pushed too hard back there with Jack. She hadn't planned to get into all that tonight, but the moment had presented itself, so she'd seized it. It was a relief to say what she'd been thinking for weeks.

"Emma."

She looked sharply to the side, searching the shadowed path to the lawn, thinking she couldn't have heard who she thought she'd heard. Her eyes, adjusting to the waning light, confirmed the worst. Mark.

531

"What are you doing here?"

"I'm here for the art auction. Just like everyone else."

"The hell you are. I want you to leave," she said.

"Well, that's not going to happen."

"Why are you still in town? You certainly haven't made an effort to see Penny."

"An effort to see Penny? I think you know I'm making an effort to be seeing *a lot* more of Penny."

"Oh, give it up, Mark! You're pathetic."

She brushed past him and hurried up to the house, her mind racing. He followed her and she stopped outside the sliding glass door leading to the kitchen. She didn't want to cause a scene inside.

"I'm pathetic?" he said. "If you weren't such a lousy mother I never would have had the grounds to take you to court in the first place."

Standing underneath the porch light, moths fluttering overhead, she told herself to stay calm, not to let him get to her. In her heart, she knew she always put Penny's needs first. Her efforts didn't always fix everything, but she tried her best every day, month after month, year after year. What more could anyone do? "I don't do everything perfectly, Mark. No mother does. No parent does. You would know this if you'd spent one day of the past decade being a real parent. But you haven't. You're incapable of it. On your best day, you'd be lucky to be the parent I am on my worst day."

The glass door slid open and Bea emerged, followed by Diane Knight.

"Here he is, Diane. I just knew we'd find him skulking around somewhere. But it seems we're interrupting something," Bea said. She poked her head back inside and called out, "Kyle, look who I found."

Why was Kyle in the house instead of helping out at the dock?

"You left Sean down there by himself?" Emma said when he appeared. He moved to her side and put his hand on the small of her back.

"Sean is fine. I'm concerned about you."

"Mark, what are you doing out here?" Diane said.

"He's just leaving," Kyle said.

"Excuse me?" said Diane. "Who are you to be so rude?"

"Diane, you do know Mark is Emma's ex-husband," Bea said.

Diane folded her arms in front of her chest. "Yes. I'm aware. But that's ancient history. Why is this somehow an issue?"

"It's an issue because Mark is here in

town fighting Emma for custody of Penny — after being an absentee father her entire life," Bea said. "He just wants to get his hands on this house. Apparently, he'd do anything for money. Even sleep with you."

"That's out of line," Mark said.

"What's she talking about?" Diane said. "You never said anything about a custody fight."

"Oh, it's not going to happen, my dear," said Bea. Then, to Mark: "I've already told Emma — and I'll say it again — I will pay any amount of money to bury you in court. You'll owe so much to your lawyers if you keep fighting this that you'll never recover. Unless Diane here is your plan B." She turned back to Diane. "He already asked me for a large check this summer. I'm sure you're next if he hasn't hit you up for funds already."

Diane nervously patted her hair and looked at Mark. "You said you were out here producing a play."

"Babe, go inside. This doesn't concern you."

"It seems like it does," Diane said, glancing at Bea.

"Don't feel bad, my dear. All wealthy women are prey to desperate men. We just have to stick together." She rested her hand on Diane's shoulder.

After a long pause, Diane turned to Mark. "You need to leave."

"Well, it seems we have a consensus," Emma said. "And since this is *my* house, I'm not asking you, I'm telling you — get out."

"That's your cue, buddy," said Kyle, grabbing Mark by the arm and pulling him away from the house. "Time to say good-bye to Sag Harbor. The party is over."

Chapter Forty-Nine

Rows and rows of white folding chairs and a podium transformed Windsong's living room into an event space, but there was no mistaking this had once been the home of an artist. A small crowd had gathered in front of *Greene Street, 1972,* and they stood there as unmoving and silent as if they were standing in an exhibit room in the painting's onetime home, the Guggenheim Museum. Witnessing this, Emma realized that acting as custodian of Henry Wyatt's art was a tremendous responsibility. His decision with the house had been capricious, and perhaps not altogether rational. She had to concede that some of Bea's disbelief and outrage had been justified.

Or maybe she was just emotional after the confrontation with Mark.

"I tried to warn you," Bea said after Kyle had forced Mark from the premises. "That's why I texted for you to come back to the house. I asked him to leave but I realized it was futile."

"It wasn't futile. You and Kyle made quite a team. Thank you."

Once the crisis was over, Emma's first thought was of Penny. Had she noticed the commotion? Had she even seen her father?

More guests filed into the room and took their seats. The front two rows were cordoned off, reserved for sponsors of the event. Emma looked around for Penny, hoping for the chance to talk to her before the auction began. She wondered if she had sneaked off to hide in her room, her anxiety triggered by the crowd.

But no. Emma spotted the unmistakable cascade of curls in the back of the room, just beyond the last row of chairs. Penny stood next to Joyce Carrier-Jones, her face tilted toward the older woman in rapt attention. Joyce held papers in front of her and pointed something out to Penny, who looked at it and nodded with a glowing expression on her face. What were they staring at so intently?

"Are you ready?" Cheryl Meister appeared by Emma's side and pressed a sheet of paper into her hands. "Don't forget these names. We have to thank the sponsors."

"I have them all written down," Emma

said, pulling her notes out of her clutch.

"One more thing," Cheryl said. "Remember to use the word *devastating* when talking about the fire. We need to rally these people to bid strong."

"Okay, okay, I've got it."

Diane strode over, reached out, and squeezed Emma's forearm, spilling a quarter of her glass of champagne in the process. "The show must go on," she said, slurring.

"Let's find our seats," Cheryl said, taking Diane by the elbow.

Emma stepped up to the lectern on the podium. It was slightly elevated, giving Emma a more complete view of the crowd. Servers made their way up and down the rows, filling and refilling wineglasses. After a few minutes, Emma knew the room had quieted as much as it was going to without her actually speaking.

"Welcome, everyone," she said, leaning toward the microphone and resisting the temptation to ask, *Can you hear me?* The room settled into silence. All she heard was the rustling of the auction catalogs, the pop of a champagne cork. "Thank you all for being here in support of a very worthy cause, the rebuilding of our beloved Sag Harbor movie theater on Main Street. Since the . . . *devastating* fire last December, the community has rallied with the creation of the Save the Cinema group. The most urgent goal is to purchase the lot where the cinema was originally built so that a chain store does not move in. Once we have secured the location, rebuilding can begin. The vision is to replicate the original facade, including the iconic Sag Harbor sign."

She paused to accommodate the light clapping, glanced down at her index cards, then back at the crowd. She spotted Penny in the third row, sitting between Bea and Joyce Carrier-Jones. Her eyes met her daughter's, and she saw something there she hadn't seen in a long time: A spark. A happiness.

Emma swallowed, her throat suddenly dry. She placed her notes facedown on the lectern. The events of the past few months rushed at her, a kaleidoscope in her mind. The shape of every moment suddenly looked different. It took her breath away.

The audience members watched her expectantly, shifting in their seats. Her pause exceeded any reasonable amount of time.

"Um, I'd like to take a moment to speak of this town's other loss this year, a far greater one than that of a building, no matter how cherished. This past May, Sag Harbor lost longtime resident and legendary artist Henry Wyatt."

The crowd stirred with murmurs and nods. She glanced at Bea, who leaned forward in her seat.

"As you know, we are gathered tonight in the house Henry Wyatt designed when he decided to become a full-time resident of this town. Henry, like some of you here tonight, discovered this town as a visitor. But ultimately, he became as much a part of this place as the people who were lucky enough to be born here. I used to see Henry Wyatt every day at The American Hotel, and for a long time I thought of him as a loner. I realize now he was not alone — he was a part of the larger family of Sag Harbor, his adopted town. Henry knew that the people and places you discover along the way in life can be as significant — sometimes more significant — than the family you're born into."

Speaking the words, she was aware that these were not new thoughts; it was a version of what she had been saying to Penny the other day by the pool. She had not fully accepted the scope of that truth herself. Not until this moment.

Henry Wyatt had *not* been capricious with his bequest of the house. In fact, he had not given Penny merely the house and the art.

He had also given her Bea.

"Henry Wyatt was a brilliant man, as we can see clearly as we sit here surrounded by his art. But I think in the end his greatest gift was drawing us together." She looked at Penny and then at Bea. She leaned just a bit closer to the microphone, her words finally sure and steady. She felt them fill the room. "For that, I'm forever grateful."

Bea nodded, just the slightest dip of her regal head. They locked eyes as the audience applauded.

Cheryl jumped up from her seat and made her way to the podium.

"And most important," Cheryl said, stepping in front of the microphone and elbowing Emma to the side, "we'd like to thank these very special sponsors . . ."

Bea slipped outside, champagne in hand, and made her way to the tent. For all of her love of art, she had little patience for auctions.

With most of the guests still in the house, Bea had the hors d'oeuvres stations and minibars all to herself. Well, almost to herself.

Angus, dressed in a light blue sports jacket and a striped tie, hovered near the crab legs. She hesitated to approach him. Their last conversation had not gone well, and she didn't know how quickly she would bounce back from another rebuke. But he did look so very handsome, and it was a beautiful evening, and, well, when had she ever been timid before?

"Great minds think alike," she said, moving next to him. "Best to get a jump on these things. There's nothing I hate more than waiting in line for food. Or, heaven forbid, for a drink."

"Hello there, Bea. I'm actually just taking a look."

Across the lawn, a string quartet began setting up.

"I begged Emma to consider a seated dinner, but the committee vetoed the idea," Bea said.

"This arrangement seems more than adequate," Angus said. "You did a fine job."

Bea smiled. "Well, thank you, Angus. I'll accept the compliment. It's highly preferable to the tenor of our last conversation."

"Do you ever stop pushing?" he asked, the hint of a smile on his lips. Just a hint — but she caught it.

"Of course not. That's how I get things done."

He didn't seem to hear her, distracted by something. She turned around and saw

Emma making her way toward them.

"I'm sorry I didn't get a chance to say hi before everything got started," Emma said to him, out of breath. "Did you see Penny?"

"I did indeed," he said, leaning down to kiss her cheek in greeting. "She looks very grown up and she was engrossed in conversation with one of the guests."

"What are you doing out here so soon? Is the auction finished?" Bea said.

"No. I needed some air — and to get away from Cheryl. I sort of went off topic in my speech and she is not happy about it."

Bea did not think Emma had gone off topic in the least. How much could one say about a movie theater? "Your speech was perfection," Bea said. "I did not expect you to mention Henry, but I appreciate that you did. And I'm sure he would have as well."

"To be honest, it wasn't planned," Emma said. "But standing up there, looking out at the audience and seeing Penny sitting next to you, it all sort of hit me, you know?"

Bea suspected she did know. But she couldn't be sure. She kept herself from saying anything, from trying to urge the moment forward. After a few seconds, Emma spoke haltingly.

"I've been going over and over it in my mind," she said. "The one thing I've been saying for as long as I can remember — and Angus, you know this is true — is that I just want Penny to be happy. I want what's best for her. I realized tonight that I can't give her that. But Bea, you can." Her eyes filled.

Bea nodded, stepping closer and giving her a hug. It was the strangest sensation. How long had it been since she'd embraced someone?

"What am I missing here?" Angus said.

Bea pulled back and opened her purse to find a handkerchief for Emma. She passed it to her and turned to Angus. "That woman you saw Penny speaking to? She's an old friend. The dean of admissions at Manhattan's best fine-arts high school. She offered Penny a spot in their freshman class. I told Emma I'd be happy to take her to the city for the school year so she can attend."

Angus appeared stunned for a second. He looked at Emma, then back at Bea.

"Well, this is an unexpected turn, to say the least. It seems you're taking my job," he said, smiling.

"I suppose I am," Bea said. It was a relief to see him looking at her with warmth once again. "So why don't you finally agree to take my room? It seems a shame to let a perfect view go to waste." She winked at Emma.

"I think we'll keep that room for you," Angus said. "For when you come back on weekends and in the summer."

"What makes you think I'll be spending weekends and summers out here?"

He reached for her hand. "Well, I'm hoping you will consider it."

CHAPTER FIFTY

Penny tried to catch her mother's eye, but Emma was busy behind the front desk. Every time Penny thought she had an opening, the phone rang and she heard her mother say for the millionth time, "The American Hotel, Emma speaking."

Penny checked the clock hanging above the backgammon table. It was getting close to noon. She shoved her sketchbook into her overstuffed backpack, pulled out the retractable handle of her suitcase, and propped both bags against the couch. She walked to the front windows, squeezing between two tables, to take a peek outside at Main Street. She looked to the right and her heart beat just a little faster. Across the street, right on schedule, the jitney passed by on its way to the pickup spot.

"Mom, it's time!" Penny said, rushing back to the couch for her bags.

"Let me help you with the suitcase," her

mother said. But Penny didn't need her help. She was so energized, she could have lifted a car by herself.

Someday you will find your own superpower.

Outside, it was sunny and hot, an August day that was meant for the beach. But Penny wouldn't have traded this moment for anything. She crossed bustling Main Street and made a left, heading to the back of the line of people waiting to board the jitney. Penny had watched visitors do this at the end of every summer weekend for as long as she could remember, but she had never imagined that one day she'd be one of the people leaving. She said as much to Bea, who stood waiting while Angus helped load her bags into the undercarriage of the bus.

"Well, I never imagined I'd be one of these people either," Bea said. "I wish you'd let me call a car service."

"This is so much more fun!" Penny said.

Really, until Penny actually stepped foot on the jitney, she wouldn't fully believe it was happening. Her father had dropped his custody fight and her mother was letting her leave town. Her wish had come true. She was getting out in the world. She would continue what she'd started with Henry in the most incredible way imaginable.

The only bad part of the whole thing was that her mom was taking the change pretty hard. At least Kyle had shown up for moral support. He put his arm around her mom, solidifying his status as hero in Penny's mind. She didn't know if she could have left her mother all alone. But now, she wouldn't be.

A woman wearing a green Hampton Jitney polo and holding a clipboard asked Penny for her name.

"Penny Mapson." She turned to give her mom one last hug and said, "I'll be back next weekend."

Her mother didn't say anything. She just nodded and dabbed at her eyes with a tissue. Penny felt a lump in her throat. "Mom, don't be sad."

"I'm not," Emma said. "How could I possibly be sad when you're so happy?" She pulled Penny into her arms. For a minute, Penny didn't want to leave. But just for a minute.

She disentangled herself from her mother's embrace, looked into her eyes, and said, "I *am* happy, Mom. I really am."

She gave her a quick kiss, then turned away and climbed into the jitney.

Weeks of careful thought and planning had

gone into this moment. And now that it was here, Emma was afraid she wouldn't be able to get through it.

She glanced behind her, back at the hotel. Jack, who was covering the desk for the few minutes she needed to say good-bye to Penny, stood on the front porch and gave her a thumbs-up. Emma had been grateful to have her job back, but perhaps never more so than in that moment. It would be important to stay busy. And as she'd told Jack the night of the auction, the hotel really was her home away from home.

With the jitney idling at the curb, the reality that Penny was on her way to New York City took on a whole new intensity. Tonight, Penny would sleep in Bea Winstead's Park Avenue apartment. By this time tomorrow, she would be touring her new school.

Emma leaned against Kyle. "Tell me I'm doing the right thing," she said.

"You don't need me to tell you that. Did you see her face?"

Of course she had. And she'd seen her expression the day they'd told her about the opportunity to go to art school in New York City. Penny had not hesitated for a second. It was as if she'd been waiting for a chance like this all along. And having given it to her, Emma felt an immediate shift in their relationship. Just like that, Penny had nothing left to push back against. She was no longer frustrated and angry.

Of course, the move would not solve everything.

"If I hear that you're not keeping up with your therapy appointments, that you're not doing the work for your anxiety and OCD, this whole thing is off," Emma warned her.

"I'll do the work," Penny said. "I promise."

Emma believed her, just as she had trusted herself to make the right decision about New York. There had been plenty of challenging moments in her fourteen years of motherhood, but it didn't get any harder than letting go.

"She'll be home next weekend," Kyle said, rubbing her shoulder. It was true, Penny would be back on weekends, for holidays, and during the summer. Sag Harbor was still her home. Bea and the school in New York were just adding another dimension to her life, like the way Penny always talked about shading and layering in her drawings.

And judging from the amount of time Bea and Angus had been spending together since the night of the auction, Emma was not convinced *Bea* was actually leaving for good. It seemed Sag Harbor had captured a bit of Bea's affection, just as it had long ago won over her old friend Henry Wyatt.

Bea hovered near the luggage hatch, checking that her bags were securely inside.

"It's fine, Bea," Angus told her.

"I do not share your confidence, but I'll have to take your word for it," she said, taking the first step onto the bus. She turned, looking at Emma. "My dear, don't fret. As you can see by my willingness to endure this entirely uncivilized mode of transportation, I am in full caretaker mode."

Emma smiled tearfully. "Bea, you always get the job done right. I have faith in you."

The Hampton Jitney attendant closed the luggage hatch on the bottom of the bus, and the engine rumbled. Emma wiped her eyes, trying to pull herself together for Penny's sake. Kyle kissed the top of her head and tightened his arm around her.

The bus pulled away from the curb. Penny's smiling face appeared in one of the front windows.

I love you, Emma mouthed, waving to her daughter.

She waved and waved, long after the bus and Penny had disappeared from view. Only then did she turn away, cross Sag Harbor's Main Street, and walk back through the wide-open door of The American Hotel.

ACKNOWLEDGMENTS

To my agent, Adam Chromy: You never fail to see the best possible version of the story — even when it eludes me. To my editor, Judy Clain: Just when I think I've taken the book as far as I can go, you take me further. I am grateful to have such a hardworking and dedicated team behind me at Little, Brown; thank you to Reagan Arthur, Craig Young, Alexandra Hoopes, my publicist Maggie Southard Gladstone, Shannon Hennessey, Ashley Marudas, Lauren Passell, Jayne Yaffe Kemp, and Tracy Roe.

Thank you to the people and institutions of Sag Harbor, especially those who helped me with my research in writing this book, including Jean Held of the Sag Harbor Historical Society; Catherine Creedon and Susan Mullin of the John Jermain Memorial Library; Captain Ken Deeg of Sag Harbor Launch Service and Mooring Rentals; Captain Cameron McLellon of Heron

Yacht Charters. A big thanks to Ted Conklin, owner of The American Hotel, and to the wonderful people who work there. A special thank you to Jack Youngs, who met with me on a frigid December day to share his remarkable family story. Any errors in detail about The American Hotel, past or present, are entirely my own. For anyone interested in an in-depth look at Sag Harbor's rich history, I recommend the book *Sag Harbor: The Story of an American Beauty* by Dorothy Ingersoll Zaykowski.

Thank you to Dr. Ariz Rojas of the OCD and anxiety clinic at the Icahn School of Medicine at Mount Sinai. A special thanks to Mikala Hanson, PsyM, BCBA.

To my two daughters, Bronwen and Georgia Brenner: It's not easy, girls, but we're doing it.

Finally, thank you to my husband, who leads me on the adventures that give me something to write about in the first place. If he had not suggested a spontaneous weekend getaway to The American Hotel, this book would not exist.

ABOUT THE AUTHOR

Jamie Brenner's previous novels include *The Husband Hour, The Forever Summer,* and *The Wedding Sisters.* She lives in New York City and spends her summers visiting the beach towns that inspire her books.